AUTLEY HOUSE
A SPY NOVEL

AUTLEY HOUSE

A SPY NOVEL

BRETT F. WOODS

SYCAMORE ISLAND BOOKS · BOULDER, COLORADO

Autley House
by Brett F. Woods

Copyright © 2002 by Brett F. Woods

ISBN 1-58160-353-3
Printed in the United States of America

Published by Sycamore Island Books, a division of
Paladin Enterprises, Inc.
Gunbarrel Tech Center
7077 Winchester Circle
Boulder, Colorado 80301, USA
+1.303.443.7250

Direct inquiries and/or orders to the above address.

All rights reserved. Except for use in a review, no
portion of this book may be reproduced in any form
without the express written permission of the publisher.

Neither the author nor the publisher assumes
any responsibility for the use or misuse of
information contained in this book.

Visit our Web site at: www.sycamoreisland.com

ACKNOWLEDGMENTS

To Helen, for her endurance, support, and numerous indulgences. And to Dr. Joe Allard and the others, especially Elizabeth, in the Department of Literature, University of Essex, United Kingdom. Their comments, criticisms, and suggestions were central to the development and completion of the manuscript. Also to John Oggero, for his unfailing encouragement and friendship. And finally, to Peder Lund and Jon Ford for their unique perspective, insight, and most remarkable patience.

Brett F. Woods
Santa Fe, New Mexico

> By nature, man is more afraid of the truth than of death—and this is perfectly natural; for the truth is even more repugnant than death to man's natural being.
>
> — Kierkegaard, *The Last Years*

THE WHITE HOUSE
WASHINGTON

TOP SECRET JADE – CODEWORD MATERIAL

NSC:ZOO2803EO
DATE: 21 January 1980
TO: Eisler [SPECAT COURIER]
INFO: OMB-DOD (NOP-231)
SUBJECT: Fiscal Authority Project QUEENWALK

Reference our conversation this date.

Pursuant to your request, QUEENWALK funding as a classified Defense line item is extended per OP-231.

Subsequent to provisions of Executive Order 12333, as amended, project remains within previous guidelines, therein preserving appropriate national security protocols.

NSC:ZOO2803EO

CHAPTER 1

THE FIRST DAY
Saturday, November 22, 1982

Guatemala City, Guatemala, 6:00 A.M.
He glanced at the weapon, then off to the east. Backlit by the rising sun, dormant volcanoes appeared through the night mist. Another clay-pink dawn in a corrugated sky.
He turned his attention to the Citroën's digital clock, *6:03 a.m.* He cleared his throat and continued to wait. Cory was a very patient man.
6:05 a.m. Shadows slowly retreated and the cobblestone lane assumed its familiar detail. Angles became visible and a slight breeze stirred the foliage.
Avenida Privado. It was a gentry kind of place. Urban. Upscale. Residential. A planned, protected enclave in which two adobe walls of bay-windowed, slate-roofed, two-story townhomes snaked around the old six-block Patron District. Even numbers on the left, odd to the right. Comfortable preservation in a country of change.
It was more European than Latin, Cory thought. Rather Dutch actually. A transplanted oasis of brass address plaques, white-painted doors, trimmed trees, and shiny new cars parked parallel to high brick curbs.
It was a peaceful place to live, and this is what Cory considered while waiting adjacent to number 16. This was Boatner's home. Boatner was the reason for the waiting.
6:07 a.m. Cory snapped open the battered Zippo lighter, lit it, then sucked the flame into the carved briar bowl. A puff, another, and the sweet aroma of cherry rum tobacco drifted from the shortly curved Charatan pipe.
It was a particularly good bowl, the fragrance reminding Cory of his youth, his grandfather, and of their summers together. He had been the only father Cory had ever known and now, like his parents in the accident, Pawpaw too was dead.
Natural causes? Cory thought this a contradiction in terms.
Everything had a reason. Nature merely observed.

Cory cracked the driver's window.

6:10 a.m. In ten minutes, Boatner would leave number 16, cross Avenida Privado, walk east to Avenida Reforma, pass the old Catholic cathedral and turn left down Calle Agua Fria where he would wait for the bus which would carry him into the central business district and to his American Embassy desk.

Boatner would walk as he always did—head down, shoulders rounded, eyes darting suspiciously. He moved sideways like a spider, Cory had decided. More of a scurry than a stalking, but predatory all the same.

After leaving his townhouse, Boatner would take 487 steps to reach the bus stop. Three minutes—from 6:20 to 6:23—would elapse. Since Cabeza's coup d'état and his subsequent ascension to the presidency, Guatemala's buses ran on schedule. Boatner's would arrive at precisely 6:25 a.m.

Cory knew the time frames. He had been watching Boatner for nine days. Boatner had not noticed. Cory was discreet.

6:13 a.m. Cory thought about the city. Upon first impression, he had decided it an anagram of architectural inconsistency. A Latin American mélange of 18th- and 19th-century buildings that had somehow survived the earthquakes and now were scattered attractively between blocks of more contemporary offices, banks, and schools. But here it all seemed to work, and Guatemala City emerged as some sprawling, brightly undulating patchwork on its lush mile-high plateau.

He would miss the vistas.

He wanted to remember them.

For nearly eighteen months, Damon Cory had called Guatemala home. A period in which he had come to understand, as well as appreciate, the country, its people and its intrinsic violence.

Nestled between the Caribbean winds to the east and the Pacific's gentle El Niño current to the west, the climate was surprisingly temperate. Similar to that of Cory's native California and his grandfather's property.

The sole heir to the estate, Cory had sold the ranch to developers, the proceeds of which were now offshore, invested and managed by the firm Calder-Lebray Ltd. of Geneva, London and Hong Kong.

At forty-nine years of age, Damon Cory was a wealthy man. But to him, such stature was meaningless. In his mind he remained a soldier.

6:15 a.m. Cory sucked on the pipe. Guatemala, he thought. Of course he would never be allowed to return. Then again, between the quick trips here and there, it had been a good tour that offered both intellectual stimulation and physical challenge. Even more promising, in the psychological sense, he only once felt compelled to exercise the hedonistic imperative to regain his emotional symmetry . . . and only then after a particularly brutal operation in the highlands around Lake Atilán. Perhaps, as he had told Eisler, he really was healing himself.

Cory took another puff on the pipe and considered the past twenty-three months. Stemming from an agreement with Washington, and sanctioned by yet another presidential finding, he had served as the primary counterinsurgency advisor to Guatemala's transient conservative leadership. His specific charge? To identify, track, and ultimately remove the remaining social democrats who voiced outrage at Cabeza's approach to quality government.

But while seldom wrong, Cory had never found the exercise quite right either. Today, Washington's support. Tomorrow, Washington's denial.

Cory had seen this agenda before, yet he felt no particular sense of duplicity.

Presidents may come and go, but QUEENWALK remained a constant.

6:18 a.m. Cory tapped out the pipe, slipped it into the breast pocket of his safari jacket and started the Citroën. He waited a moment for the engine to warm, for the tappets to quiet.

6:19 a.m. He shifted the vehicle into gear, rolled from his spot, drove to another, and double-parked the Citroën so its right door was between the rear bumper of a Fiat and the hood of a second Citroën. Through the passenger window, the brass plaque of number 16 was now visible, the white townhouse door less than fifteen feet away.

The positioning was acceptable, the perspective more than adequate.

Cory pressed a button. The passenger window slid down eight inches. There was a small rectangle of black rubber glued along the top center of the glass.

Cory waited.

6:20 a.m. The brass plaque winked in the sun. The door opened and Boatner emerged.

Cory tooted the Citroën's horn once.

Boatner, keys in hand, looked to the car. He appeared perplexed. Leaning over from the waist, he peered inside. *Cory?* he thought.

6:21 a.m. Cory took a deep breath, released half of it and held the rest. Reaching over, he raised the muzzle of the .22-caliber High Standard Competition Match automatic, aligned it atop the rubber strip, aimed, and feathered the trigger impassively.

Boatner had no additional thoughts.

The silencer coughed, the weapon flexed and, like raisins in a sauce of creme, three dark spots stained Boatner's face. A cheek, the forehead, the bridge of the nose—raisins in procession to brain tissue. A requiem, thought Cory.

Boatner, his eyes an impulse of disbelief, collapsed to the cobblestones, choked in his own mucus, and died.

The eyes remained open. They died more slowly.

6:22 a.m. Cory put the Citroën into gear, drove quietly east, turned left toward Avenida Reforma, and flowed with traffic toward the center of the city.

He had two thoughts in mind.

First, the airport and the plane. It would be leaving for Mexico City within the hour. He had two weeks' leave coming, and he planned to spend the time between assignments diving the Pacific coast before continuing on to South Africa for his next extended posting.

This was not a problem. Sufficient time remained.

The *problem*, he decided, had been the rubber on the window. It had not been soft enough to cushion the weapon while firing. The shot pattern, although effective, had been entirely too loose. Unacceptable. At fifteen feet, the hollowpoint rounds should have stacked, not sprayed.

Yes, he thought. In theory, the rubber strip had been a practical modification. He just hadn't taken it far enough. The next time, he would try soft Styrofoam, perhaps a damp sponge. Something with a bit more absorbency. More volume. Anything to control the recoil and ensure a tighter grouping.

As for Boatner? A matter of convenience.

His alliances were simply unacceptable.

CHAPTER 2

Aeromexico Flight 006, 9:35 A.M.
In the extreme rear of the aged L-1011, Cory adjusted his window seat and watched the ground passing below.
Mexico City in one hour. Cabo San Lucas in four.
Executive prerogative. His crimes again absolved.
To be sure, he felt somewhat fortunate. Through nothing more than luck of the draw, the flight was nearly deserted. Now if he could only manage to convince the hostess he really wasn't interested in magazines, headsets, or the rest of her peddlings, a nap was well within the realm of possibility.
But then what? He couldn't sleep forever. After Mexico, it would be Pretoria and a fresh round of clandestine grazings: the hotel meetings, the assurances of protection, the drops, the intercepts, the cryptic notes and the lies and the bribes that drove the machinery of state.
Tradecraft games. The things men played with such serious guile.
Of course it seemed odd, but after so many months south, somehow the thought of heading east left him with a certain amount of . . . of what? Apprehension? Dread? Something in between?
He wasn't sure. Wasn't really sure he wanted to be sure.
The beach in four. Sleep would be nice.
"Mr. Cory?"
He looked over to the stewardess. It was the same fleshy brunette who had bothered him before.
"Yes?"
She passed him a white envelope. The flap was sealed with a clear plastic tape. It showed no signs of tampering.
"The man in 4-C asked me to give that to you."
Cory nodded. On the front of the envelope was Cory's seat number. On the reverse, the initial E. The writing, he noticed, was in black ink—felt tip—and scrawled as if its author had been rushed.
"Thank Mr. Eisler for me," he told the stewardess.
She smiled. Her teeth were short and somewhat canine.
"Will there be anything else, Mr. Cory? Something to eat? Drink?"
"I'm fine," he reassured her.

"Well if there is, just ring and . . ."
"I will."
A dip, a bow, a wave of the hand and hostess turned, walking quickly back to the first class section.
She moved stiffly, Cory noticed. Buttocks tucked forward under hips. He wondered about her sexual adeptness. He smiled. Eisler would probably know. Eisler always seemed to know the lesser details. Perhaps he would ask the old man about her later, but first things first. The envelope felt sticky in his fingers.
Sliding from his seat, Cory pulled on his round, wire-rimmed spectacles and wished, briefly, that he had not developed the astigmatism in his left eye.
But as he headed for the restrooms, he just as quickly dismissed the thought for, somewhere along the line, he had matured into a pragmatic man—at least when it came to his body—so should he need glasses to stop the headaches? So be it.
Cory despised dilettantes. He had no time for foolishness.
Stepping into the foul-smelling closet, Cory closed the door behind him and slid the *ocupado* latch into place. From somewhere a light flickered. Not on, not off. Just the usual pale pulsings that annoyed as much as they illuminated.
He tore the envelope open.
Inside was a single sheet of onionskin paper. A telex copy. New orders.
He began to read:

PAGE 01 GUACTY 01 OF 01 287114H
S6 SI/RD QUEENWALK [RESTRICTED DISSEMINATION] ACTION SS-22
O P E R A T I O N A L I M E D I A T E
INFO: NOV-04 SSD-00 CCD-92 NSCE-J2W
D//R: 287114H QUEENWALK
FM: EISLER [TPOD-GUACTY]
TO: QUEENWALK OPS [FILE WESTERN HEMISPHERE H021]
INFO: AMEMBASSY GUACTY [HAND DELIVER EISLER-CORY]
AMEMBASSY MANILA [PASS TO QUEENWALK OPS]
AMEMBASSY PRETORIA [PASS TO QUEENWALK OPS]
SUBJECT: CORY [QUEENWALK H021]
REF: WESTERN HEMISPHERE [QUEENWALK OPS] TWX 719901
1. EFFECTIVE THIS DATE, PREVIOUS TWX CANCELLED.
2. REASSIGNMENT PRETORIA NEGATED. REROUTE MANILA.
3. H021 REASSIGNMENT EFFECTIVE IMMEDIATE PER VERBAL ORDER UNDERSIGNED.
S6 SI/RD SI/RD QUEENWALK
GUACTY 201186 [EISLER]
END COMMUNICATION......NOTHING FOLLOWS......287114H

Refolding the telex, Cory began to tear it and the envelope into small pieces.

The Philippines. They were kind of like the Grand Canyon. Once you'd been there, not much reason to return. You'd seen it all before.

Besides, he remembered, his last trip to the rim of confusion, to Mindanao most specifically, had borne a particularly sour fruit. As the lead American *consejero* to Ferdinand Marcos' counterinsurgency forces, his Guardia Libertád, the communist consolidation of power inside Mindanao had proved itself a remarkable exercise in humility, at least for those advisors who survived.

On the other hand, Mindanao also had afforded him the opportunity for the subsequent rotation to the Western Hemisphere: the Salvador, Honduras, and Guatemala shuffle. And all things considered, Central America was much easier. And, no, it was not due to any expertise on his part. Not at all.

The basic fact was that it was infinitely more expedient to fight insurgency, any insurgency—including those suspected or presumed—when the press was censored, public meetings prohibited, and detentions of up to two months were permitted without having to bother with any formal charges, again suspected or presumed, against the accused.

Cory lifted the seat on the toilet.

Strange, he thought, but wasn't it remarkable how tactics that worked so well elsewhere had failed so miserably in the Philippines? He decided it had something to do with commitment. Despite Washington's largesse, Marcos had been no statesman. Just another petty tyrant motivated by greed—nothing more, nothing less. And should the current Filipino president come into displeasure?

Cory shrugged.

He, too, would be replaced and Cory would be rotated once more.

New orders. New targets. New matters of State. QUEENWALK could go either way. The dictators, their visions of self, would have no impact.

He dropped the torn orders in the toilet and cleared his throat.

What was the latest catch phrase? *Low-intensity conflict? Peacekeeping? Nation building?* Cory scoffed. True, he admitted, they sounded conscientious. Much like *police action* did in the late sixties and early seventies. But, in reality, Cory had never believed that one either and now, having been allotted the opportunity to firsthand experience both low-intensity conflict and nation building, he finally had come to realize the real definition of these terms—both sides killing those trapped in the middle. A ruthless round robin of excess wherein the beasts and the children lived without blessing.

As for commitment? At times it seemed an ambiguous syndrome.

Cory looked back to the torn orders floating in the toilet. He waited to ensure all were damp, then flushed the bowl and closed the lid.

He stepped to the miniature sink, twisted on the hot water, then leaned back against the door to study his reflection in the mirror. The image stared back with thinly veiled insolence.

Engaging, he thought, aware of his appearance. What with the round wire glasses, the illusion was that of detachment. Of a cool intellectual superiority tempered with the physical agility of some nineteenth-century Russian revolutionary. A man who worried political trivia and pondered the responsibility of bloodshed as legitimate partisan doctrine.

The image was tall, six-two, and deeply tanned. Under the clothes? With the exception of a long surgical scar traversing the abdomen from the left hip to the tip of the sternum—Laotian shrapnel—the body remained reasonably attractive, although age was finally claiming its due and his collegiate swimmer's physique was slowly being left behind.

He leaned closer to the mirror and observed the reflection do likewise.

It was an arguably aggressive face. Lean, with that tenable trace of aloofness reticent opponents found compelling. Hard, but not cold. Lined, but not necessarily aged. It was clean-shaven and wind-burned, with startling direct china-blue eyes peering skeptically above what some would term a classic Roman nose. The mouth was wide, with a hint of cruelty, and the jawline well-defined, itself slightly indented at the chin.

The hair was dark, rather long at the nape and thick without being coarse. It was brushed back from the forehead, and some graying was evident at the temples.

He grimaced. The teeth were straight, white, and even. The cheekbones pronounced and high, and the ears were set close to the head.

Admittedly, in rare moments of conceit, Cory would acknowledge his appearance as effective. The image of an arrogant man whose features, as well as general persona, demanded he be taken seriously. At times, very seriously.

Raising a hand, Cory touched the glass and allowed himself to become one with the mirror man.

He considered the moment.

In there, he knew, in the mirror, was where the other part of Damon Cory lurked—the Cory known to QUEENWALK. To Eisler. To the men he'd known, to the men he'd killed.

In there lurked the Damon Cory who accepted reincarnation and had long ago assimilated the process of war into two distinct categories: the defeated, those chained to the victor's chariots; and the victors, those who drove the chariots.

The face in the mirror? The Roman proconsul selected by Caesar to wage punitive war against Macedonia. The warrior known to history as Lucius Aemilius Paulus. The specter who engendered Cory's judgment of self.

168 B.C. The Battle of Pydna. Lucius Aemilius attacked across the Aesom River and emerged the victor. Of the enemy, some 20,000 Macedonians were killed while another 10,000 were captured and enslaved. Rome thereafter controlled the eastern Mediterranean.

Skeptics? Cory knew many. In college, the U.S. military academy at West Point, he once mentioned reincarnation to one of his professors. The instructor, an older Signal Corps colonel, had listened politely, then smiled while remarking that it was probably better to be Lucius Aemilius than the traitor Benedict Arnold.

Cory felt humiliated and had never again mentioned Lucius to anyone. But following his instincts, he began to research the phenomenon of reincarnation. After weeks in the West Point library, he decided himself in exceedingly good company. Wellington, Pershing, MacArthur, and Patton. Dozens more. All believed in some sort of process of reincarnation. All had identified with a particular historical figure. All had seemingly found some measure of fortitude from those who had prevailed in the past.

The significance? Patton had written it was the warrior's soul—the wellspring of duty, honor, and devotion to country. The seed of virtue from whence men can kill and order others to kill. The root that allowed a moral wrong to blossom into an honorable right.

Cory had accepted Patton's logic and, since that particular day, Lucius Aemilius had always been central to his being. The mirror man was his voice from within, the essence that permitted the violence to be principled.

Glancing down at the sink, Cory removed the glasses and returned them to his pocket. And as he did so, he was aware of the inner voice—Lucius Aemilius—sounding somewhere in the back of his brain.

The whisper, Cory knew. Little more than silence, it always took place in his mind.

"So, Damon," Lucius was mocking. "Manila? Again? Are we really ready for a new adventure?"

Cory looked back into the mirror. The same face. The same expression. Only the eyes seemed different. The blue was darker and the pupils were dilated.

"I suppose," he whispered.

"But Damon," Lucius taunted. "How can we consider new adventures when we are still considering Boatner?"

Cory weighed the question for a long moment. Then, chancing supposition, he shrugged.

"You should know," he answered. "After all, *you* are the visionary of our twosome. Or has something changed?"

"Nothing has changed," Lucius said. "But am I still confined to being *only* the visionary?"

"What more do you need?" Cory asked.

"Conscience," Lucius said flatly. "Conscience and vision are what I must have, what I must be, if you are to remain a warrior. If you are to excel as a warrior."

Cory declined comment and lowered his eyes.

Conscience, he thought. Again that shitty request. Even the word, the way Lucius uttered it, it was like theory and accusation in two, even shittier syllables.

Cory looked back into the mirror.

"Boatner was wrong," he said slowly. "I have righted his wrong."

In the mirror, the image seemed to nod approval.

"This being the case," Lucius said. "Then perhaps we are prepared for a new adventure."

Cory said nothing.

"Damon," Lucius provoked. "Why do you continue to avoid my question? To reveal our passion for a return to the islands?"

Cory stared deep into the mirror's eyes. The blue was almost black now.

Was he ready for a new adventure? It was a question to which he had no answer. Or, even if he did, it was one he must refuse the share. Some secrets were never to be spoken. Not even to himself.

Cory waited, but Lucius, at least for now, had retreated. Still, Cory realized his reappearance, the thought talk and the conscience tugging, was far from over.

He took a deep breath and released it slowly. No matter. He felt somehow recharged now. Resigned to the new assignment. Emotionally prepared to speak with Eisler.

The Philippines? No doubt he would be there soon. Another trip into its political sparring ring, a ring where the referees remained blind and the only rest corner was an unmarked grave.

"Blessed are the peacekeepers," Cory whispered, as he leaned over and splashed the warm water onto his face.

Given enough opportunities, they would eventually annul the earth.

CHAPTER 3

Washington, D.C., 9:40 A.M.

Hershel Bechtel was an unwieldy, ponderous man in his early sixties. He was tall, but stooped, and his face hung jowlishly beneath a thinning paste of slate-gray hair.

From his father, most assumed, he had inherited the demeanor of a federal judge—for that was what most people thought him to be. And, had circumstances been different, perhaps he would have followed his family's judicial tradition.

But Hershel Bechtel, like so many others of his generation, had found himself caught up in yet another American military escapade, Korea. And after Pusan, Chosin and so many other now forgotten places, he had discovered his values forever altered. After returning to his native South Carolina, he graduated from law school, but instead of the bench he opted for a more, in his opinion, serviceable practice and had forsaken the robes for an oath to protect and defend the Constitution of the United States of America.

Since 1958, Bechtel had lived by this oath and never regretted the decision. Now, as one of four deputy assistant directors of the Federal Bureau of Investigation, he held the reputation of being both a stickler for detail as well as a harsh disciplinarian. Attributes that, over the years, had earned him the sobriquet "the headmaster." But Hershel Bechtel believed in discipline and did nothing to change his image. Besides he rather enjoyed his role as custodian of the director's hatchet.

Like any senior government official, Bechtel's office befitted his position. Three walls were paneled in dark pine and the fourth was glass, which overlooked Washington from the fifth floor of the FBI Headquarters building at 9th Street and Pennsylvania Avenue.

It was a quiet room suited to soft-spoken conversation. Furniture was dark, vaguely Chippendale in design, and consisted of Bechtel's desk with sideboard, two matching brass Steiffel table lamps, and five high-backed tufted Chesterfield chairs. One, in dark blue leather, was behind the desk; the remaining four, in simulated blue leather, sat facing it. An American flag drooped listlessly from its pole in a corner by the window.

The walls were as organized as the desktop. Directly behind Bechtel's head was a four-color plaster replica of the FBI seal. On the two remaining walls hung four autographed presidential photographs. Bechtel was a dedicated Republican and contrived no apologies for his preference. Eisenhower and Nixon locked eyes across the office with Reagan and Ford. There was no wall for Kennedy or Carter. Their "best wishes" remained in a sideboard drawer.

There were no plants, ashtrays, or other nonessential memorabilia scattered about. Even to the casual visitor, it was clear the office was a place for work, not idle chatter.

Leaning forward in his chair, Hershel Bechtel placed his elbows on the desk and looked over to the man standing by the window.

"No reservations, Jonathon?" he asked softly.

The man did not respond. He was lost in thought, Bechtel knew. His mind anywhere as he silently stared out past the National Archives Building to the National Gallery of Art.

Bechtel wondered what he was thinking.

He realized he would probably never know for, intrinsically, Jonathon Weall was cool, detached, and objective. The same qualities that, three years before, had led Bechtel to select Weall out of a pool of more than seventy qualified candidates for the position of Inspector-in-Charge, Special Intelligence Activities.

It had been an excellent, if intuitive, choice.

Weall was both a listener and a finder of skeletons. It seemed to come to him naturally. Another case of a father's genes being passed on.

The son of a career naval intelligence officer, Jonathon Weall had worked his way through both undergraduate and Yale Law School. Upon graduation, he had been recruited into the FBI's legal attaché section where, under U.S. State Department cover, he spent nearly eighteen years in various overseas intelligence posts.

As it turned out, few in the embassies even suspected his fluency in French, Spanish, or Italian. Weall had exploited this oversight by listening. His reports had been introspective, lucid and, uniquely, totally devoid of emotional conclusions. This last characteristic Bechtel saw as critical for the individual who was to serve as his principal liaison with the murky, confused souls who migrated toward the intelligence world.

The decision made, Bechtel had recalled Weall from Brussels, promoted him out of order, and given him the position. Jonathon Weall was now forever out of the shadows. But the time overseas had left its mark: at fifty-two, he still appeared more European than American. And after a conversation, one could not help being left with the impression of having just been allowed audience with some monied aristocrat.

Of course this was an illusion, Bechtel realized. A misconception that had been finely honed so Weall could move easily among the diplomatic elite and snatch their secrets from what was *not* said during the course of innumerable social affairs. But what had been an actor's part in the beginning had, through the intervening years, now become second nature. Weall had matured into a master illusionist whose physical characteristics served only to further enhance the misconception of superiority.

Jonathon Weall was a sleek, small-boned man with a thin, well-bred face and beguiling dark eyes. The cheekbones were pronounced; the nose slim and straight; the lips compressed but full. He was not particularly tall, perhaps five foot eight at most, with a compact, somewhat sinewy body. This, coupled with a full head of light blond hair, impeccable dressing habits and a soft, discriminating voice, separated him from the crowd.

No stranger to the Bureau's legendary infighting, Hershel Bechtel could well understand why detractors inside the bureau envied Jonathon Weall. He had looks, intelligence, position, and access. And if these were not enough? Well, Jonathon Weall had one more thing going for him.

Bechtel smiled at the thought.

He also had enjoyed "the headmaster" as a mentor and friend.

Hershel Bechtel would have it no other way.

"Jonathon," he repeated, raising his voice a bit. "I asked if you had any reservations about this one?"

Weall did not turn around.

"Actually, I think not," he said. "Read between the lines. You'll find the measure of the man."

Bechtel grunted and returned his attention to the single computer printout sheet in the center of his desk.

ADM REF: WEALL - FOREIGN INTELLIGENCE BRANCH [FBI]
           112286 K0912
FRANCO, SALAMON PATRICIO 321-42-6671 Current Position:
           Senior Special Agent.
DOB: 3-27-48, St. Theresa Hospital, Dade County, FL.
FATHER: PATRICIO FRANCO: Retired: Miami Police Department
           [Deputy Chief]. Deceased 5-17-76.
MOTHER: HANNAH FRANCO: [Institutionalized in Miami
           nursing home - Alzheimer's Disease]
EDUCATION: St. Edward's Academy, Miami, FL; 1966.
           University of Miami, Coral Gables, FL; B.S., 1971,
           Criminology.
           George Washington University, Washington, D.C.; M.S.,
           1976, Foreign Affairs.
CAREER: 1966 - 1971 Miami Police Department. Assigned patrol,
           narcotics and homicide divisions.
           1971 - 1978 United States Navy. Commissioned
           Lieutenant (j.g.) Intelligence.

	Office of Chief of Naval Operations [Analyst - Latin Desk]
	Naval Attaché - U.S. Embassy Caracas [1977-1978].
	Resigned Commission 4-16-78 [Terminal Rank -Lieutenant 03].
FBI:	EOD 5-16-78. Sponsor: Weall, Legal Attaché - Caracas.
	5-16-78 TO 9-17-79 [Miami Field Office].
	9-18-79 TO 2-23-81 [San Juan Field Office].
	2-24-81 TO PRESENT [HDQS-Foreign Intelligence].
COMMENDATIONS [FBI]:	
	Miami FO [1] Superior Performance Case 105-22861.
	San Juan FO [1] Superior Performance Case 97-33213 X 32-33109.
	San Juan FO [1] Valor Case 32-33209.
MARITAL:	Divorced KAREN ANN MOBLEY 1-16-78. No Children.
CREDIT:	Slow Pay.
POLITICS:	Not a registered voter.
OTHER:	Capable. Resourceful. Above-average intelligence. Disassociates with fellow workers during non-duty hours. Moderate drinker. No membership affiliations. Fluency in Spanish.
NOTE:	Currently resides 4 Bradford Lane, Falls Church, VA with KAREN ANN MOBLEY.

END ADM REF: WEALL - FOREIGN INTELLIGENCE
[FBI] 112286 K0912

Bechtel finished rereading the document. He remained unimpressed.

"Franco?" he said dubiously. "I don't know who he is. And *looking between the lines*, Jonathon, what I see is a man who doesn't pay his bills on time, is probably a loner, cares less about voting and who, for some unfathomable reason, is living with a woman he has already divorced. Why is this man still working for us?"

Weall smiled at Bechtel's summation.

"He likes to be called *Sal*," he said, nodding to the abstract. "What else did you see?"

Bechtel glanced back to the paper.

"Well, most obviously, he's one of your fair-haired boys. You recruited him, you have him working for you, and now you're pushing him for this assignment. Any particular reason?"

Weall walked over to one of the chairs facing the desk and sat down.

"He's good," he said with the wave of a hand. "The commendations should have given you that clue, Hershel."

Bechtel grunted. "So what do you have him doing now?"

"The Latin desk," Weall answered. "Central America and the

Caribbean. He tracks extremists. Franco's a realist. Keeps his feet on the ground. No pipe dreams, no seeing subversives behind every ragtag regional editorial. Besides, he's traveled to every country down there. He knows the players, knows those who think they're players."

Bechtel thought for a moment.

"No problems? Complaints?"

"Only once," Weall admitted. "Puerto Rico. He finessed the Agency when they tried to keep him from finding one of their indigenous assets."

"I never heard about that," Bechtel admitted. "Then again, I quit listening to their critiques a long time ago. It seems they're always grousing about one thing or the other. They haven't been worth spit since Allen Dulles left."

"I quashed the complaint," Weall added. "Besides, Franco was right. As it turned out, the informant Langley wanted protected was only a functionary of some splinter San Juan nationalist cell. Nothing special, just your typical homegrown anarchist. Franco arrested him after he told the Agency he wouldn't. Even after they offered to let him look at the cell profile files if he would back off."

"Franco see the files?"

Weall nodded. "He even managed to copy them. Good break for the New York Field Office. They were able to use the Agency's material to identify the expatriate nationalists who kidnapped that Puerto Rican banker from the Chase-Manhattan economic conference a year or so ago."

Bechtel vaguely remembered the incident. The banker, a nephew of Puerto Rico's governor, had been freed unharmed by the Bureau's hostage rescue team. He nodded appreciatively. Opportunities to finesse the CIA were few and far between.

"Remember," Weall continued. "Franco is Cuban. He knows the Latin mind because it's part of him. Excellent interrogator."

But Hershel Bechtel could still not place Sal Franco's face.

"Why haven't I seen him around the building?" he asked. "Seems like I should have."

"He avoids you," Weall said simply.

"Avoids me?"

"Nothing personal," Weall explained. "It's just that Franco has an aversion to neckties. He's afraid you'll see him without one and write him up for violating the headquarters' dress code."

"Like I have nothing else to worry about." Bechtel shook his head.

"It's not just *you*," Weall chided good-naturedly. "In the military, when he was in the Caracas Embassy, the head of the military attaché section was an academy air force colonel. Franco was hardly ever in uniform. One day this colonel told him the next time he saw him, he wanted it to be in full-dress whites. Know what Franco did?"

"Pray tell."

"Put on the correct uniform, had a full-length, formal portrait taken, then hung it on the colonel's office wall. There was a note attached. As I remember it said, 'Whenever you want to see me in uniform, just look to your left.'"

Bechtel had to smile.

"Irreverent bastard, isn't he?"

Weall shrugged.

"It's a Latino thing. But in all seriousness, Hershel, if State wants us to take an impartial look into this Honduran bombing, Franco's our only choice. He knows as much, if not more, about Latin terrorist infrastructures as anyone in government."

"And he's your boy too, right, Jonathon?"

"No contest there." Weall answered quickly. "Like you unto me, it's me unto him."

The eternal rabbi system, Bechtel thought. Some things remained constant.

"Okay," he said. "We'll give him first shot at it. I assume you know where he may be hiding today?"

"In your anteroom," Weall smiled.

"Well, get him in here. The director is waiting to hear from me before he talks to the secretary of state again."

As Weall stood and walked to the office door, Bechtel pulled open his top drawer, slid Franco's readout inside and pushed the drawer closed. Then, as Weall led Sal Franco into the office, he leaned over the desktop and put on what he called his "headmaster" face—stern, but benevolent; wise, but understanding. And as the introductions were made, Hershel Bechtel realized he really *hadn't* ever laid eyes upon this agent before.

Sal Franco did not strike Bechtel as looking particularly Hispanic. In fact, for some reason, Bechtel thought his appearance more Mediterranean, rather like a young man who may have served in the Greek resistance during the Second World War. Appearing younger than his years, he was taller than Weall, dark and thin and somewhat feral. His hair was black, a bit curly, trimmed short on top and brushed back to where it was left longer at the collar. There were no sideburns, and the top of his ears were visible.

The face was unlined but seasoned, with faint acne scarring visible on the cheeks. He wore a moustache. It was thick, black and much too large for headquarters assignments. It covered his mouth, which evidently was filled with gum for Franco appeared to be chewing something. Bechtel didn't like his agents chewing gum, nor did he like moustaches. He thought facial hair unsanitary, but decided not to mention it.

Franco's eyes were small and olive green, and the eyebrows were bushy like the moustache. The eyes held Bechtel's own effortlessly. This was an unusual sensation for the deputy assistant director and left him with the same uneasiness he had once felt when reviewing a videotaped interview of Charles Manson.

Bechtel looked away.

"Please sit down, Agent Franco," he said after a moment. "You, too, Jonathon."

As the two men selected chairs, Bechtel noticed the younger man's clothes. He wore a short leather aviator's jacket with epaulets, a blue oxford cloth shirt with the top two buttons undone, starched blue jeans, and western boots that looked to be made of some dark-stained reptile hide. A western belt of a similar material was at his waist and as he leaned over, Bechtel could see a thin gold chain around his neck. He noticed Franco's hands, where his attention was drawn to Franco's rings. Another curiosity. On both hands he appeared to be wearing wedding jewelry. The ring on the left hand was much wider. Yet Franco wasn't married, so the rings prompted more questions than they answered.

Narcotics and homicide. Bechtel could now understand Franco's assignments while on the Miami Police Department. He looked like a man who would enjoy working nights. Who would feel comfortable on the streets.

"Sorry to have to bring you in on a Saturday, Franco," he said, an obvious reference to the clothing. "But Jonathon here tells me you're our resident expert on Central American affairs."

Franco smiled and Bechtel caught a brief flash of even white teeth beneath the moustache. He also caught the notion that the smile was lost somewhere in the facial hair because it never made it to the eyes, which were now casually examining the presidential photographs.

"No Democrats," Franco said, referring to the photographs. "Why?"

Bechtel was taken aback, nobody ever had asked before. He cleared his throat. "Well, during some of the terms I was . . ." Unsure of where they were leading, he let the words trail off.

Franco looked back to Bechtel.

"If I voted at all," he said thoughtfully. "I would probably register as an independent. Keeps things simpler, don't you think?"

Bechtel glanced over to Jonathan Weall who was barely hiding a smug smile.

"Perhaps you should explain the Honduran situation, Hershel," Weall suggested

"Of course." Bechtel looked back to Franco. "What do you think about the insurgency problem in Honduras?"

"What they do, or what we are doing about it?" Franco asked.

"What we are doing about it," Bechtel said.

Franco nodded. "The government's elected, of course. We supported that and still do. If we didn't, they'd be out in about a week. But it's a shell power base. No local support. It's the same traditional powers behind the scenes—the wealthy, the military. The little man realized nothing new and won't. That's where the insurgency gets its support. Unless we influence some changes at the top, nothing will change in the hinterlands. It's kind of like cancer. You assume you have it, or are going to get it, but unless you know for sure you're content living with the status quo."

Bechtel thought the answer as good as any.

"Well, the cancer claimed a victim yesterday afternoon," he said. "I want you to find out who was responsible and if it was an isolated case, or if we can expect the start of something more protracted. Since we have no Bureau attaché in Honduras, you were selected for the inquiry based upon your background and familiarity with the region. Give him the details, Jonathon."

Weall explained in concise sentences.

"At 1700 hours, Honduran time, a satchel charge blew up a convent school in the capital. Tegucigalpa. There were thirteen dead. Two nuns, a priest, and ten children all between the ages of six and seven. The children were practicing for their first communion ceremony, which was supposed to take place this morning."

"So why is the Bureau involved?" Franco asked.

"One of the children was the daughter of the American ambassador to Honduras. He asked the State Department to have us investigate her murder."

"Any witnesses or suspects?"

"No witnesses," Weall told him. "But the Honduran military has a suspect in custody. Her name is Alicia Carrera. She's allegedly a Cuban and currently is being held at the Honduran military base at Chuloteca. Evidently she was captured while attempting to get out of Tegucigalpa."

Franco understood. "When do you want me to leave?"

"Two hours," Weall said. "State and CIA are pulling together everything they have on her as are our people. I'll see that it's all formatted and have it to Dulles by the time your flight leaves at noon. You need a lift to the airport?"

Franco shook his head and stood. "No, I'm in my personal car. I'll just leave it at the airport. Any special instructions about how you want this handled?"

Hershel Bechtel spoke first.

"Just be careful not to offend any Honduran officials," he said. "State feels the Hondurans are letting us talk to the woman only as a courtesy and are treating the crime as a Honduran problem, not an American one. Am I making myself clear?"

"Perfectly," Franco said simply. "No big productions."

"None," Bechtel nodded.

Franco stood, glanced over to Weall, then turned and began to walk toward the office door.

"Agent Franco?" Bechtel called after him.
Franco looked back over his shoulder. "Sir?"
"Mind if I ask you a question, a personal question?"
"No, sir."
"It's about your rings," Bechtel said. "Why do you wear two wedding bands when you're not married?"
Franco nodded thoughtfully and held up his right hand. "This one was my father's younger sister. She left it to me in her will." He then raised up his left hand. "This one was given to me by my wife when we were married."
"But you're divorced now," Bechtel said.
Franco shrugged. "Only according to some paper somewhere in Caracas. I don't put a lot of faith in Venezuelan legal documents. Do you, Mr. Bechtel?"
"Well, I don't suppose I've ever really thought about it."
Franco glanced back to Weall. "Besides, I've been told by a former Venezuelan legal attaché that the document has been mysteriously misplaced. Without it, I'm afraid Karen and I are still legally married. Any other *personal* questions, Mr. Bechtel?"
Hershel Bechtel could feel his face flush. "Uh, well, no, Agent Franco," he said softly. "I'll see that your personnel file is updated to reflect your correct marital status."
Franco opened the door and stepped out into the anteroom.
"Thank you, Mr. Bechtel," he said, all too sincerely. "I'll be back in a few days." Then he was gone without additional comment.
As the door closed, Bechtel turned back to Weall.
"He made me feel like an idiot," he said, making it an accusation.
"No," Weall disagreed. "You made yourself feel like an idiot. If you wanted to know about his *personal* status, you should have asked me."
"Maybe it's just his attitude," Bechtel said. "Or his appearance, for that matter. Explain to me this marriage arrangement one more time."
Jonathon Weall shrugged. "His wife left him in Caracas because she hated the country. You remember a senator named Goodson Mobley? He supported busing in the early sixties."
"The Maryland oyster king?"
Weall nodded. "Well, Sal is married to his youngest daughter. She couldn't handle the Venezuelan lifestyle, so she came back home. Sal got back together with her when I brought him into my section. One day he asked me about the Venezuelan divorce. I told him I would see that the documents were purged from the archives and I did."
Hershel Bechtel could think of nothing to say.
Weall continued the explanation.
"As far as his wearing his aunt's wedding ring, she was a nun original-

ly from Cuba. After Castro came into power, he ordered her whole convent out of the country. The nuns moved to San Juan where they lived quietly until the FALN decided to kidnap them as an example of the government's inability to deal with crime in the city. Sal was stationed in Puerto Rico at the time and was one of the first agents on the scene when the convent's burned-out bus was found in an abandoned warehouse. His aunt and three younger nuns were inside the vehicle. All had been raped before they were murdered. The ring was the one given to his aunt when she was a novice and took her initial vows. She had worn it for over thirty years."

Bechtel felt even more foolish.

"Why isn't all of this in his personnel abstract?"

"I'm special intelligence," Weall said offhandedly. "You need to take that up with administration. That's why I told you to look between the lines, Hershel."

"Humph," Bechtel grunted, deciding to change to subject. "I don't like that moustache either, Jonathan. And I really don't like agents chewing gum when they're talking with me."

"Let it be, Hershel," Weall said. "He's always worn a moustache and as for the gum, he's trying to stop smoking. He runs with a long leash, Hershel, and only needs two things from us: the latitude to work his own cases and freedom to work them his own way, however unorthodox it may seem."

Jonathon Weall stood and began to walk slowly toward the door.

"Oh, one other thing, Hershel."

Bechtel looked up.

"What's that?"

"Franco stays under my direction. His contemporaries hate him as much as mine do me. I'm teaching him how to handle it."

"Like I taught you, Jonathon?"

"I'm a survivor," Weall said.

"Okay, Jonathon," Bechtel said, after considering the request. "You keep control. Let's just get some answers."

"We will, Hershel. We always do."

CHAPTER 4

Aeromexico Flight 006, 9:54 A.M.
    To those around him, he seemed a gentle, even humble man. Scholarly, but not superior. Refined, but not courtly.
    His age was indeterminate. One would guess seventy, but never sixty or eighty. He wore no jewelry and his suit was gray, inexpensive, and a bit too large in the shoulders. It was an old suit. At least twenty years. But this was not an issue. He cared little about fashion. Even less about pretense.
    However, the old man did care about people. He cared about what they did, about what they refused to do. Sometimes, rarely, he failed to comprehend the *why's*; but he always confirmed the *who's*. He labored a complex and weighty charter: in time of ambiguity, he demanded fact; in time of gross corruption, he required morals. It was more than an avocation. Such actions were required by law. For he was not a submissive man, he was a placer of blame.
    Physically, he appeared quite unassuming—three inches over five feet and weighing less than 140 pounds. His hair was white, neatly trimmed, and parted more in the middle than the side. With the exception of the bushy white eyebrows, he wore no facial hair.
    His eyes were brown, expressive, and surprisingly quick. Glasses were not prescribed. The nose and chin were somewhat pointed, and the ears, hands, and feet almost too large for his small frame. Still, he was not altogether elfin. There was just a hint, just enough for the magic.
    But the man was aware of the magic. Understood it. Cultivated it.
    To him, it was a precious thing. The gift that made other men believe in him. Listen to him. Tell him the secrets of nations.
    Those who had witnessed the magic, the handful, thought him genius.
    Others, the unknowing, thought otherwise. They described his demeanor as passive and his affectations those of some retiring professor emeritus.
    The university? Warsaw in the thirties.
    His curriculum? Perhaps the Torah.
    The man seemed a throwback to an earlier time. And as for the fact that he was now occupying Cory's window seat?

He did not appear concerned.
Eisler held the power. Cory worked for him.

***

Leaving the restroom, Cory returned to his aisle. Of the three available seats, only the outer one was now vacant. Someone had released the center tray table and on it were two plastic cups with ice, a wad of napkins, four packages of smoked almonds and four small bottles. Two contained scotch, the others bourbon. The liquor was unopened. There were no mixers.

Taking the aisle seat, Cory leaned back, adjusting the headrest so he would be at the same angle as Eisler. The seat creaked audibly.

Cory respected Eisler and, out of deference, he waited for the older man to begin the briefing as he would also wait for the him to open the bottles. Eisler was like that. He expected subordinates to follow his lead.

Cory lit his pipe.

Eisler continued to stare out the window.

Cory continued to wait.

QUEENWALK was an index of waiting.

Eisler broke the silence.

"I've had a thought, Damon," he said, his voice betraying a hint of Polish-accented English. "Do you realize that for all the generations man has lived on this planet that ten percent of all the people who have ever lived are living as we speak?" He did not look at Cory.

"No," Cory said simply.

Eisler continued to gaze toward the ground.

"They are down there, Damon. They are down there and few have any impression of what deceptions they endure."

He turned and looked at Cory.

"Do you remember what Dostoyevsky wrote?"

Cory said nothing and Eisler nodded.

"He told us deception will be our suffering, for we shall be forced to lie."

"*The Brothers Karamazov*," Cory whispered.

Eisler was pleased. It was a small test, but Cory had passed.

"Yes," he said. "Then was not unlike today. We must never forget that life cannot be ruled by intellect alone. *Feelings*, Damon. *Justice*. These things too must be examined."

Eisler watched Cory nod in thoughtful response. But he knew Cory well and was aware of his uneasiness when discussing the abstract. Changing the subject, he reached over and gripped Cory's forearm. It was paternal.

"I'm an old man, Damon," he smiled, nearly openly. "These are the things upon which old men dwell. Do not think of me as foolish."

Cory looked at the hand on his sleeve. It was more skeletal than he had remembered. More veined. Still, the grip remained surprisingly strong.

"I never have."

Eisler relaxed, the grip becoming a series of pats, like those from a favorite uncle.

"Fine, fine," he said sincerely, indicating the bottles. "May I offer you a cocktail?"

Cory accepted and they selected bottles. Eisler the scotch. Cory the bourbon. Twisting off the caps, they filled their respective cups. One bottle, one drink. Eisler raised his for a toast.

"To whom?" he asked.

Cory thought about it.

"To Dostoyevsky," he suggested, after a moment.

Eisler smiled. Cory again had pleased him.

"To Dostoyevsky," he repeated, touching his cup to Cory's. "May we learn from what we suffer."

As they sipped their drinks, they discussed urbane little footnotes: weather, politics, but mostly the smoked almonds. Eisler learned that Cory preferred toasted cashews. Cory discovered that Eisler was plagued by diverticulitis and was unable to eat nuts, although in fact he did so at Christmas. Eisler termed his seasonal munchings an "iconoclastic fall from grace."

Cory thought this witty and told Eisler so. They laughed together.

But it was not Christmas, so the smoked almonds remained sealed as they poured their second drink. There was no second toast and the conversation idled briefly.

Eisler kept it moving. New directions.

"I was sorry to hear about Mattman," he said regretfully. "You two were very close. His death must have been difficult for you."

Close? Cory thought. Although Eisler hadn't meant it that way, to describe their relationship as close was nearly an insult. Mattman had been like a brother. *Tight* they called it. Tight since Culver, grades six through twelve. Military academia. Tight through West Point, class of 1968. Cory graduated twentieth in standing. Mattman twenty-first. Then the real army. Together through the Kennedy Unconventional Warfare School at Fort Bragg, to the Laotian operations a year later.

Eisler had found them there. QUEENWALK became a job. Traveling together. Still tight. Thailand. Panama. The Marcos islands, then Latin America together.

"He's been dead three months now," Cory said.

Eisler nodded. "It was the Mexican national oil company, wasn't it?"

"PEMEX," Cory said. "He thought it was a good job. Lots of perks. Women. Booze. Corporate jets. Company villas on the Pacific." He took a sip of the bourbon. "I've yet to understand why he would resign his commission to . . ." He failed to find the right words and, self-consciously, feigned interest in his pipe.

"You thought about it too, Damon, did you not?"

Cory nodded, but declined additional comment.

"But you chose not to resign," Eisler pressed.

"No."

"What do you think motivated your decision to stay?"

Cory looked at Eisler. Their eyes locked.

"The real reason?"

Eisler made a permissive gesture with his hand. Cory took a sip of his drink, then answered his own question.

"It's me, or maybe it's what you've made me. In either case, it occurred to me that after twenty-odd years of manipulating governments—supporting them or undermining them depending on the winds—the idea of running around in *private* security, sounded asinine."

Eisler understood.

"It's pride, Damon," he said. "Your pride precludes your involvement in such amateurish endeavors."

"My sanity too," Cory sighed, then he added. "The Mexicans mailed me Mattman's note. You know what it said?" He did not wait for Eisler's answer. "It was ten words: *Fucked up job. Not real. Have to beg off. Regards*."

Cory drained his drink.

Eisler watched him closely, then finished his own.

"Let's have two more," he suggested, not really wanting them himself but realizing Cory did.

They ordered the liquor.

The stewardess, hips still forward, had come and gone and Cory was well into his third bourbon when Eisler decided it time to mention Boatner and the assassination in Guatemala.

"Your communication indicated he was a homosexual," he said.

"Boatner?" Cory nodded. "Evidently he was being blackmailed . . . a young boy and his father."

Eisler shook his head slowly.

"Unfortunate," he said. "What is our exposure factor?"

"Worst case scenario is that our financial arrangements may have been compromised. At least the London-Guatemala City channel. Nothing back from there though . . . at least I don't think so."

"Personnel?"

"No penetration there," Cory said flatly. "Boatner's in-country duties were limited to desk audits. Even if he were to sniff around, it would have only been financial records, nothing operational. I was still using the *La Prensa* news conduit, so any real exposure should be minimal."

"Boatner knew you, of course," Eisler speculated.

"Knew of me. Knew me on sight. Knew I was attached somewhere in the American MILGROUP contingent. But he never had time to put QUEENWALK and me together. He really wasn't that deductive, I don't think. Probably didn't even realize the potential value of the material he was passing over."

"How are we controlling it?"

"*La Prensa* initially, then Radio Guatemala. By tonight they will both have received a communiqué from the old social democratic government-in-exile—Calderón's group—claiming Boatner was executed for crimes against the people and that he is only the first execution in their 'return to power' mandate. Same old spin."

Cory waved a hand in the air as he continued.

"As for the rest, nature will take its course. Our ambassador will express shock and outrage. The Guatemalans will vow to bring those responsible to justice. Security will be tightened at the embassy, in the streets, and in the military districts. As for Boatner? His family will get the body, a flag, and some suitable State Department tribute, probably an obscure foreign service medal. Then he will be ceremoniously buried in 'the highest tradition of the American diplomatic service.'"

Cory looked at Eisler.

"Kind of makes you feel warm all over, doesn't it?" he said sullenly.

Eisler ignored the question. The bourbon was releasing Cory's cynicism. His contempts. Those bitter questionings men of purpose held just beneath the surface. It was all in the voice. Its tone. Its inflection. The sequence in which the words were uttered. All part of the process. Part of the learning.

In time, Eisler predicted, Cory would reach the point at where he would instinctively keep his questionings unspoken. In time he would become more politically astute that way. In time, Eisler knew, but not just yet. Learning through example. Such was the nature of apprenticeship.

"Perhaps we should have some lunch," Eisler suggested.

Cory summoned the stewardess. They selected the chicken breasts mornay. For both of them, Eisler declined additional alcohol. The point was not wasted on Cory.

The meal, they decided, was standard and grim: peas, potatoes, salad, bread, butter, cake, and fowl long dead.

They nibbled cautiously, leaving as much as they ate.

"Blemishes on a plastic plate," Eisler observed, as the stewardess removed all that remained.

"Airline spoor," Cory added.

They humored each other and ordered coffee, black, no sugar. Cory lit his pipe. Eisler leaned back in his seat.

"So, Damon," he said. "What do you know of the situation in Manila as it now exists?"

Cory considered his answer.

"I'm sure it's still somebody's leftists trying to overthrow the incumbent rightists so that the winner can start a new rightist government."

Eisler chuckled wryly.

"Something like that, I suppose. But I was referring to the internal political situation. Do you think the Filipinos will be able to stabilize their economic policy once our bases at Clark and Subic Bay have been turned into free trade zones?"

"I can't really predict that," Cory admitted. "The old players are changing too fast. Besides, it's been too many years now, and I never really thought you would rotate me back to Manila."

Eisler understood and, although mildly displeased at Cory's failure to keep abreast of regional power shifts, he saw no reason to manufacture issues.

"Your candor is commendable, Damon," he said. "But in this case it too becomes irrelevant."

"I'm not sure I understand," Cory said.

Eisler nodded thoughtfully.

"Tell me, Damon," he said. "Is there any particular reason why you would want to return to the Philippines?"

"Of course not," Cory said quickly. "It was one of the worst tours of my career."

"Exactly," Eisler smiled. "Which is why you will not be returning."

"But the orders . . ."

"A ruse," Eisler interrupted. "I have in mind for you something, shall we say, a bit more sensitive.

Cory said nothing. A response was unnecessary and unexpected.

"Item," Eisler continued. "Some three weeks ago a man by the name of Avraham Sergov approached one of our latents inside a French medical team that had been invited to study Soviet morbidity trends. Sergov's story was familiar. He claimed to be a senior technical analyst in the Glavnoe Razvedyvatelnoe Upravlenie and wanted to emigrate to Paris."

"Motivation?" Cory asked, well knowing that his life and the tale of some Russian army military intelligence type were already on a collision course.

"The traditional demons," Eisler said, without rancor. "Avarice and hubris. He wants money and someone to assuage his bruised ego. Sergov has been in the GRU for nearly twenty-five years and is only a major. He sees no future in Russia. At least for him. There are no funds available for pay or for his retirement. His wife evidently left him for an automobile mechanic, no less. And now the Soviet Army's General Staff has ordered selected GRU personnel, those with technical backgrounds, to be reassigned from Moscow proper to other, more rural areas. Sergov is slated for some obscure power station on the Estonian border. He is not a happy man, Damon. Not in the least."

"I can imagine," Cory said. "But why doesn't he just leave? After so many years in the business, he shouldn't need our help."

"But he does," Eisler said. "His current position is within the GRU's Directorate of Technology Assessment, which bears direct responsibility for the acquisition of Western high-tech processes. Industrial spies, if you will. And considering the current economic conditions inside Russia, this has become the most important aspect of Moscow's present, and future, intelligence-gathering efforts. Sergov knows the GRU's foreign infrastructure, its assets, and its future plans. If you were his supervisor, would not you take certain precautions to ensure his continued allegiance?"

"I suppose so," Cory said. "Then why transfer him in the first place?"

"His relationship with our French latent," Eisler shrugged. "Evidently, due to the knowledge he possesses, his superiors suspect he is in danger of being compromised. After all, I've been led to believe our French latent is a very attractive woman, some fifteen years Sergov's junior."

Ah, a third demon rears its ugly head, Cory thought. Lechery. Another case of penis leverage. Not that he could blame Sergov, of course. Spring in Paris could be considerably more festive than a winter in Estonia. "So what strings went along with his emigration?"

"The usual," Eisler said. "New identity, funding, protection. None of this is really a problem, and Sergov is intelligent enough to realize it. But he was also intelligent enough to realize that if he was to be taken seriously, he would have to provide some bonafides. He did so of his own volition. He offered us a GRU *avanpost*, a spy cell, in Washington. It was in the form of a list. Five names."

Reaching into his left breast pocket, Eisler extracted a folded sheet of monarch-sized stationary and passed it over to Cory.

"Here is Sergov's information, Damon. I will entertain your comments."

Taking the paper, Cory scanned the contents:

BIRTH	NAME	POSITION
17 Mar 1912	POINTER, William	DARPA
4 Dec 1911	ROUSE, Robert	DARPA
29 Apr 1909	WYLIE, Miles	DARPA
3 Nov 1910	CELT, Gustav	APG
9 Aug 1912	JARVIS, Steven	APG

Cory was confused, yet curious as he glanced over to Eisler. "These men are all over seventy."

"Correct," Eisler agreed. "Nonetheless, according to Sergov all five are conduits for the GRU."

Cory refolded the paper and handed it back to Eisler.

"Maybe so," he said. "But they seem a little long in the tooth to . . ." He caught himself, but it was already too late.

Eisler reached over and patted his arm.

"Please, Damon," he smiled. "No offense is taken. I am well aware of the differences in our ages. Particularly from your point of view."

Cory could feel his face redden. "I just meant that normally, to stay operational, you would think . . ." He searched for words. None would sound genuine, he realized. Eisler was at least equal in age to the names on the paper, and he remained about as operational as anyone could ever hope to become. He turned the conversation back to the note.

"DARPA," he said. "Defense Advanced Research Projects Agency?"

"Yes," Eisler nodded. "High-risk, high-payoff technology research: adaptive optics, STEALTH applications, that sort of thing."

"Then that would make APG the Aberdeen Proving Ground," Cory reasoned.

"Precisely," Eisler said. "Laser applications, C3I communication fields and their collateral support systems."

To Cory, the next question was obvious.

"You've attempted to verify their affiliations?"

"Yes," Eisler said softly. "Indicators unfortunately confirm Sergov's allegations."

Cory understood the tone. "So how bad is the damage?"

"Incalculable. All five are still, or most recently were, senior administrators in the various projects of the two agencies." Eisler turned and stared into Cory's face. "They all worked in American defense-related areas for well over thirty years, Damon. A few still remain in the system. As for what they may have passed? The list is endless. They were working for us when the Soviets launched the first Sputnik satellite, when we commissioned our first nuclear submarine, tested our first integrated ocean sonar nets."

Eisler sighed heavily. "Fortunately there was a paper trail, Damon. We reviewed the individual assignment records for each of the five, placed them in a date-project-time grouping, then compared it with what the Soviets developed during the same general timeframe grouping. We found 184 incidents when the Kremlin unexpectedly developed an identical technology to what we were refining in the same period.

"In 132 of the 184 cases, the Kremlin product was even superior to ours, particularly in their levels of sophistication concerning tertiary chemical processes. Of course, this can only stand to reason. Since we were de facto conducting all of their basic research, they could concentrate on taking a fundamental system design intact and directing their efforts to fine-tuning what we erroneously assumed was state of the art."

"Kind of like they started a fifty-yard dash at the twenty-yard line," Cory said.

"More like the forty in all too many cases. No, Damon. I'm afraid our investigation only supports Sergov's contention. For over three decades now, five of our top military technocrats have been passing information to the Kremlin. As I've said, the damage is incalculable."

"Who hired these men in the first place?" Cory wondered.

Eisler made a dismissive gesture with his hand.

"Originally, the U.S. Army European Command, which controlled our occupation forces after the Second World War. As I recall, it was headquartered in Germany, outside of Heidelberg."

"No background investigations?"

"Only cursory," Eisler said. "Sheer numbers precluded anything more extensive."

"But considering the positions they eventually assumed, surely there had to be something more? Something later?"

Eisler shook his head somewhat regretfully.

"I agree," he said after a moment. "There should have been a thorough vetting. But then, well, consider the times, Damon. The late forties. World War II was finally over. Europe was divided. Do you realize how many homeless there were? How many refugees? How many were desperate to begin new lives?"

"No," Cory said simply.

"In Germany alone, there were hundreds of thousands. Hundreds of thousands of men, women, and children who needed to be fed. To be clothed. To be sheltered."

Eisler paused to take a sip of his coffee.

"We obviously had planned on this," he said. "In Potsdam, when Germany was first divided, there even had been some talk of a centralized effort wherein we, the French, British, and Russians pooled resources to deal with the refugee question. However, as events unfolded, no cooperative program was ever implemented."

"Nobody really cares about refugees." Cory asked. "Never have, never will."

"Perhaps," Eisler nodded, pleased with Cory's insight. "But, then, any responsible nation could never acknowledge that fact. And, as victors, we were charged with that very responsibility. Besides, in the final analysis, we were the only ones who could even begin to afford to help the homeless. France was destroyed, the Brits were all but bankrupt, and the Russians? All they ever really desired was to gain control over more territory which, of course, they did."

Cory nodded in understanding and Eisler continued.

"Item. Soon after the Russians began occupying their zone, the stream of refugees became even greater as many began to suspect that living under the Soviet boot conceivably could become worse than existence under the Nazis had been."

At the word "Nazis," Cory could discern an unfamiliar tenseness in Eisler's voice. Fear? Hatred? Something even stronger? He let is pass.

"So they fled to the western sector?" he asked instead.

"In droves," Eisler said. "Polish, Latvian, Czechoslovakian, Hungarian, alone and with families, educated and ignorant, all wanted freedom and most wanted to emigrate to America. Then something happened, Damon. In Heidelberg, our immigration review officers began to notice that some of those desiring American visas were actually brilliant men, not unlike those who had escaped in the early war years and eventually had come to work on our atomic bomb project, who had served as scientists and inventors, and who had not been able to leave when their countries were overrun by Hitler.

"Their collective potential had been commandeered to bring Germany to the very edge of discovery in chemical warfare, aeronautics, and missile guidance systems. Remember, Damon, these individuals were not Nazis, nor even Nazi sympathizers. They were unfortunate people caught in unfortunate times. And under the threat of death to themselves or their families, they had been forced to create."

"So when identified," Cory said, "they were hired by our government."

"It was more than a simple hiring process, Damon. When we realized the available talent, the Office of Strategic Services mounted an operation codenamed PAPERCLIP to round up the scientists to prevent them from falling into the hands of the Russians. That was the project that brought Wernher von Braun and his team of V-1 and V-2 rocket experts to the United States.

"By 1952, our suspect group of 459 individuals had been identified and given permission to emigrate to the United States under government sponsorship. Once in the United States, they were assigned appropriate duties in various defense research laboratories. In any case, the numbers involved, the stringent security and censorship requirements, plus the necessity of rapidly moving them out of the packed European refugee centers, precluded anything but the most perfunctory of background checks."

Eisler turned and stared out the window.

"An error in judgment, Damon," he said softly. "But, then, the human factor was an imperfect equation. It remains equally imperfect today."

"So," Cory asked, after a moment. "Of the 459, how do you know that only five are intelligence agents?"

"The paper trail isolated them." Eisler turned back and looked at Cory. "Out of the 459, 230 are now dead, 187 retired with no government contact, and of the remaining 42, a review of their date-project-time groupings suggests no relation to any unexpected Soviet breakthroughs. And if this was not enough in itself, the Heidelberg immigration records indicate that all five of those identified originally came into the western sector from Czechoslovakia."

"Which," Cory remembered, "had gone directly from German to Soviet control."

"Yes," Eisler sighed again. "No, Damon, objectively, we must take Sergov's allegations as valid. We have been suffering an incredible penetration of our technological wherewithal. Consequently, the targets must be removed."

Enter me, Cory thought irreverently. "Then I guess I know why the ruse in my orders. I'm to be somewhere I'm not. But why the force option and not a more conventional intelligence operation?"

"It's a presidential decision," Eisler answered. "He feels, and I concur, that these five have been in place so long that they all have initiated their own individual cells. Who knows where? And, what with the Russians so in need of foreign currency, there exists a real threat that they could conceivably simply become middlemen, stealing our technology and selling it to someone with hard currency. Someone toward which we are not so indulgent: the North Koreans, Muslim factions, possibly even the Japanese or Chinese.

"To preclude this scenario, the president has issued a finding authorizing the action. His line of thought is straightforward. To save American lives in the future, he is willing to sacrifice five Russian lives today. Additionally, once they are compromised, conventional counterintelligence surveillance will be enhanced so that any of their subordinates can be identified and dealt with in a less severe manner."

Cory understood the real rationale. Not yet two years into his presidency and the Reagan approach to the *weltpolitik* was making itself felt.

"It's all changing back, isn't it?" Cory asked.

"Yes," Eisler nodded. "And with it, the counterpoint: the biases of the intellectual left and the inevitable suspicion and misgivings concerning American intelligence functions. There is even talk of legislation to place the FBI in charge of all counterintelligence operations, including the overseas activities which are now being directed by the CIA."

"Kind of irrational," Cory observed.

"Of course it is," Eisler agreed, pausing for a moment. "We need to stay the course. To do as we have always done. We must delete the threat and protect our network. Accordingly, what with their collective tenure, to eliminate the five Russians, well, you can imagine the mad scrambling as lower ranking operatives jockey to fill the void."

"A blind man should be able to pick them out," he said.

"And perhaps even the FBI," Eisler said, smiling. "No, the Russians will be pushing hard. Consequently, they will make mistakes. We will capitalize on this and, if fortunate, perhaps we will be able to, as it is said, *persuade a few of theirs to become a few of ours*."

"Maybe I was wrong," Cory said. "Maybe all the old players aren't changing."

"Oh, they're changing," Eisler smiled. "And so is the playing field. It's not so much territory anymore, Damon. It is all currency and industry driven. I envy you your future. The assignments will be less prejudicial. Moderation will be required. Like the drivers, they too will become commerce. More inviolate."

Cory looked away. There was an unmistakable touch of sadness in Eisler's voice, as if he had come to grips with his own mortality and the realization that tomorrow would not be his and Cory's to share. Cory wondered briefly whether his grandfather had pondered similar thoughts. Then, as much for himself as Eisler, he shifted the subject back to operational realities.

"What about logistics?" he asked.

"Of course," Eisler said. "Your liaison will be Boudreaux Pock."

Cory smiled openly. "I thought Pock was somewhere in the Middle East?"

"Actually it was Pakistan," Eisler said. "However, he ran into a bit of trouble with our hosts, so I was compelled to order his back. He currently is working in a support capacity attached to the Joint Special Operations office in the Pentagon. Boudreaux is expecting you and has instructions to provide anything you deem necessary."

"Who makes the initial contact?" Cory asked.

"Pock will communicate with you. You will be preregistered at the Stouffer's National Center Hotel outside of Washington. It's adjacent to National Airport and, since all five individuals live near Washington, also close to your targets. Pock will secure a vehicle for your use. After completion of the assignment, return it to the hotel parking garage. Boudreaux will ensure that it is sanitized and returned to the rental company.

"Now," Eisler continued. "About documents. When we land in Mexico City, we will remain in the transient passenger area so as to avoid the Mexican authorities. Once in the terminal, I will provide you with a packet. In it will be an American passport under the name Brian Kellogg. You will employ your agricultural advisor fabrication, I presume it's second nature now, and will find the necessary documents, a driver's license and credit cards, to support the identity. You may use only one of the credit cards, VISA. The others are invalid.

"Airplane tickets. We will not travel to Washington aboard the same aircraft. You will become Brian Kellogg in Mexico City, then fly direct to Washington with an intermediate stop in Houston where you clear U.S. Customs. You will give me all of your papers when I pass you the Kellogg packet. With the exception of Pock and myself, anyone even remotely connected with QUEENWALK will be led to believe you are performing some highly classified assignment in the Philippines, the details of which were authorized by my direct verbal order. Any questions?"

"One," Cory said. "Any specific egress plan?"

"Yes," Eisler smiled. "Once you have completed your assignment, you will use the VISA card to purchase a ticket to San Juan, Puerto Rico. No permits are required for Americans, and the Kellogg passport will serve as your identification. Upon arrival in San Juan, you will find public transportation to our safehouse. Do you remember the location of the villa?

"Is it still the one adjacent to the old town Ramada Inn?"

"Yes," Eisler nodded. "You will wait for me to contact you at the villa. Now, a word as to your demeanor with the villa's residential staff. You are nonspecifically to give the illusion of just having returned from Manila and some advisory action with NISA, the Philippine National Intelligence Authority. As to why you are in San Juan, you may explain that I am to debrief you personally. Once I have learned of your safe arrival in Puerto Rico, I will join you there. You will return all the Kellogg documents to me, and I will return yours to you."

Eisler paused for a moment. Then, almost as an afterthought, asked, "Since I'm to assume Manila is unsatisfactory, where would you like to be reassigned after this?"

"I'm not sure," Cory said.

"Well, consider it, Damon. I'll need three choices."

"You'll have them," Cory told him.

"Fine," Eisler smiled. "Now then, since the administrative details are finished, shall we have some fresh coffee?"

Cory nodded and Eisler reached up to press the stewardess call button.

As he did, his left suit sleeve slid down his forearm and there, on the flesh some four inches above his wrist, Cory saw something he had never seen before. A faded gray tattoo: 27675.

Eisler noticed him looking.

"Birkenau," he said simply.

"I didn't know," Cory shrugged. "I guess I should have thought . . ."

But the stewardess arrived before Cory could complete the sentence. And as they ordered their coffee, talk turned away from the past and to generalities. Neither Birkenau nor Heidelberg was mentioned again during the remainder of the flight to Mexico City.

***

Mexico City. Hot, crowded, humid, and polluted.

Eisler, with his diplomatic passport, was ushered to the transient waiting area. Cory wandered through the exercise with the other common travelers.

He found Eisler waiting for him in the far corner of a lobby adjacent to the duty-free shop. "By the way," he said as Cory joined him, "I meant to tell you. You've been promoted. You are a full colonel as of today."

Cory was surprised. "I never expected that."

"You realize it also will be your last promotion," Eisler added, without apologies.

This did not surprise Cory. He nodded.

With few exceptions, the army—for that matter, the entire military hydra—tended to possess an unspoken yet ingrained hostility toward officers whose entire careers were spent in the clandestine arts, even those who, like Cory, had walked the long gray line out of West Point.

Guerrilla warriors never generals become.

Such was the old adage, Cory remembered. No, generals were those with command experience. Time endured in companies, battalions, brigades, then divisions. The line marching onward, upward. Swaying in drone-like obedience to administrative tangos.

Privately Cory despised regulations, their typists, and, quite obviously, their authors. But even more to his ire was the very idea that his service was considered inferior to that of some Pentagon paper wizard struck him as patently ludicrous. Then again, there surely was no shortage of absurd military traditions. So why question this one?

He smiled at Eisler.

"Well, it's not like I need the money."

Eisler chuckled at the typically honest comment.

"And how are your good friends at Calder-Lebray?" he asked.

"Still taking their eight percent off the top, I imagine. In any case, I do appreciate the thought."

"Nonsense," Eisler said, with a wave of the hand. "It was more than deserved. Your work in Guatemala was beyond reproach."

Reaching into his coat pocket, Eisler casually passed Cory two thick envelopes. One held the identification materials. The second, information abstracts and photographs on the five Russian scientists.

"You're senior man now, Damon," he said softly.

Cory took the envelopes as he handed Eisler his own documents.

"Really?" he asked as they began to walk together. "And just how many of us are there now?" It was a good-natured probe. A tease mostly.

Eisler's eyes danced mischievously.

"More than few, less than many."

Cory nodded. It was Eisler's stock answer and although he himself had crossed paths with any number of other QUEENWALKers over the years, he still had no real idea of how many individuals Eisler had in the field.

"I thought rank had its privileges," he said.

"In time, Brian Kellogg," Eisler said, becoming serious as he offered an outstretched hand. "But for now, we must be going. Select an appropriate deception, Brian. I shall be watching your progress."

Brian Kellogg, Cory thought. As was his way, Eisler was using the name to ease him into character. It was a subtle little trick, but a proven technique.

He shook the older man's hand. It felt gristly, the skin loose and dry. They held the grip for perhaps a second too long as a look that was not quite conversation passed between them—that of men who knew each other well. Who understood one another. Who even cared.

Cory spoke first.

"Goodbye, ambassador." It was said sincerely.

At the word, his title—for he did carry the honorarium of ambassador—Eisler blushed slightly.

It passed.

"Goodbye, Brian Kellogg," he smiled.

Cory turned and disappeared amid the airport's confusion.

For a long moment Eisler stood quietly, a rather plain little man in a large, brooding world. Then he moved, shuffling slowly to the gate where his own flight was boarding for Miami en route to Washington, D.C.

Fait accompli. The magic was passing.

"Take care, Damon Cory," he whispered to himself.

You need only reap its bounty.

CHAPTER 5

THE SECOND DAY
Sunday, November 23, 1982

United Airlines Flight 143, 12:07 A.M.

"... indicating our final approach into the Honduran capitol of Tegucigalpa. We request you please extinguish all smoking materials, bring seats and tray tables to an upright and locked position, and please remain seated until we come to a complete stop in the terminal area."

Figures, Sal Franco thought. The bastards never lowered the wheels until he'd decided he was finally tired enough to actually sleep. Wishing for a Marlboro, he unwrapped another piece of chewing gum and popped it into his mouth.

Franco rolled his head around on his shoulders. He was irritable and admittedly surly. His tongue felt like the first draft of a Dead Sea scroll and the airplane seat not unlike some prostatic cyst requiring surgical removal. He had not been able to sleep, so in the twelve-odd hours since leaving Washington he had done absolutely nothing but wait. Washington to New Orleans, wait. New Orleans to San Salvador, wait, and now, finally, the landing in Honduras. The plane was a gulag with wings.

The litany back to English: "On behalf of our pilots and your entire flight crew, I would like to thank you for flying United and hope you will fly us again when your plans call for air travel."

"Count on it, princess," Franco whispered, as he tapped his fingers on the armrest. He'd sooner call for a root canal.

***

Franco was *comercial*—traveling on his personal passport rather than the official documents issued by the Bureau. Normally he preferred to keep his arrival low-key in a country, but now he was wondering if perhaps he'd made a mistake.

Looking up from Franco's papers, the Honduran immigration officer, a particularly reptilian specimen, considered the clothes of the passenger standing before him: leather jacket, jeans, and boots. He then directed his attention to the rest of the belongings now pulled from the canvas flight bag and divided into three distinct heaps on the long steel table and guarded by two Honduran soldiers with American surplus carbines at the ready.

First pile: additional clothes.

Second pile: toiletries and camera equipment.

Third pile: blister packets of gum, four legal pads, an envelope filled with papers written in English.

"Your name is Franco?" he asked.

"Yes," Franco answered.

"And you are American?"

No, asshole, Franco thought. I'm a Knight Templar on a secret mission for the World Health Organization. "Yes."

"And what is the purpose of your visit, Mr. Franco?"

"Tourism."

"Tourism?" The officer began snapping at the passport with soiled, fleshy fingers.

Franco glanced to the two soldiers standing behind the table. Their efforts to appear intent made them look even younger.

"Yes," he repeated. "Tourism."

The officer flipped through the passport with a splayed thumb.

"You travel much, Mr. Franco," he commented.

So it can read, Franco thought. "I'm a journalist."

"A generalist?"

"A writer."

The officer nodded mechanically, more horizontal than vertical.

"Do you realize we imprison terrorists, Mr. Franco?"

A knee-jerk reaction to the bombing, Franco suspected. He would play along. "Terrorists?"

"It is a crime to plot against my government, Mr. Franco."

"Sounds like a good plan."

The officer looked back to the passport.

"You have traveled to El Salvador," he said, referring to the document. "And Colombia. And Grenada. And Mexico. And Panama."

He looked up.

"When have you traveled to all these places, Mr. Franco?"

Evidently it didn't read numbers, Franco surmised. "I don't know. Within the last couple of years. The dates are stamped in there somewhere."

"I know that, Mr. Franco."

Raising a leg, the officer perched himself on the corner of the table. He smiled broadly revealing a particle of undigested food wedged between two crooked front teeth. Franco wondered the availability of dental floss in Honduras.

"But the dates are not important," the officer continued. "I must know why. Why have you traveled to all these places? You are American CIA, yes?"

No, I work for a living. "I told you. I'm a writer. I write stories."

"I like stories, Mr. Franco. Good stories."

"Everyone's a critic."

"I like stories about women, Mr. Franco. Do you write stories about women?"

And I bet you really break the hearts, Quasimodo. "Occasionally."

"Do you have any of your stories, Mr. Franco? I see no stories here, and I would like to read one of these stories."

Franco said nothing. The officer was getting under his skin with the banal line of questioning.

"So, Mr. Franco. It seems we have no proof you actually write stories, do we? "

Back to asshole. "You can call the American Embassy. I'm sure you will find their reply most enlightening"

The officer held out his hands in a typically Latin gesture.

"But Mr. Franco. I have no telephone. I have only you. Perhaps I should imprison you until you admit the purpose of your visit?"

Franco had had enough. It was time to terminate the moronic interrogation. Leaning over the table, he lowered his voice to its more intimidating level.

"May I leave now?" he asked, speaking for the first time in perfect Spanish. "Or would you rather I find the telephone and make the call?"

An expression, more than distress, but less than fear, flashed across the officer's face. Franco knew what he was thinking: Call? Call who? His embassy? My superiors? Who is this man? Can he hurt me? Have me transferred? Sent to the border stations? Better not risk it. The airport was good duty. Safe with many bribes offered.

"Well?" Franco asked. He jingled some coins in his pocket.

Suddenly, the officer began to laugh.

"Of course, Mr. Franco. Of course. Do not worry. I make joke. My government does not imprison its visitors without reason. We believe in democracy. Of course you may leave now."

Guns and butter. "Whatever's right."

While the officer busied himself with all the appropriate stampings and initialings, Franco roughly jammed his belongings back inside the flight bag.

"And here are your papers, Mr. Franco."

Franco took the passport and slid it into a jacket pocket.

"Just one more question, please?" The officer was all smiles.

"What's that?"

"Where will you be staying while visiting Honduras?"

"The National Cathedral," Franco said with a straight face.

The officer looked puzzled, but Franco did not wait for a response. He hefted his bag, proceeded though the immigration checkpoint and stalked toward the outside parking area.

He checked his watch. It was well past midnight. As he reached the curb, Franco noticed a black Jeep Cherokee slide from its parking slot and wheel toward him. Armored with tinted windows, the Jeep was known as a *blindado*. In every Latin country, the vehicles were identical.

As the Cherokee stopped, Franco tossed his bag into the rear cargo area, then climbed into the front and reached under the passenger's seat.

"Chuloteca," he told the young Latino driver from the embassy motorpool.

The driver eased away from the curb.

"You want woman first?" he asked.

"Not tonight," Franco told him as, from beneath the seat, he retrieved a Browning 9mm pistol, worked the action, placed it on safe and slid it into the waistband of his jeans. "Just make sure I'm in Chuloteca by dawn."

"*No problema*," the driver grinned. "You sleep, I drive. You can get woman later."

Trying not to smile at the driver's juxtaposition of priorities, Franco punched open the glove box, shoved aside two boxes of 9mm ammunition, and pulled out the obligatory half-pint of scotch, the usual bit of cheer arranged by Jonathon Weall.

Twisting off the cap, he took a small sip and looked out through the windshield. With the exception of a few military vehicles and soldiers loitering in small packs on various corners, the streets were dark, wet, and deserted. Franco was acutely aware of their mission and, unexpectedly, found himself experiencing a fleeting pang of melancholy.

Another dead city. Another curfew. Another third world political promenade with dawn's facade of freedom ensured only by the previous night's oppression.

Sadly enough, even the air tasted of contradiction.

He took another sip of the liquor.

Fuck it, he decided. It was too late an hour for humanist scrutiny. Besides, he needed to stay detached.

He looked to the driver.

"What's your name?" he asked.

"Qito," the man answered.

Franco unwrapped, then popped a fresh piece of gum into his mouth. He noticed the driver watching him.

"You want a piece?" he said.

The driver declined and Franco shrugged.

No problema, he thought, as he snuggled deeper into the seat.
Within a few minutes, Sal Franco was asleep.
His dreams were those of rings.

CHAPTER 6

Chuloteca, Honduras, 10:20 A.M.

A synapse, Franco decided, considering himself. Another spark in the word games network.

A noun? No. Perhaps an adjective? A preposition? No, not those either. What then? He considered the options—his function.

Simply a conveyance to prompt an occurrence.

Yes, he thought. From this point of view, he knew. He was a *verb* . . . a dismal little verb wandering its way through the sullen vector of interrogation.

But wait? Another question now. Tense use. Which tense was he? Past, future, present? He poked through the papers on the desk. Tense was not important, he decided. At least not for the moment. Things were all beginning to sound the same anyway.

Another prisoner, another interrogation.

Another question, another answer.

And him? Relegated to finding those reticent little truths occasionally hidden within them both. It was funny that way at times—word surgery, that is. *A conveyance to prompt an occurrence.* Such a splendid little craft.

It was also the worst part of his job.

Located less than twenty miles from the Nicaraguan border, Franco's interrogation bunker was adjacent to the sprawling military training complex at Chuloteca—the Honduran-flagged base from whence American dollars and supplies began their clandestine journey to the Contra rebels fighting in Nicaragua.

Trendy times, Franco realized. But although the CIA's efforts to destabilize the Nicaraguan junta were only less than a year old, the bunker was already in disrepair and signs of decay were readily evident. Tattered bits of green cloth hung from the fibreboard ceiling, and sandbagged walls disgorged their contents onto an unswept, rotting floor.

The air was heavy, fouled with diesel-stained drafts, and Franco coughed periodically. He swallowed the aftertaste reluctantly, deciding it the flavor of truckstop mildew. A belligerent condiment only accentuated by the distant throbbing of an unseen helicopter. It was all so uniquely military, so exclusively hostile.

Life in the tropics.
Franco leaned over the rusting metal desk and coughed again.
Appropriate, he thought. The dankness of the bunker was an ideal accoutrement to his pestering mood swings. Those wayward soundings of shallowing gloom that seemed to be getting even shallower by the minute. The cool winds of Virginia were but a pleasant memory already tarnished by the pervasive Honduran humidity. He didn't like this place, but his likes were unimportant. Once again, he forced Virginia from his mind and returned his attention to the woman.

They were alone in the bunker.

Perhaps too alone, Franco was thinking.

Bound hand and foot to a small wooden chair, she glared back across the desk with a pure, almost raw hatred. Yet, Franco considered her attractive even in the torn camouflage uniform.

Middle twenties and small-boned, her dark Cuban skin seemingly liquefied the intensity flashed by violet eyes narrowed in arrogant concentration. She was exotic looking with long, dirty hair hanging waif-like over her shoulders. Her mouth, full beneath sunken cheeks and wide nose, trembled almost imperceptibly.

The quiver was absolutely no indication of weakness, Franco knew, remembering the previous two hours as he flipped casually through his notes. It was rage.

Then again, he would expect nothing less from Alicia Carrera, for she was a political prisoner. She was also, by virtue of curriculum, a terrorist.

Looking up from his notes, Franco continued the questioning. They spoke in Spanish.

"Your dossier is extensive," he said softly.

"You are not amused?"

"No. Why? Should I be?"

"Shocked?"

"Not really. Actually, it's more or less what I have come to expect."

She displayed her bindings. "So it appears."

Franco made a grand show of leaning back in his chair and rocking slowly, watching the dust motes drift down to where they stopped, suspended in a low thin cloud inches above the desk.

"Why the children?" he asked again.

"I told you before, they are a commodity."

He stared into her eyes. The white seemed jaundiced and sallow. An illusion, he decided, conjured by the two low-wattage bulbs pulsating in harmony with mobile generators.

"Do you enjoy the killing, Alicia?"

"You have killed before."

Upon hearing her all-too-correct supposition, Franco's mind reflexively flashed back to Puerto Rico: the botched arrest, the loose weapon, the fugitive he had been forced to kill. True, the woman had been one of the extremists charged in the murder of the nuns, of his aunt; but despite, or maybe because of, the Bureau's valor citation, he had never been able to completely resolve the issue in his own mind.

"Not children," he said.

"You have been in war before . . . ." She let the statement trail off momentarily. Skeptical. Testing him. "Who then?"

"There are different types of war, Alicia."

"Of course there are. But Americans always have others fight their battles." She strained against the chair. "You see your enemy only like this, bound, unarmed, alone."

Franco feigned a yawn.

"But we are not at war," he suggested.

"No," she agreed. "Not you and I. Not even your country and mine. But there is war. People are dying and children are victims. The fact that you and I are even speaking of it only indicates it cannot be changed."

Franco toyed with a pencil.

"You have no remorse?"

"Remorse?" She laughed at the question. "I will be dead within two hours. I have no time for remorse."

Shift to empathy, Franco thought. He stood and walked over next to her.

"Not necessarily," he said softly. He leaned on the corner of the desk and softened his expression. "If you cooperate and talk to me . . . ."

"What?" she interrupted with a hiss. "Cooperate and tell you what?"

"I will see that . . . ."

"Pointless." She spit the word.

"No, not in the least."

Franco lowered his voice. Mellowed it. Tincture of clemency.

"I'm in a position to help you. But you must want to help yourself."

He paused to let her consider the enticement.

"Work with me, Alicia. Let me help you."

She looked into his face.

"Free my hands."

"Will you cooperate?"

Outside, the crack of a single pistol shot echoed into the bunker and, for brief instant, they both remained motionless. Sighing, Franco moved behind the chair and untied her arms.

He returned to his chair and sat down behind the desk.

"How long have you been operating with the insurgents?"

"I don't remember," she answered, rubbing at the angry red welts braceleting her wrists.

Like shit, he thought. "Well, how long do you think you've been operating with them?

She nodded to the file at the corner of the desk. "You already know that answer."

"You said you would cooperate," Franco told her.

"I said nothing."

Cunt. "You are Cuban," he probed.

"You are American."

"You were trained by the Soviets. *Boyevaya* assassination teams."

She dismissed the accusation.

"I know nothing else about you except your government supports the puppet *coronel* in his escapades of terror."

"Which *coronel*?" Franco asked.

"Rico, the Honduran."

Franco knew the name. It had been mentioned in the State Department file. Rico was the commander of the Honduran military border police.

"You know the *coronel*?" he asked.

"Yes," she whispered. "Butcher."

At this, Alicia Carrera slowly, even leisurely, unbuttoned her shirt and exposed her small breasts to Franco. They were horribly disfigured. In the place of nipples, there existed only yellowed lumps of fibroid scar tissue. Two fleshy knobs which, for some reason, reminded Franco of the fatty waste removed from raw poultry prior to cooking.

"He did this to me," she said clinically.

Franco averted his eyes.

"I'm sorry," he whispered, realizing how much he for once meant it. "I had no idea."

"No, I'm sure you didn't." She rebuttoned the shirt. "But the American military officer did."

Franco keyed on the word *American*.

"What American?" he asked.

"*Now* you sound surprised," she said, taunting him.

I'm good, he thought, changing the subject. "Where did this happen?"

"In Dulsuna. To the east."

"Dulsuna is in Nicaragua," Franco said. "We have no ground people across the border. It's against our policy."

"In Dulsuna," she repeated, as if anticipating the denial. "About three months ago."

Franco stared at her for a long moment.

"Tell me about this American." He made the words sound almost off-hand as he began taking notes again.

Nodding, her response came in carefully measured phrases.

"About three months ago, one of our camps was attacked by the *coronel* and his men. I assume we were informed upon; but in this type of struggle, it is always to be expected."

Franco didn't comment.

"After the fighting stopped," she continued, "four of us were captured and held for questioning."

"You?" Franco asked.

She nodded.

"Myself, Luis Blanc, and two others. I cannot remember their names now."

"Who is Luis Blanc?"

She smiled slightly.

"A comrade. A friend. We trained together and fought together."

Another Cuban, Franco thought, scribbling the name on the yellow legal pad just beneath his doodling of Pinocchio in drag.

"Go on," he told her.

But Alicia Carrera said nothing, and Franco became aware of her searching his face for something.

He knew what it was—understanding.

Not yet, he thought, making sure she found none.

"I told you to go on with your story."

"I know," she sighed. "I was just . . . ."

Stay cold, he admonished himself. Not time for real softening yet.

"Just continue, Alicia. Nothing more."

Her eyes kindled something; but it passed so rapidly Franco was unable to identify the emotion.

"Alicia?" he pressed.

Finally she resumed talking.

"The morning we were captured, they led us to a clearing in the jungle. The *coronel* and the American were waiting for us. The soldiers forced us to kneel at their boots and . . . ."

"And what?"

She twisted on the chair.

"And the American winked at Rico and . . . ."

Franco knew what was coming.

"And Rico pulled his American pistol and shot the other two in front of Luis and me."

"Why them?"

"They were not Cuban. They were Honduran."

Divide and conquer. "And?"

"And then the *coronel's* soldiers decapitated them . . . ."

A bit much.

"And placed the severed heads in front of Luis' and my eyes so we were forced to look into the bleeding stumps of their necks."

Unacceptable, Franco thought. Simple sickness.

He was aware of his fingers tapping on the desk as he consciously attempted to retain some measure of objectivity while evaluating her most likely self-serving interpretation of events.

True, insurrection made for dirty little wars and, again true, the details were repugnant, *if factual*.

Two thoughts now. One, he was not a field correspondent for Amnesty International. But, two, there was really no legitimate reason for her to manufacture lies.

Back to square one. More information was required.

"What happened then?" he asked.

"The torture, of course." Her voice was low. The timbre somewhere between defiance and loathing.

Franco rubbed his eyes. The words *same story* strobed in his mind. Large, back-lit, and in high-contrast Technicolor, it was always the same story. Identical. Regardless of the time or place in history. Regardless of the issues. For that matter, even regardless of any personal motivations, the petty wickedness of mankind always floated to the top. A scab of violence drifting loosely between periodic clots of rational thought. Consuming, even viral, it had become the accepted definition of Third World equity.

"How?" he asked her.

"Rico's usual way of dealing with women. I was stripped nude and tied over a watering trough. Then the soldiers had their way with me."

Franco watched her carefully.

Remarkable, he thought. She spoke as if she had been some spectator at a sporting event. So very, very casual. As for him? All the difference. He suddenly realized that, noxiously, out of crude prurience, he was now primed, even eager to hear the details of the violation. She was the ticket scalper and he was the buyer. Would the game be a good one? It would depend on how truthful the trivia.

"And?" he asked simply.

"I was raped for what seemed like hours. I looked to Luis once. They were forcing him to watch. He could do nothing. There were tears in his eyes, but, but . . . ."

She looked to her hands. The fingernails were chipped and soiled. "I vowed to hurt the *coronel* for the pain Luis suffered."

Franco assumed a more caustic posture.

"And I'm to assume the American watched all of this?"

She nodded, rather childlike.

"And laughed. He once commented on the virility of the *coronel's* men. I had to take him with my mouth. The *coronel* next. Not the soldiers though. Only the *coronel* and the American in my mouth. They called it 'skulling.' Rico said only officers were afforded this tribute."

Franco found himself uncomfortably flushed with anguish.

"But your scars?" he asked. "The soldiers?"

"No. After they completed their mountings, the *coronel* took a machete and began slicing. The American approved. He told Rico they wouldn't have to worry about me nursing anymore guerrillas. 'Field weaning' was the term he used."

A spidery chill feathered Franco's spine.

"What happened to Luis?"

"Yes," she sighed. "Luis. He was a professional. He wanted no personal recognition. He saw himself as only a small part of a people's movement destined for ultimate victory."

Bullshit communist rhetoric, Franco thought. He disregarded her statement.

"You didn't answer my question."

She again twisted in the chair.

"The *coronel* realized Luis was willing to sacrifice his life for what he believed. That he was committed to serving the combined will of the peasants. That he would . . . ."

As before, they both stiffened as the shock of another pistol shot reverberated into the bunker.

Franco parlayed the moment. The threat was self-evident.

"That he would do what, Alicia?"

"That he would die, of course. But to suffer a mutilation that removes a person from the struggle and makes them a burden, someone to be cared for . . . ."

Franco understood. Dead was dead—one on the tally board. Mutilated was one, plus how ever many others were needed to care for him. More could be removed from the field with mangled people, severely mangled people.

"You think that is why Rico is so preoccupied with torture?" he asked.

She thought about the question.

"As a means to an end, I suppose. But I really think it was something altogether more than that. What do you think?"

Franco paused. She was probing his weaknesses. His conclusions. He cut it off.

"What do *you* think?" he countered.

She shrugged.

"Luis was a professional. I told you that."

Dime a dozen. "So?"

"So even if he could be made to talk, Rico knew anything he said would be useless. Old information. Disinformation at best."

Franco set down the pencil and moved it slowly to the exact center of the desk. Then he stood.

"In other words, Alicia, you're not going to tell anything either."

"I don't know," she answered. "May I untie my feet?"

Franco made a permissive gesture with his hand.

Bending over, she quickly freed her ankles, then looked up at Franco.

"You said it is against your country's policy to have American military advisors inside Nicaragua."

Leaning against a wall, Franco was making small mounds in the spilled sand with the toe of a boot.

"I'm not here to discuss American foreign policy," he told her.

She stretched her legs.

"I know. But could it not be part of your duties to report such violations of American foreign policy?"

Perceptive bitch, Franco thought as he returned to the desk and flipped through his notes. But this was dangerous ground to be covering.

"What's your point, Alicia?"

Her eyes went cold.

"I am well aware of your function, Mr. Franco. You are merely attached to your country's diplomatic staff. You do not belong here. You are an outsider and may bypass conventional reporting procedures at your own discretion. Correct?"

She was definitely no novice, Franco reminded himself.

"Conceivably," he nodded

"There are no secrets in this place. Besides, I've been kept alive for the sole purpose of your interrogation."

Reaching to the desk, Franco picked up the pencil and pointed it at her.

"No," he said. "You have the option of . . . ."

"You have read my dossier," she interrupted, her voice softening slightly. "I am not a fool. I, too, have some measure of expertise in these matters."

Nodding in agreement, Franco experienced an escalation of nervous admiration for the woman. It left him with an empty calm.

"But back to the point," he prodded. "You feel the incident with Rico was more than torture for information?"

"In Luis' case, it was sheer brutality."

Fervor, Franco thought. Still no tangible evidence.

"Did Luis cooperate?" he asked.

"No. I told you he would not."

Back to word gaming.

"But they tortured him anyway?"

"Murdered him."

"Rico?"

"The American."

Franco lowered his voice an octave.

"What is the name of the American, Alicia?"

"It is not important."

"It is, if I'm to verify your story."

Her eyes widened.

Good, Franco thought. Got to keep that hope springing.

"It is," he repeated. "You know it is."

"You will report what he did?"

"I merely asked for a name."

Watching her closely, Franco could sense she was beginning to collect her thoughts. Starting to open up. Good signs all the way around. He decided to allow her a few moments of silence. Feigning disinterest, he began to paced around the bunker. Soon, she began to speak.

"After the mutilation of my breasts, I became unconscious. When I awoke, I could hear Luis whimpering. I looked in the direction of his voice. He was being tortured . . . *la boya*."

Talk to me, Cuban. "*La boya?*"

"You are not familiar with the technique?"

"No," Franco admitted. "What is it?"

She explained in that casual spectator voice again.

"It means the float. That the brain is not anchored to the skull. That it floats inside the bone of the head. Like a buoy or a cork inside a bottle."

Franco found his mind swirling with a fresh new round of morbid fascinations and congealing visual images. Try as he would, they could not be denied. With what was not quite eagerness, he nodded her on.

She seemed not to notice his fascination.

"The American had wired Luis' forearms together behind his back and his legs together at the knees and ankles. Then Luis' body was bent backward and another wire tied around his neck. Its opposite end was twisted into a noose and looped around his testicles. If Luis did not keep himself in that backward position, the wire would tighten and he would eventually castrate himself."

Jesus, Franco thought. Just imagining the man's helplessness caused a hollow emptiness to reach from his own groin. Cold hauntings radiating from somewhere behind his snug little prostate and ascending to the throat. He thought to speak, but decided against it.

Her voice began to quiver as she fought back tears.

Franco listened closely, very closely. Emotion made the story real. Made for better truth.

"As I said," she continued. "The brain floats inside the head. The theory being to upset the equilibrium of the solution, cloud the thought processes, and overcome an individual's reluctance to talk."

Upon the word "talk," she suddenly began to shake. Involuntary tremors seizing nerve endings.

A saucy *danse ganglia*, Franco observed. Another good sign. He exploited it.

"What then?" he asked.

She stared across the desk.

Franco kept his face impassive. No empathy yet. Information first.

"What then?" he repeated.

Her lower lip fluttered. Tears streaked her cheeks.

"Alicia?"

Her words came in halting wet breaths.

"The American kept hitting Luis in the temple trying to induce shock. But Luis refused to talk. After about ten minutes, blood began dripping from his ear and he died. The American urinated on his body and walked away."

"Luis told them nothing?"

"No," she whispered. "That is precisely the point. They knew of his training. That he would die before cooperating." Her tears ran openly now. Cheek to lip, lip to jaw. "No, Franco. There was no tactical reason for hurting Luis. The *coronel*, the American, they murdered Luis for amusement."

In the distance an artillery battery commenced firing, and inside the bunker the bare lightbulbs flickered in silent protest.

"How did you escape?" Franco asked.

"I did not escape. I was allowed to live." Each word oozed loathing. "My breasts are to be an example to others."

Time to back off a bit, Franco decided. Give her a moment to slide back down the emotional scale.

Closing his eyes, in his mind he counted to sixty while outside the sounds of the artillery intensified, then dissipated. The lights regained their cool translucence as the generators stabilized.

"Sounds like they're shelling another hamlet," she told him. "I wonder how many children are being maimed?"

Franco was surprised by the calmness in her voice.

"It could be training," he said. "Or it could not be."

She shrugged vaguely.

"Does it really make any difference?" she asked.

"Probably not," Franco answered, surprising himself with his candor.

She understood his meaning. In either case, her participation was no longer a factor.

"People used to care," she said. "Some still do."

"Do you, Alicia?"

Thoughtful, she paused for a long moment before responding.

"I don't know. Just then, when I was listening to the artillery, I was trying to remember. Trying to . . . ."

Get inside the bitch's head. "Trying to what?"

"It's not important now. Anymore, I'm not sure it ever was."

Cunt. Pushing back from the desk, Franco stood and walked over to her.

"What is the American's name, Alicia?"

She stared up at him, the tears were now dried flakes that discolored her skin with pale irregular lines.

"Devlin," she murmured.

Ladies and gentlemen, we have a bingo. "Where is he now?"

She shook her head.

No problema, Franco thought. Continue the chipping.

Returning to the desk, Franco thumbed though a folder containing blank yellow legal sheets.

"There is no Devlin attached to the American contingent," he said, after an appropriate length of time.

"That is none of my concern." Her voice sounded far away. Somehow artificial.

Climb the scale again. "You and Luis were lovers?"

"Yes. We were together for many years. I had his child."

Child? Exquisite. Yet another ingredient for the emotional bouillabaisse.

"A child?" Franco asked, his voice level.

"A boy. Last year. It was stillborn. We were in the jungle. There was no doctor so . . ." Her voice choked off.

Work the emotions. Keep pushing. "You were alone?"

"No. Luis was there. But he could do nothing. After failing to revive his son, he fell asleep in my arms. There was the same whimpering then, like when Devlin was torturing him." Her lip began to quiver again. "Those were the only times I ever heard Luis cry." She glanced up at Franco. "He was a strong man. A brave man. The tears were not for himself. They were for the torment he felt. His inability to help his woman and child."

Franco could not comment. Her words had provoked another uncomfortable surge of compassion. He averted his eyes. Damn, he thought. Pity? *Me*?

It was an unnerving experience; yet he could not excise it anymore than deny it. It just lurked there. Kind of like some sinister gene on a newly discovered paradoxical helix.

"These are difficult times," he finally mumbled, not so much for her, but to give himself a moment for composure.

She kept talking.

"Do you know how much pain Luis must have felt when Devlin forced him to watch me raped and mutilated? How much anger? How much . . . ."

Franco got that gut feeling. He was losing direction.

"Enough," he told her.

"Luis knew he could never avenge me . . . ."

"Enough." He made it an order.

". . . comfort me."

Franco said nothing. He needed to listen. He made himself listen.

"We buried our child in the jungle. We both knew we would never visit the grave again, but neither of us mentioned it. It was our personal loss and we both tried to deal with it alone. The child was the only thing Luis and I had together. And now we will never have anything. Devlin did that. Devlin and the *coronel*. They took Luis away from me."

Fighting the urge to share her loss, Franco walked over and squatted down in front of her chair.

"But I told you," he said softly. "There is nobody named Devlin operating here."

Her eyes flashed a new razor of loathing.

"And I told you that it was none of my concern. People like Devlin are never on any lists. They may become an embarrassment. But he worked for your government."

Standing, Franco sighed as he leaned against the desk corner.

"I'll see if I can confirm it."

"Don't even bother to waste your time."

"Meaning what, Alicia?"

"Meaning that you should not take me for an amateur. Your government is not going to admit to him anymore than Havana will admit to me."

"I think you have some misconceptions," Franco countered, immediately realizing the recklessness of his statement. Where the hell was his mind? *Get the direction back. Get the control in place.*

The woman spoke first.

"Misconceptions?" she snapped. "I think not. Terrorism, be it your side or mine, has made its slot in politics, particularly here, in the revolution."

Franco disagreed.

"No, Alicia. You murdered children. That's different. Senseless."

"To you, perhaps. In a war, no. They are just statistics, numbers. Nothing more."

Start pushing again. "That's absurd."

"Absurd?" Her eyes glazed with released zeal. "Violence, whether to children or adults, that is selected by the people, planned by the people, and committed by the people makes it possible for the masses to understand the moral justification of the act. It frees the oppressed from the inactivity of despair."

Franco moved from the desk and stood before her, arms folded across his chest.

"Spare me the worn-out Leninist propaganda, Alicia. You cannot possibly believe in the moral justification of murder solely for its own sake. Think of Luis."

She bared her teeth in a mocking grimace.

"It's not me, Franco. It's not even propaganda. What about your Devlin? Was his violence justified simply because he happened to be American? Were his actions somehow more acceptable?"

Closer now, Franco thought. Keep the pressure on. The big question was coming up again.

"You have no proof about this Devlin."

"Me?" she screamed. "It's not *me*, you self-righteous fool. *You're* the one who wants proof."

Good, Franco thought. Good. Back off a note or two now. Go easy. Keep her talking it out.

"This is pointless," he told her. "You have no conscience . . . no sense of right and wrong."

She shook her head.

"Fuck your right and wrong arguments, Franco. Conscience is only another of your moral fabrications and it is not conscience that is the issue. No. The issue is the question of ethics and responsibility. You have not seen life on the other side. The millions of your dollars doled out to the little countries. The medical supplies. The military aid . . . ."

Standing, she stepped in close, her face inches from his.

"The people never see the money. The people never benefit. It's always the *jefes*, the generals, the *coronels*, the Ricos . . . ."

"Sit down," Franco told her.

She moved even closer.

"Check their Miami bank accounts. Their Swiss banks. The money's there, not here."

"I said sit down."

Again he was ignored.

"And *your* government," she hissed. "The very essence of hypocrisy. When things go wrong. When the people have had enough. When they want their share. You send in your Devlins to make sure things remain the same. To take care of any little problems."

On the edge now, Franco thought.

But who? Him or her? Unknown factor. Keep the pressure on. Keep it on line. Reaching over, he grabbed her arm. It felt incredibly thin through the ragged camouflage cloth.

"Down," he repeated for the third time.

"No," she screamed, spitting in his face and pulling away. "Don't you touch me, charlatan. Don't you ever touch me."

Outraged by the spittle, Franco forced his anger into check. He watched her eyes. The terror therein, not of him, but that special terror only the desperate and lost could ever experience. Inside he felt a familiar rush of power, then it was gone, replaced by a gnawing realization of sympathy that devoured even the most remote thoughts of domination.

"Please, Alicia," he whispered, as he wiped the mucus from his chin, then reached over and gently eased her back into the chair. "There is no need for this."

She refused to look at him. His tenderness was forcing her own composure to return.

"I'm sorry," she said softly.

Franco thought a subtle threat appropriate.

"It's time for you to go, Alicia."

Her eyes softened.

"Wait, please?"

Franco looked down at her.

Finally, he thought. She seemed to be changing before his eyes. It was in the shoulders, the posture, the nervous bouncing of her knees. No longer was Alicia Carrera some dedicated terrorist spouting revolutionary theory. He had broken her. Cringing. The process was intact. Working.

Another moment and she would be transformed into an empty shell, devoid of emotion. Little more than another dead impulse smothered by the acceptance of reality.

Of course, realistically, he had anticipated nothing less. After all, interrogation was his specialty. But somehow, with her, the success seemed discouragingly dishonest. Even lamentable.

But why? Why this time? Why with her?

The answers flared with nauseating clarity.

Christ, he thought bitterly. His objectivity had evolved into understanding and the understanding into empathy. Even worse, he was unable to stop thinking about the damned baby rotting somewhere in the jungle. What was the deal here? What kind of mind games were going on? Had he become nothing more than another fucking priest?

El cura. El cura. Please save my soul for I've forgotten the ritual.

Fuck. Even this was starting to sound acceptable.

"Please?" she repeated.

The bitch, he thought. Her words had cut deep. Too deep. *Charlatan.* No fact had ever been more literal.

"Franco?"

He glanced down at her, then his watch.

"All right, Alicia. We can wait for a few more minutes."

She nodded and slumped in the chair. A moment later, she was again talking quietly, her voice filled with an almost reverent conviction.

"The peasant watches the child die, the government does nothing.

"The peasant pleads, the government does nothing.

"The peasant complains, the government soldiers attack the village.

"The peasant fights, loses, is taken prisoner, and is executed as an enemy of the government."

She looked up at Franco.

"Don't you see? Can't you understand? Won't you allow yourself to understand?"

No, Franco told himself. It would only make things that much murkier, and he wasn't sure how much more murkiness he could tolerate.

"I have no control over that," he gently reminded her. "I have no input into foreign policy."

"No, perhaps not. But you can report Devlin."

"I have no proof."

She searched his face.

"Is Devlin sufficient proof?"

Franco nodded.

"And you will help me if I tell?"

Again Franco nodded and waited. She was being cautious, and he was more than aware of her evaluating him. Studying him. Remembering the conversation. The questions. Answers. Attitudes.

Franco gave her his most practiced expression of sincerity. It was a token, he knew. But she really had no other measure of hope.

"There is a village," she whispered, after a few terminal seconds. "Manchia. His body is there."

"But Manchia is in Nicaragua," he told her. "I am prohibited from going there for confirmation."

She held out her hands. Cupped them together. More than hope, less than prayer.

"Besides," Franco sighed. "If he is dead, then it would be all for naught anyway." He looked down at her. "You killed him?"

She nodded.

"Tortured him?"

"With vengeance."

"*La boya*?"

"How did you know?"

"It's probably what I would have done," Franco admitted.

"So you will help me?"

Franco glanced back to his notes.

"Why the children, Alicia?"

"Two of them were *Coronel* Rico's," she answered softly. "Now, he too lives with a loss."

"But the American child?"

She shook her head.

"She was not the target. She was only there."

"So be it," Franco whispered, as be leaned over and gently urged her to a standing position. "It is time for you to go, Alicia."

Walking next to him, she stepped in close.

"You will help me? Speak to Rico's soldiers?"

"Yes, Alicia," he smiled, pausing for a moment at the bunker entrance. "I will speak to Rico's soldiers."

Returning the smile, she took Franco's hands and, placing them inside her shirt, allowed him to feel the mutilation of her breasts.

"Talk to Rico, Franco. See how he lives. See the kind of man he is. Then report Devlin and him. Please," she begged. "Report them both and end this madness. Not for us, for the children."

Unable to find words, Franco could only nod as she left him alone.

Then, for a long minute, he stared into the emptiness of the bunker before moving to the desk and flopping heavily into his chair.

As he reached for his notes, the sound of a single pistol shot filled the enigma of his mind. As per Rico's orders, Alicia Carrera was dead.

Franco swallowed and with the touch of her scars etched on his fingertips, began methodically to destroy his scribblings. Soon, they were but worthless shreds of paper abandoned to the cluttered floor.

No, Franco did not see the flickering lights. Nor would he recall hearing the deep throbbing of an approaching helicopter. At that precise moment, Franco's brain was inundated by cryptic images of maimed breasts while his ears replayed sound of his own *I will speak to Rico's soldiers* lie.

Retching in self-disgust, he forced the time to pass.

For charlatans, he hoped, transitions were brief.

So who was responsible for the cancer?

He knew the answer. Within the hour he would be leaving for Dulsuna and the headquarters of *Coronel* Umberto Rico.

No, he had not forgotten the rituals of interrogation. But now he wished he could, for, inside, he knew it was all different now. The bombing of children and jungle *la boya*. For the first time in his life, Sal Franco knew his cup had indeed runneth over. As for Alicia Carrera?

Somehow the word *crucible* seemed all too appropriate.

CHAPTER 7

El Fuego Airfield, Chuloteca, 12:20 P.M.

The heat was stifling and the air putrid. An endemic puree of fuel, feces, and rot.

Franco cleared his throat, while mentally his list of negatives lengthened.

No wind.

No clouds.

No air conditioning on the cargo plane.

No way to change any of it.

A droplet of sweat splashed into his left eye. He ignored the assault and glanced out the aircraft's open hatch.

Freedom's best, he thought sarcastically. Still allergic to order, I see. *Anyone for cholera?*

Franco chuckled at his mordancy. It really was legitimate, though. Yet another hopeless display of romanticism and realism that persisted despite the futile mediocrity of the whole affair.

In the hard midday sun, the Honduran air facility at Chuloteca seemed the unceremonious parody of a black historical comedy—the Boxer Rebellion, the Crusades, and the Charge of the Light Brigade all rashly stirred together in yet another insurgent skirmish. Unequalled squalor nurturing parasitic waste. A fitting backdrop as the lumbering C-47 shuffled one slot closer to the runway.

Inside the transport, the sound was deafening: metal on metal, rubber on rubber. Mechanical protests of toneless hissings, grindings, and hydraulic scrapings punctuated by sporadic bursts of cockpit radio traffic. Franco was the sole passenger. The embassy had arranged the space.

He decided the noise was a symphony of belligerence. The precise articulation of ugly's sound. Of its feeling.

Another roll, another hold. Then a groaning turn to the left and more waiting. More sweating.

On the far side of the tarmac Franco could now see the control tower, its sandbagged roof and concrete blast walls hazy in the low, lateral waves of heat generated by mother sun and countless numbers of ceaselessly running engines. Closer, between the runways, was equipment, litterings of militaria lying untouched, spilling from abandoned pallets and becoming useless.

There was waste on the horizon where hot filth reeked and sewage seeped wetly between torn bags of garbage. A salad bar of delights for large, green-bellied flies to sample, then regurgitate at leisure.

Rodent munchings prospered.

"Bon appétit," Franco whispered to himself, as a village of white Quonset huts slid into view. The impression was that of broken windows and colorful flags.

Honduran soldiers were everywhere. Fresh army recruits just arriving at the training camps. Veterans rotating back to nameless units. Others simply foraging around lost, sloshing through the septic tank overflow—bowel gumbo, Franco christened it—in sheep-like columns of two and three.

Ahead, a flight of Honduran F-4 Phantoms blasted into the sky, their afterburners scorching the air with billowing clouds of oily black smoke.

Rocking, the C-47 chugged one slot closer. Then another.

Finally, clearance was given, and the pilot wheeled the transport onto the parched runway and immediately began his takeoff roll.

Franco spit.

After baking in the sun for the better part of an hour, the howling bitch of the turboprops clawing for lift was a pleasant annoyance. Since the bunker, *since the woman*, Franco had decided he loathed Chuloteca. In fact, he had broadened the scope of his loathing to include the entire Pacific slope of Honduras.

Dulsuna was farther east. He hoped this would make it more hospitable. Cooler. Quieter.

Of course on the negative side—another factor to be added to his list—Dulsuna was where he would also have the opportunity for audience with Umberto Rico and, contemplating this eventuality, he tried to remain impartial and not allow Alicia Carrera's allegations to prompt any preconceived notions about the man.

He found this to be impossible. Unlike himself, Franco knew the woman had not been lying. And Rico, he suspected, would turn out to be like the majority of other Latino officers he had met through the years. Arrogant, politically connected, and morally blemished. The very indicators that made the skulling and *la boya* stories all too believable. No, Alicia Carrera had spoken the truth; any lies would be his and Rico's to share.

Suddenly, violently, the aircraft shuddered, bounced twice, then lifted off with the pilot torquing into a steep climbing arc out over the Bay of Fonesca.

His mind numb, he continued to stare out the hatch.

The flight to Dulsuna would take fifteen minutes. He wished it were longer, but he didn't know why.

"Screw it," he whispered. Wishes were for dreamers and children. He was neither suit nor was glad, for both were tough cards to play. Tough on the streets, but substantially tougher in the jungle.

Franco shifted in his seat as the C-47 droned south paralleling the Honduran coast. He passed a few seconds watching the water. It was surpassingly clear: a pale, almost aquamarine blister upon which small Honduran patrol boats steamed in aimless circles around a much larger American destroyer. The image stayed in Franco's mind. It seemed to symbolize the whole of Washington's Nicaraguan destabilization efforts.

A moment later there was a slight flutter in engine pitch. Franco sensed it and braced himself as the transport banked east and crossed over the coastline, heading deeper into Central America.

Beneath him, the water became earth. The blue, rich hues of parrot green inching up from the surf to the mountains beyond.

The pilot, he realized, was skirting the Nicaraguan border for he was now able to pick out the various military encampments scattered along the imaginary line that divided the two perpetually belligerent countries.

He looked to the south as the pilot pulled back on the throttles. Low in the distance, he could see the cloud-screened crags of the Darien Cordillera, the natural volcanic spine separating Nicaragua's western population centers from the Caribbean lowlands of the Miskito coast.

Below, the Rio Coco sliced through the jungle. Shallow and sandy, it too was a natural boundary. Not unlike a liquid line of challenge drawn in the dirt and over which each side dared the other to cross. One country scared, the other glad, Franco predicted few would ever get wet feet in a conventional war. The Rico types would see it remained a guerrilla action. They needed things to remain the same.

"Three minutes," the pilot shouted back over the engines.

Franco forced a smile he did not feel and responded with a thumbs-up as he flicked his gum out the hatch. Seconds later, the aircraft's nose dipped sharply and the C-47 plunged toward the ground.

No matter how many times he flown with them, he was always surprised at the way in which military pilots chose to land. It was as though they lined up on the end of the runway from miles away and simply aimed at its end until they hit. There was never any slow, gradual approach as in commercial aviation; but rather nothing more than a controlled fall until the final jolt of touchdown.

He had once asked why this was, and a U.S. Navy pilot had explained it came under the general heading of tactical efficiency—the accepted military term for cowboying it. Franco had doubted this at the time. He had already decided the pilots, like most everybody else who worked in government, just didn't give a rat's ass about the equipment. After all, *they* weren't paying for planes and Uncle Sugar was nothing if not a charitable employer.

As expected, the transport slammed down on the tarmac indicating some semblance of a landing. With the tires screaming in protest and the reverse thrust of the engines beating his ears, Franco gripped the canvas seat to avoid being thrown forward. Soon they slowed, turned, and began to taxi back toward an area bordering the extreme western end of the runway.

Franco stood and walked to the open hatch. He was dumbfounded at what he saw. Whatever he had expected, soldiers, weapons, anything even vaguely military, he had obviously been mistaken. Dulsuna, at least from the outside, appeared as removed from the hostilities as Sarasota, Florida.

In the center of the compound was a large, sprawling, hacienda-like ranch house surrounded by at least four matching outbuildings. All were set behind a white, four-rail wooden fence and defined by a well-manicured expanse of dark green coastal Bermuda grass and pebbled concrete sidewalks. All the buildings were constructed of white stucco and capped with roofs of deep-red tile. The sidewalks had been tinted to match the roofs.

Kind of pretty, Franco thought. Out of place, but pretty nonetheless. Much like some rich South American's thoroughbred horse ranch, without the horses. But not only were the horses missing, he realized, the compound also appeared to be deserted. He could see no people or even vehicles. The only transportation in sight was an old, white, single-engine Cessna Skywagon, and a much newer blue and silver Beechcraft King Air. Both aircraft were civilian models.

The C-47 pulled to a stop adjacent to the Cessna and the pilot cut the engines.

"How long do I have?" Franco asked him.

"Long as you need," the pilot answered. "I'm just driving the bus, you're making the schedule."

"Probably no more than an hour," Franco told him. Then, taking a deep breath, he hopped to the tarmac and began to walk toward the main ranch house where he assumed *Coronel* Umberto Rico would be waiting.

And now, he thought. The truth knotting.

Rico. Franco knew the tone to set. Let the *coronel* take the lead. It would be important to him. Latino military officers were like that, adolescent posturing meant everything.

As for himself? Keep remembering that, if past experiences were to be any counsel, the whole interview would come down to nothing more than the two of them talking, circling, scrutinizing, then eventually coming to appreciate all they didn't have in common.

Of course what Rico wouldn't realize, and Franco inherently did, was that the questions were the easy part. Deceptive answering was where the real art of truth splicing emerged.

Franco? His merit badge was gold.

Rico's? Probably nothing more than bronze.

***

Sal Franco walked into the main hacienda and paused to let his eyes adjust to the dimmer light.

In marked contrast to the gentlemanly illusion conveyed by the outside architecture, the building's interior offered the ambience of an army dayroom: coolly official and smelling of coffee, disinfectant, dirty ashtrays, and floor wax.

A number of walls had been removed to provide a larger working area, space that was now cluttered with conference tables, gray metal desks, swivel chairs, telephones, and green IBM typewriters.

A yellow cat yawned, then stretched atop one of the dozens of four-drawer black-metal file cabinets that lined the walls. Cardboard boxes seemed to be stacked everywhere, as were dark-blue three-ring binders and dog-eared copies of *Time, Newsweek, Penthouse,* and *Playboy*. It was well-established bureaucratic disarray illuminated beneath a brace of low-hanging, fluorescent ceiling lights.

On the walls, above the cabinets, hung *National Geographic* topographical maps. Tight stretchings beneath protective acetate coverings and slashed with red, blue, and yellow grease pencil markings. While it could have been a Washington "war room," it most definitely was not.

The reason, Franco realized, was the stark absence of American flags and the portraits of Washington officials. Here, only one photograph was displayed, that of a Latino officer in a color, three-quarter pose. To Franco, he looked to be another fat, no-neck rhino with a Mussolini complex.

He was formally bemedaled. Enough decorations to open an Army-Navy store, Franco thought. Weird crap, too. Things he had seen at diplomatic receptions. French medals. German medals. Even something that looked African and was about the size of a Honda Accord.

And although Franco had no idea who the officer was, he did note that the eyes did not follow him around the room. The reason, he suspected, was myopia.

To the left a hallway disappeared into darkness, and to the right all windows were concealed behind heavily floraled, lime-colored drapes, which had, Franco guessed, come with the original hacienda.

Strangely enough, with the exception of one man, a ratty-looking Honduran Air Force captain, this room too was deserted.

"*Capitán*," Franco called. "Where is everybody?"

The officer looked up beneath thick eyebrows. He did not bother to stand.

"You are the FBI man?" he asked.

"Sal Franco."

The captain nodded slowly. "It is Sunday, FBI man. We do not work on Sunday. It is the Lord's day." His voice was thick with sarcasm.

"But I was supposed to meet *Coronel* Rico?"

The officer continued to nod.

"And so you will. The *coronel* is resting in his office." He waved a hand in the direction of the darkened hallway. "A word of caution, FBI man."

"What?" Franco asked him.

The captain smiled crookedly.

"The *coronel* is unhappy with you, FBI man. The *coronel* feels you should have met with him before speaking to the Cuban woman."

This irritated Franco. Rico had already been talking behind his back. He shrugged off the warning and attempted to remain pleasant.

"What can I say? It was just a matter of timing."

"We have little time for you, FBI man," the officer said coldly. "We have no use for you. But, then, that is for the *coronel* to explain. Please, go back, FBI man. Discuss it with *el jefe* for yourself."

For an instant, Franco considered telling the good capitain to take his uses and stick them up his ass. But then he remembered Hershel Bechtel's admonishment regarding offending Honduran officials. He swallowed his anger instead.

"I'll do just that, *capitán*," he whispered, as he headed down the darkened hallway. "Thanks for the warning."

***

Sal Franco was again bewildered.

To suggest Rico's office was richly furnished would be akin to describing Chopin as a piano player. Opulent, it was obvious no expense had been spared. All Franco could think of was pass the powdered wigs, *por favor*.

On the other hand, as was the case with most of the *coronel's* phylum, all evidence of good taste apparently remained well entrenched in his mouth. And the private office left Franco with the distinct impression of having encroached into the court of Louis XIV. Louis or, perhaps more pointedly, a peasant's notion of how wealthy people were licensed to live.

Franco shook his head. As Henry James once remarked of Newport, "It was simply too much."

About twenty by forty with a twelve-foot frescoed ceiling, the chambers reminded Franco of a miniature Sistine Chapel, at least that is what he assumed it originally had been designed to resemble. Someone had elected to ruin this effect by covering the walls with an assortment of brown and green colored tapestries, which Franco decided were probably ninteenth-century, possibly Basque, and definitely looted from their original owners.

At one end of the room was a hand-carved Spanish marble fireplace. Faintly pink in color, it embraced an entire wall. At the opposite end of the room were the windows, whose original panes were gone and replaced with stained glass inserts that reminded Franco of those in the old churches in Miami's Little Havana district. He suspected these were also stolen and wondered how they found their way to Honduras. The clear explanation, of course, was that Rico was wealthy and that he spent his money on antique mismatches.

Franco stepped farther into the room. The furnishings just kept coming: wool Persian rugs, pastel and thick; carved jades, marbles, and woods; rare curios, small things, conspicuously displayed on a variety of pewter and teakwood occasional tables. Crystals, golds, coppers, and silvers. All the trappings, only not so pleasing. Only a darkly repressive den in which to display one's treasures amid a subtle glaze of indirect lighting.

It was all so out of context. So cloistered. So garishly opulent.

Franco began to wonder about this man. This Rico. Who was he? What was he? A butcher? The *la boya* devotee he had been led to believe he was? Curious, he moved to the center of the chambers.

His name was called. The voice deep and loud. An exorcised *FRANCO* that hung in the air like an indictment.

Franco's neck hair twisted. He looked to his left. He saw the man in the photograph examining him.

"*Coronel* Rico?" he asked, realizing it could be nobody else.

Rico said nothing.

Showmanship, Franco thought. Role-playing.

Sitting in what could only be described as an alcove draped with dark velvet curtains, Rico was hidden in the shadows to the left side of the fireplace. It was like a little burrow concealed in the corner and protected from the remainder of the room by a massive, intricately carved mahogany desk. Facing the desk, their backs to Franco, were two Florentine-looking side chairs. Gold leafed and upholstered in a velvet that matched the curtains, they reminded Franco of something in the lobby of a Palm Beach hotel.

Franco decided not to wait for an invitation. He walked to the chair closest to the wall and sat down. The seat was hard and uncomfortable, but he said nothing. Franco would role-play too. Rico could begin the conversation.

But Umberto Rico refused to be rushed. He, too, said nothing, and for several seconds they simply stared at each another. One the cobra, the other the mongoose, neither knowing which the other would be.

He had pegged the photograph right, Franco remembered. Rico did tend to remind him of a rhinoceros, without the horns of course.

His head was shaved, and with the exception of a thin moustache, he was hairless. A sort of Idi Amin *español* whose neck had failed to sprout from his shoulders and who reeked of English Leather cologne.

The resultant appearance?

In his early fifties, Umberto Rico was a short, slick, fleshy specimen. A dark, low-browed, even ox-like man whose physical attributes, thick, moist lips, tiny bronze eyes, heavy loose jowls, and flat, wide nose could easily be mistaken as clues to some genetic deficiency begat from sibling love.

But Franco would not allow himself to be mistaken. Experience had taught him that men like Rico were usually shrewd and masters of self-preservation. If not, they would never be able to attain and *hold* their positions of power. Familial ties, particularly in the tropics, could only take a man so far. How he protected his territory was up to the wits of the individual.

Eventually Rico broke the silence. Reaching behind his back, he extracted a silver platter and offered its contents to Franco.

"Cheese?" he said, his tone measured.

"I'll pass."

"Then perhaps something else?"

Franco shook his head, observing as Rico again reached back into the burrow, pulled out a second platter and placed it on the desk between them. Larger than the first, this one offered grilled shrimp and was garnished with slices of avocado.

Must have a deli back there, Franco thought as he looked behind Rico and into the nest. It was like a Pullman sleeper. A small vestibule, a berth really, where Rico could relax, feed, then go to work by merely swinging his legs over the edge and sitting behind the desk.

Not unlike a moray eel, Umberto Rico had reduced the science of time and motion to its most efficient level. He could attend to his duties, whatever they may be, without ever actually leaving the bed.

But where were the medals? Franco thought. He felt somehow cheated. He wanted the complete man, not some resting lord of spoils who now found merit in concealing his true self behind a costume of gold chains, gold bracelets, and a blue oriental-silk dressing gown.

For Franco, a man who had always thought one was either dressed or undressed, the gown was near infuriating. As for the gold embroidered letter J over the left breast, this was momentarily confusing.

J? he thought. Then he realized the significance. J did not stand for Rico's name. The J was for *jefe*—chief, leader, head. The Spanish term of art for those who doled out the largesse.

Christ, Franco thought. What a pretentious parasite.

Watching his visitor closely, Rico placed a slice of avocado in his mouth, then dabbed at his lips with a small linen napkin. "The avocado is excellent," he said. "It pleases me."

"One must have one's priorities," Franco shrugged.

Rico nodded in understanding and peeled a shrimp with small, manicured fingers.

"So you are Franco," he said, without looking up from the platter.

"Yes," Franco said. "Sal Franco."

"Sal-Franc-O," Rico repeated, accentuating the syllables. Then he ate the shrimp with a loud smacking noise, wiped his fingers and tossed the soiled napkin to the center of the cheese plate, thereby indicating the end of lunch.

"So, Sal Franco," he continued. "Your embassy tells me you are with the FBI? That you are a senior special agent for the FBI? This is correct?"

"It is."

"Well, Agent Franco," Rico said. "You should know that I am not a happy man. No, it is more than unhappiness. I am distressed. Do you know why I am distressed, Agent Franco?"

"No," Franco said, deciding to toy with him.. "Have I somehow offended the colonel?"

Rico answered quickly.

"Yes, Agent Franco. You have. You interviewed the Cuban terrorist without speaking to me first. She was my prisoner. I could have saved you a considerable amount of time and effort."

"There must have been some misunderstanding, " Franco said, reasonably.

"Yes," Rico said dubiously. "A misunderstanding."

Franco was already tiring of this charade.

"But colonel," he said. "I come not to question the colonel's authority, but to praise him for the skill and expertise in which he so quickly captured the woman responsible for the death of our ambassador's daughter."

Purposely, Franco's words were laced with sarcasm and woven through with rudeness. But Franco couldn't care less. The anger on Rico's face confirmed the desired effect.

"Surely the colonel can understand why the ambassador would want me to interview the woman? He is a diplomat and knows nothing of police techniques. Hopefully, my report will be able to give him some measure of comfort in his hour of personal grief."

Rico dismissed the explanation with the wave of a pudgy hand and Franco caught the flicker of a diamond ring reflecting the light.

"It is not praise that is the issue, Agent Franco. Your speaking with her without talking to me first is unauthorized. You are only a guest in my country, and I cannot approve any questioning of political prisoners without my being fully apprised, in advance, of the interview parameters."

As he spoke, Franco was aware of Rico's eyes beginning to pulse and of a thin film of perspiration forming just above the moustache. Good, he thought. Rico was upset. Probably wondering whether the woman had told anything that could hurt his career. This only further served to validate Alicia Carrera's story. Time to push now before Rico could relax.

"What do you know about an American named Devlin, colonel?" he asked.

"Nothing." Rico's face remained impassive. "Where did you get that name?"

"What about a torture method called *la boya*?"

"It is a Cuban procedure," Rico answered, a bit too quickly.

"So it seems," Franco said softly. Then he stopped talking and began watching Rico's face. He was practiced, Franco thought. His face still remained impassive. Practiced, but not totally inscrutable. Below Rico's chin, in the neck, Franco could see the muscles begin to tremble. Most people who habitually lied could keep the muscles of the face where they wanted them due to frequent use. None could control the neck. None were that practiced.

He wondered if Rico knew he was caught. He decided to push harder.

"The woman told me she bombed the children because two of them were yours, colonel. That the ambassador's child was not the target. Did you lose two children in the bombing, colonel?"

"Yes, I did, Agent Franco," Rico said cautiously.

"And why do you suppose they were targeted?" Cory asked.

"They were not the targets. The ambassador's daughter was the target."

"I don't believe you, colonel," Franco said flatly. "I believe all the children were murdered because of something you did to the woman."

"I had never seen that woman before." Rico snapped.

"I don't believe that either, colonel," Franco shot back. "I believe you and this American, Devlin, whoever he was, tortured a man named Luis Blanc, killed him, then mutilated the Carrera woman. The bombing was simple vengeance, nothing more. My investigation just doesn't support your government's contentions that it was a terrorist act directed against American interests."

Rico eyed Franco suspiciously. Then he lowered his voice.

"And this is what your report will indicate?"

"Yes," Franco told him.

"Then you leave me no alternative, Agent Franco. I shall be forced to report to your embassy that your conclusions are based solely upon your questioning of the woman. That you made no effort to review my files on the incident and that you were both insubordinate and superficial in your regard for Honduran military authority."

"That, obviously, is your option, colonel. However, I should remind you that the appropriate *civilian* authority has already been obtained. Since this is the case, I needn't tell the colonel that his contacting my embassy could result in—how shall I say it?—a needless exposure of the colonel's authority?"

Franco stopped talking. It was difficult. He actually enjoyed talking to someone in the third person, as if they weren't privy to the conversation. Besides, this one was working very well indeed. He had just politely told Umberto Rico that if he questioned Franco's investigative techniques, he could expect the American Embassy to press for the colonel's being relieved of his command.

Admittedly, Franco had absolutely no hope of this happening. But the notion of raising its possibility, of perhaps worrying the colonel, was too expedient to let pass.

For his part, Rico had obviously understood the thinly veiled threat for, now, he looked pensive. Rather like some cheesy topping sprinkled on a humble pie.

Debasement au gratin? Franco thought. Another bowl for *el coronel*. He wears it so very well.

So now it was up to Rico. He could do two things, Franco predicted. Complain to the embassy, which would take it to Washington where the complaint would eventually end up with Jonathon Weall for disciplinary action. Franco considered this stretch. Rico was no doubt connected; but probably not *that* connected.

What he expected Rico to do—what he *should* do—was withdraw and let everything die down. He would play the grieving father if possible—although Franco had seen no evidence of grief as of yet—and fall back to protect his position and some measure of dignity. Latinos were predictable and there were entirely too many Latino egos involved to risk alienation from Washington.

Across the desk, Rico's jowls fluttered as he sighed heavily.

"I suppose the children make it a civilian matter," he mumbled.

Ah, Franco thought, he's read the script.

Rico offered a toothy smile.

"Please, Agent Franco. We are both professionals, there should be no reason for misunderstandings between us."

Franco shrugged, and Rico reached back into the berth. He pulled out a thick manila envelope and placed it on the desk.

"That is my report on the bombing. I would ask you to include it as an attachment to your investigative report."

Franco's brain effected a brilliant strobe of scar tissue. Ready to conclude the meeting, he stood.

"I'm sorry about your children," he said softly.

Rico nodded solemnly.

"Thank you, Agent Franco. This is a difficult time for all of us."

Franco held Umberto Rico's eyes for a long moment. Then, declining comment, he backed from the desk and walked stiffly toward the door.

"Franco?"

Franco paused at the hall. He did not turn around.

"What?" he called back.

"You forgot my report."

Franco looked back to the desk and stared at Rico's face. He wanted to remember Rico like this. The weakness. The puffery. The meaningless, self-serving document clutched in his miserable little fingers.

"No, colonel," he said, after a moment. "I didn't forget your report. But in time, I'm sure I will."

Without waiting for a response, Franco turned around, left the chambers and hurried toward the waiting aircraft.

His work here was finished. Now, all he wanted was to get back to Washington, give Jonathon Weall his report, and forget about Honduras.

But as he climbed aboard the transport, even these priorities were shoved to his subconscious by something even stronger, something more visceral. His palate was seeping with the odor of shrimp. He cleared his throat and spit out the open hatch.

Haunting in its bitterness, the taste remained. It metastasized. Another sense touched. Visions of breasts and bombings, scents of grilled seafood and rotting flesh. One feeding the other, each feeding itself.

He spit again, then swallowed. Pointless efforts. Like succinct little *soulsnacks*, the visions beckoned him darkly as his revulsion with Rico thusly congealed.

No, he realized. Honduras could not be forgotten. His sense of probity precluded rationalization.

The next step?

Atonement.

Rico, sometime, somehow, would pay for his sins.

CHAPTER 8

Washington, D.C., 3:10 P.M.

As Sal Franco was leaving Dulsuna, Damon Cory was arriving in Washington. More specifically, he was at that exact moment one of two passengers sharing the complimentary limousine service from National Airport to the Stouffer's Concourse Hotel. For a Sunday afternoon, traffic was impossibly snarled and they were already twenty minutes into the five-minute trip.

To pass the time, Cory lit his pipe, snapped the Zippo closed, and continued watching his fellow passenger out of the corner of his eye.

Was he or was he not Desmond Tutu?

Probably not, Cory decided. Looks aside, this one had no Nobel Peace Prize suspended from his neck, and *everyone* knew the good archbishop had never removed the trinket since its award. No medal, no Tutu. Such was the way of the cloth.

The cleric had his props out and was fingering rosary beads with the fervor of a nesting water beetle. He was also quite drunk, an impious vision of alcoholic veneration replete with food-soiled collar and mismatched socks.

Hypocrite, Cory thought, imagining him naked, strip-searched by government soldiers, murmuring hollow incantations to his absent god while a teenaged squad leader asked the timeless question: *Will no one rid me of this meddlesome priest?*

Cory had attended that rite before. No, no, *comandante*. Not I, *comandante*. I am but an observer to your culture. Please play through.

Why thank you, *comandante*. But I have no time to watch, you see I'm late for a very important meeting with *el presidente*.

But of course, *comandante*. Brunch would be nice. Perhaps after tomorrow's coup d'état? I understand completely, *commandante*. Politics leave me ravenous also.

Bemused by his own wit, Cory realized that the limousine had just pulled into the hotel's entrance. To his right, the cleric broke wind with gusto. Cory laughed out loud. Welcome to Washington. It was all so remarkably becoming.

***

Barefoot, a towel around his waist, Cory stepped from the shower and padded across his tenth-floor suite to the window. Outside, to the northeast, Washington was little more than a muted tapestry of shadow and light with the afternoon sun hanging low beneath a distant gathering of storm clouds spawned from the distant Canadian Arctic. The blandness of the light was almost tangible. It would snow before dawn. In the morning, when the shopping mall opened, he would purchase heavier clothing. His was much too thin for winter.

Across Route 1, the Pentagon squatted thickly near the banks of the slate-blue Potomac River. In there, he thought, the conventional planners were planning for conventional operations. And eventually, following these plans, conventional people would die conventional deaths.

Cory felt no trace of sympathy. Such was their choice and such were the realities in conventional tours de force, a consequence he had long before determined the most archaic demonstration of military theory. Then again, he was surely no Lawrence or Mao. And probably some generals still believed it chic. *Another star for that collar? Take two, they're small.*

Cory thought about the planners for a moment. Anyone, he decided, could analyze; nobody could change facts. As for him, there had never been enough. Enough what?

Mirrors? Yes, that was it. There were never enough mirrors to ever make conventional operations look right, not at all. QUEENWALK was the route. Safer to be dissociated from conventional units. More illicit. Silkier.

"Silkier," he whispered, savoring the word. Indeed, the perfect description. In reality, it was probably the prime reason he had been drawn to QUEENWALK in the first place. That and Eisler.

While not exactly military, QUEENWALK was not exactly civilian either. It was an administrative hiatus whose personnel were drawn from the cream of the various services and answered only to the little ambassador. By design, QUEENWALK was all done with mirrors. Because it was not considered military, its staff was exempt from any random congressional guidelines limiting the number of *military* advisors in a particular area.

In a like manner, because it was not civilian, it did not come under the direct control of any particular embassy. As Eisler had initially put it, "QUEENWALK is the flame from which there is no ash."

Eisler's ruse had worked well, Cory acknowledged. And in the autopsical years following Vietnam et al., QUEENWALK had emerged as the instrument of choice when addressing the more ambiguous national security investments.

Undeniably, at times, as on Mindanao, the assignments proved bittersweet; but then such was the reimbursement for a Flying Dutchman *de guerre*. Just another consideration coming with the exercise. Another gathering of emotion to be rejected.

Operating with Defense Department logistical support and employing National Security Agency communications networks, the however-many QUEENWALK consultants, either through chance or design, simply roamed around the clandestine world, getting paid, taking the good with the bad and dispensing the sanction of Eisler's blame.

Most would term it an arguable calling, Cory suspected. And this was probably valid. There was always contention when public posturing ran counter to private policy. Nonetheless, Nicaragua, Somalia, Haiti, and all the other headliners had at one time or another served as platters for QUEENWALK's clandestine grazings.

Covert wars and secret numbers. Traditional American gunslingings. The Russians in Washington? No exception.

All was right with the world.

The phone in the suite rang softly. Cory walked over to the end table and picked it up.

"Ten-twenty."

"Got any used farm equipment for sale, Mr. Kellog?"

Cory laughed. It was Boudreaux Pock.

"But of course," he said. "For you, Boudreaux, everything has a price." Pock chuckled.

"So, how you doing?" he asked.

"Fair to middling," Cory answered. "You?"

"Keeping on, keeping on. Want to drink some whiskey?"

"Sounds good to me," Cory said. "Where and when?"

"The Ondine Lounge," Pock suggested. "Your hotel. It's off the lobby. I'll see you in about an hour."

"You got it." Cory replaced the receiver and returned to the bathroom to finish dressing.

Boudreaux Pock, he smiled. It would be good to see him again. Boudreaux told some of the best stories in the business.

***

Cory ate pretzels and glanced around the hotel bar. It was furnished in a striking, if cold, contemporary decor and, like most Washington hotels on a Sunday evening, was packed with all manner of patrons, most of whom planned to conduct Beltway business during the upcoming week.

Cory listened to the conversations around him. He found them to be routinely predictable.

Two State Department types in dark pinstripe suits: "Actually, Rodney,

I feel that strategic engineering analysis is the most viable alternative to regional stabilization."

A Midwestern businessman: "Price supports. All we need is price supports and, by God, I'm gonna get 'em this trip. I'm talking to Congressman Garrity."

Three Marine privates with slick sleeves and no decorations: "Semper Fi, my man. I'll kick his fucking ass 'til I get tired."

The international weapons reps: German, "Buy Heckler & Koch." Israeli, "Buy UZI." Belgian, "Our Fabrique grenade clearly displays the best operability."

A middle-aged prostitute: "Do you like me? Do you think I'm pretty?"

The Marines once again: "Fuck a bunch of ragheads. Back in Mobile, the only folks with rags on their heads have ringworm."

Cory yawned and checked his watch. 6:30 p.m. He glanced toward the door. Right on time, Boudreaux Pock was looking around the lounge.

"Need an usher?" Cory called, waving a hand in the air.

Pock smiled and began limping toward Cory's table.

A legal bastard, Boudreaux Pock had never attempted to conceal the fact that his existence was owed to a brief, albeit carnal, liaison in the swamps of a nameless Louisiana bayou, specifically that between a fourteen-year-old mulatto girl and a fifty-year-old white ornithologist on field study sabbatical from the University of Vermont.

But as Cory remembered the story, when Pock was in high school, someone found out about his lineage and called him "the tweet." Pock thought this an insult and had immediately, and most unkindly, "rooted" the name caller. Cory had never been able to determine exactly what "rooting" entailed, but he assumed it was serious, for Pock had been given the choice between twenty years in the Louisiana State Penitentiary at Angola or voluntary induction into the military service. Pock had selected the army. No one had ever called him "the tweet" again, not even from behind his back.

"I got your usher hanging," Pock grinned, as he sat down and shook Cory's hand. "Feel frisky?"

"Not that frisky," Cory laughed. "Get you a drink?"

"I've already got them coming."

At that moment, a waitress appeared and sat two tall glasses on the table. Both were bourbon and water. As Pock paid for the liquor from a thick roll of $50 bills, Cory studied him closely.

It had been at least five years since their paths had last crossed and, with the exception of an ugly white scar running from his left eye down to his nose, the time had done little to alter the man's appearance or manner. Both still reminded Cory of a Mississippi River tugboat captain.

In his late forties, Boudreaux Pock was short, dark, hairy, powerfully straightforward and mean looking. He was built like a brick and nonpolitical to a fault. Had it been the 1890s, Cory suspected he would be shanghaiing drugged sailors in old San Francisco. But Pock had been born too late. He'd settled for QUEENWALK.

Cory knew him well. Eisler had recruited them within two months of one another and Pock, although always ready to party, remained serious about his work. Cory considered him a friend.

"Nice touch," he teased, nodding to the scar. "Been dueling again?"

"Building character," Pock said, declining to explain.

"Looks like it was stitched with a logging chain."

Pock shrugged. "The embassy doctor was a obstetrician."

"Must have thought he was doing a cesarean."

"You've got a lot of room to talk," Pock smiled. "What's the deal with those wire glasses? You look like a fucking cockroach."

"Half the time I feel like a fucking cockroach," Cory said, half-seriously. "Too many years poking around in other people's garbage, I guess."

Pock nodded and raised his glass. "Welcome home, Damon."

"Wherever it might be," Cory added.

For the next few moments they drank in silence, then Cory lowered his voice so those at the other tables would not hear the conversation.

"So what's going on in the world, Boudreaux?" he asked. "Anything special I should know before jumping in the Washington sandbox?"

"Not really." Pock shook his head. "Just the same old shit. We chase, they run. They chase, we run. But it's kind of getting all fucked up lately. Everybody's out for themselves and everybody's becoming a prima donna."

"Kind of makes you feel like a bounty hunter, doesn't it?" Cory said. "Doing what we do just because we've been doing it so long."

"Yeh," Pock agreed. "Now we've got you with glasses and me with a gimpy foot. Shit, Damon, we're old bounty hunters now."

Cory knew Pock was right. Lately, even the bad guys were starting to look like seniors on their way to a high school prom. No point in dwelling on it though. Better to change the subject.

"So," he asked. "How was Pakistan?"

"A real shithole. We were backdooring some of the Agency's cross-border operations in Afghanistan. Nothing real. Smuggling weapons, bribing Paki military officers, a little training, shit like that. Hell, after a year of that lightweight stuff, I was beginning to think I was going to lose my touch."

"I doubt it," Cory disagreed. Eisler, he knew, considered Pock one of the best ground men in QUEENWALK. "Besides, everything can't be a cakewalk."

"Maybe it was just the target then . . . when I finally got one."

"Lot of contact?"

"No, not even that. You really haven't heard about it before?"

"Not a word," Cory said. "It's not like we've got a newsletter to keep us all posted on everyone else's travels."

Pock snorted then took a sip of his drink.

"Get this master stroke," he began. "Some idiot in the National Command Authority—that's what they're calling the White House now—decides we should find out where the Afghans are getting the chemicals to refine their petroleum products, right?"

Cory nodded.

"But everyone knows it's from Russia, right?"

"Wasn't exactly a state secret," Cory shrugged.

"Kind of what I thought," Pock said. "But, as usual, old Boudreaux was wrong. They wanted a *raw* petroleum product. A sample before it was processed through the Afghan refineries, so that they could compare it to a refined sample. Anyway, they decide we should take a stroll to the outskirts of Orgun—about forty klicks inside the Afghan border—tap a pipeline, grab a couple of gallons, and stroll back."

"That's crap," Cory told him.

"No shit," Pock agreed. "Now, I'm no petroleum engineer and I don't know a damn thing about pipelines. No issue, they say. They pouch me this little drill that's supposed to puncture the pipe, allow the oil to run out for the sample, then automatically seal the hole when the drill's removed."

"You get the samples?"

"Sure I got the samples. Filled our containers, sealed them and was packing up to leave when things turned to shit."

Pock took another gulp of his drink before continuing.

"Get this," he said. "I couldn't get the fucking drill out of the fucking pipe. God knows I tried. I pulled on the damned thing for almost an hour and it just wouldn't budge. Couldn't turn the damn thing off either. Oil was running all over the place, my scout, this shithead *mujaheddin* goat farmer, was getting nervous, the sun was coming up, and yours truly was developing a royal case of the ass."

"So what'd you do?"

A little-boy smile creased Pock's weathered face.

"Made a command decision. I blew up the whole fucking pipeline."

Cory laughed. It was a typical Pock response.

"Any repercussions?" Cory asked.

"What do you think?" Pock grinned. "Of course there were repercussions. I was launching out of a place called Kotahpuh, just across the border inside Pakistan. The whole area was run by this asshole Paki general named Safdar, Amir Safdar. Ever heard of him?"

Cory shook his head.

"Remember the Chicom light colonel we fucked over in Laos?" Pock asked.

"Yeh," Cory said. "The one whose face looked like it had been stung by a bee?"

"That's the dude. Except Safdar makes that lardass look like a piker when it comes to political bullshit."

"Lot of stroke?"

Pock nodded. "Big time stroke. Supposedly his cousin is the Paki minister of defense, or something. Since Safdar considers himself the only one holding back the Afghan hordes from taking over Pakistan, you can imagine how he acted when I came trooping back across the border with a six squads of Afghan dickwads chasing me. I guess he thought he was getting invaded."

"What happened then?" Cory asked.

"Safdar was going to hold me for questioning," Pock said. "For violating the terms of some mutual assistance treaty. That's when I really lost it. I told them to fuck off and left. My orders were to turn in the samples to our embassy in Istanbul and that's what I was going to do.

"The short story is that I had to borrow a Paki army truck to make the trip. Safdar complained to his cousin, who complained to our ambassador, and that spineless little turd complained to Washington. Eisler got the call, and I was ordered back here.

"Be glad you're missing that whole lick, Damon. It's really fucked up. But that pipeline explosion," Pock whispered, touching his scar. "I caught some shrapnel, but damn, what a fucking masterpiece. You should have seen them, Damon. Talk about pissed. The Afghanis chased me for two days until I finally got my goat farmer scout off his ass and we got back over the border. But the Pakis were just one thing; my real problem was when Mr. Eisler told me the smoke was blocking the ground from surveillance overflights. He was madder than Safdar had been. Hell, I offered to reinsert and snap a few frames for him, but that just pissed him off more. Sometimes you just can't win for losing"

"I've been there," Cory agreed.

The both fell silent. Pock watched as Cory lit his pipe.

"You really like that thing?" he asked.

"It's better than cigarettes," Cory said.

"I guess." Pock stretched his shoulders. "Guess who bought the farm?"

"Who now?"

"Devlin."

"Where?"

"Somewhere in Central America. Word is he got tapped about a month ago."

"Mattman's dead too," Cory sighed. "Mexico. Pulled his own plug."

"Tough call," Pock grunted. Nothing else was necessary. Death happened.

"You know, Damon," Pock said, changing the subject. "Mr. Eisler's been pissed off at me ever since that pipeline mess. He told me this thing with you was my last chance and not to fuck anything up. I don't want to get run off, Damon. I'm just an uneducated coonass and too set in my ways to learn a new life."

"I know," Cory said softly. *Piece of shit. Not real. Have to beg off.* He didn't need any more suicide notes.

He forced a smile.

"Hey, Boudreaux. Some people just have a hard time recognizing your kind of talent. You're working with me now, and when this is over I'll speak with the old man. Maybe you and I can both find a new place to live. That is, of course, unless you like that circle jerk over at the Pentagon?"

Pock rolled his eyes. "Give me a break. All they do there is study old operational after-action reports that have been rewritten so many times that nobody knows what really happened in the first place. That and fucking push-ups and haircuts and shit like that."

"Like I said," Cory told him. "Let's make it through the next week or so and we'll figure something out. That's what we do, remember? Figure things out."

"Thanks, Damon," Pock smiled, his mood considerably brighter. "Let's get the whiskey lady back over here."

The waitress came and went. Cory took a taste of his fresh drink, then leaned across the table.

"So, how much do you know?" he asked.

"Not that much," Pock admitted. "Mr. Eisler just told me to get you a room, wheels, and follow your lead from there."

Cory nodded.

"It's an extended action," he said after a moment.

"How extended?"

"Five."

Pock's eyes narrowed and Cory could see his jaw muscles tighten.

"What kind?" Pock asked.

"Russian." Cory said. "Inside Defense."

"Shit."

"We've handled worse."

"You need me to work a parallel?"

"Not at first," Cory told him. "Maybe later. Depends upon how fast it all comes together."

Pock thought about this for a few seconds.

"You better watch your ass, Damon," he said. "The local law around here is better than the national police from where you're used to working."

"I know that," Cory nodded. "But I've sketched out a plan. If it takes, I think it will throw them off track long enough for me to finish up and get out."

Pock understood his meaning. The misdirection.

"Political or criminal?" he asked.

"A little of both," Cory said flatly. "Shining Path."

"Good choice," Pock whispered. "They're on everyone's shit list. How are you going to work the peg from Peru to here?"

"Parlay the Defense link," Cory explained. "Everybody knows that the Agency and DEA are snooping around down there. Add to that all our Defense Department types dragging around Peru advising, training and trying to identify narco-terrorism connections, and you've got a perfect scenario. I'll make a couple of calls, let the locals here connect the dots, and suddenly Washington believes they've got a spillover resulting from their 'imperialistic meddling in internal Peruvian politics.' What do you think?"

"That dog could damn sure hunt," Pock nodded appreciatively. "They'll be months trying to figure out who did what to who and why."

"And I should be out within a week."

"What are you going to need?" Pock asked.

"Nothing too sophisticated," Cory said. "Shining Path's not very creative, just effective. They shoot, stab, and bomb. I want to stay in character."

"What's your pleasure, then?"

"I'll need a Steyr package?"

"When and where?"

"Where is my transportation?" Cory asked first.

Pock reached into his pocket, then tossed a set of car keys on the table.

"Silver Camaro," he said. "It's in the basement. First floor. The last three are two-niner-six."

Cory picked up the keys.

"Can you have the package in the trunk by 1800 hours tomorrow?"

"Can do," Pock nodded. "What about explosives?"

"That can wait, I think. I'll let you know. But if I decide on it, it'll be something straight, C-4, Semtex. I need to make sure its a controlled site. Too much chance for someone else getting hurt in the process if it isn't."

"I hear that," Pock said. "By the way, I left two little somethings in your room before coming down here. One's on the dresser, the other's in your duffel's outside pocket."

Cory could guess what the little somethings were.

"I appreciate that, Boudreaux," he said.

Suddenly, Pock stood up and tossed some bills on the table.

"You finished drinking already?" Cory asked him.

"For now," Pock grinned. "I've got a sweet young debutante waiting to wash every inch of this body with scented oils."

Cory laughed. Pock's reputation for being able to locate the most offensive women on the planet was unmatched in the annals of military history.

"If you need me," Pock added. "I'm hanging my hat at the Guest Quarters over in Alexandria. My phone number's on the key chain. Just leave a message, I'll get back to you."

"Later," Cory nodded.

At this, Pock gave Cory a wave of the hand, turned, and began limping toward the lobby.

Gimpy foot, he had called it.

Cory knew there was much more to the story.

Laos, 1974. OPERATION HEAVY HOOK. Pock had rappelled from a helicopter to extract two downed air force fighter pilots. The Pathet Lao discovered him, began shooting, then began dying. Final tally: twenty-two dead Laotians, two saved pilots, and gimpy foot.

DIAGNOSIS: Traumatic amputation of all toes on right foot.
ETIOLOGY: Hostile small-arms fire.
PROGNOSIS: Poor. Patient will be unable to walk without prosthesis.
FUTURE: Pock, Boudreaux (NMN), Staff Sergeant, 5th Special Forces Group Airborne [detached service MACVSOG], will be medically retired from active duty.
Disability Percentage: 66.

But the doctors were wrong. Within two months Pock was walking without a prosthesis. In six months, he was running and, by the tenth month, he had placed sixteenth in the Fort Bragg, All-Airborne Marathon. His retirement was deferred, and QUEENWALK came six weeks later. Pock had been looking for a new war. Eisler had given him several.

Boudreaux Pock was a gutsy man, Cory remembered. Results oriented. He was also the only man Cory knew personally who had actually received the Congressional Medal of Honor. It was awarded for the Laotian extraction and it had not gone to his head. When asked, Pock always denied the commendation by stating, "No. That's the other Pock . . . the white guy."

So Cory would do as he had promised. He would talk to Eisler and appeal to the older man's commitment to fairness and decency. Pock was as peerless as most others were common. He would just wither on the Pentagon vine.

The Medal, if nothing else, entitled him to better than that.

CHAPTER 9

THE THIRD DAY
Monday, November 24, 1982

The Stouffer's Concourse Hotel, Arlington, Virginia 12:16 A.M.
    Sunday became Monday. Cory shifted on the bed and rubbed his eyes. Since meeting Boudreaux Pock in the hotel lounge, the remainder of the evening had passed rapidly. He had returned to his room and ordered dinner. He had declined a larger meal in favor of two oranges, a small bowl of dry cereal, and six ounces of broiled, highly peppered fillet of red snapper.
    The mission was beginning: the evaluation of targets, assessing their relative vulnerabilities, deciding the sequence of their sanction. The body, as well as the mind, had to be prepared. The meal—fish, fruit and bran—would see that his was.
    After eating, Cory had taken another shower. At precisely 10:05 p.m., he had stepped into the tub and spent fifteen minutes under the hot spray. He had then planned on going to sleep, but in the two odd hours since, he was still awake. There were two reasons. One normal. The second unforeseen.
    The normal. For as long as he could remember, Damon Cory had suffered from varying degrees of insomnia the nights immediately prior to a mission. Its basis, he knew, was anxiety. Tonight was certainly nothing new, and he had taught himself to expect it. Appreciate it. Understand it for what it was and not try to read anything else into it.
    No, Cory knew, the insomnia was not an issue. Its absence would be.
    The unexpected. As he had stepped from the shower, a soft knocking was audible in the bathroom. Wrapping a towel around his waist, Cory walked to the hotel room door and opened it to find the Korean girl. Saying nothing, she passed him a note: "To cut the edge." The message was signed "Pock," and now, as the clock nudged toward 12:30 a.m., it was this same girl Cory left sleeping as he slid from the sheets and picked his way to the bathroom. He poured a glass of water and looked back through the mirror toward the bed.

Her name, not that it made any difference, was allegedly Nisi, and Cory knew she was Pock's way of wishing him well on the assignment.

Cory appreciated the gesture, at least at face value, but there was a downside. Now, one day, he would have to return the favor. Like sending flowers FTD, he would have to provide Pock a woman in return for this one tonight. Then, upon receipt, Pock would be left owing Cory a favor rather than the other way around.

Always better to give than receive, Cory reminded himself. Always better to have others owing him.

Cory set the glass on the sink, turned back toward the bed and continued to stare at the girl. She was young, probably only eighteen or nineteen, and not at all practiced enough to understand the prurient chaos in which some men, himself included, delineated their needs.

A prostitute? The term had never offended him. On the contrary, vague thoughts of the other men she had taken only served to make his own pleasure all the more intense.

And what if time was not an issue? How long would it take before he tired of this one? A day? A week? As long as a month? Surely no longer than a month. She was too young. More than a month and she would only become dependent on him. For everything. Food. Clothing. Why, she may even elect to initiate conversation. Then what? He knew. He would start pulling away. She, sensing this, would commit herself even more, the commitment serving only to push him further away. Then, as was destined to happen, the relationship would quickly degenerate. Him hating her because he hated himself for allowing her to become so attached. Her hating him because he discarded her. Why did this always have to be the price of his sexual arrogance?

Cory deliberated this singular *why*. Again, no credible resolution manifested itself. He had never bothered to understand younger women. They always seemed to want all or nothing and he viewed them with indifference.

As for loving women, naturally he had, but they tended to be older. Better versed. More resigned to unspoken negotiation. Then again, he had always saved a bit of love for himself in the process. It was simpler that way. Made it easier when the splitting-up process, as it inevitably did, began its slow parade around reality's maypole.

Walking to the dresser, he splashed two fingers of bourbon—a bottle of Wild Turkey was the first something Pock left in the room—into a plastic drinking cup. Then he quietly moved to the room's single window and squatted nude before the glass.

He took a sip of the bourbon, cracked the window an inch, and sniffed at the fringes of the cold night air. It tasted of wet—the heavy, promising flavor of snow.

Winterkills. Blood upon the ice.

It would make the violence that much starker.

Cory stared into the night. In the distance, Washington beckoned, a hushed invitation to night-pace streets where lights bounced up, then off the low, sullen sky of clouds.

Winterkills, he thought again, and as he did so, he became aware of the silent presence within him. Lucius. The warrior was ready, Cory knew. Ready, even impatient to effect the assignment.

Directing his breath to the window glass, Cory watched the condensation form and considered his feelings.

"Shit," he whispered. For the killing he needed Lucius. For the living he did not. Tonight was for living, for himself. So why was Lucius so close?

Cory sighed heavily, despondently.

He was attentive to the ramifications. As before, Lucius was becoming anything but a sense of duty; he was starting to control the night again. Becoming too Mephistophelian. Taking too much and leaving too little. Honing the intensity of isolation that this Nisi girl, however lewd, could never begin to blunt.

Cory looked into his cup, then set it gently on the carpet. Tonight is for me, he thought to himself. Lucius and his duty could wait for the sun.

Standing, Cory looked back to the bed.

Still asleep, the girl had turned onto her stomach, and in the small of her back tiny beads of perspiration reflected the bathroom light. He moved closer. He thought the moisture erotic, yet coarse and common at the same time.

Pock had been undeniably right about one thing. It was all getting fucked up lately. Everybody was just out for themselves and everybody was becoming a prima donna. Himself? No different. Evil spelled backwards was live.

Reaching the bed, Cory leaned over, touched a finger to her lower back, then placed it to his lips. He curled his tongue and smoothed the flavor to the roof of his mouth. Brothish. Not beef, nor fish, nor fowl. Just brothish in a gamey sort of way, an enduring sort of way.

Awakened by his presence, Cory observed her stretch as he slid in next to her. This time would be better than before, he thought. More intense. Purer.

But soon, all thoughts of purity passed and, as they moved together, he again felt the familiar onset of pain, pleasure, and absolute control. It was both shadow and dance. The methodical consumption of private ecstasy and personal excess. Sensations he had no inclination to share.

And later, after his passion was spent, after tissue and nerve endings had acquiesced, he sent the girl away. He no longer desired her youth. No longer fancied her broth.

Then he slept. A deep repairing sleep, while outside a steady snow filled the sky with winter's frigid weepings. The games would begin most shortly.

Warriors and weapons would be mandates for the day.

CHAPTER 10

FBI Headquarters, 11:15 A.M.

As Jonathon Weall read the first draft of the Honduran report, Sal Franco looked casually around the windowless office.

It was much smaller than Bechtel's. It was also as cluttered as Hershel Bechtel's was neat. There were no flags or photographs and only two chairs, one behind the desk where Weall sat and one facing the desk where Franco now slouched, fingers laced behind his head and booted feet crossed at the ankles.

The walls were lined with bookcases, every inch of which were stuffed with reports, files, magazines, and books. The desktop was even more disorganized, as if someone had slipped in and gently shuffled hundreds of pages of documents into a random heap that more resembled the office of an absent-minded professor of physics.

But the appearance was misleading, Franco knew, for there was no doubt in his mind that Weall, if necessary, could remember, and find, any particular page at any particular moment.

"So how many times you going to read the thing?" Franco wondered out loud.

Jonathon Weall looked up from the paper. Franco's eyes were rimmed with red, and a splotchy growth of beard shadowed his face and neck.

"When's the last time you slept?" Weall asked.

Franco shrugged. "Couple of days. Why? Does it show in the report?"

"Not at all," Weall said. "It's all very concise, to the point and quite thorough."

The word hung in the air like the *Graf Zeppelin*. Franco asked it.

"But?"

Weall placed the document on the desk, then leaned back in his chair.

"I think we're going to have a problem," he said.

"I don't," Franco said impulsively. "I wrote what I saw and heard."

Weall lowered his voice.

"What you wrote, Sal, are the grounds of a homicide indictment for this Colonel Umberto Rico. I would place him under the heading of co-conspirator or, maybe, some kind of accessory before the fact."

"So?" Franco asked. "Bechtel wanted to know who was responsible for the bombing, and in my opinion it's Rico."

Weall nodded slowly, as if considering the implications of each word.

"The report's bullshit and you know it," he said. "You come off sounding like some whimpering social moralist, Sal. Trying to place blame. Trying to figure the cause, at the expense of the effect."

Weall picked up the report and flipped to a particular section.

"You say here the Miami Field Office should conduct a survey of Dade County banks to verify the existence of any bank accounts this Rico may have."

Franco thought briefly of Alicia Carrera, of her mutilation.

"It's a legitimate inquiry," he explained. "Based upon information I developed."

Weall shook his head.

"It's witch hunting, Sal. The presence of any bank accounts has nothing whatsoever to do with the incident at the school."

"But the woman told me . . . ."

Weall raised his hand, interrupting Franco.

"I don't care if she told you she was the Pope's love slave," he said. "I've read the report three times. You're way out of line."

"So, you think she was lying?"

"No," Weall said. "Not at all."

"But you want me to change my report?"

"It's necessary."

Considering the order, Franco stared back across the desk for a long moment. This was not like Jonathon Weall, he thought. This was not how Weall identified priorities.

"Who sandbagged me?" he finally asked.

"Officially?"

Franco nodded.

"The Under Secretary of State for Latin American Affairs."

"Who touched him?"

"It's not important," Weall said.

"Who?" Franco pressed, his anger visible.

"Honduras." Weall averted his eyes. "Our ambassador."

"Our ambassador?" Franco repeated, raising his voice. "It was his daughter, for God's sake. He's the one who asked for the investigation in the first place."

"Settle down, Sal," Weall said. "Personally, the ambassador sincerely appreciates your efforts. However, as a representative of our government, he feels the need to mitigate any hostility you exhibited during your interview with Colonel Rico. Did you express any hostility, Sal?"

Franco was incensed. He could not imagine any man, ambassador or not, caring more about political niceties than his own child's murder. Foggy Bottom shitheads. Franco suspected the motivation. Now, should one of the prime postings become available—London, Paris, wherever—the ambassador could produce his "daughter's death" card and be immediately propelled to the top of the selection list. Just because this scenario was so genuine, he found the whole line of thought leaving him ill.

"Rico's an asshole," Franco said softly, more for himself than Weall.

"I'm sure he is," Weall agreed. "Which is why I want you to rewrite your report and take out all the negative comments on the colonel."

"I won't do it," Franco said.

"Yes, you will."

"It guts the investigation."

Not at all," Weall said. "On this bombing thing, the ambassador made a deal with the Hondurans. If they would allow us to interview the woman, they could see a copy of our report without any deletions."

"So?"

"So that is what we're going to give them, Sal. You don't have to do it. I'll rework the report so it tells what the Hondurans want it to, namely that Alicia Carrera's primary target was the ambassador's daughter and that the Honduran authorities, specifically your Colonel Rico, were professional and straightforward in aiding us in our investigation. I'll even have the director sign a commendation letter for the ambassador to pass to Rico."

The zeppelin floated by again.

"Then?" Franco asked.

Jonathon Weall smiled slightly.

"Then we take steps to, as it is said, resolve your differences with Colonel Rico. Observe and learn."

As Franco watched, Jonathon Weall poked around the desk and found his telephone. Picking up the receiver, he punched in a four-digit code from memory and waited while the connection was made.

"Good Morning, Miss Quill," he crooned. "This is Jonathon Weall, and how are things in Racketeering this fine November morning?"

Franco started to smile. Mildred Quill was a sparrow-like spinster who had worked in Racketeering's Intelligence Section since before Franco had been born. She was a crusty, no-nonsense, prick of a woman, who was generally rude to everyone.

Everyone but Jonathon Weall, Franco realized. Who was now smiling and teasing his way into the woman's good graces.

"I know, Miss Quill," he was saying. "Copy for this, copy for that, tit for tit, tat for tat. Which is exactly why I decided to call you personally rather than putting it in writing. Do you have a minute?"

Weall paused, then continued.

"Good. It seems I need some information, but I need it discreetly. It concerns the financial arrangements a foreign military officer may be having with certain banking institutions within our country.

"Well, yes, I suppose embezzlement could be the word." Weall nodded thoughtfully. "Just rumor though. Yes. Yes. Well, anywhere we may have jurisdiction, including San Juan and the Virgin Islands, I suspect. Of course, Miss Quill. Well, I'm sure you would know much better that me. Just a moment."

Weall flipped through the report.

"Last name," he read out loud. "Rico. R-I-C-O. First name Umberto. U-M-B-E-R-T-O. He is some type of colonel in the Honduran Army. Age?"

Weall glanced up at Franco who held up five fingers on one hand and made a zero with the other.

"About fifty," he told the woman. "Yes. Yes. Fine, Miss Quill. Of course. No, two will not be a problem. I'll see to it personally. Fine. Thank you and enjoy the game."

Smiling, Jonathon Weall hung up the receiver.

"What?" Franco asked.

"You owe me a ticket to the next Redskin's game," Weall told him. "Miss Quill is obsessed with professional football. She wants to take her sister to a game. We'll split the difference for the two seats."

Franco arched an eyebrow.

"And what am I getting for my money?" he smiled.

"Umberto Rico's bank accounts, if there are any," Weall explained.

"You're working a deal, aren't you?"

Weall nodded casually.

"Of course, I'm working a deal. How else would you do it? You put all that nonsense about banking into a report going to the Hondurans, and Rico will know we're taking a peek at him. This way he gets your report, sees you didn't try to ruin his reputation, and, at least on the diplomatic level, no feathers are ruffled between State and the Honduran government."

"And suppose we find his money here?" Franco asked.

"Well, first of all," Weall said, "if there are any American bank accounts, Miss Quill will find them and let me know. If there aren't, then doing it this way, as a personal favor, leaves no pesky written requests that would leave me explaining why I was nosing around in somebody else's section."

"And if we find the accounts?"

"Simple," Weall said. "You still have friends in Miami?"

"A few."

"Then you just pick up the phone, have them call our field office in Miami, tell our people they heard on the streets that some Honduran is stashing funds in bank accounts X, Y, and Z. The Miami field office, since it originated locally and is a foreign matter, will route the information to me, and because you're my Latin affairs man, I will route it to you."

Weall leaned back in his chair again.

"Granted," he said softly. "You won't be able to make a murder case on him. But you can make a play for banking violations, seize the funds, and, if you find a decent prosecutor, you may even be able to get him indicted, at least until his cronies in the Honduran government figure out a way to get the charges dropped. This isn't exactly the Kennedy assassination, Sal. Keep it in perspective."

"Fucking with his money is not enough," Franco sighed.

"Maybe not, but realistically it's probably the best we're going to be able to do."

"Whatever."

"Look at it this way, Sal. It's cost only one phone call and two football tickets so far. Before you start grousing about it, let's first see what Miss Quill uncovers. We can always revisit our options later. Besides, you've got something else to occupy your time . . . at least for tomorrow."

Franco looked up.

"What something else?"

"You're teaching tomorrow afternoon," Weall told him.

"Teaching what?"

"A four-hour block on Latin extremists. A basic agent class is coming over from Quantico for their headquarters tour."

Franco groaned.

"Can't someone else do it?"

Jonathon Weall shook his head and smiled.

"It's your turn, Sal," he said. "Just try not too be too cynical. Their fertile little minds will be poisoned soon enough. No point in expediting the process."

"Indeed," Franco said, as he stood. "You mind if I beg off the rest of the afternoon?"

"Not at all. Just let me know where you can be reached." Weall said. "Something might come up."

Franco nodded.

"And make sure you're in here tomorrow by noon," Weall added. "You're on stage from one until five."

"I'll be there," Franco sighed, as he walked to the door then paused. "You'll keep me posted on the Rico thing?"

"You'll know something when I know something," Weall nodded.

"The son of a bitch needs to be shot, Jonathon."

"Then that would make us no different than him, would it?"

Franco thought about this for a moment. He decided he was too tired to respond.

"I'll see you tomorrow," he finally said. Then he left Weall's office for the garage and his car.

He felt better. But not that much better.

Umberto Rico? Intellectually, he supposed Weall had been right to want to handle the diplomatic consideration the way he had. After all Rico was just one man. Nothing really special. Simply another embolism in the vein of time. And, like so many before him, he, too, would one day detach himself from diplomacy's wall and ride his politics to a stroke-dead brain.

The bank accounts?

Only a tool. Only the scalpel with which to expedite the process.

***

Forty minutes after leaving Weall's office, Sal Franco reached the split-rail and flagstone fence of his Falls Church, Virginia, home. There was no name on the black mailbox, only snow and the small white letters stating 4 Bradford Lane.

As usual, he and Karen had argued about leaving their last names off the box, but Franco had been adamant. It was a question of embarrassment: 4 Bradford Lane was far too luxurious a place for a lowly FBI agent to live without gossip. And, as he well knew, those who did not know complete stories always gossiped.

The truth of the matter was that 4 Bradford Lane had initially been purchased by his wife's father shortly after he was first elected to the United States Senate in the early 1960s. Then, it had been a working farm, some 350 acres all central to and managed from a large fieldstone mansion built in 1874. The house originally had been designed to resemble Jefferson's home at Monticello and the only significant difference was that the masonry was of natural rock instead of red brick. Most thought this more attractive. Franco tended to agree.

But the mansion aside, Senator Mobley was no farmer. His fortune had been made harvesting the crab and mollusk of Chesapeake Bay, not dirt crops. So sometime during the course of his two Senate terms, he had divided the initial 350 acres into seven 50-acre tracts and sold them to colleagues in Washington's inner power circles.

What resulted eventually became to be known to the locals as Bradford Estates numbers 1 through 7. And now, with the exception of Franco's, all were currently owned and occupied by former U.S. senators, bankers, and one retired Supreme Court justice. As could be expected, all of the tracts now also boasted mansions of their own, but only number 4 held the history. Monticello in rock. It was a trimmed, landscaped, beautiful piece of property. It also was owned free and clear by Karen. A gift from the senator when she had returned from Caracas. A little sweetness to help her get over the divorce.

Still, Franco would readily admit, not unlike her present of his Rolex, the very idea of living here made him feel rather ridiculous. After all, he was still driving the same 1962 Corvette he had purchased used when first joining the Miami PD. It was a champagne-gold roadster with black convertible top.

True, the top leaked, the clutch slipped, and the air conditioning had never worked, but for Franco, a man who had grown up with the old "Route 66" television series, the car was a dream fulfilled. So when he found it, he purchased it without thinking, and as far as he was concerned, it would be the only vehicle he would ever own. It was like a comrade. Something that could never be replaced.

Downshifting into third, Franco wheeled the old Corvette through the twin flagstone entrance markers and accelerated up the winding drive toward the house. Its dome, twin wings, and portico flashed into view through a stand of leafless birch and maple trees.

Unfolding, the scene was like a Christmas card. Clean and white under a thin dusting of new snow and black smoke drifting from two of the seven chimneys.

It was all so different than Florida, he thought. So much more than the green frame house of his youth.

Here, there were rooms he never bothered to enter. An entire wing never even heated or air-conditioned. As a practical matter, even what was lived in, the three bedrooms, three baths, studio, and combination den, dining, and kitchen area, was arguably too elaborate for only two people. But it was Karen's house, and it made her happy. He had adjusted to the lifestyle because he loved her. No, not just loved her, he was in love with her. The same feelings he had experienced during their first chance encounter nearly ten years ago.

1973. The Smithsonian. An oriental art exhibit at the Freer Gallery. He was twenty-five, in uniform, and she thought him dashing. She was twenty-eight, in jeans, and he thought her artsy. They had talked art, then politics. President Ford had just pardoned Nixon. Both approved of it. This was unusual. It became a common ground. He bought her lunch, then a movie: Bergman's *Scenes from a Marriage*. Dinner and Irish coffees followed. Soon, nights together became weekends. Weekends, whole weeks. They were married in Annapolis six months later, and since that time, Sal Franco had never been with another woman.

Certainly in the intervening years he had had any number of opportunities. But he had always thought to decline. The reason was simple. In his mind, it just wouldn't be right. And now that they were back together, well, that just made the time apart and her visits to Miami and San Juan while "divorced" all the more special. Like everyone, they had their difficulties, but they also had their memories. As for his monogamy? He had never regretted the decision.

Franco pulled the Corvette under the portico and parked next to Karen's dark-blue Volvo coupe. Setting the brake, he grabbed his bag, climbed out, and walked quickly into the house. His nostrils immediately were assaulted by the unmistakable odor of turpentine. He smiled and headed toward the studio.

The studio was a long, narrow room just off the rear kitchen area. One wall was windows and overlooked the grounds and the pond to the north. The remaining walls were for the most part occupied by shelving and held an assortment of paints, clays, chemicals, and dozens of plastic boxes holding whatever tools, brushes, or potions a serious amateur artist might deem desirable. In the center of the studio a large workbench with stainless steel sink divided the room, and above, racks of spotlights, canvases and paint-spattered palettes hung in no particular order.

Normally, Sal Franco avoided the studio for he was always afraid he would touch something, spill something, or inadvertently spoil some project currently in progress. And, with Karen, there was always something in progress.

In his unspoken opinion, Franco thought his wife approached the creation of art much like Hitler had approached the concept of war in Europe, blitzkrieg. One day was sculpture, the next, lost-wax casting. Another day was pottery, the following one, jewelry design. And every day there was the painting, the acrylic, oil or watercolor done while something else was drying, hardening, or cooling.

But today was turpentine, so today was also oil painting. And it was standing before her easel that Sal Franco found his wife. Her back was to him, and he said nothing for a moment as he watched her work.

At thirty-seven, Karen Mobley had, of late, become a substantial woman as her mother's German lineage finally rose to the surface. She was short, two inches over five feet and, as Franco thought, sturdy and getting sturdier by the hour. But she was not fat and her substantial bosom, hips, and thighs retained an acceptable amount of muscle tone. She had borne no children and her stomach was flat, well, reasonably flat, Franco told himself. Flat enough for him. Strange, but the older he got, the less he seemed to care about bodies anyway, particularly hers. It was the face he had fallen in love with, and although he knew it had to have changed in the past ten years, he was unable to put his finger on anything specific.

Her hair was a medium brown and long, reaching to the center of her back. Her eyes were blue and open as if she perpetually were surprised at life's experiences. They sparkled when she talked and crinkled when she smiled. They were trusting eyes, and Franco never tired of looking into them. Her nose was small and, without makeup, a sprinkling of freckles was visible across its bridge. The mouth was full, and now, as was the usual case when painting, Franco suspected a tendril of hair was probably between her lips as she pondered the easel in front of her.

In all honesty, Sal Franco could not have asked for a more perfect mate. Karen was a vibrant, caring woman and he could think of only one negative trait. The more she immersed herself in her work, the more she became the flaky artist. But he had decided it was probably better this way. Before, when she had tried to keep abreast of his work, they had found themselves having problems. Now, since they had decided to again live together—and with the possible exception of the names on the mailbox—they had not had one real disagreement. Both of them had helped the other mature. Neither now felt jealous of the other's avocations.

"Been jogging?" Franco asked, a direct reference to the red sweatsuit and running shoes Karen was wearing. "Better be careful, you might get frostbite."

Startled by the voice, Karen wheeled around. Her face split into a wide grin.

"Ten miles before breakfast," she said proudly.

They both laughed. It was a blatant lie. Whereas Franco really didn't consider her to be fat, Karen did. The sweatsuits, therefore, held a twofold significance. Primarily, they concealed the additional pounds; but secondly, she hoped by wearing the sweats, she might one day find herself getting into the exercise frame of mind. She had been waiting for this inspiration for six months. It had yet to make its presence known. But as an artist, Karen Mobley appreciated the importance of inspiration. Never to be rushed, she would continue to wait for what she defined as the "mood of sweat."

Franco walked over, gave her a quick kiss on the forehead, then glanced down at her painting. It was a hopeless swirling of blues and white. He looked outside toward the pond. He could find no clue as to what the swirling was supposed to represent. Not knowing what to comment, he felt fortunate Karen when spoke first.

"Now, can you tell me where you went?" she asked.

"What difference does it make?" Franco shrugged. "I was only gone two nights."

Karen smiled slightly.

"I'll make you a wager?"

"What?"

"You tell me where you went, and I'll tell you what this painting is."

"How do you know I don't already know what the painting is?"

Karen placed the palette on a shelf and crossed her arms.

"Because you have never known what any of my paintings are."

Franco smiled and touched her cheek.

"Ask me no questions, I'll tell you no lies."

Then he put his arm around her shoulders.

"Okay, I'll bite, what is your painting?"

"You first," she said, enjoying the teasing.

"No. You first," he countered.

Karen sighed. "I'm calling it *Bedford Snow Misting*."

"It looks more like an Arctic squall," Franco said dryly.

"Well, it's not finished," she nodded. "I think I need some more blue."

"Some more something."

"So, your turn," she smiled. Where did you go?"

"Come on," Franco said. "I brought you something."

Their arms around each other's waist, he led her to the kitchen where his flight bag was in the center of the floor. Reaching into an outside pocket, he pulled out a folded cloth, then stood and turned to face her.

It was a white T-shirt with HONDURAS—ADVENTURES IN PARADISE stenciled in red across its front.

"Honduras?" Karen breathed. "Sal, they're killing people down there. I just heard where our ambassador's daughter was murdered by terrorists."

"I know," Franco said. "But I was careful though. The press always blows everything out of proportion so they can justify their combat pay, I guess. It really wasn't that bad, just busy. I haven't been to bed since I left."

"Well, you better get some sleep," Karen told him. "Did you forget we're supposed to have dinner with Senator Rossett tonight?"

Franco abhorred the very thought of going out for dinner.

"I'm not going over there," he said.

"Yes, you are," Karen told him. "He's our neighbor, he's a lonely old man, and he's one of daddy's oldest friends."

"Just tell him I'm still out of town."

"I'll do nothing of the sort. Now go upstairs and go to sleep. Dinner is at eight. I'll wake you at seven."

"Are you sure I can't get out of it?"

"No way, Sal."

Franco sighed heavily, picked up his bag, and began to plod toward the stairs.

"Make it six-thirty," he called back over his shoulder. "And bring me a drink when you come."

"You can have a drink at the Senator's."

"Scotch," Franco told her.

Karen said something else, but Franco couldn't make out the words.

"Thank you, Karen," he yelled back. "I love you."

In the bedroom, Franco tossed his flight bag to a corner and fell into bed without bothering to undress. He was asleep within seconds.

CHAPTER 11

Crystal City Underground Mall, Virginia, 5:25 P.M.

"Thank you, Mr. Kellogg," the young girl smiled, as Cory handed the VISA card across the counter. "And will there be anything else today?"

"Not today," he told her. "Just the coat."

The clerk smiled again, rang up the price, then passed the receipt back to Cory. He scrawled "B. Kellogg" on the form and slid it to the girl, waiting while she verified the card and put the coat in a large cellophane bag.

Cory took the bag, opened it, and put the two smaller bags inside with the coat. Then he left the store and continued walking around the underground shopping mall. Although it was not even Thanksgiving, the mall was alive with early Christmas shoppers all scurrying here and there, amid the sounds of carolers, piped-in Christmas music, and the squeals of happy children.

To his right costumed elves danced with remarkable merriment, while to the left Santa was hearing the wants of another giggling child. A flashbulb popped and the giggle was suspended in time: *Tommy with Santa, age 4.*

Cory turned away. He felt out of place here, removed. Having forgotten the enthusiasm with which Americans celebrated the holidays, the sight of families joined together left him with a perception of marked isolation. But it was really more than just the people, he realized. What made the place seem so alien were all the lights.

There were nearly a hundred shops, restaurants, and boutiques in the mall, which was adjacent to the hotel's parking garage. A hundred shops, and each one had Christmas decorations blinking, sparkling, pulsing, and twinkling in every imaginable color.

It was like Norman Rockwell with wattage, he decided. An all too tactile *baño de lumbre* that washed everything and everybody in elaborate bursts of reflected illumination. Greens to peach. Blues to apricot. These to coppers and coppers to vibrant reds, teals, and lavenders. All changing before his eyes. So ethereally commercial in its perfect orchestration.

It was quite striking. Even he found himself tempted to buy, to give. But a gift? For whom should he buy? Pock? Of course not. Eisler? No. That would be sentimental. Inappropriate.

He felt something akin to loneliness welling up inside him. He had no family. No children to sit on Santa's knee. To ride in Santa's sleigh. To dance with Santa's elves.

Perhaps he should buy himself a gift? But what? He had already purchased the only things he really needed: the floor-length, black leather overcoat with fur collar, the Russian-looking fur-lined hat, the gloves and the sixteen-inch-tall leather and rubber hunting boots. All the clothing for cold weather.

Maybe he should look at handguns? No, there would then be the background checks, and besides, Pock had already provided one. The "little something" in his duffel had been a surplus, Soviet Army 9mm Makarov pistol he now wore concealed in the small of his back. An inferior weapon, but effective at close range and untraceable.

Suddenly, across the mall, Cory saw something he wanted. Something for himself. Shifting the bag to his left hand, he walked quickly to the store with the sign flashing NUTHOUSE.

"Cashews, please," he told a sallow-faced teenager.

"How many?"

"A pound," Cory told him.

The clerk said nothing as he grabbed a scoop and shoveled the nuts onto a scale, then into a white bag.

"Ten-fifty-three."

"You take VISA?" Cory asked.

"Who doesn't?" the teenager shrugged.

Cory passed over the card, signed "B. Kellogg" on the slip, waited while verification was obtained, then took the card and cashews and returned to the hotel garage at the end of the mall.

Locating the silver Camaro, he popped the trunk and inside found the forty-two-inch canvas case—the Steyr package. He looked around. The garage was deserted. Reaching into the bag, he pulled out the leather overcoat and draped it cloak-like over his shoulders. He then leaned into the Camaro's trunk, looped the case's sling around his left arm, and stood. The weapon slid around under his arm and was concealed by the coat. Satisfied he could now walk through the lobby without raising suspicions, he closed the trunk, grabbed the shopping bag, and headed quickly to his room.

War was such a simple art when tempered with deception.

CHAPTER 12

3 Bradford Lane, Falls Church, Virginia, 9:18 P.M.

". . . to be assumed from any preemptive policy decisions on the part of the administration and NATO. Don't you agree?"

"I suppose that's a possibility," Sal Franco said, caring less as he took another sip of the after-dinner cognac.

"So then you can see why this course of action with respect to the Asian subcontinent is curiously short-sighted. You know, Karen, your father and I were faced with a quite similar situation back in '64 when the North Vietnamese attacked our destroyer Maddox in the Tonkin Gulf. Why I remember . . . ."

Franco looked across the table to his wife. She appeared to be interested, hanging on every word coming from Senator Blanton Rossett's bird-like mouth. He took another sip of the drink, turned back to their host and arranged his face in what he thought most resembled an intelligent expression.

In the dim chandelier light, the senator looked to be a frail, but wealthy man dressed in the casual elegance of an English country squire on safari. A vision of tan, linen, epaulets and canvas hiking boots—his estate dress.

A widower for ten years, he was a short man with the body of a mantis, the mind of a scholar, and the demeanor of a Scottish chieftain. His hair was white, long, and combed back from the forehead. His eyes were small and, of late, a rheumy brown in color. His nose was large and his mouth pinched. Franco thought this odd, for as much as the senator liked to articulate the arcane, he would have expected the mouth to be large, at least from all the exercise it received, if not naturally. And if the talking weren't enough, even the old man's accent was irritating. Originally from somewhere in upstate New York, when he became excited, words like "tar" became "tah," and "car," "cah."

But, as Karen told him, the eighty-year-old senator was a close friend of the Mobley family. And, in this, Sal Franco forced himself to be polite.

"So you see, Sal," Rossett continued. "There are universal laws behind historical change. And it is these laws we must understand if we are to be able to have the knowledge to predict future historical patterns."

Realizing some response was now necessary, Franco, for the hundredth time this evening, considered telling the senator that discussing Third World politics was too much like work. But, as in the previous times, he held his tongue. There would be no percentage in offending the man. It would serve only to irritate Karen.

"History is important," he finally said.

Rossett smiled indulgently.

"It is crucial," he said. "Now, let us predict, for a moment, what the political theorists might eventually tell us about the current situation. I would imagine it will be much like the time in '58 when Ike and I were discussing Lebanon and . . . ."

As Rossett droned on, Franco's mind began to wander. He found it wandering back to Honduras, back to the interrogation bunker.

What would the theorists eventually say about Central America? he thought. Another wasted effort? A new byproduct of Marxism's approach to the riddle of history? Slash and burn? Contain and control? Another fallacy, another country, another stretch of conquering and conquering and then being conquered in spite of themselves.

One could only accept the irony, Franco realized.

It was a regional madness.

Obviously the insurgents were also buying the storyline. At least the rhetoric part. But why? He supposed, if for no other reason, than to be able to share Havana's enthusiasm for continuing revolution elsewhere despite the resultant economic dysfunction of Cuba itself.

Too esoteric? Franco wondered. Conceivably. What was it Alicia Carrera had told him? Something about freeing someone from the inactivity of despair? Perhaps this really was the reason Marxism seemed so palatable. Maybe it was the means to alleviate the boredom drawn from day after day of waiting. But for what? Some obscure political powering? Some temporary authority spit from the mouth of another temporary revolutionary? Orders to kill children? To torture women?

Not enough, Franco decided. There had to be something else. Something in addition to the ritualized reliance on Marxist afterthought. He took another sip of cognac and allowed it to drip slowly down the back of his throat.

Maybe the rhetoric was the way the Cubans planned to feed their new Latin recruits? After all, Latin America was the soft underbelly of Havana's expansionist efforts and if you don't have food, anything is better than hunger. Better than letting the recruits turn to Washington for meals. *Prime rib? It's Iowa beef. No, gracias. I'll have the Cuban word casserole instead. It's impolite to eat while I'm talking. The children? They've many new words to learn. Much too many for beef.*

Franco shook his head with disgust.

Central America, he thought. God, what a mess. And Nicaragua. The Sandinista takeover had been so very simple. Too simple, thanks to Washington's abandonment of Somoza, its liberal blind eye. Conversely, and thanks to Washington's now conservative blind eye, in El Salvador the military rightists were methodically assassinating priests and nuns. Honduras? Neither conservative nor liberal, it seemed. Just Washington meandering along, feeling its way with nothing particular in mind.

But no, he corrected himself. It was not Washington. Not all of it anyway. In the final analysis, all responsibility fell upon just one man . . . the president.

Franco wondered whether any American president could even begin to really understand the Third World. He doubted it. The White House was too insulated from reality, and statesmanship was a far cry from snake oil.

Franco drank the remainder of the cognac in a silent toast to posterity.

To you, Mr. President, he thought. May you one day learn the difference between politics and prudence.

". . . so you can see why our efforts are wasted then?" the senator asked.

"Well, when you put it that way . . ." Franco nodded blankly.

"Exactly," the Senator agreed. "Now what would you propose we do about it, Sal? Better yet, what do you think Ike would have done?"

Franco had no idea. In fact, he had no idea exactly what the senator had been rambling on about for the past twenty minutes. He felt like an idiot for having been caught daydreaming. Fortunately, no answer was necessary. Karen redirected the conversation. Franco could have kissed her.

"Some other time Rossey," she smiled, patting the old man's hand. "It's getting late, and both you and Sal need some rest. You can come to our house next week and continue your conversation. Isn't that right, Sal?"

"I'm looking forward to it," Franco smiled.

Soon thereafter everyone stood. Kisses and handshakes were exchanged. Thank you's given and received.

Outside, as Franco walked Karen to the Volvo, she leaned up and kissed him on the cheek.

"What's that for?" he asked.

"For letting Rossey reminisce about his friendship with Eisenhower. It was nice of you."

Franco shrugged.

"I suppose he does know what he's talking about."

"I don't know how you would know," she said, a measure of concern evident in her tone. "Your mind was a million miles away most of the night. You need to talk about something?"

Franco offered a bland grin.

"Not really," he said softly. "It was probably just the cognac. It left me with a headache. Let's head for the house. I have to teach a class tomorrow."

There was no conversation during the five-minute trip. But as they climbed out of the Volvo, Karen decided to find out why he was acting so introspective.

"What happened in Honduras, Sal?" she asked. "One word."

One word, Franco thought. It was a game they had played since first meeting. They allowed themselves one word to describe how they were feeling about something at any particular moment. Both felt this helped the other to immediately know the other's mindset before a discussion.

But in this case, Franco knew one word would never suffice. He whispered two instead.

"*La boya.*"

She looked at him curiously.

"I don't understand?"

"I'm not sure I really want you to understand."

"Let's go upstairs," she said, taking his hand. "We'll just start at the beginning."

Later, in bed, they talked until midnight. Franco told her everything. About Alicia Carrera, about Rico, even about the nameless child buried in the forgotten jungle. Then he fell asleep in her arms.

The last words he remembered Karen saying were, "I love you, Sal."

He had been too sleepy to respond.

CHAPTER 13

The Stouffer's Concourse Hotel, 9:30 P.M.

While Sal Franco drank cognac, Damon Cory continued to study the five, single-sheet identification abstracts now spread out on the bed. All were identical formats: 8 x 10 inches, double-spaced, each with a black-and-white, passport-size photograph stapled to the upper left-hand corner of the page.

Cory nodded thoughtfully. Upon first observing the images, he had experienced a fleeting, yet disquieting sense of misgiving, of *unfairness* even, for the faces in the photographs looked so very, very old. Indeed, effecting their deaths would present little challenge.

Then again, the presumption of unfairness was certainly not to be confused with inequity and, drawn from this subtle distinction, he felt his qualms subside. What with their age and tenure, he could well understand why these five had remained well above any real-time level of suspicion. Physically, nobody could appear more benign than Eisler's targets. All were blemished, and all seemed the typical male septuagenarian.

Considering their death, Cory popped a cashew into his mouth, sucking off the salt before chewing. He reflected on the targets in a theoretical way, wondering about the gravity of their collective offenses, about the finality of the sanctions, and about the legitimacy Eisler envisioned when balancing the two. Cory had, of course, killed men for lesser offenses, just as he had surely killed others for greater wrongs. Still, he did not envy Eisler's circumstance. The killing, Cory's part of the equation, was relatively easy, a technical exercise at most. Deciding who was to die was a much more entangled exercise.

Cory lit his pipe, then reached down and selected the center abstract. Eisler had indicated no particular order of importance. So the first man to bear witness would be—Cory glanced at the top of the paper—Gustav Celt.

"So again it begins," he sighed sullenly. Then he ate another cashew and turned his attention Celt's vitae.

To ensure clarity, Eisler had delineated each abstract into three sections. The first was PHYSICAL DESCRIPTION. Celt was five feet seven inches, 185 pounds, with brown-gray hair, brown eyes. Eisler noted him to be a careful, ponderous man, rarely given to displays of humor.

The second section was ADDRESSES, residence and work. Celt lived in Manassas, Virginia, and commuted daily to his Aberdeen Proving Ground office in Maryland.

Like the first, Cory skipped the second section and dropped down to the third, COMMENTS. There, Eisler had provided what Cory considered to be a sentimental, but, for his purposes, critical factor concerning Gustav Celt's behavior patterns: *Since her death in the autumn of 1981, subject visits his wife's grave [Holy Cross Cemetery, Manassas VA] each morning between the hours of 0700 and 0715.*

Cory looked back up to the photograph.

A fat man, he decided, committing the image to memory. A fat man. Tired eyes. The flesh of his face resembled wax on a melting candle.

And so Gustav Celt would die, Cory thought, as he returned all the abstracts to their envelope. He would die at Holy Cross Cemetery between the hours of 0700 and 0715. It would be effected without ritual and in a manner that would preclude unnecessary suffering for Celt himself.

Climbing off the bed, Cory walked to the suite's sofa, unzipped the tan canvass case and extracted the weapon, a modified 7.62mm Steyr SSG sniper rifle. Painted a drab olive, it was a state-of-the-art instrument featuring a twenty-six-inch barrel with a chrome bore of one turn in eleven inches. To reduce tempering stress, all castings were hammer-forged and the action had been converted to single-shot to preclude metal fatigue.

An Austrian design, the SSG actually had two triggers placed front to back, like an old double-barrel shotgun. The first trigger—the "constant actuator"—was normal, having a crisp release pull of two pounds. However, when the rear trigger—the "variable actuator"—was simultaneously pulled, the front trigger's release pressure was reduced to only two ounces, thus giving the shooter a hair trigger upon request.

Atop the SSG, was QUEENWALK's scope of choice, the ART IV 3–9X variable ranging, automatic telescope. Simple and reliable, once the scope was laser-aligned with the barrel, the weapon remained sighted until the scope was removed. Flipping the weapon to its side, Cory inspected the ART mounting brackets. The red wax seals remained intact at four mating points between the breech and the scope tube.

Matchless, he thought. Before adoption of the Steyr package, other rifles always needed to be sighted in before shooting. But, normally, QUEENWALK had insufficient time for such luxury. With the Steyr and the ART laser-sighting capability, the time problem had been eliminated. If the wax seals were intact, the SSG was zeroed at 500 yards, and taking the weapon as it was here, Cory knew his capabilities. With rudimentary, on-site adjustments to the ART scope's ranging mechanism, at 1,000 yards he could hit a 9-inch pie plate nineteen out of twenty times, a 95 percent "effective" rate. At 800 yards, the ratio increased to 100 percent.

Gustav Celt? Depending upon terrain and weather, experience told Cory the target would most likely be between 400 and 600 yards.

Cory nodded in assent. The parameters would be adequate.

Laying the weapon on the bedspread, Cory reached to an end table and picked up a blue, waterproof plastic case. Similar in design and about the size of a band-aid box, inside was the SSG's ammunition.

He popped open the packet, poured the contents to the bedspread and counted. There were twelve 7.62mm hollowpoint bullets, the normal Steyr load.

Such graceful little tokens, he thought. So shiny and brassy. So prominent.

Cory tossed a handful of cashews into his mouth, then lined the cartridges up on the bedspread as he thoughtfully chewed the salty nutmeat.

The bullets, like the Steyr, had been modified for QUEENWALK, and these were versions of what had originally been Springfield Armory's 168-grain Match King rounds.

Cored for the hollowpoint, they were developed to be shot at a target in a crowd, yet keep the projectile from completely penetrating the target's body so those adjacent to it would not be injured inadvertently.

In this, the hollowpoint version, the bullets actually blossomed inside the target, causing what was known as a Jell-O effect, the massive internal tissue damage that results when the round penetrats the skin, expands, and releases its velocity into the soft vital organs. In a chest shot, Cory knew, heart, lungs, spleen, and liver were reduced to nothing more than a useless mass of inoperable sinew. Because of this internal blossoming effect, this particular kind of hollowpoint was termed a *roseround*.

"Roserounds," he whispered. They were an efficient and, at least externally, a tidy way to die.

Humane, thought Cory. But sometimes a bit too humane. Sometimes he had felt a lingering death in order. But he dismissed this reservation as inappropriate for the old Russians and checked his watch. 10:15 p.m.

It would probably take him an hour to find the cemetery, another to find the grave and be in position. If Celt was expected to arrive by 0700, Cory would have to be on the road by at least 0500. That meant waking up at 0430.

If he went to bed now, he would get six hours rest. More than enough to be able to deal with a seventy-year-old man.

Quickly scooping the roserounds into their case, Cory tossed the packet to the bedside table next to his pipe and flipped off the light. He was under the covers and asleep minutes later.

The insomnia was gone now. He was not preparing for a mission, he was now well into the exercise.

Lucius discerned the difference.

No dreams would be conjured tonight.

CHAPTER 14

THE FOURTH DAY
Tuesday, November 25, 1982

Manassas, Virginia, 6:55 A.M.

Holy Cross Cemetery was a cold, wind-swept acre of abandonment perhaps five miles north of the city proper. In Cory's opinion, it seemed lamentably apropos for the task at hand.

The grounds had gone to seed, and in the faint light of dawn, weeds and shrubbery poked their bristly heads through the six inches of snow that covered the area. All of the growth appeared taller than the tombstones, and much of it even outstripped the rusting wrought iron fence that defined the cemetery's perimeter.

There had been two Civil War battles just northeast of here, Cory remembered. He wondered if any of the veterans were buried here. He suspected some probably were. Holy Cross looked like a place that could have been around in the 1860s. But that was then and this was now, so that war and its victims would remain forgotten. Cory had other things on his mind.

Fortunately, the cemetery's minimal size had made his choice of a surveillance point all the easier. It was roughly a 50-by-100 yard rectangle of land situated between two intersecting farm roads. The entire area was deserted.

After finding the cemetery, Cory had driven the Camaro to the corner, turned left, and proceeded no more than 100 yards up to the top of a rolling hill. Parking the vehicle, he had taken the Steyr, climbed through a four-strand, barbed-wire fence and walked carefully back, angling his path through the ruts of an old cornfield to the windward slope of the hill that overlooked the cemetery below. The terrain drop to the cemetery's exact center was a gentle twenty degrees. The distance, 650, maybe 680, yards. Cory squatted at the base of a gnarled, leafless oak and waited, mindsetting himself as he anticipated Celt's arrival.

Cory weighed his emotional symmetry. How he must look. How he must feel.

The image was there, he knew. The solitary hunter. An application of isolated power who, considering his costume—the long leather coat, fur hat, and knee-length boots—probably more resembled someone plucked from Chichagov's officer corps as the Russians stood to repel Napoleon's Berezina River attack.

And the feelings? Cory knew them central to appearance. Commitment. Duty. Making things just. From Lucius Aemilius at Pydna, to Chichagov at the Berezina, to Patton at Bastogne, the awareness was both chaste and timeless.

"Making things just," Cory whispered to himself.

The mind-set was locked into place.

"He comes, Damon," Lucius reported from somewhere. "He will be old and sick and appear quite pathetic. Ignore these factors, Damon. For he is the enemy. He must be prosecuted. The mission is desistance."

Desistance, Cory thought, as he looked to his left. Its headlights still on despite the dawn, an old brown Ford station wagon had pulled to a stop near the gate to the cemetery.

Cory reached into his pocket, selected one of two roserounds, worked the Steyr's action, inserted a cartridge, and closed the breech. He did not look at the weapon while loading, his eyes remained fixed on the station wagon and on the man who was now climbing out the driver's side.

Gustav Celt closed the car door behind him, glanced up at the sky, then began to walk slowly through the wrought iron fence toward the center of the cemetery. He moved painfully, Cory thought, as if he suffered from phlebitis of the left leg—a limping heap of adipose tissue dressed in a threadbare overcoat, plaid muffler, and Irish walking hat.

Celt paused at a grave marked by a mildewed marble cross.

Cory smoothed the leather coat across his abdomen, pressed his back against the tree, and pulled his knees up. Raising the Steyr, he brought the scope to his right eye as he rested his elbows on his knees for support.

Through the telescopic sight, Celt blurted into view. Cory reached up with his right hand and adjusted the variable-power ratio to obtain the correct proportions. The process was a smooth, nearly instinctual transition wherein he adjusted the ART's optics until two parallel, ratio enhancement lines were superimposed beneath the horizontal member of the crosshairs and corresponded to an eighteen-inch measurement on Gustav Celt's chest, roughly the distance from the chin to the waist. Since the range was about 670 yards and the weapon zeroed to 500, a minor compensation was necessary. Doing such, Cory aligned the crosshairs on Celt's mouth instead of thorax center. Then he slid his right middle finger around the rear trigger and depressed it fully. The front trigger remained untouched.

AUTLEY HOUSE

Cory took a deep breath and released it through clenched teeth. A low hiss was audible as he continued to observe his target through the scope. Stationary now, Celt's head was bowed and his eyes closed as if in prayer.

The *moment*, Cory thought briefly, as he lightly touched the front trigger with his right index finger. He began to apply pressure. A sensitive caress. Not too much, not too little. Just a steady, practiced easing as he remembered the old BRASS acronym while the trigger tension closed in quarter-ounce increments: 1 ounce, *B*reathe; 1.25, *R*elax; 1.5, *A*lign on target; 1.75, *S*lack muscle tension; 2.0, *S*queeze.

7:03 a.m. The Steyr slammed into Cory's shoulder as the crack of the roseround splintered the morning calm.

A millisecond later, the upper chest cavity of Gustav Celt was reduced to a pulpy soup. As desired, it was humanely concluded: a painless death even before he collapsed into the snow covering his late wife's grave.

By the time the echo of the rifle had dissipated, Cory was already standing. He could feel the adrenaline rush and was aware of a trembling in his knees and fingers. It was a familiar and not an altogether unpleasant sensation. He took another deep breath. There was no reason to inspect the cemetery more closely, to confirm the obvious. As he watched for any movement below, he worked the action on the Steyr. The expended casing ejected. It flipped through the air, landing ten feet to Cory's right rear.

He turned to retrieve it. Moving to the spot, he found where it had penetrated the snowcrust. Reaching down, he felt into the small hole, found the casing, and put it into his coat pocket.

Standing upright, he looked to the northern sky. Forecasters had predicted a heavy snow by noon. Good, he thought. If so, all evidence of his trespass would be covered under a thick blanket of slush by evening.

Suddenly, he became aware of the intense pressure in his bladder. The excitement of the previous few minutes was making itself known and he was unable to deny the hollow sense of urgency.

Slinging the Steyr behind his shoulder, he unsnapped the long coat, unzipped his trousers, and, with gloved fingers, freed his flaccid penis.

The urine was yellow and warm. It steamed in the cold air as he saturated the small hole made by the casing. Then, his bladder empty, he turned to leave.

Zipping up his trousers, the rifle still slung, Cory began to walk quickly back across the cornfield to the waiting Camaro. He would drive back to Washington, find a public telephone, and at exactly 1000 hours, call the main switchboard of the Department of Defense.

And while bureaucratic nature by rote followed its course, he would return to the Stouffer's and to the four remaining abstracts.

This evening would present another scenario.

It would also deliver a second desistance.

CHAPTER 15

FBI Headquarters, 2:25 P.M.

"I've got a question about that, Agent Franco."

Sal Franco glanced to a young, attractive black woman in the lecture hall's second row. She was one of the fifty-three attending his class. "Yes, ma'am?"

The woman looked back to her notes, as she began to speak.

"You said the relative absence of political terrorism in this country was attributable to our social and political safety valves. Do you see this changing?"

Franco shook his head.

"I believe what I said was that the relative lack of terrorism here could probably be attributable to certain of our sociopolitical safety valves. But, regardless, with respect to Latin groups—and that is the subject during this block—I don't really think there should be any hard and fast rules. One act of violence, large or small, could change everything."

"I don't understand?" the girl admitted.

"Well, look at it this way," Franco explained, as he leaned his elbows on the podium at the front of hall. "Look at terrorism like beauty. It is all in the eyes of the beholder. The number of incidents actually indicates very little. To us, to the terrorists for that matter, even to the general public, perceptions as to the severity of terrorism are determined by how spectacular the acts may be, not on their statistical occurrences. We must prepare for reality, and assume it will eventually occur."

Another hand shot up toward the rear of the hall.

"Yes?" Franco asked.

"But why worry about the Latin groups so much?" a short-haired, athletic-looking man asked.

"Simple," Franco told him. "Their roots are the closest to our borders, and their people are the most likely to be responsive to the United States for any number of economic, political, and even social motivations."

"So there are no home-grown groups operating here?"

"Sure there are," Franco smiled. "Croatian émigrés, IRA, Cuban exiles, neo-Nazis, various militias, all kinds. But the important thing to remember is that intelligence information is the key to preventing loss of life. So when you get to your field offices, remember to keep your ears open. If something sounds suspicious, take the time to ask a few more questions. And if you are still concerned, bring the matter to the attention of your supervisor."

The black agent-trainee spoke again.

"So who do you think are potentially the most dangerous Latin groups around today?"

"Well, let's start with Mexico," Franco answered. "There are at least four groups currently operating there, the Zapatista Urban Front; the Revolutionary Armed Forces of the People; the 23rd of September League; and the National Revolution for Civic Action. All of them are opposed to our economic influence on Mexican politics.

"Now, let's take the Civic Action group first. Believe it or not, this is a pro-Chinese movement that seems to specialize in ambushing military and police patrols. Some of you may remember . . . ."

"Agent Franco?"

Franco looked down. Standing immediately to the right of the stage was one of the headquarters runners, an intern who was working his way through college.

"Yes?" Franco asked the young man.

"From Mr. Weall." He passed Franco a folded slip of paper, then disappeared through the door behind Franco's platform.

Rico, Franco thought hopefully, as he unfolded the note.

But the message said nothing about Rico. Only a terse, typed. "My Office, Immediately. JW"

Right in the middle of a lecture? Franco thought. What the hell. What Weall wanted, Weall got.

He refolded the paper and looked back to his audience.

"Well, looks like you people got lucky. I've got something to attend to now. Why don't you just go on break and be back in your seats in about half an hour."

There was a brief sprinkling of applause and Franco smiled. He held up a hand to get their attention.

"Just a minute, good people. Before I let you out, I've got one question. I want to see if anyone has learned anything so far. Now listen up. Who can tell me why the members of Latin terrorist groups have accents?"

There were murmurs in the lecture hall as the trainees exchanged curious glances.

"No takers?" Franco asked.

No hands raised.

Franco raised an eyebrow. "It's so young, innocent FBI agents will know who to arrest."

The class broke into laughter.

"See you at three," Franco told them. Then he left the lecture hall to meet with Jonathon Weall.

***

Franco walked into Weall's office without bothering to knock.

"*Qué tal?*" he asked, as he took a seat in the single vacant chair.

"Plenty is happening," Weall sighed, glancing up from his desk and leaning back in his chair. "Update me on a Peruvian group. *Sendero Luminoso*. I want the short course." "Shining Path," Franco said. "They're a Marxist-Leninist splinter faction. Why?"

Weall ignored the question.

"What's their pedigree?"

"Off the cuff?"

Weall nodded.

"In one fashion or another, they've been around a long time," Franco said. "Since the early '60s. They were one of the Cuban-backed groups who followed all that nonsense of developing a *foco* theory of rural revolution in Peru. When the Peruvian military clamped down and started spoiling their party, a bunch of them split off. Since *foco* wasn't living up to its expectations, they decided to try something else. They puttered around with the Maoist Party in Bolivia, eventually split from them, and around 1970 assumed the title Sendero Luminoso."

"So how much capability can they muster?"

"Well," Franco shrugged. "They're committed, that's for sure. Besides that, they've got a substantial amount of rural support for their cause, particularly in the last couple of years."

"What happened then?"

"Narcotics," Franco said flatly. "Shining Path is mainly being financed by the Peruvian cocaine traffickers. They work a trade. Shining Path gets arms, ammunition, and money. In exchange, they protect the traffickers' coca-growing plantations in Peru's more remote regions. It's a hell of a business, Jonathon. Big dollars. The last figure I read indicated Peru is now responsible for about thirty percent of all the cocaine entering the United States."

"Any local successes?" Weall asked. "Penetrations? Chances for interdiction?"

"Slim and none," Franco told him. "With all the money involved, plus the lessons the traffickers learned in Colombia, Shining Path is a black hole when it comes to intelligence operations. We get virtually nothing. Nobody talks because they know if they do, they will end up dead with their cock and balls in their mouth. On top of that, they're probably as well armed, if not better equipped than the Peruvian Army."

"A couple of months ago, some rural mayor started complaining about the narcotics trafficking. He was assassinated. The army sent in about 200 troops to restore order in the area. Big surprise for the army. The soldiers were met by 300 of Shining Path's finest. Only about twenty of the soldiers made it out. Our narcotics types in the Lima embassy figure they were outgunned because of antiquated equipment and lack of training. Consequently . . . ."

"Why do I have the feeling I know where this is going," Weall whispered.

"Because it's been going the same way for years," Franco told him. "It's panning out to be like Vietnam was in the early '60s. To 'train' the Peruvian Army in narcotics interdiction, we've all kinds of military and law enforcement types rummaging around down there: chopper pilots, defoliation specialists, guerrilla warfare instructors. I understand we've even got people on the ground, special forces teams, actually running offensive actions with the Peruvian authorities."

Franco paused for a moment, then he asked, "Why all these questions about Shining Path? Am I going to Peru?"

"I wish it were Peru," Weall said slowly. "Only it looks like they've come to us."

Reaching to the desk, Weall picked up a single sheet of paper and passed it over to Franco.

"That is the transcript of a call received over at Defense at 10:00 a.m."

Sitting upright in the chair, Franco took the paper and began to read:

OFFICE OF THE ASSISTANT SECRETARY OF DEFENSE
WASHINGTON, D.C. 20301-1400

U-4, 678/RTS-1
Transmission Transcription: SPECAT EXCLUSIVE PER OASOD
2511871001................................. 2511871002

Gustav Celt has been executed subsequent to conviction by the people's court of the Partido Comunista del Peru en el Sendero Luminoso de Mariategui. He is but the first to receive sentence as a result of American military oppression directed against our brothers and sisters in Peru who are now calling out for justice.

We have but one demand. Immediate withdrawal of all American oppressors from our country. If all American military personnel are not withdrawn from our homeland within 24 hours, executions will continue until this demand is met. We are prepared to sacrifice ourselves for this belief.

END SPECAT EXCLUSIVE
U-4, 678/RTS-1

Franco glanced back over the transcript a second time, then handed it back to Weall.

"Gustav Celt?" he asked.

"They discovered the body two hours ago," Weall explained. He was chest-shot at a cemetery in Manassas sometime this morning. Probably close to dawn."

"Cemetery?" Franco asked, wondering about ritualistic implications.

Weall nodded, knowing what Franco was thinking.

"It's not that way, Sal. He was visiting his wife's grave. He went there every day."

"Who was he?" Franco asked.

"A scientist," Weall told him. "He worked for the Defense Department at Aberdeen Proving Ground."

Franco thought back to the transcript.

"Was the call in Spanish or English?"

"English."

"We have the original tape yet?"

"Not yet," Weall said. "We will by this afternoon."

Franco understood.

"I guess it's my case, right?"

Weall nodded.

"I've already cleared it with Bechtel. You've got the lead and you're detached from everything else. How do you want to work it?"

Franco considered his answer.

"Where else did the call go, Jonathon? The press have it yet?"

"No," Weall said. "Only Defense and us. Why, what are you thinking?"

"That I want to segment the investigation," Franco said quickly. "I'll need Forensics, of course. And Linguistics, for the tape. As for any site work, I think we should use the local field offices. If we work it right, maybe we can keep it quiet. But we need to make sure there are no leaks. This place is a sieve when things get up to your level, Jonathon. At least the field offices remember something about security. The fewer people who connect the killing to a terrorist threat the better, so try to make sure it stays closely held."

Weall accepted Franco's pointed, and valid, concerns regarding the headquarters senior staff and made a mental note to ask Hershel Bechtel to handle this invariably touchy matter. Then he narrowed his eyes and changed the subject.

"So you think we can expect additional homicides?" he asked.

"What makes you think I believe that."

"You used the term 'field offices,'" Weall said. "As in plural."

"You think the White House is about to pull our advisors out of Peru? We just spent I don't know how many millions to stabilize the Peruvian government. No, they're not going anywhere."

Weall nodded in agreement.

"I see your point," he said. "What do you need from me?"

"Celt's personnel file for starters," Franco said.

"I ordered it when I called for the original of the tape."

"Good," Franco smiled. "Have you stirred up the legal attaché in Lima yet?"

"I will," Weall said. "I'll have her touch base with DEA and the MIL-GROUP contingent. Somebody may have heard some rumors."

Franco grunted his approval.

"Well, if you can get me a fox for a ride to the cemetery, I'd like to take a look at the crime scene before it gets too disturbed."

"I'll have one on the roof in ten minutes."

Franco stood from the chair and looked down at Weall.

"I appreciate the nod on this one, Jonathon. I think I need a field hunt."

Weall offered a slight smile.

"Who else?" he said. "You're our Latin expert. Just catch the bastards, Sal. I'll keep everyone else out of your hair and make sure you get whatever or whomever you need."

"We'll catch them, Jonathon. They're on our turf now."

As Franco turned to go, Weall called after him.

"Oh, and Sal? Why don't you get out of that suit and into something less formal."

The suit, Franco thought. He'd forgotten all about the class waiting in the lecture hall.

"What about the . . . ."

"Forget it," Weall said, with a wave of the hand. "Those who can, do; those who can't, teach. I'll get someone from Administration to pontificate about something. You just get your jeans on and get moving. The feces is already in the fan on this one. I want to make sure we're upwind of it."

The old "teaching" adage made Franco feel good. The idea of getting out of the suit even better.

"I'll be in touch," he said. Then he turned and left the office.

Franco gone, Weall picked up his telephone and punched in four digits from memory.

"Communications," a male voice answered.

"This is Weall, get me the attaché in Lima, and while that's being put through, I want a helicopter. Roof pad, ten minutes. The destination is Manassas and the passenger is Senior Special Agent Sal Franco."

The order given, Weall replaced the receiver and leaned back in his chair. In the universal melee, he thought sourly, there were no beginnings and certainly no ends.

There was only a timeless milling about.

***

Painted a flat black and sterilized of all external markings, the tiny Hughes observation helicopter shuddered, then lifted no more than three feet above its pad atop the FBI Building. A quick check of the instruments and the pilot to Franco's left dipped the nose. Gathering ground speed, they cleared the building, passed low over the swirling Potomac River, then flew west. Manassas was twenty-five miles away. They would be on-station in twelve minutes.

Dressed comfortably in jeans, boots, and short leather jacket, Sal Franco watched the snow-spotted tapestry of Virginia passing below. But soon, shifting in the seat, he closed his eyes and released his lesser senses to experience their perceptions in order of occurrence: the smell of burning fuel; the whine of the turbines segueing into the hypnotic *fluckata-fluckata* of slicing rotors; the pressure of the shoulder harness biting into his chest and across his thighs. All the things he knew so well.

If asked, Franco would admit he liked the *fluckating* best. It reminded him of the hours spent overflying the Puerto Rican jungles. The out islands. The hundreds of boats, trucks, and countless other craft that may have hidden the insurgents, their weaponry or their support cells. The *fluckating* was bringing all of this back and, not unlike a rush of adrenaline, it honed his perceptions more sharply.

All rise, he mused thoughtfully, pleased with his life. Court was again in session and the session held promise of a chase.

Smiling, Franco allotted the recollections a few more moments, then opened his eyes and released the small vent window at his elbow so he could smell the air.

Ahead, through the Plexiglas bubble, he saw only overcast, and the horizon appeared just another stroke of gray on gray. The helicopter, he knew, was probably no more than another dab tossed somewhere in between.

Abruptly, to his left the pilot dipped the cyclic control stick forward and the helicopter dove toward the ground. They skipped over a tree-capped swale, then followed the slope of a snow-dusted glen until bisecting Route 234.

As they crossed the highway, the pilot banked the helicopter to the north and, seconds later, Franco could clearly see the reflections of emergency roof lights and the convergence of government vehicles upon a site perhaps two miles east of the main highway and near the intersection of two, poorly graded, iron-ore farm roads.

They roared over the scene an instant later, the pilot banking hard as he whipped the helicopter into a tight clockwise turn and selected a small, clear area just behind the cemetery for landing.

Rotors popping, they flared into a gentle touchdown amid a thrashing of wind, snow and swirling leaves.

Franco glanced at his Rolex. 3:52 p.m.

As the turbines slowed, Franco climbed out of his door, attached his badge to the upper right lapel of his jacket, and started walking toward the knot of uniformed and plainclothes officials who were now moving in his direction.

Homicide. After countless months in intelligence, he was finally back in his element, the one-on-one search for the killers of man. He felt good. Charged. Filled with a nearly visceral excitement.

The trail was less than nine hours old and already he was in the field and tracking.

Shining Path? No issue.

He'd cut his teeth on hard, fast hunts.

CHAPTER 16

The Stouffer's Concourse Hotel, 4:10 P.M.

Cory lay motionless on the still unmade bed. His room was dark and the washcloth felt cool to his eyes. Cool, yes; effectual, no. The cloth was doing nothing to control the pain, and with each carotid pulsebeat his brain continued its throbbing in green. Cory could taste his mind's eye weeping.

Outside, hanging on the doorknob, the NO MAID REQUIRED card eased into its sixth hour of service. No employee had questioned the instructions. None would. Stouffer's ran a tight ship. Room 1020's linens could remain soiled until the guest indicated otherwise. A marketing decision, such neglect was lumped under the general heading of hospitality. Mildewed towels and dirty sheets? The laundry could save soap today.

But Cory's thoughts were not of soap. Alone, awake, and fully dressed, he was aware of only two entirely dissimilar perceptions: the soft country rhythms drifting from the bedside clock-radio and the enduring strobe of the sinus headache.

"Fucking weather," he whispered, as he pressed the damp cloth against the bridge of his nose. The morning's trip, specifically his nasal breathing of the cold air at Manassas, had bred the pain even before leaving the site. And as for the commercial Tylenol-Sudafed combinations, a baker's dozen of each in the past eight hours, it looked as if they had only succeeded in upsetting his stomach while now, like further insult to injury, on the radio John Denver had begun yet another pointless ditty about the Rocky Mountains and their endangered flora and fauna.

"Fucking music."

As he suffered the music, Cory decided that all John Denver music should be permanently enjoined as a crime against humanity. And, at this, he jerked the washcloth from his eyes, tossed it across the room and sat on the edge of the bed.

He flipped off the radio and glanced at the clock. Notwithstanding the headache, it was time to get moving again. The pain? Eisler would expect him to tolerate it.

Eisler would not be disappointed.

Standing, Cory walked to the bathroom, splashed cold water on his face, dried his eyes, then returned to the bedside table and turned on the lamp. Kneeling at the side of the bed, he reached under the box springs and up into the small angular slit he had cut into the gauze that covered the bottom of the frame. Finding the manila envelope, he stood, leaning against the wall as he pulled out the abstract sheets and began to select the next target.

Why stand on routine, he thought. It really made little difference who would be next. But as he set Celt's vitae aside and studied the four remaining targets, he found himself returning to the photo of William Pointer.

He wondered why. Then it dawned on him.

It was to make it equal.

Whereas Gustav Celt had been the most obese of the original five, William Pointer was definitely the most delicate. A nice balance, thought Cory. Pointer it would be.

Cory glanced at PHYSICAL DESCRIPTION: 5'7", 132 pounds, short brown toupee, brown eyes.

He looked to the photograph. Pointer reminded him of an old Ichabod Crane. He was cadaverous thing with a long neck and heavily bagged turtle eyes. The toupee was a cruel joke. It was rawly chopped and perched atop two large ears like some windblown nest of straw.

Cory skipped down to Eisler's comments: A veritable recluse when not attending to DARPA duties. Subject is addicted to late-night cable television. Subject has never married and lives alone.

Pointer's home address, Cory read, was 119 Sheridan Acres Drive, Takoma Park, Maryland. In brackets beneath the address, Eisler had added the words, "mobile home."

Well, Cory thought. Mr. Pointer would no doubt miss his old movies tonight. A more invidious priority would add a bit of variety.

Cory refolded the abstracts, slid them into the envelope, knelt and returned the packet to its box-springs cache. Then he stood and looked around the room.

But what to do until Takoma Park?

God knew this place was boring. Boring and inanimate. Perhaps he would go for a drive? Maybe get a bite to eat?

He found himself smiling. No, he knew what he would do. What might prove interesting. He'd drive over to the Guest Quarters and see how Boudreaux Pock was living now. If he was lucky, maybe Pock could find something a little stronger for the headache.

He pulled on his leather coat and left the room. As he walked to the elevator, his thoughts turned once again to his mission. He then remembered an old Chinese adage first told to him by Eisler during a discussion of assassination.

You kill the chicken to frighten the monkey.

Such a succinct rationale for political death.

CHAPTER 17

Manassas, Virginia, 5:12 P.M.

Sal Franco sat astride a chipped concrete tombstone and chewed his gum. Around him, like some trained procedural squid, analysis of the crime scene continued to progress. Attention to detail was critical but time consuming, and Franco eyed the activity impatiently. He envisioned the squid on thorazine.

Currently, by virtue of his orders, the Virginia State Police controlled the roads while county sheriffs secured the cemetery's perimeter. Inside the isolated area, Celt's station wagon and corpse remained unmoved, while around them, the five-man FBI team plodded through its particular motions.

Operating from a mobile laboratory, a converted Winnebago without windows, two forensic experts had fingerprinted, photographed, and examined Celt, while two others searched, vacuumed, and dusted his vehicle for latent prints.

Franco had done nothing to interfere with the forensic efforts. He appreciated the fact that tiny clues were what made cases, eliminated suspects, and ultimately identified killers. He also believed in the notion that if there was something to be found—and there always was *something*—the technicians and their scientific esoterica eventually would find it.

But that was all the forensics experts did, find evidence. It was Franco's responsibility to take their findings and determine how any physical evidence fit into the grander investigative scheme.

As for what the technicians had found so far? Franco had no idea. Since their arrival on the scene, they had seen fit to speak only among themselves . . . not that Franco was really that surprised. It was relatively normal behavior. Forensics considered agents the offshoot of some lesser intellectual phylum.

As he played in the snow with the toe of his boot, Franco glanced to the sky. It was getting colder, and the snow that was already long overdue probably would arrive shortly after nightfall.

Turning up the collar on his leather jacket, Franco allowed the impatience to get the best of him. He shoved off the tombstone, stalked to the mobile lab, and pounded on its locked rear door.

"Who is it?" a voice called from within.

"Archduke Ferdinand," Franco shouted back. "Goddammit, Dunnigan, open the goddamned door."

A moment later, the electronic lock released and the door was opened by Dunnigan Cox, a pasty, middle-aged man who looked to suffer from the human equivalent of soil erosion. Holding a doctorate in applied physics from M.I.T., Cox was the forensic team leader. He was also, at least in Franco's opinion, entirely too taciturn in his duties—pleasant, yet evasive in a distinctively aggravating manner. It was almost as if he felt nothing could be a truth until it had been reduced to a written report.

"Yes, Agent Franco?" Cox asked, standing in the door so that Franco was forced to remain outside.

"I hesitate to interrupt the scientific muses," Franco said. "But I only have about forty five minutes of light left and I need to know what you've found so far."

"I'm afraid there really isn't much," Cox shrugged. "Nothing on the vehicle and just preliminaries on the deceased. I would hate to venture any conclusion until we've examined the data more completely."

"Humor me," Franco suggested. "What about Celt?"

"Single gunshot wound," Cox whispered, as if betraying a confidence. "Shoulder weapon, probably a NATO round weighing between 140 and 170 grains. No exit wound, though. Seems to indicate some type of hollowpoint. Of course I cannot confirm this to the exclusion of all others until after the autopsy, when we are given the opportunity to examine any metal fragments."

"Any guesses as to the shooter's location?"

"I don't market speculation," Cox said, shaking his head. "I rely on facts, facts I will submit to you only after I see the autopsy report, examine any fragments, and complete both our ballistic and trajectory enhancements."

"No initial findings?"

"Nothing is verified, and anything less would be solely speculation based upon incomplete data." Cox crossed his arms in front of his chest.

"Speculate." Franco's tone said it all. Both a threat and an order in three quick syllables.

Cox glanced around suspiciously, then reached behind him where be picked up a yellow legal pad, tore off the top page, and passed it to Franco.

"That's far from complete," he apologized. "In fact, it may be completely erroneous. I won't know until I can confirm it with the enhancements."

Franco looked at the paper. To him, it was a scribbled crisscrossing of lines, arcs, and mathematical formula graphs.

"Do you mind translating this for us commoners?" he asked, as he handed it back to Cox.

A pained expression spread across the scientist's face.

"*Now* would be a good time," Franco added.

"Very well," Cox nodded, sighing as he glanced down to his notes. "My initial findings, and I stress the word initial, are based upon *A*, the positioning of the corpse; *B*, the external entry wound angle; and *C*, generally accepted trajectory principles. Taking these into consideration and extrapolating from known to possible predicted activity, these data seem to support the hypothesis that the shooter, or shooters, was located somewhere along an imaginary line drawn between the corpse and the rise directly to our northwest."

Cox pointed behind Franco. "See that tree up there? The one at the ridgeline?"

Franco looked around. "The old oak?"

"Yes," Cox said. "If you begin at the corpse and walk directly to the tree, our unsupported findings suggest the shooter, or shooters, were most likely concealed at some point within five feet to either side of your path."

"But no definite distance?" Franco asked.

"Not even for you, Agent Franco," Cox shrugged. "If you can wait until all the information is analyzed, I will be able to tell you the exact shooting point within a two-foot radius. But again, that will be sometime tomorrow after our enhancements are completed. Once we have determined the point, we will conduct a thorough examination of the entire sector, in accordance with controlled standard operating procedure."

Franco looked back to Cox.

"You might want to dust off your snowshoe procedure first," he said. "By tomorrow it could well be piled up to your ass and you won't be able to find anything."

"Well," Cox grunted, nonplussed. "That will be tomorrow. As for this afternoon, may I get back to my work? Or do you desire additional companionship?"

Franco chuckled. "I've had enough for now. Give my best to the muses."

Cox returned the smile. "I suppose you're now planning to take a stroll?"

"I am."

Cox nodded knowingly. "We'll remain available should you need us. Good day, Agent Franco."

"*Pax vobiscum*, Doctor Cox."

As Cox retreated to the Winnebago, Franco walked over to Gustav Celt's corpse and squatted at its feet. He looked up to the ridgeline, centered the oak, then visualized a ten-foot-wide lane from the tree back to Celt. The bullet's probable path now identified, he stood, moved quickly to the cemetery's rusted fence, hopped it, and began counting strides as he ascended the slope.

AUTLEY HOUSE

The ground remained frozen, covered with perhaps a three-inch layer of snow. Fortunate, Franco thought. Somebody should have left something behind. He watched the ground carefully as he continued toward the oak: 200 strides, a small rabbit hole; 370, a second hole, even smaller; 740, the oak, its base, footprints, depressions in the snow.

Franco moved closer: 778 strides; 779; 780. He stopped less than two feet from the tree. Turning around, he looked back toward the cemetery. 780 strides at about 30 inches each was about, 700 yards?

Jesus, he thought. Even with a scope, 700 yards was a hell of a shot. But could the shooter have been closer? Probably not. If Cox had been correct about the trajectory, then this was the place. It was the only area even close to the lane where someone had obviously been tramping around.

But tramping from where? And to where?

He would follow the footprints.

As he turned to his right, Franco noticed the stain at his feet. It looked oddly out of place against the white backdrop. He dropped to one knee and inspected it closer. He began to smile. *Never eat the yellow snow.* It was urine. Frozen urine. Frozen shooter urine, he'd bet. Enough for a specimen? He doubted it. Most of it had seeped through the snow into the soil below.

But wait? he thought. What is this? Small, curly, was it brown? He leaned over even closer.

"Hello," he whispered. It was a hair! A hair with one end frozen into the urine. Could it be a shooter hair? A possibility. He would save it for the lab.

Reaching into his pocket, Franco pulled out a piece of gum. He pulled off the foil wrapper, removed the gum and popped it into his mouth. He then reached down and plucked the hair from the ice and placed it on the empty gum wrapper. Standing, he refolded the wrapper and placed it in a jacket pocket for safe-keeping.

Cox could analyze the hair later. Now, it was back to the footprints.

For the next ten minutes Franco methodically followed the tracks across a cornfield, through a barbed wire fence, and finally, to the old farm road where the footprints ended and vehicle tire tracks began.

Footprints and tire tracks. Solid collaborative leads.

He trusted forensics had brought flashlights.

They'd need them when casting the molds.

CHAPTER 18

Alexandria, Virginia, 5:58 P.M.

It was just after dusk by the time Damon Cory shoved through the double glass doors and entered the Reynolds Street high-rise.

Guest quarters. The lobby was painted an anemic gray, with lighter shades of pastel furniture lined up like seed rows. By design, it was one of those in-between kind of places. More than a hotel, but less than a condominium, it supposedly offered the benefits of both. Another routine building that catered to government employees who, like Pock, were visiting Washington, and others who, for whatever reason, opted for longer occupancy simply because it was easy.

Cory glanced at the Camaro's key chain. Pock had written extension number 802 on the reverse side. Ignoring the desk clerk, Cory walked directly to the elevators, stepped inside and pressed the button for the eighth floor. The doors slid closed and the car jerked into motion.

Riding up, Cory directed his attention to a large poster bolted in Lucite to the wall. The advertisement presented an artist's rendering of the guest quarters building and detailed four reasons to prefer it over the similar area hotels:

1. Daily, weekly or monthly rates.
2. Convenient to commercial, academic and official activities.
3. Lobby restaurant and pub.
4. Maid service [optional at extra cost].

All, Cory read, were central ingredients in guest quarters: *We do it so you don't have to, purpose in life.*

He shook his head. More bullshit sloganing designed to attract new recruits into the quarters' middle-class coffers.

8th floor. The elevator jerked to a halt, the doors opened, and Cory stepped into the hall. His nostrils were immediately assaulted. There were two odors, one as distasteful as the other was pleasing.

The distasteful. To his left it wafted like discharge from a nightsoil pot. It was probably another extra cost option, but the guest quarters needed a plumber somewhere.

Cory turned to his right and the pleasant. Here there was onion, tomato, Tabasco, and shrimp in the air. Cory smiled. Jambalaya. He followed his nose to 802 and rapped on the door.

There was no answer but, leaning closer, he could clearly hear the sound of music playing inside, zydeco. Upbeat Cajun tunes with fiddle, accordion, and harmonica. He rapped on the door again. This time Pock responded.

"Yo?" came a muffled voice.

"Farm implements," Cory said. "We're making housecalls to qualified buyers."

As Pock opened the door, Cory noticed two things: he was carrying a Beretta .9mm semiautomatic pistol, and he was soaking wet with a towel around his waist.

Cory nodded to the weapon and stepped inside.

"Late on the rent?" he said.

"Just finished entertaining," Pock grinned, closing the door. "Make yourself a drink. Everything's in the kitchen."

"I need something stronger than aspirin first," Cory said.

"What's the problem?"

"Headache." Cory said. "A real crown of thorns."

"Above the sink. There's some codeine in the Tylenol tin."

Pock turned and walked to a closed door—a bathroom?—at the room's left rear. As Pock opened the door and stepped inside, Cory could hear a shower running. The door closed and Cory glanced around, assessing the apartment: a one-room efficiency with kitchenette, sofa-bed, cocktail table, and bookcases from where a small stereo continued to play the zydeco music.

From the kitchen the aroma of the jambalaya was stronger now, but so too was the apartment laced with the scents of human lovemaking. Cory smiled. *We the People*. Wasn't that what made America great? The freedom to chose one's own vices?

He moved into the kitchen and looked above the sink. Finding the Tylenol tin, he took out two small pills and popped them to the back of his throat. Then he located a reasonably clean glass, rinsed it out and poured two fingers of bourbon from a bottle on the counter. Gulping half of it, he washed down the codeine and turned back to the living area just in time to see a woman emerge from the bathroom. She wasn't pretty and appeared to have that pale, sickly persona Cory had always associated with redheads. Plain in that "let's sit on the porch and talk" sort of way.

"Hello," Cory said. "And how are you today?"

Obviously embarrassed, the woman clutched a purse and headed to the door without comment. As it slammed shut, Cory grunted and drained his glass. He walked back to the sink, poured in another two fingers of bourbon, then lifted the lid on the jambalaya pot. Taking a large spoon, he stirred the stew until a shrimp bubbled to the top. He trapped it in the spoon, raised it to his lips and smelled the aroma. Thick and heavy with Tabasco as it should be. He ate the shrimp. Perfect. Soft, yet still retaining its texture.

"Hey, Boudreaux," he called out. "I think this is about ready."

He waited, but Pock didn't respond. Cory put the lid back on the pot and taking his bourbon, walked into the living area and sat down on the sofa.

He leaned his head back against a cushion and closed his eyes. His mind, in a kind of intellectual voyeurism, began to game. This time, the exercise focused on the redhead who had just left the apartment. The woman no doubt had a name like Ann, Catherine, or maybe Mary? Surely something plain. Whatever, he smiled. Mary would do. In fact, she rather looked like a Mary. Looked like a Mary from, say, Omaha. Midwest Mary. Midwest Mary from a house on the farm, the two dogs barking, and the blueberry-pie-cooling-on-mom's-kitchen-counter place. No Sarah Lee pie in Omaha. This would be homemade blueberry, good dirt-farmer blueberry.

So there it was, Cory thought. Midwest Mary with her family back in Omaha, now in D.C. with her pantry filled with Shredded Wheat and Frosted Flakes, her red Toyota Tercel in the parking lot and a half-eaten pint of Haagen-Dazs waiting in her freezer. She would have torn the ice cream's lid. Now, it would be covered with a piece of wax paper held in place with the rubber band from last week's Sunday newspaper that she always purchased just to read the employment sections for jobs she would never be offered.

But where did Midwest Mary work now? Where was she spending her eight hours a day, five days a week for the next twenty years or so? The government, of course. But where? She was not flashy enough for Capitol Hill or the more showy departments like State or Defense. No, Mary was more the Housing and Urban Development genre. The "send me your form 88A and I'll send you back a 76C" type of worker. Her apartment was doubtless in one of the nondescript Arlington buildings: a $550-a-month, one-bedroom, one-bath flat. Inside, it would be painted white and on the walls there would be baskets and plastic-framed prints of happy green frogs, mushrooms with eyes, and Robert Frost sayings. Her favorite magazine was probably *TV Guide*; her favorite movie, some old Tracy-Hepburn thing; her favorite celebrity, Meryl Streep; and her favorite book, something like *Why Men Leave Women Who Love* or whatever other drivel the predictable were reading these days.

Cory took a sip of his bourbon as he refined his cynicism and continued the game, admiring, as always, his own cleverness in the process.

Women like Mary, he knew, tended to live in clusters, like grapes. He suspected Mary's apartment building friends would be no different. On Saturdays they gathered together, ate avocado dip, watched a rented movie on a borrowed VCR, and planned vacations they could never afford on their meager salaries. Then it was back to clusters, back to themselves, and back to the masturbation with one of those "deep tissue massagers" purchased from obscure mail order houses in Southern California. Batteries were not included. Mary had purchased her C-cells at a grocery store.

But allowing Pock to sample her wares? Variety, Cory supposed. Certainly not love on a high and windy hill. More like a perfunctory rutting. But at this, Cory began to speculate about Mary's sexual history. To what might have been her first tentative steps on the path to Boudreaux Pock.

Relaxing on the sofa, he continued to find diversion in the random musings.

Midwest Mary, he smiled. She no doubt had lost her virginity back in Omaha. Probably the old boyfriend. Probably some kid named, named what? Bob? Yes, Bob would do. It was a good strong American name. A good son-of-another-dirt-farmer name. Bob and Mary. Cory could see them now.

He visualized an old Dodge truck, perhaps a rusted blue in color. Bob and Mary sitting alone in the cab. The senior prom was two weeks away. Bob was eager and inexperienced; Mary timid and anxious. It was night, and they were parked in the far corner of a deserted corn field. In the distance, cars on the interstate could be heard, moving fast, moving anywhere just to be out of Nebraska. The truck's engine was turned off and on its radio, the sounds of, well, the sounds of nothing were audible. It was a beat-up farm truck. It had no radio.

Bob and Mary had kissed for a long time. Bob was physically excited and Mary was aware of his condition. She had rubbed him before, but never directly. Always with the back of her hand or her forearm until he kind of shivered and the wet spot appeared on his jeans and he had stopped wanting to touch her.

Bob had touched Mary's breasts before, but never had he delved below the waist, never there. But this night was different. This night, Bob took his . . . .

"So what's going on?" Pock asked, walking in from the bathroom

His thoughts interrupted—and a bit too soon at that—Cory opened his eyes and looked over to Pock. Straight from the shower, the Cajun was wearing a black sweatshirt with U.S. ARMY emblazoned in gold across the chest.

"Just thinking," Cory smiled.

"Anything in particular?"

About what an elitist I've become, Cory thought.

"About young girls and the rites of passage," he said. "Do you think there's any domination that doesn't feel natural to those who possess it."

Pock walked over and turned down the stereo.

"What in the fuck are you talking about?"

I'm not sure, Cory thought. The codeine and the bourbon were working his brain quite nicely.

"Your little friend," he said. "Not much on conversation."

"She's not bad," Pock said, heading for the kitchen. "Not much curb appeal. But she makes that up in effort."

"In the dark all cats are gray," Cory whispered. And that being the rite of selection, when Adam delved Eve, who then was the snake? God? Man? Lucius? Unknown. Unknown in the who cares mode.

Cory shook his head. The codeine was bastardizing his thoughts, conjuring those penitent, belly-of-the-beast sensations again. He stood and walked to the kitchen.

"How's the head?" Pock asked.

"Better," Cory said.

"Another drink?"

"I'd rather eat first."

"I hear that," Pock grinned. "Go sit down. I'll dish this up."

Because Pock had no dining area, Cory ate at the coffee table. Pock had turned off the zydeco music and turned on a nine-inch portable television he found adjacent to the sofa. Setting it in the center of the table, he sipped a drink, his eyes traveling between the game show and Cory, who was eating, and obviously enjoying, a large bowl of jambalaya.

"Ain't she fine?" Pock asked, sitting cross-legged on the floor.

Cory didn't look up from his meal. "Who?"

"That blonde in the evening gown."

Cory glanced at the television. He had already decided the woman had too many teeth.

"I guess," he shrugged, after a moment. "What's the point of this show anyway?"

"You've never watched it?" Pock asked.

"No," Cory said, sarcastically adding, "I like the host, though. I bet he wears pantyhose."

"Probably," Pock smiled.

Cory grunted and took another bite of the jambalaya while, on the television, the prissy-looking host, tooth lady, and a prideful husband were clapping while a woman attempted to stuff herself into a tiny Mazda truck.

"You did it!" the host heralded. "You won the truck!"

There was a wild round of applause as the camera zoomed to a tight shot of the winner's face—a teary harvest moon beaming through the windshield from the interior of the cab.

Curious game, thought Cory. Plump Americans could win small Japanese trucks if they could fit into them. Little wonder Japan had cornered the vehicle market.

"By the way," Pock said. "I was going to call you tonight, anyway. Mr. Eisler wants us to come over to his place Thursday, high noon."

"What's the occasion?"

"Thanksgiving."

Thanksgiving? Cory thought. He briefly thought back to the shopping mall and the crowds. He couldn't even remember the last time he had eaten a formal Thanksgiving meal.

"Are you going?" he asked Pock.

"Naw," Pock said. "I told him I couldn't make it because I already had other plans. I hate to hurt the old man's feelings, Damon. But, shit, Eisler's so fucking smart that every time I'm around him I feel like an asshole because most of the time I don't know what the hell he's talking about."

Pock reached over and turned the volume further down on the television.

"I mean, look at it from where I am," he continued. "If you go, then you and him will be sitting around bullshitting old wars and weird philosophy crap that I don't even want to think about. I'm not an officer and I'm not a diplomat. I still wear stripes on my sleeves, Damon. I always will."

Cory said nothing. Thanksgiving. As a practical matter, the only one he could really remember was during his plebe year at West Point. On that cold November morning, as snow dusted the statue of Patton and the sarcophagus of Winfield Scott, the entire corps of cadets had donned their dress grays and marched across the Plain. Although not unique in itself, for Cory the event held special significance. That evening he had come to grips with the realization that he was truly alone in the world. Simply another tarbucket hat in a brace of hundreds. *The Corps, and the Corps, and the Corps.* Such was his family of man.

"I guess I'll go," he whispered. "Where does the old man live now?"

"Over on Virginia Avenue," Pock told him. "The Watergate. He's got a neat little place over there. Just like him too. Small and organized."

"Do I need to bring anything?" Cory wondered.

"He didn't tell me anything," Pock said.

"Okay," Cory said. "Give him a call and tell him I'll be there."

"Can do," Pock said, returning to the kitchen to fix himself another drink. "You need anything else?" he called out.

"Not right now," Cory said. He finished the bowl of jambalaya, placed it on the table and leaned back on the sofa, closing his eyes, clearing his mind.

"You want to sleep here tonight." Pock asked, returning to his seat. "You can have the sofa bed. I can make a pallet here on the floor."

"Can't," Cory said. "I'm working tonight."

"How's it going so far?"

Cory flipped a palm back and forth. "One down and four to go. Heard anything yet?"

"Nothing," Pock said. "I guess the police are sitting on it. Want a little company tonight? I could use the action."

"Not yet," Cory smiled. "I do need one thing though. I'm thinking I may not want to use the Steyr all the way around. I'm still not sure of the application, but I want to be able to have an option with explosives."

"Pick your poison," Pock said. "Detcord, C-4, Semtex."

Cory opened his eyes and looked at Pock.

"Something simple," Cory said. "I'm not a specialist with that shit. It has to be prepackaged, probably trip or pressure release. I'm thinking some kind of small antipersonnel mine. Any old Soviet stuff around?"

"Tons," Pock grinned. "You looking along the lines of the PMN-PMD series?"

"You tell me," Cory shrugged. "I want it small and directional. I don't need any flechettes flying all over hell and back. Somebody could catch one by accident. No sanity in that."

Nodding, Pock took a sip of bourbon and considered the problem.

"You want a MON," he said, after a moment. "The MON-100 series. It's small, directional, and even officer proof."

Cory chuckled. "Can you get one?"

"Not by tonight," Pock said. "Probably tomorrow though."

"What about tracing problems?"

"What tracing problems?" Pock laughed. "With everything that has gone on everyplace, I don't think there's anyone who knows where anything is supposed to be. Why I'd bet my old maiden auntie in Morgan City could probably pick up a MON at the local Wal-Mart and not look back."

"Let's run with it then," Cory said.

"Whatever's right," Pock nodded.

"Oh, one more thing, Boudreaux?"

"What's that?"

"I do need a little nap before heading out tonight. Mind waking me up in two hours?"

"Can do," Pock smiled. "You need a blanket or a real pillow?"

"I'm fine," Cory said, as he crossed his arms across his chest and snuggled deeper into the sofa. But just as he dozed off, he was aware of Pock turning the television's volume to a barely audible level.

"You're right," an announcer was saying. "The correct response is Virginia ham. You know what that means don't you?"

A shrill squeal of delight was the response.

"That's right," the announcer continued. "You get to try for the Honda."

Another squeal. Applause. Computerized music and beeping tones.

Fucking morons, Cory thought. Then he wondered the point no more. Japanese cars and Virginia hams.

He found himself missing the jungle.

CHAPTER 19

En route Washington D.C., 7:40 P.M.

"Lucky we lifted off when we did." the helicopter pilot shouted. "Five more minutes and we'd be spending the night in that cemetery."

"What do you mean *we*?" Sal Franco yelled back.

"You mean you'd have left me out there to watch this thing by myself?"

"Can't leave government equipment sitting around unattended," Franco teased. "Someone might steal it. Guess who'd be responsible?"

The pilot laughed.

"Whoever checked it out?"

"That's right," Franco smiled. "I don't remember signing my name on anything."

"I heard special agents didn't know how to write their names."

It was Franco's turn to laugh.

"I can scribble my X with the best of them," he said. "That's the first thing they teach you in the academy."

Chuckling, the pilot eased forward on the cyclic control. Franco glanced out his window. They broke through the clouds at 400 feet. The snow had reached Washington and, while not heavy, only the most familiar landmarks, the Capitol dome and the Washington and Jefferson monuments, were readily discernable.

"Glad I'm not down there," the pilot said.

Franco looked beneath them. Traffic was snarled and the 14th Street bridge was a parking lot in both directions. He recalled the Florida Air jet slamming into the bridge.

"The traffic reminds me of last January when the jet went in," he said.

"Pretty close," the pilot nodded. "A friend of mine flew the Park Service chopper. That was a hell of a mess, wasn't it?"

"Yeh," Franco said. "Really brought out the freaks, too. You know the company got all kinds of calls asking the price for a one-way ticket from National to the bridge."

"There're some sick fuckers out there, aren't there, Agent Franco?"

"And getting sicker every day. This place draws them like gypsies to a fraud."

125

"I guess that's what keeps us in work."

"I'm not complaining," Franco said.

"Neither am I," the pilot smiled. "Hang on. We're heading for the barn."

Shoving the cyclic forward and to the left, the pilot banked the helicopter into a slow left turn taking them directly above the Botanic Gardens, then the Federal Trade Commission building. Descending, he passed low over the Federal Triangle, banked right over Pennsylvania Avenue, turned into the wind and flared to a landing atop the FBI Headquarters building. He kept the turbines powered up.

"Watch your head, Agent Franco. I'm gone as soon as you're out."

Franco understood.

"Don't want to spend the night here?"

"Uh-uh." The pilot shook his head. "Both me and this baby are going to be hangared tonight."

Franco popped open his door.

"Well, it's been real inspiring," he said. "Let's do it again sometime."

"What do you say we wait until the weather's better?"

"Maybe we can," Franco said, climbing out. "Thanks for the ride."

Already torquing up the turbines, the pilot responded with a theatrical salute. Franco returned it, secured the door, and stood back as the helicopter shuddered, lifted up, then launched into the night amid a furious cloud of rotor-whipped snow.

Pilots, Franco thought. Unique breed. They always enjoyed the bitching nearly as much as the flying. Only a weathered-in pilot could have nothing to do all day, do nothing, then that night gripe about the nothing being only half done.

"Don't let the bedbugs bite," Franco smiled, as the thwack of the rotors faded. Then he turned and quickly walked to the roof access door.

First stop? Weall's office.

About the shooting, Weall would have a number of questions.

About Umberto Rico, Franco would have only one.

Where was the money?

Forgive your enemies, but not their names.

It was half-past time for an answer.

***

As expected, Jonathon Weall was sitting in his office. Franco found him with his tie loosened, his sleeves rolled up and hunched over his desk. He was eating snack bar fare, a microwaved sandwich of nebulous origin.

"So how was Manassas?" he asked, as Franco walked in and flopped into the chair across from the desk.

"A lot like Donner Pass," Franco shrugged. "Cold, isolated, a corpse frozen in the snow, and not a Wendy's in sight."

"Hungry?"

"Yeh," Franco nodded. "It wasn't that much like Donner Pass."

Weall chuckled wryly and held out half a sandwich.

"Take some of this."

Franco eyed it skeptically.

"What do we think it is?"

"Dutch Lunch," Weall said warily. "I think with that kind of turkey that tastes like ham, or maybe its the ham that tastes like turkey. I never can tell the difference. The bread's fresh though."

"I'll chance it," Franco said, reaching over and taking the half.

Weall watched as Franco took a bite and began to chew.

"So what do we have?" he asked, after a moment.

"Not as much as you want us to have," Franco answered, as he collected his thoughts. "One shot, upper chest, no exit wound. Ballistics are pending until after the autopsy."

"What type of weapon?"

"Some kind of rifle," Franco said, taking another bite of the sandwich. "We isolated the shooting point. A rise northwest of the cemetery. It was a long haul, Jonathon. Damn near 700 yards."

"Seven hundred yards? That's nearly half a mile."

"Sure is," Franco agreed. "It appears someone sure knows their capabilities."

"Any witnesses?"

Franco shook his head and popped the last of the sandwich into his mouth, chewed and swallowed.

"The cemetery is in a rural location off two back roads. On a good day it probably wouldn't see more than one or two cars in the area around the time of the shooting."

"What about crime scene forensics?" Weall asked.

"We might get lucky there," Franco said. "Cox's people gave everything a pretty thorough going-over. We retrieved some shoe and tire impressions. He's running them against the reference file samples and should be back to me sometime tomorrow."

"Anything else?"

Franco smiled slightly.

"Yeh," he said. "Two things. The impressions indicate there was only one person moving around the shooting point. It snowed a little the night before last and just one set of prints were visible today."

Weall nodded slowly.

"What's the second thing?"

"The shooter took a leak. It stained the snow yellow."

"Could have been an animal," Weall suggested. "Was there enough for a fluid analysis?"

"No. But I'm sure it was the shooter's urine. We found a hair frozen in it. Of course, Cox told me he couldn't analyze it until later, as usual, but I persuaded him to examine it while the others were out casting the footprint impressions. Guess what?"

Weall leaned forward and placed his elbows on the desk.

"Not an animal?" he guessed.

"Not at all," Franco said. "It was a human pubic hair. Guess what else; it didn't shed from any Latino groin either. Cox put it under a microscope. Preliminarily, he isolated it to be anglo, from a caucasian with dark brown, Cox called it 'chestnut' colored, hair."

"Too bad we can't fix gender from hair."

"We don't need that, Jonathon. The shooter was male. The footprints were relative large. Cox will give me the exact size tomorrow with the his other findings, but just looking at them, they appeared to be at least as large as mine."

"Still," Weall said. "That might not prove anything one way or the other. A lot of woman have big feet."

At the comment, Weall noticed a broad grin spreading from beneath Franco's drooping moustache.

"What?" he asked.

"Oh, I was just remembering the urine stain," Franco explained. "No, the shooter was definitely a male. The closest footprints were about two feet away. If it were a woman, there would have been foot impressions on either side of the stain, right?"

"A reasonable assumption," Weall agreed. "Why is that so amusing?"

"I don't know. I just had a mental picture of some big-footed woman trying to piss in a puddle two feet in front of her. The thought just struck me as funny. Sorry, Jonathon. Must be your Dutch Lunch coming back on me."

Weall smiled politely.

"Must be," he said. "Anything else besides waiting for lab analyses."

Franco shook his head.

"Not as far as the actual crime scene offered. What about here? Anybody get a shot at the Defense tape yet?"

"They just finished up about an hour ago," Weall told him. "The forensic linguists seem to support the pubic hair theory if, in fact, the shooter and the caller were the same person."

"Caucasian?"

Weall nodded.

"White male, probably between 40 and 50 years of age." He glanced at a paper on his desk. "Sounds college educated and, based upon the pronunciation of the English words, the linguists suspect he is either a foreign-born, naturalized American; or an American who has been living in a Spanish-speaking country for an extended length of time. Speech patterns support . . . ."

"Wait a minute, Jonathon," Franco interrupted. "I don't understand that. You mean they can't tell the difference between American or foreign-born?"

Weall glanced up.

"Not based solely on the linguistic evidence, I guess. Evidently, other than being American English in nature, his pronunciation has no particular regional link to it. The lab described it as 'generic.'"

"How does one go about doing that?" Franco asked. "Everybody comes from somewhere."

"I asked the same question," Weall answered. "They came up with three possibilities. First, he could actually be a foreigner who learned English from the tapes supplied by our embassies. They're purposely designed to have no regional accents and they're also passed out like popcorn. Free to anyone who asks."

Franco said nothing as Weall continued.

"The second possibility is more plausible, I think. The linguists believe the caller may be an American-born child who grew up with an American expatriate mother and father someplace. The family probably would have spoken the local dialect outside the home, but English within the home. After a few years the English would lose its, as they put it, *geographical bias*."

"That's reasonable," Franco said. "Most countries that have a large American population have English-speaking schools. What's the third possibility?"

Weall glanced back to his desk.

"That the caller is an American who has been living overseas for an extended period of time. So long that he now considers English a second language and speaks it only with indigenous people who want to practice their own English."

"That they presumably learned from our embassy tapes," Franco surmised. "That sounds even more remote than the first two."

"I agree," Weall nodded. "Which, of course, brings us back to possibility number one."

"Or possibility number four," Franco said. "That Linguistics really doesn't know."

"That, too," Weall agreed. "There really wasn't much to go on."

Franco leaned back in the chair and stroked his moustache.

"What about the Spanish words in the transcript? I suppose they think he learned those from Cuban Embassy tapes?"

"They didn't say," Weall smiled. "But they did notice a marked pronunciation pattern. Curiously enough, though, it was not considered Peruvian in nature. The fact of the matter is that it was not really anything in nature. The lab felt it a more Castilian form of diction. Upper class. The type of Spanish spoken at the ministerial level throughout Latin America."

"That's a big help," Franco said sourly. "Latin America? That could be anywhere from Brownsville, Texas, to Tierra del Fuego."

"You didn't let me finish," Weall told him. "One word on the tape did have a particular geographical bias."

"Which one?"

"*Par-ti-DO*. The computers broke down the syllables and determined his enunciation to be identical to a verified regional syntax."

"Where?"

"Guatemala," Weall said softly. "In the region around Guatemala City, the word is accented with the emphasis on the *do* instead of the *ti* like it is elsewhere."

"*Par-ti-DO*." Franco repeated the word as the caller had said it. "Sounds strange that way. It's like pronouncing party, par-TY."

"I know. Supposedly, Guatemala is allegedly the only place in the Spanish-speaking world where it's pronounced that way. Could be an important distinction."

"Maybe," Franco nodded. "What about the psycholinguists? They get any handle on threat validity?"

"Nothing you could grab. Only that the caller's voice displayed no emotional interaction with the words. Voice inflections indicated more of a reading rhythm, as opposed to anything spontaneous."

Franco unwrapped a piece of gum and put it in his mouth.

"That could be good," he sighed. "Or it could just as easily be bad."

"What do you mean?"

"It tells us two things, Jonathon. If the caller was reading his demands, chances are he was just following instructions. If he was speaking off the cuff, then it means he probably really doesn't mind the killing."

Franco flicked the gum wrapper into a metal trash can.

"You realize," he said. "Since the hair was Caucasian and the caller's voice is most likely American, it appears we've got either one or two anglos doing Shining Path's dirty work."

"Could be more than that," Weall added. "What kind of anglos do you think Shining Path would offer this type of subcontract to?"

Franco chewed the gum slowly and considered his answer.

"Personally," he said, after a moment. "Although it's a fine line, I'm not sure Shining Path subcontracted the work to anyone."

"Because the caller and shooter aren't Latino?"

"Well, that, too," Franco admitted. "But I was more thinking about what they've done in the past. Do you remember me telling you they were a rural-based group?"

Weall nodded.

"Well, I was speaking in the strictest sense of the word. For the most part, even in Peru, they've avoided Lima like a bad habit. It doesn't stand to reason they'd just pop up here out of the clear blue. In a faction like Shining Path, they usually begin with something small, move to something larger, then to something larger still. Now if we're to believe this alleged claim of responsibility, we would have to accept the fact they've jumped from ambushing Peruvian Army patrols in the jungle, to assassinating a government scientist in the capital of the United States of America. It's not right.

"They're Marxist-Leninist, Jonathon, not impulsive Islamics. And because they're Marxist-Leninist, they're indoctrinated to believe that nothing can be changed overnight. Ideologically, they're committed to the philosophy of small bites making a meal. And I think they would consider killing people here much like having breakfast, lunch and dinner at one sitting."

"So who did the subcontracting?" Weall asked.

"Who knows?" Franco shrugged. "Until we get the rest of the forensics evidence, we could sit here and speculate for weeks. As it stands now, we've got probably two anglos, one of whom spent some time in Guatemala, shooting a man here, and threatening to kill more, in the expectation of our government suspending narcotics eradication efforts in Peru. The most obvious question is who benefits if we pull out?"

"The narcotics traffickers," Weall said. It was not a question.

"Logically, yes," Franco nodded. "But why Gustav Celt and not someone else?"

Jonathon Weall realized he had no clue why. He felt somewhat annoyed with himself. Too many hours on the embassy cocktail beat and not enough time working genuine crime.

"Because he was there?"

Franco smiled slightly and ignored the impulse to chide Weall by making the applicable Mount Everest reference. He decided to make Weall's answer correct.

"Exactly," he said. "Gustav Celt was a target of opportunity. He was a employee of the Department of Defense and in a location where he could be reached, a soft target. But back to the original question. Why Celt? Defense has over a million and a half other employees. And why Defense, in general, and not our army, which is specifically carrying out the bulk of the eradication efforts? It doesn't add up. There has to be some reason Gustav Celt came to the attention of whoever wanted to make whatever point."

Weall said nothing as Franco continued.

"I want to take a good hard look at Celt," Franco told him. "Did you get his personnel file from Defense?"

"With the tape." Reaching to his desk, Weall picked up a three-inch-thick manila folder and handed it across to Franco. "He's been around a long time."

Franco flipped through the file. He predicted at least two hours of reading.

"I'm going to take this home tonight."

Weall watched as Franco stood.

"Where do we go from here, Sal?" he asked.

"We wait until tomorrow," Franco shrugged. "Cox will be back to me with the forensic findings, and I'll have had a chance to review Celt's file. After I get an idea of everything we know so far, I'll start compiling a psychological matrix on the shooter and see if we can narrow him down based on the evidence. What about you? Any financial information on Rico yet?"

Weall shook his head.

"Not as of five o'clock this afternoon. I'll check with Miss Quill the first thing in the morning."

"Don't back-burner it, Jonathon," Franco said softly. "I want his ass."

"Easy, Sal. It hasn't even been thirty-six hours yet."

To Franco it felt a lot longer.

"Give Miss Quill my regards," he said, walking to the door.

"Sal?"

Franco looked back.

"What?"

"Don't let this Rico thing get out of hand. I don't want it affecting your judgment in any way, shape, or form. Understand?"

Affecting judgment? Franco thought. In Miami, they called judgment *justicia*—making things right.

Then again, Weall had not meant it as an admonishment. It had been said as a friend.

Franco offered a measured smile.

"Sometimes judgment is a fine line too, Jonathon."

There was silence in the office and, for a terminal second, they simply stared into each other's eyes, each taking account of the other's preoccupation.

Weall decided to leave it alone.

"Give my best to Karen," he said.

Franco nodded.

"I'll be at home if you need me, Jonathon." Then he left the office without further comment.

Jonathon hadn't touched the mutilated breasts, Franco thought. Jonathon hadn't been forced to braid the lies.

But perhaps it was better that way, Franco decided.

Justicia.

He needed it all for himself anyway.

CHAPTER 20

Falls Church, Virginia, 9:15 P.M.

Sal Franco parked his Corvette in its slot, climbed out, and walked to the beveled glass door of 4 Bradford Lane. Unlocking it, he stepped into the lighted foyer, double-locked the door behind him and slid the brass security chain into place.

"Is that you, Ward?" his wife called, from the rear of the house.

Franco chuckled. Karen was obviously in a good mood. The *Leave It To Beaver* reference was a distinct indication.

"Yes, June," he called back. "Where are you?"

"The kitchen."

Kitchen? Franco thought. God, he hoped she hadn't decided to cook again. Regardless of the recipe, of late everything seemed to end up tasting like poppy seeds or oregano.

But his fears proved themselves unfounded for, as he entered the large country kitchen, he found her sitting on a barstool at the sink. She was dressed in jeans and a paint-spattered denim workshirt. A towel was wrapped around her head, and she was reading a copy of *Southern Living* magazine.

Franco discreetly glanced around. Not a meal in sight. He felt his stomach relax as he kissed her on the cheek.

"So, how are the boys?" he asked.

Karen smiled openly.

"Wally's fine," she told him. "The governor called and gave him a stay of execution."

Franco nodded gravely.

"And the Beave?"

"He called this afternoon," Karen said, matching Franco's seriousness. "Yoko Ono wants to have his baby."

"She's a good woman," Franco said solemnly. "What did you tell him?"

"To clean up his room first."

Franco laughed out loud. Karen smiled.

"Have you eaten yet?" she asked after a moment.

"Not enough. How about you?"

"Earlier. You want me to fix you a sandwich?"

Franco shook his head.

"I'll microwave something," he said.

Franco walked to the refrigerator and opened the freezer door. Inside, was a low-calorie tundra: Weight Watchers this, Lean Cuisine that. Throwing caution to the wind, he selected a small box of cheese cannelloni Lite Choice and closed the freezer door.

"Why the towel?" he asked, as he opened the box and moved to the microwave.

"I frosted my hair," Karen told him. "Remember, you said you used to like it that way?"

Franco didn't remember, but said he did as he placed the cellophane packet into the oven and set the timer for three minutes. Hearing water running, he glanced back over his shoulder. Karen was now shampooing her head at the sink. Exactly why people frosted their hair, he was never sure and had no time to speculate on the reasons. A soft beeping tone indicated that the meal was ready.

He grabbed a plate and extracted the packet from the microwave. Burning his fingers in the process, he tore open the cellophane and poured out the contents.

It looked like an uncooked egg roll. A dismal little doughy thing sliding around in a watery red sauce.

"So what do you think?" Karen asked, as she turned off the water.

"I think I'm not hungry anymore."

"Not that," she corrected him. "My hair."

Franco looked up. Her head was still wet, the hair itself curling frizzily. He could detect no difference whatsoever in its color.

"Looks good," he smiled. "I'll bet when it's dry, you'll really be able to see the frosting."

Karen grinned and eyed his plate.

"What'cha eating?"

"Cheese cannelloni."

"Mmmm. Can I have a bite?"

Franco looked down at the slider, then back to his wife. He handed her the plate.

"Go ahead and finish it off," he told her. "I don't think I feel like Italian tonight, anyway. Besides, as good as you look with that new hair color, you're going to need to store up energy to keep the carnivores away."

"But what about you?"

Franco leaned over and kissed her on the forehead.

"I've got a hour or two of reading to do. You coming to bed?"

She shook her head.

"Not just yet. I'm sketching tonight. Unless, of course, you have something else for me to do?"

Franco chuckled at the innuendo.

"Why, June," he said. "What would the Beave say?"

"Beave's got Yoko," she winked. "What does he know?"

"Not much, I guess," Franco said, turning away. "If I'm asleep, wake me when you come up."

"Is Ward sure about that?" she called after him.

"Yes, June," he shot back. "Ward is sure."

As he left the kitchen, Franco could hear Karen digging through the silverware drawer. Enjoy the slider, he thought fondly. Regardless of her weight wars, blonde or white, he would not trade a hair on Karen's hungry head.

***

Upstairs, the master bedroom suite of 4 Bradford Lane was a substantial yet serene effort. Originally created from three smaller rooms, it had been remodeled to meet a previous owner's needs and included two separate dressing areas, a double-mirrored bathroom and a raised sleeping platform now dominated by a hand-carved, ivory-painted bed canopied in quadrille cotton. At one end of the suite, a huge nineteenth-century armoire stood silently, while at the opposite end an elaborately detailed gas fireplace hissed amid softly dancing flames.

With muted off-whites and fine-lined gilded highlighting, it was a pale room, Franco had once mentioned. Peaceful, even ethereal in mood, its presence was only further enhanced by the bleached hardwood floors, embroidered lace draperies and the brace of various antique occasional pieces all upholstered in a milky Old World weavers' silk.

But Sal Franco was not thinking of Old World weavers or the hissing fire. Propped up in bed, he was reading intently. The time was 10:40 p.m., and the subject was Gustav Celt.

Franco was anything but happy. It was taking too long to learn too little. Thus far the personnel file was, in his most professional opinion, bullshit. It touched only highlights of Celt's federal service and told nothing of the man himself. Merit raises, awards, and performance evaluations, yes. But nothing to answer the question *Why Gustav Celt?*

Vitae? Nothing there. No children, no dependents; even the beneficiary for his life insurance was, in Franco's estimate, a most eccentric choice, The March of Dimes, with Celt's funds earmarked for polio research?

Evidently, Celt had not revisited this issue in a day or two, Franco surmised. But maybe that in itself was telling him something about the man. Celt saw no reason to change beneficiaries. He just didn't care. Seventy-five years old and no wonder he stayed on the job: the poor bastard had nothing else.

Franco sighed audibly and flipped to the next page: 3 February 1956, attached to the Little John missile development program. Another page: 17 April 1955, temporary duty at Redstone Arsenal, binary munitions development.

Franco yawned and closed his eyes. He had begun reading the file at the most recent addition and was now back to 1955. Over twenty-five years and zero. No reason to pick Celt. He was too low profile. Too removed. Not even remotely related to anything so far.

Franco yawned again and snuggled deeper into the pillow. Still, like a crone first wife, the original issues returned to haunt: Why did they select Gustav Celt? And how had they culled him from the vast defense herd?

The questions repeated, swirling into one another, then into disjointed thoughts: Aberdeen; Little John; no dependents; Redstone Arsenal. Whys? Hows? But nothing connected and before it could, sleep intervened.

From somewhere, a clock chimed eleven. In the studio Karen continued to sketch, while upstairs, in her bed, the remainder of the file went unread as the black dream's mindwings began to unfurl.

For Sal Franco, he took the journey as it came. Facing into its wind, he was guided onto the plane of helplessness.

Charlatan.

The smelltaste of shrimp returned, but sleep precluded spitting this time.

He took a breath, then another, and forced himself to swallow.

Charlatan.

Even the word rang more wicked than before.

CHAPTER 21

Takoma Park, Maryland, 11:50 P.M.

Cory shifted in the Camaro's seat. The engine was off, the interior was cold, and flakes of snow melted against the glass at his left shoulder. Disregarding the weather, Cory continued to stare through the windshield toward 119 Sheridan Acres Drive. He had been watching the residence for forty minutes. He had yet to observe any human activity. The residence remained dark save the flickering of a television set behind a solitary window.

"He waits for our coming," Lucius Aemilius whispered. "For the consequence to his actions."

Cory said nothing.

"I feel him, Damon," Lucius added. "Can you feel him with me?"

Cory could, but again declined comment. It was not time for Lucius yet, he told himself. Not until the moment. He rubbed his eyes, then surveyed his surroundings once more.

Sheridan Acres. The name was derived from the property available to each home. All were one-acre lots with the various structures set back from the street. William Pointer's property was identical to the others, a 50-by-100-yard tract. Each acre was offset from the lot across the street and each was surrounded by a tall hedgerow presumably grown to ensure the owner's privacy.

But the hedgerow, as well as the fact that the residence was across the street and some 100 yards away, was not Cory's current problem. The main difficulty, he decided, lay in the actual design of home itself.

William Pointer had elected to live in one of the old, silver Airstream trailers. Due to its smaller size, perhaps fifty feet in length, it had been placed at the extreme rear of the property line and was elevated on a deck-like affair that then raised the windows to a height of at least seven feet above the ground. To make matters worse, the top of the windows were concealed behind awnings of brightly striped cloth that endowed the Airstream with a somewhat carnival flair but, at the same time, made Cory's tactical decisions all the more vital. So, as he waited and watched, he coerced his mind to continue rejecting Lucius Aemilius and to evaluate the variables once again:

1. Pointer could any moment, or never, appear in the window.
2. Due to window height, the shot would be a difficult upward angle.
3. Shooting through the glass would cause deflection of the round.
4. The snow could again start in earnest, with visibility dropping to zero.
5. A neighbor could become suspicious of the Camaro and alert authorities.

The prudent course of action? Forget the Steyr. Take Pointer with the Makarov.

The decision made, Cory reached up and snapped off the plastic cover of the interior dome light. Setting it on the seat, he then slid a finger next to the exposed fuse-like bulb and popped it out. He replaced the lens cover and placed the bulb in the ashtray. The vehicle was safe now. He could open the door without illumination.

Leaning forward, Cory reached around to the small of his back and extracted the Makarov, caressing the hard rubber grips as he recalled its specifications: weight: 1.46 lbs; length: 6.3 inches; cartridge: 9 millimeter; effective range: 50 yards. It was an admittedly unromantic but highly utilitarian weapon.

Originally manufactured outside Moscow, the Makarov was the most widely issued pistol in the Warsaw Pact countries, and this one, like the others, held a fully loaded, box magazine with eight rounds of ball ammunition. As it was, both the weapon and the ammunition were virtually untraceable due to the vast quantities in circulation.

For a brief instant, Cory thought to check and make sure the weapon had a round in its chamber. He decided against it. A waste of time. He had chambered one himself the day before. He knew it was there. To fire, all he had to do was flip the thumb safety down and pull the trigger. The limited range would not be an obstacle. Pointer would be less than six feet away.

Taking a deep breath, Cory slid the weapon into his long coat's right front pocket and opened the Camaro's door. Stepping out, he closed it gently behind him, ensuring that the door remained a bit ajar.

"Again the stalking, Damon," Lucius Aemilius whispered. "Will you concede your reluctance."

"No," Cory said softly. Then he began to maneuver toward the trailer.

Cory approached from the right, moving slowly, keeping himself in the shadows of the hedgerow. He paused at the halfway point and looked back to the Camaro. Its low profile was invisible against the backdrop of taller shrubbery. He glanced to the sky. It was murky with low, scudding clouds, and he had the impression of snowflakes misting his face.

He turned toward the Airstream and quickly covered the remaining fifty yards to its right rear corner. From the back side, he could see the television flickering through a rear window.

He arrived at a conclusion. The television room ran the entire width of the trailer. Two options then. Front or back. Double them. Four options:

window, window, door, door. Which entrance to select? Which one was preferable, safer? To know, he would be forced to look inside. Holding his breath, he eased toward the rear television window, stepped up on the decking and, more from the side than the sill, peered into the trailer's interior.

Through the window Cory saw Pointer immediately. It was a peculiar scene, one that reminded Cory of the young girl watching the blank screen in the movie *Poltergeist*. Sitting in a chair, Pointer was in shadow, his back to Cory, his profile defined by an extremely large television, a rear projection model with a sixty-inch screen.

But something was different. It was the head, Cory realized. In the photo Pointer was wearing a hairpiece. Here, the toupee was absent and the skull had conspicuously evolved into a smooth, pointed thing.

Could it be someone else? Cory wondered. No. The distinctive ears were present: two repellent flaps of flesh, which looked as if they had been attached to the skull as an afterthought.

Cory measured the distance through the glass. Three feet. He tried the window. Locked. So would the others be, as would the doors.

More options. One, go around to the front, knock on the door and shoot as it was opened. Not good. Too many variables. Two, smash the glass with an elbow and shoot as Pointer looked around. Variables? None. Pointer would look toward the sound. People always looked to unexpected sounds. Option two it would be.

Turning at an angle to the trailer, Cory reached into his pocket and pulled out the Makarov. Raising it up, he flicked the thumb safety down and aligned his elbow to the window. Considering the temperature variance between the icy outdoors and the trailer's heated interior, the glass would be brittle. A sharp thrust would easily shatter the window.

"The tactic is flawed, Damon," Lucius interrupted.

Cory paused.

"What?" he whispered.

"Listen, Damon. Listen for the sound."

Cory lowered his arm and closed his eyes. He concentrated for a moment, but was aware of nothing but the low wind and muffled conversation from the television.

"To the right, Damon. To the right and behind this place."

Cory squatted on the deck and leaned his head toward the rear of the trailer. He heard the sound. A steady hissing that drifted on the wind. Yes, he thought. A better tactic. Silkier.

Engaging the safety, he slid the Makarov back into the pocket, eased off the decking, and moved toward the rear of the trailer. He squatted to the side of a large metal cylindrical tank. Butane or propane? It would make little difference. It would all be over before Pointer realized the malfunction.

Reaching down, Cory inspected the flexible two-inch copper tubing that attached the gas to the trailer's heating system. He found the faucet-like valve and rotated it. Full on to the right. He eased it counterclockwise and found it moved smoothly. Copper fittings. It made it all easier.

His mind ran through the considerations: two-inch pipe, fifty-foot trailer, the heating system located a bit closer to the rear than the middle. Distance? Fifteen feet, eighteen maximum. Thirty seconds would be enough. Half a minute with the gas supply curtailed would allow the heater's pilot light to burn itself out.

Thirty seconds. He thought back to Fort Bragg, to the exercise that taught young officers how to measure time without a watch. Sergeant Major Dunn's litany. All Special Forces officers had learned it by rote. Twenty-five, however illogical, phrases which, when recited with the proper cadence, would indicate the passage of two minutes.

But Cory did not need two minutes. He needed thirty seconds. His training took over. The phrase count would be ten.

Gripping the valve, he turned it full to the left and cut off the gas supply. He then began to repeat the phrases in his mind, careful to keep the cadence correct:

One hen;
Two ducks;
Three squawking geese;
Four limerick oysters;
Five corpulent porpoises;
Six pair of Don Alverzo's tweezers;
Seven thousand Persians in full battle array marching side-by-side;
Eight brass monkeys from the sacred, holy crypts of Egypt;
Nine apathetic, diabetic, sympathetic old men on roller skates with a marked procrastination toward envy and sloth;
Ten mangy, menacing, marauding denizens of the deep who quo at the quay of the qui all at the same time.

Finish ten-count, thirty seconds. Cory twisted the valve back to the right. The hissing began again. He left it on, sprinted to the hedgerow, and followed his original path back to the Camaro.

Climbing inside, he pulled the door shut, reached to the right front seat, and popped open the Steyr package. Taking out the weapon, he laid it in his lap and selected two roserounds from their packet.

Working the bolt on the Steyr, he inserted the first bullet and closed the breech. The second roseround went into his mouth, holding the cartridge between his teeth like a cigarette.

"Sufficient time has passed, Damon," Lucius whispered.

Yes, Cory thought. The moment was at hand.

Reaching down, he started the Camaro but left the gear in park. He pressed a button. The driver's window slid into the door. Cory raised the

Steyr and aimed it out the window, steadying his elbows against the rear and front roof posts. He adjusted the ART scope. Pointer was not visible; but the television was an adequate ranging point. Cory sighted through the Airstream's front window at a point just beneath the canopy awning. The television image sharpened. He could see a desk on the screen and hands upon the desk.

He fired immediately.

As Cory ejected the spent casing and chambered the second, the first roseround shattered the window glass, then itself into fragments. Cory now had an unobstructed trajectory to the actual television.

As the crack of the rifle dissipated, Cory slammed the bolt closed on the second round, again steadied himself and found the television through the scope. He depressed both triggers almost simultaneously and as the Steyr slammed against his shoulder, he threw it to the seat without ejecting the second round.

The Airstream exploded an instant later, as the television's shattered electrical components ignited the gas inside the trailer. As Cory expected, it was not a large explosion. A few windows broken and perhaps a fire later. But this was not an issue. William Pointer would be dead. His lungs would be destroyed as the gas flash-fired through the trailer's oxygen supply.

His work finished, Cory depressed the accelerator, pulled the gearshift into drive, and began to speed away. For an instant, he almost lost control when the tires slid on an unnoticed patch of street ice.

Jerking the steering wheel in the direction of the skid, he overcompensated and the Camaro slid back to the right. Again he turned into the skid but, just before he regained control, he saw the brief flash of an object at the edge of the street.

He let off the accelerator, but a second too late. The metal trashcan smashed into the Camaro's right front fender just behind the wheel well opening.

Cory cursed his inattention to detail. With all the moisture in the air, he should have anticipated the street's icing over as night lowered the temperature. It was an amateur's mistake.

But as he sped away into the night, his thoughts turned back to operational details. He would make the Pointer call before driving to Arlington and the home of the next target, Robert Rouse. Lucius asking the "reluctance" question had exposed the anguish nerve—the raw, preserve-one's-sanity nerve—and now, like metal scraping bone, it demanded compensation.

But with only two men down and three to go, the match was far from over.

For Eisler, for his own coherence, Cory would once more keep the nerve at bay.

CHAPTER 22

THE FIFTH DAY
Wednesday, November 26, 1982

Falls Church, Virginia, 4:54 A.M.

Karen spoke gently, "Sal?"

Franco scorned the intrusion. It seemed to repeat anyway.

"Sal?" She touched his shoulder.

No, the *dreamseed* cautioned. Ignore this woman, this *wife*. Require her to wait, to doubt. Savor your fantasy without the meddling.

Franco listened to the dreamseed and obeyed. He disregarded Karen and willed the vision to continue.

But it did so jerkily now. Fragments becoming vignettes. Vignettes, whole captions of whatever lurked between something past and that which should have never been. A dark beckoning from whence Alicia Carrera again emerged.

She was smooth now, her body flawless. Slow dancing as she lured him farther past the warm amber of the threshold.

"Sal? Wake up. Jonathon Weall is on the phone."

No, Franco thought. Not yet. Alicia first. Yes, this lovely Cuban. *His* lovely Cuban.

Alicia moved slower now. Shifting even poetically. Seductive turns and breasts upraised in undefiled perfection.

Franco leaned down and took a perfect nipple between small white teeth. *Gentle. Gentler.*

He began to nurse. Impressions of lactose as he tasted the *dreamseed*.

"Sal?"

He again forced the voice away. Karen an irritation. Alicia more trothing.

He moved to the second breast. Another taste and, from somewhere, he became aware of increased sensations . . . of cruelty.

FRANCO.

Franco groaned as Rico's voice loomed in his subconscious.

FRANCO.

Franco's groan became a moan as the lactose seemed to jell on his lips. Not as sweet, he thought. Not sour, nor distasteful just . . . *singular.*

FRANCO, Rico taunted. *You are a charlatan, FRANCO.*

Franco dared to pull back, the nipple distended, remaining affixed to his lips. Stretching itself. Transmuting itself into a cold putty-like thing.

A charlatan, FRANCO. CHARLATAN.

Franco pulled back further. Her flesh continued to distend.

A growth? Tumor?

Was he attached to it? Or was it attached to him. Unknown. An unfamiliar urgency pressing hard now.

Now, FRANCO. Do it, NOW.

Franco knew the *it.* Rico was demanding a decision. A judgment call.

Do it, FRANCO. You must. It is required.

Franco heeded the command. He bit down hard. The nipple was severed by his teeth.

Rico laughed out loud.

CANIB, he screamed. *FRANCO, you are CANIB.*

Franco awoke with a start. He was covered with sweat and momentarily disoriented. He found Karen leaning over him.

"What?" he asked.

She eyed him curiously.

"The telephone," she said, holding out the receiver. "Jonathon Weall."

Franco glanced to the bedside clock. 4:56 a.m. Nodding knowingly, he reached for the phone with trembling fingers and pressed it to his lips.

"Where?" he whispered.

"Takoma Park," Weall told him. "119 Sheridan Acres Drive. Another defense scientist."

"I'll be out of here in ten minutes."

"I'll meet you there," Weall said.

The phone went dead in Franco's ear.

"What's happening?" Karen asked, as he handed her the receiver and climbed out of bed.

Franco looked down at her and, for a questioning second, considered explaining. He just as quickly decided against it.

"It's Wally," he smiled. "He's escaped again."

Karen offered a smile she didn't feel and, as Franco walked quickly to his dressing room, she realized that something wasn't right.

It was the dream. A nightmare was normal. A nightmare with the sweating even understandable. But Sal had been whimpering. This was completely alien to his normal behavior. It had only happened once before—Puerto Rico, when his aunt was murdered by extremists and during their first attempt at reconciliation. Then, like tonight, Sal had suffered from the whimpering. The whimpering had lasted for two months. The course of the investigation.

Eight weeks. A time frame wherein he had drawn further and further into himself, while she had only watched and, instead of helping, had only criticized him for his inattention to her.

Well, she reminded herself, that was then and this was now.

Then, she had again run when he needed her. Then, she was still a selfish child.

Now it was different. Now she would stay.

Karen looked up as Franco stepped out of the dressing room. As usual, he was in boots, jeans, and his short leather jacket.

"I'll be here if you need to talk," she told him.

Franco winked at her. No response was necessary.

He left her sitting on the edge of the bed and ran down the stairs two at a time. With the second killing, the pattern would become evident.

Franco felt a surge of vitality, of control.

The delineations could now begin.

CHAPTER 23

Arlington, Virginia, 6:10 A.M.

A considerate man, Robert Rouse was careful not to disturb the nubile young college student who shared his queen size bed. Easing himself to a sitting position, he turned on the bedside reading lamp and angled it to illuminate only the document. As the chief of the Defense Advanced Research Projects Agency's life sciences section, he had to read the material, understand it, and be prepared to either recommend or decline additional DARPA funding of the proposal.

In his mid-seventies, Robert Rouse was a tall, still vigorous man with thinning gray, combed-back hair, quick blue eyes, and a rather large, bulbous nose. But to Rouse his appearance remained a lesser concern. He was a research scientist and an expert in synthetic molecular applications. Two talents that, as he read the document's title-synopsis page prompted the return of that pleasing, if intellectual, cognitive challenge:

BATRACHOTOXIN
The Active Principle of the Colombian Arrow Poison Frog
[Phyllobates Bicolor]
Organic and Biological Chemistry Branch, Chemistry Division
 U.S. Naval Research Laboratory, Washington, D.C. NRL Report 61503
SECRET/NOFORN
Synopsis: The venom obtained by NRL team K035 from the skin of the Colombian arrow poison frog, Phyllobates Bicolor, is the most active natural venom so far known. The recent expedition (June - October, 1981) to the Choco rain forest of Western Colombia netted 2400 frogs whose skin extracts yielded a total of 30 mg of the crystalline major active principle which was named batrachotoxin. The exact molecular weight of the batrachotoxin was determined by high-resolution mass spectrometry to be 399.2412, which corresponds to the empirical formula $C_{24}H_{33}NO_4$ [mol. wt. calculated 399.2409].

Rouse laid the twelve-page document on his lap and closed his eyes. Intriguing, he thought. *The most active natural venom known so far.*

More powerful than the cobra's. More lethal than the lion fish's. But simple. Much simpler than most synthetic venoms. Carbon-hydrogen-nobelium. He could see it as a powder, like sugar. A liquid, almost clear, like saccharin. Of course, saccharin. What was saccharin? Carbon, hydrogen, nobelium, and something else. His mind raced. Sulfur! What with various molecular numbers, eliminate the sulfur, realign their proportional relations, and one could actually manufacture this batrachotoxin even in the most rudimentary lab. It would be field-expedient.

Taste? It would be sweet. The applications, particularly in the more clandestine sense, could be devastating. Whole water supplies tainted for months, down to a drop in a cup of coffee, a sweet cup of coffee.

He thought about Washington, the capital's water supply. Would the sanitary treatments render the toxin benign? No. The nobelium would keep the chemical balances intact. Preserve the lethality. After all, nobelium was what kept saccharin together when mixed with tap water. What kept it . . . .

Unexpectedly, Rouse's thoughts were interrupted by the long tapered fingers now trailing along the inside of his left thigh. It was more irritating than erotic. He had had enough of this child the night before.

Reaching down, he gripped the probing fingers and squeezed hard.

"Not now," he said, his voice low. "It's almost seven. Don't you have a class this morning?"

"But I don't want to go to class," a sleepy voice murmured.

Rouse smiled tenderly as he reached down, tilted up the boy's face and stared into the pale blue eyes. It was a beautiful face. Strong cheekbones and a small nose amid a tousled head of thick blonde hair. He ran his index finger along the boy's jawline.

"But you must," he explained. "Both your grades and attendance must be beyond reproach if I'm to see you're awarded another scholarship next semester."

As Rouse watched, the young eyes flashed misgiving.

"Now, quickly, get going," Rouse said. " I will meet you here tonight at nine."

At this, the boy offered a perfect smile, kissed Rouse's palm and hopped out of bed. He dressed openly, but slowly, allowing the older man the pleasure of watching a young body struggling into tight, faded jeans and a black T-shirt.

For his part, Robert Rouse did in fact watch, but for purely personal reasons. It was not because Kurt was an exchange student from Germany's Bohemian Forest region; nor was it because Kurt had been sharing his bed for the past three months.

The reality of the matter was that, in this manchild, Robert Rouse saw himself as he had looked some fifty-odd years earlier. Of course the boy hadn't realized it; nevertheless Rouse did, and to him the physical resemblance, with the exception of the nose, was remarkable. Tall, blonde, with wide shoulders and a slim waist and hips, all set beautifully in a tightly muscled frame. Kurt, like Rouse thought himself as having been, was the perfect specimen of youthful health. To actually make love with the boy was an obscenely erotic discipline and, in his fantasies, Rouse felt he was afforded the privilege of sampling his own youthful flesh.

He had yet to regret any of it. To him, the distance between molecular application and prurient avocation was indeed less than one would imagine.

As Kurt finished dressing, Rouse reached up and caressed the younger man's buttocks.

"Now, go," he ordered. "You will end up making *me* want to stay here again."

Kurt stood and looped his thumbs into the jean's pockets. Rouse smiled. How he loved the arrogance of the boy. So proud. So unabashed. He pointed a finger toward the bedroom door.

"Out," he stated firmly. "Before I summon the authorities."

Kurt laughed out loud and turned toward the door.

"I'll see you tonight," he said, as he left the bedroom.

Rouse waited until he heard the front door close. Then, the apartment silent, he returned his attention to the document, opened it to the first page, and began to read the report in its entirety. A quarter of an hour later, he had just turned to page 8 when the apartment door bell chimed.

Who in . . .? Kurt. He must have forgotten something. No doubt he needed money for gas or to have lunch with his friends. He was always forgetting something. Smiling, Rouse climbed out of bed, pulled on his old blue terrycloth bathrobe, and walked to the door.

He opened it just as the bell rang a second time. Surprisingly, it was not Kurt. It was a tall, studious-looking man with round, wire-rimmed glasses. He was holding a winter hat in his hands and appeared rather unassuming.

"Yes," Rouse asked.

"Robert Rouse, please?" the man asked.

"I'm Robert Rouse."

The man reached into his pocket and pulled out a small black notepad. Flipping it open, he referred to some scribbled writing as he began asking questions.

"Mr. Rouse, are you the owner of a 1977 Volkswagen, Virginia license plates David, Boy, George, six-niner-three?"

Kurt's car, Rouse thought. The used vehicle he had purchased for him last month.

"Yes," he nodded.

The man flipped the notebook closed and returned it to its pocket.

"Why?" Rouse asked. "What about it? Is something wrong?"

The man nodded pensively.

"There has been an accident," he said slowly. "The young man driving the Volkswagen is your son?"

Rouse felt the bile rise in his throat. Accident? Kurt? No, not Kurt. His mind began to fill with dreadful images.

"Mr. Rouse?"

Rouse forced himself back to the present.

"Yes?"

"The boy," the man repeated. "He is your son?"

"My nephew," Rouse lied.

The man nodded thoughtfully.

"Yes, your nephew," he said. "Well, whatever, he had no identification. He is being transported to Saint Elizabeth's Hospital."

Hospital? Oh, my God. Kurt *was* injured. But Saint Elizabeth's? Why, it was no more than a cruel atrocity staffed by Third World sadists. Kurt must have better than that.

"What are the extent of . . . ."

The man smiled.

"It's not that serious, Mr. Rouse," he explained. "Just a few bruises. Unfortunately, the accident was your nephew's fault, and I'll need to see proof of the Volkswagen's public liability coverage for our report."

Rouse nodded blankly. Bruises. *Not that serious.* He sighed with relief.

"Of course, officer . . . uh . . ."

"Kellogg," the man answered with a curt nod.

Rouse regained his composure.

"Of course, Officer Kellogg. Please come inside. I'll give you whatever you may need."

Stepping out of the way, Rouse allowed Cory to enter, then closed the door behind him.

"The policy is in the back," he explained. "Just give me a moment."

Cory smiled politely.

"I'll just wait here," he said, as Rouse walked quickly down a hall and around a corner.

But Cory had no intention of waiting, nor did he hesitate for long. Easing to the corner, he listened and heard Rouse rummaging through bedroom furniture. He began to move quietly in the direction of the sound.

Finding the insurance policy, Robert Rouse stood back from the tall chest-of-drawers and flipped through the papers to make sure all were attached and in order.

Curiously, he suddenly observed the writing on the policy's cover melt from black ink on white paper to a spectacular blue on bright yellow.

A synapse later, the yellow became orange and the blue some shocking pastel color he had never before seen. This he wondered about briefly, too briefly, he decided, for it was soon gone. All pastels fading. Shadows instead. Shadows from some undefined edge now spreading exponentially, a cool flushing of browns into grays and grays into blacks as the fertile dissipation of memories—Kurt, the Volkswagen, the toxin—merged together, then vanished into nothing as his mind turned inward, inflected, then filtered into abject darkness.

A humane death, thought Cory.

Rouse had felt no pain. Cory had approached from the rear and the slim Phillips screwdriver had penetrated the skin at the depression just behind Rouse's right ear lobe. Following the auditory canal, the membrane, occicles, and cochela were already obliterated before Cory redirected the four-inch steel shank to the rear and down.

Four inches. *Textbook.* From the lobe of the ear, to the exact center of the medulla oblongata was precisely four inches. And as the starpoint slid home, Cory had paused, not long, just a moment, just long enough to ensure that this particular segment of the brain had been violated. It had. The medulla regulated breathing and heart rate. Rouse's responses were in order.

At the exact instant of the medulla's perforation, Rouse's heart had raced as his breathing became an irregular series of shallow pants.

Cory had concluded these to be acceptable reactions and the rest, on his part, became nothing more than a swift, skilled continuation of the process.

Holding Rouse by the back of the hair, Cory had slammed his left elbow between the older man's shoulder blades and pinioned Rouse against the chest-of-drawers. His right hand still holding the screwdriver, Cory then made a deft circular motion with the plastic handle while, inside Rouse's brain, the opposite end, the metal tip, responded in concert with four tight 360-degree revolutions within the medulla.

Similar to carving the core from an apple, Cory had cored the life from Robert Rouse. Recovery was inconceivable. Rouse's autonomic brain functions had ceased to exist.

Exitus acta probat, thought Cory. This death too was justified.

But if so, Cory wondered, why was he waiting? Why was he still embracing the man as opposed to letting him drop to the floor?

Sight, touch, and smell, the answers came in a stinging rush of sensations.

Was not Rouse's robe terrycloth?

Was not its color a familiar shade of blue?

Was not its scent that of yesterday's Old Spice cologne?

Yes, yes, and yes.

Cory squeezed his eyes shut and cursed the moment. Lucius was spawning memories.

Back to youth, California. Back to childhood and his grandfather. Pawpaw's old terrycloth robe. Pawpaw's Old Spice.

Cory thought to vomit.

The Pawpaw link. Not good. It was weakness. What if the mission had been Pawpaw? Could he have done it then? Effected the prosecution? Still justified the death?

Cory smelled spice with a cherry-blend base . . . Pawpaw's tobacco.

Too much conscience was bubbling up, too much anguish. None of it could be denied. None of it deferred. He must regain perspective.

Cory sipped air like a fine old wine. He felt his pulse rate double.

The gnawing demanded offset, *compensation*. Exorcism by the self-defined hedonistic imperative. It had been over a year since its last onset, the last time he had felt the need for recompense. But he felt more out of context now than he had in Guatemala, so this time would be more intense. It would not be as with the Korean girl; there were distinct differences, requirements really, between perfunctory rutting and the art of conscience cleansing. A certain distance to be maintained. A certain balance to be attained.

For the conscience, neither age nor appearance were issues. Yet restrictions dictated a woman who had endured her own measure of suffering. An affinity? Conceivably. Or perhaps it was more similar to his proclivity for rescuing wounded animals and nursing them back to health. In doing so, Cory knew, he also nursed himself.

Hedonistic imperative.

Eisler, Cory remembered, had once alluded to codependence, yet was too much a gentleman to actually utter the word. So, as neither secret nor sin, his limits and the means through which he maintained his emotional symmetry were, at least to Eisler, common knowledge.

Cory took a deep breath, swallowed, then slowly, a muscle at a time, began to release Rouse's body. Stepping back, he removed his forearm from between the shoulders and angled the screwdriver a bit more downward at the tip.

For a passing moment, Rouse remained motionless. Then, like syrup off a butter knife, he dripped smoothly from the tip and collapsed to the carpet.

Conscience, Cory thought. Such a disgusting precept. Lucius Aemilius had made madness from memory. Pawpaw from Rouse. A friend from an enemy.

Weakness? Damn the affront to his calling. Damn the . . . .

A sob choked off in Cory's throat.

Making wrongs right? His mind swirled.

He took a deep breath and stared down at Rouse's body while he mechanically reached into his breast pocket. He extracted a small plastic bag, deposited the screwdriver in it, and returned the bag to his pocket. Later, at the Memorial Bridge, it would be tossed into the Potomac River.

It was time to leave, he reminded himself. And dejected and upset, he turned and walked stiffly to the hall and the apartment's front door.

The night had taken its toll. Physically, he was exhausted. But this could be readily cured. A meal would quell the sour grumblings of his stomach and sleep, the granular burning in his eyes.

No, Cory told himself. The body would endure as it always had.

But the mind? The psyche?

This continued to give him pause.

Rouse, Pawpaw. Pawpaw, Rouse. The transposition of memory and mission with conscience in the middle was scalding, as if his emotions were being fed to themselves. He felt a sharp pain behind his right eye and pondered his acute need for compensation.

The woman must be intelligent. The more intelligent, the more productive the application. The more severe her interest, the more profound his cleansing. And after his symmetry was restored? As was the cycle, he would reluctantly walk away, telling her nothing and, by default, abandon her to her own interpretations of inadequacy. He, of course, would experience similar feelings, but since he lived the cycle, any protracted anguish was generally leveraged toward the woman.

As he reached the Camaro and climbed inside, Cory tasted a tear as it touched the corner of his mouth. He angrily wiped it away with the back of his hand.

No, he knew. He could kill no more this day. He would dispose of the screwdriver, return to the hotel, and spurn alcohol in favor of a large meal somewhere in the mall. Perhaps the brush with humanity, the lights, the shoppers, would help.

Then, after the meal, he would make the Rouse call to Defense, go to his bed and sleep.

Tomorrow, during the Thanksgiving meal, he would speak to Eisler. Ask to be released from the final two actions. Pock was here. Pock would do just as well. Eisler could understand.

Hopefully, he would.

CHAPTER 24

Takoma Park, Maryland, 6:40 A.M.

Waiting inside the mobile forensic van, Sal Franco had already sipped three cups of rancid coffee by the time dawn finally broke over what remained of William Pointer's all-but-melted Airstream trailer. Outside, Dunnigan Cox's crime scene team continued its search, while inside, both Franco and Jonathon Weall counted the passing minutes.

There was little conversation. Weall dozed in a corner chair, while Franco slumped at a small desk and slid his tongue along the bottom, bristly side of his moustache. There was a sore spot at the tip of his tongue. Franco had decided it the beginning of a cold sore and, even though the moustache hair hurt, he continued to touch it to the spot. The pain, he thought, was human in nature. Everyone toyed with their cold sores just to make sure the pain was still there.

"You're going to lick that thing off," Weall commented from his seat at the van's opposite side.

Franco glanced up.

"What thing?"

"The moustache," Weall said wearily.

Franco shrugged.

"I wouldn't worry about it," he said caustically. "As long as this is taking, I could probably grow a new one by the time Cox finishes his appointed rounds."

"Lighten up, Sal. He couldn't even begin until the fire trucks pulled out."

"I guess," Franco mumbled, not quite regretting his tone. "It just seems to me we spend an inordinate amount of time waiting for Cox to bless us with his wisdom. We need to get out of this defensive box we're in and move into a more offensive role."

"I agree," Weall nodded. "Want to tell me how you plan to do that without any of Cox's wisdom?"

Franco considered this for a moment. Simple answer? He couldn't. For all that had happened, the shooter remained an unknown quantity. Unless there was an informant, which Franco doubted there would be, quantification would come only through Cox and the forensic data. He looked back to Weall.

"I guess I'm not," he said. "Still, aren't you even feeling a little antsy?"

But before Weall could respond, the van's rear door flew open and a very cold Dunnigan Cox climbed inside. Franco thought him to look even more tired and disheveled than usual.

"So?" Franco asked him. "Anything?"

Cox wiped his red nose on a sleeve and sniffed.

"An internal explosion of undetermined origin."

"A bomb?" Franco asked.

Cox shook his head.

"I said an *internal* explosion, Agent Franco. In the vernacular, bombs are codified as *external* stimuli."

"That makes absolutely no sense," Franco said tersely. "You're telling me that this trailer just happened to blow up and our caller just happened to telephone and claim responsibility?"

Cox looked to Weall, then back to Franco.

"I'm not saying that at all, Agent Franco. I'm saying it was an internal ignition source and not due to the introduction of any external incendiary device. I would venture to say your caller did, somehow, precipitate the explosion. As to the specific methodology, well, we've really only just begun. I've ordered both a spiral and a zone search, as well as a sifting of all debris. Until then, the best I can offer is that the assassin employed some as yet to be determined means to effect the explosion."

Jonathon Weall felt as if he had missed something.

"Excuse me, Dunnigan," he said. "But what was there in the trailer that would cause such destruction?"

Franco already knew.

"The butane, I'm sure."

Cox nodded in agreement.

"Actually, it was propane. But, strangely enough, the outside storage tank remained intact, which would lead one to believe that one of the appliances served as the ignition point."

"How many appliances were gas operated?" Franco asked.

"Heater, stove, and water heater," Cox said quickly.

"Want to venture a guess?" Franco arched an eyebrow with the question.

"No, Agent Franco. I do not. After my team has completed their initial survey, I will be . . . ."

Franco held up a hand.

"Never mind, I know where this is going. What about yesterday, though? Any conclusions as to the cemetery yet?"

Cox's face brightened considerably.

"Any number of things," he said, as he reached into an upper cabinet and extracted a yellow legal pad. "My report's been dictated, but not transcribed. If you don't mind my speaking from my notes . . . ."

"Please," Weall told him.

Cox flipped through a number of sheets.

"Where would like me to begin?" The question was directed to Weall.

Franco spoke first.

"With the weapon."

Cox nodded, turned two more pages, found the spot and began to paraphrase the information.

"Ballistic analysis indicates the actual projectile to be a modified version of the Springfield Armory 168-grain bullet known as a Match King. It is a commercially available bullet and, unfortunately, due to numbers annually distributed, the particular batch number is virtually impossible to trace."

"Domestic or international distribution?" Franco asked.

"Both," Cox advised. "Domestic until 1974. International the following year to the NATO countries."

"It's a military round?"

"Originally," Cox answered. "A 7.62 millimeter, to be exact. But as I indicated, there were millions manufactured. One can only assume they've found their way into certain civilian circles. Wouldn't you agree?"

"Could be," Franco said. "What about the batch? Any rough estimates as to this particular bullet's manufacture date?"

"Of course," Cox nodded, as he glanced back to his notes. "Springfield Armory indicated this bullet came from their batch number MK78-001." Cox looked up at Franco. "January, 1978. From its initial development in early '72, the Match King was only cast every other year."

"So it's had a long time to travel around before it ended up in Mr. Celt chest."

"So it appears," Cox shrugged. "I'm sorry, gentlemen. But we simply cannot trace it after so long a time."

Franco realized he was tonguing his moustache again. He stopped.

"You mentioned the bullet was modified," he asked. "In what way?"

"It was cored," Cox explained, drawing an imaginary circle in the air. "In its factory form, the Match King is not a hollowpoint. The projectile that killed Gustav Celt was. Obviously, the modification was done after leaving the factory."

"Professionally?" Franco guessed.

"Not *un*professionally," Cox told him. "The fact of the matter is that all it takes is a small drill and a steady hand. As for the coring itself, it could have been done last month or last year. There is no way to even attempt to pinpoint a date."

Cox turned a page and continued.

"On the other hand, I can tell you the exact type of rifle."

"What?" Franco and Weall said the word almost simultaneously.

Cox felt a surge of pride. He enjoyed the brief moment of one-upmanship. "A *Steyr Scharfgeschütze Gewehr*," he smiled smugly. "An SSG for short."

"German?" Franco asked.

"Austrian," Cox corrected. "Definitely a military weapon. One specially designed for sniper operations. Very expensive and very well machined."

Franco sighed audibly. This was what he didn't want to hear. The shooter was a professional. He forced himself to ask the next logical, if unnecessary, question.

"Are you sure?"

"To the exclusion of all others," Cox said, making it a known variable. "The projectile was detailed for rifling and, singularly, we determined it to have been fired through a barrel, a chromium barrel, no less, of 26 inches in length and possessing a land-groove twist of one turn in 11 inches. We took these characteristics, isolated them within the 7.62 millimeter caliber grouping and conducted a computer interface against the known traits of the 13,000 weapons in our cross-reference collection. No, Agent Franco. There is no margin for error. The murder weapon was most definitely the Steyr."

"So how many of these Steyrs are out there?" Franco asked.

"Unfortunately," Cox sighed, "we really have no way of knowing. As a matter of policy, the Austrian government treats all weapons sales as proprietary information."

Franco didn't like the sound of this either.

"You mean they won't tell us?"

Cox made a helpless gesture with his hands.

"No," he said softly.

"That's bullshit," Franco said, his voice a threat against Cox. "Get goddamn Interpol in on it. Austria's supposed to be our goddamn friend, for Christ's sake."

Weall held up a hand. This was something he *did* know about, and it surely wasn't the fault of Dunnigan Cox.

"Hold it, Sal," he said, making it an order. "Doctor Cox has no control over it. It's an internal Austrian agreement. All Austrian weapons manufacturers are, for the most part, financial partners with the Austrian government and all weapons sales are covered under the Austrian Financial Secrecy Act."

"So then they're not our friends this week," Franco said sarcastically.

"Of course they are," Weall snapped. "At least in principle. However, when it comes to weapons sales, all records are sealed for diplomatic reasons."

"What diplomatic reasons?" Franco asked.

"Trade pacts," Weall explained. "Whereas Austria generally refuses to deal with patently outlaw countries, it does trade with fringe regimes like those in the Balkans and the sub-Saharan areas. The business includes the sale of weaponry. To keep politics out of it, Vienna has adopted a policy wherein it does not tell anyone where it sells it materials. Anyone includes the United States."

Franco thought for a moment.

"No way our legal attaché in Vienna can get the records?"

"None," Weall said. "And as for Interpol, you know as well as I do why they won't get involved."

Sure I know, Franco sullenly remembered. Interpol. The only thing they wasted more than money was time. He knew this to be a fact. While assigned in San Juan, he had once occasioned to visit its Secretariat Headquarters—the rue Armengaud concrete-and-glass coffer in the Parisian suburb of Saint-Cloud.

But what was supposed to be a conference on the FALN terrorist infrastructure turned out to be little more than some group encounter session conducted on the grassy knoll behind the headquarters building. There, overlooking the Seine, Franco along with twenty other "experts" were forced to sit cross-legged on the ground and say nothing while some retired French lawyer—from service at the Hague—offered two days of reasons why Interpol could not involve itself in any *political* crimes. Political, of course, being the Secretariat's synonym for terrorism.

Franco had decided this decision was based solely on greed. Interpol was publicly funded, and anything "controversial" could well end up alienating a member-nation and hence, cutting a few francs, riyals, or pesos, the ordained sustenance for this particular paper tiger.

"Sal?"

"I know, Jonathon," Franco said begrudgingly. "The responsibility claims make this all political in nature."

"Exactly," Weall nodded. "So attempting to trace the weapon is out."

Franco thought for a moment before responding. He wasn't really ready to give up on it yet and felt he was forgetting some angle but wasn't sure what, and the only thing on the tip of his tongue was the cold sore. Give it time, he told himself.

"We'll see," he told Weall, then he turned back to Cox. "What else?"

"That's about all on the weapon and ammunition."

"What about the casts of the footprints and tires?"

Cox flipped through two more pages and again spoke from his notes.

"The footprints were made by a boot. Size 11 and rubber with a crepe outersole vulcanized to the vamp and heel. The pattern is described as 'chain tread' and is manufactured by Gorthram Polifyns. Their home office is in Paramus, New Jersey."

"Can they be traced?"

Cox shook his head.

"We doubt it. Gorthram is a wholesaler. They manufacture only the rubber outersole and sell to the retail outlets like Sears and Oshmans, as well as most of the mail-order chains like Eddie Bauer and L. L. Bean. The retailers buy the outersoles, subcontract the attachment of the soles to whoever makes the boot uppers, and then sell the finished product through their normal retail distribution channels."

"But it was a size 11?" Franco asked.

"Yes," Cox said. "No question. Gorthram only manufactures whole sizes."

"Humph," Franco grunted, thinking aloud as he glanced down at his own boots. "I'm about six foot and I wear a size 10. So this guy is probably taller than me?"

"Conceivably," Cox nodded. "Somatotypical averages would probably place a size 11 somewhere between, say, 5'11" and 6'2"."

"What about weight?"

"How much do you weigh, Agent Franco?"

"About 170," Franco answered. "Why?"

Cox smiled slightly.

"We used your foot impressions as the constant for comparison against those of the unknown individual. His depressions in the same area were no more than perhaps one-tenth of a millimeter deeper."

"So he is heavier than me?"

Cox nodded.

"By about ten, maybe fifteen pounds. We estimated your weight to be closer to 185."

"You're probably right," Franco admitted. Finally, he felt as if he were getting somewhere. "I assume you put all this into your computer?"

"We did," Cox told him. "We set the boot size, weight estimates, and, of course, the length of stride between footprints. Programming these data against somatotype base averages, we developed what I feel should prove to be a fairly accurate portrait of the suspect: 6'2", 190 pounds. Add to this the data gleaned from the pubic hair you discovered and, as we've already discussed, he should be a Caucasian with dark brown hair."

Dunnigan Cox gave neither Franco nor Weall time to respond. He flipped to the next page and continued to hold their attention.

"Now," he said precisely, "about the suspect's vehicle. Two factors were isolated. First, the tires. These were determined to be Goodyear P215/65R15, steel-belted radials. Secondly, due to the relative positioning of the tires, we determined the vehicle to have a wheelbase of 101 inches."

Cox glanced up from his notes.

"Actually, the tires caused us a bit of consternation initially. You see the Goodyear 65R-15 is relatively standard, particularly in car enthusiast circles. However, when placed within the 101-inch wheelbase constraint, this problem resolved itself rather nicely. Fortunately, this particular tire, when mated with this particular wheelbase, indicates the vehicle as having been a General Motors product and one of only two possibilities: the Pontiac Firebird or the Chevrolet Camaro, both of which have a 101-inch wheelbase and carry the 65R15 as standard equipment."

Jonathon Weall was genuinely impressed.

"Nice work," he said.

Cox dismissed the compliment.

"I suppose," he shrugged. "In any event, we wanted to further isolate the vehicle's identification and ultimately we did. One of my technicians observed that between and to the rear of the rear wheel impressions, there were two additional depressions in the snow."

"Exhausts," Franco said impulsively.

Cox nodded appreciatively.

"That's what we determined them to be. Well, what with this in mind, we were then able to isolate two additional facts about the vehicle. First, exhaust positioning indicated it was a 1982 model. Secondly, and perhaps even more important, the fact the 65R15 tires were on a 1982 vehicle with dual exhausts, as opposed to a single tailpipe, further delineated the vehicle to be the more sporty version of either the Pontiac or Chevrolet. Both models offered the 65R15 Goodyear tires and dual exhausts on only one each of their respective models."

"Bottom line?" Franco asked.

Cox looked Franco directly in the eyes.

"Your suspect was driving either a Pontiac Firebird TransAm or a Chevrolet Z-28 Camaro.

"This year's model," Franco stated.

"Yes," Cox said softly. "This year's model."

Franco took a deep breath and let it out slowly.

"Anything else?"

Cox again shrugged his shoulders.

"Nothing here yet. As for the cemetery investigation, the usual. Find me the boots, the Steyr, or the tires and I'll prove them to have been at the scene."

Franco smiled knowingly.

"To the exclusion of all others, Dunnigan?" he teased.

Cox returned a tired grin.

"To the nth degree, Agent Franco."

"Thanks, Dunnigan," Franco said sincerely, then he turned to Weall. "You ready, Jonathon?"

"I suppose," Weall answered, as he glanced at his watch. "It's almost seven-thirty and Bechtel wants my smiling face at an eight o'clock meeting." He looked up at Franco. "You mind dropping me at the White House?"

Franco arched an eyebrow.

"The White House?"

"Next door, really," Weall said. "The Executive Office Building. The meeting is with Defense. I guess they wanted neutral ground. I wish you were going with me."

Franco understood. Discussing homicide, Weall would find himself out of his element. Franco envisioned a table of assistant deputy secretary-level bureaucrats sleuthing the crimes by quorum. He politely declined Weall's not-so-veiled offer.

"I'll drop you off," he said. "But what about your car?"

Weall looked over to Cox who took the hint.

"One of my technicians will drive it in, if you like."

"Fine," Weall said, turning back to Franco. "So, Sal. Are we going in that old Corvette of yours?"

"We sure are," Franco smiled.

"Is the heater working yet?"

"Like a fine Swiss watch."

"I doubt that," Weall chuckled. "But I'll chance it anyway. Let's get moving."

Allowing Dunnigan Cox to return to his data, Franco and Weall left the forensics van and began to walk the twenty yards to the waiting Corvette. As they reached the driver's side, Weall noticed Franco beginning to smile.

"What?" he asked.

"Dunnigan Cox," Franco explained.

"What about him?"

"He rather enjoys the soothsayer role, doesn't he?"

"Amazes the hell out of me," Weall admitted, as he walked around the Corvette's rear and climbed in the passenger door.

Franco flopped in the driver's seat and started the engine. A low guttural exhaust growl filled the car. He shifted into first, released the clutch, and began to pull away.

Weall stifled a wide yawn, leaning back in the seat and closing his eyes.

"How many more do you think there will be, Sal?"

Franco didn't answer. He glanced over at Weall, then back to the road. "Kind of funny though."

"What?" Weall asked.

"The Airstream trailer."

"What about it?"

As Weall half-listened, Franco began to explain. Something about his childhood and associating Airstream trailers with trapping migrating land crabs in the Florida keys.

But Jonathon Weall was not really concerned. In fact, the seemingly nonsensical rambling was quite expected. It was Franco's way of dealing with the stress, and the more he talked about nothing, the more he was thinking about the investigation.

His interest in *trailers*?

It could just as easily been roofing nails, and Franco, he knew from past experience, neither needed nor wanted any response.

Just as well, Weall decided. The heater was performing quite admirably, and the car was now warm and cozy.

Squirming deeper in the soft leather seat, Jonathon Weall crossed his arms across his chest and allowed the throaty exhaust modulations to lull him to sleep.

Glancing over, Franco realized that Weall was napping. He suffered no hurt feelings. Currently, his brain was focused on one specific item: the psychological profile he would begin once back in his office.

Looking back to the road, Franco depressed the accelerator and the Corvette surged forward heading into Washington and the White House.

The meeting with Defense? Franco was glad he wasn't to be a participant. They would solve nothing and, besides, he had something much more meaningful to complete, the *profile*.

He had an appointment with the shooter's mind.

***

Dunnigan Cox hated interruptions, and now, less than ten minutes after Franco's, in Cox's opinion, none-too-soon departure, the soft knocking on the forensics van's rear door indicated he was again being disturbed.

"Who is it?" he snapped.

"Tombs," a voice called back.

Tombs, Cox thought. The technician responsible for periphery examination. He must have found something.

Stepping over to the door, Cox released the lock and opened it to find two people standing outside: Tombs and a woman Cox had never before seen. They were an odd-looking pair. Tombs was a middle-aged black man with white hair, an open pleasant face and the posture of a comma. He was dressed in a fur-lined military parka.

"Yes, Tombs," Cox said, observing the woman out of the corner of his eye.

"This is Mrs. Kanter," Tombs explained. "She lives next door to the deceased."

Cox nodded politely. She was an ugly hag of a woman, probably in her late sixties. Her face was lined from a lifetime of frowning, and her nose and chin pointed, respectively, down and out. Dressed in an old plastic raincoat draped over a nightgown, she wore a threadbare brown beret on her head and large red galoshes on her feet. Cox thought briefly of disease. Even from a yard away the odor of Vick's Vapo-Rub was ripe. He looked back to Tombs for an explanation.

"And?"

AUTLEY HOUSE

"Mrs. Kanter's a witness," Tombs said flatly. "She was kind enough to direct me to two areas of interest."

Reaching to the side of the van, Tombs pulled a metal trashcan into view.

"This belongs to Mrs. Kanter," he said.

"Uh-huh," Cox muttered, hoping Tombs would soon elaborate.

Tombs didn't. Reaching into his pocket he pulled out a small evidence envelope and held it up for Cox's inspection.

"And this is ours," he smiled self-righteously.

Cox looked at the glassine envelope, then back at Mrs. Kanter. He could feel his own "public relations" smile creeping across his face.

"Coffee, Mrs. Kanter?"

"You have milk?" she asked. "I don't take no powder. I need real milk."

Cox froze the grin on his face and reached down and offered his hand.

"For you, Mrs. Kanter. I think we can find some milk. Please, come inside where we can be a little more comfortable while we talk."

Moving aside, Cox allowed the woman, followed by Tombs and the trashcan, to enter the mobile lab. He continued to smile as he secured the door behind them.

"Now, Mrs. Kanter," he said softly, "sugar with that coffee?"

"Three lumps."

Cox prepared the coffee, made sure Mrs. Kanter was given the softest chair, and then began the questioning.

Dunnigan Cox was thorough as usual.

The conversation would last the better part of an hour.

CHAPTER 25

Crystal City Underground Mall, 11:02 A.M.

For two hours, since the mall's nine o'clock opening, Cory had passed the time walking from shop to shop, talking with shopkeeper after shopkeeper. Some had been quite pleasant, others all but rude. Cory wondered why this was. Once, in a clothing store named Norman's, he had asked a shoe salesman the reason for his insolence. The salesman, a young Middle Eastern immigrant with crooked teeth and bad breath, had thought about it for a moment then shrugged an apathetic, "I am only part-time employee."

Cory had suggested Lysol for the breath and moved along. The irony made it comical. The mall seemed to run on part-time employees.

The final stop before brunch was a bookstore. Cory had always enjoyed bookstores and the Globe Book Shop offered a large and browsable selection. Avoiding the best-seller and how-to sections, he located the military history and political science aisles and it was here he spent nearly a half-hour studying the titles and reading the jackets.

He decided to purchase two trade paperbacks. One was a study detailing American relief efforts during the Truman administration, the other a somewhat lengthy treatise addressing the socialization of Mexico as predicted by some Princeton professor whose name was mostly composed of lower-end consonants.

The professor was touted to be an expert. Cory doubted if he even spoke Spanish. In his experience, few American "Latin experts" even bothered to learn the language.

That notwithstanding, at least he now had something to occupy his time while eating and, books in hand, he left the store to begin the search for a restaurant. The choice was more difficult than he anticipated. A concourse placard indicated that fifteen eateries were available. They ran the gamut. For the fat there was The Pastry Palace. For the thin a kiosk called Defile, which offered a forgettable selection of yogurt and rice cakes. In between there were any number of Mexican, French, Italian, Vietnamese, German, Greek, and, listed last, American restaurants.

Cory decided on the Florakis Grill and found it near the end of a plant-lined, patterned concrete lane. The choice proved quite satisfactory. Despite the newness of the mall, the grill looked old and reminded Cory of some Greek-run deli which, tended to feel the same whether in New York or Nairobi.

It was one of those old fashioned places. A counter in the front where mall regulars sipped thick coffees with sugarmilk, ate microwaved sweetrolls, and discussed western civilization as defined by Madison Avenue's media. In the rear there were tables. Rickety-pedestaled, Formica-topped, and cheap, these were serviced by young, mustachioed Greek men in their early twenties who, like illegal siblings, all shouted in identical broken-English phrases.

The counter was full, but the rear was reasonably vacant. Cory was in no rush, so he selected a vacant table in the smoking section underneath a large, cheap mural depicting Mediterranean fisherman, ordered from the menu, and began glancing through the photographs contained in the center of the Truman book.

By 11:18 a.m., Cory had finished his meal, a three-egg omelet with wheat toast, and decided it excellent. Now, as the waiter refilled his coffee, he leaned back in his chair and lit his pipe. He had just snapped the Zippo closed when he became aware of a heated exchange in Central American Spanish drifting from the table behind him. Resisting the urge to turn around, his curiosity engaged, he began to listen. It was obvious the argument had begun long before the speakers had been seated:

A woman's voice, fervent and intelligent: "Absurd. The Pope is unable to even understand the concept, much less its impact on belief. Consider the numbers. Latin America is where half the world's Catholics now live and where, by the end of this century, more than half the world's Catholics will live."

A man's voice, tired and pedantic: "Perhaps. But your *el Dios de los pobres*, this God of the poor, is heresy. No more than another means of effecting the consolidation of power through some structured symbiosis of the Nicaraguan revolution and Holy Mother Church."

The woman: "Not at all. Besides, it did not even begin in Managua. It began in Colombia, in 1968, with the conference of Latin bishops. The bishops were the first to realize that it all needed some measure of political mediation."

The man, sighing heavily: "Perhaps. But not to the point of this theological schism with Rome."

The woman, argumentatively: "I disagree."

The man: "There cannot be two churches, Monika."

The woman: "There already are two churches. At least in Managua where the poor have some say in the matter. The Sandinista loyalists required it."

The man: "The poor have no idea what their say is. They repeat only what they are allowed to repeat, and this liberation theology of yours is nothing more than another political exercise. Control of the population through the use of Marxism disguised in the cassock of a priest? It's rubbish."

The woman, sarcastic and low: "At least it is a cassock that serves the poor and does not ignore their needs."

The man: "A cassock that is Marxist is not Catholic, Monika. It is only a ruse, a sophisticated ploy to exploit religion as the means for control. As I said, it is heresy and I no longer have any inclination to continue the conversation."

The scrape of a chair.

The woman: "You are not eating?"

Cory listened. No male response. Shortly, out of the corner of his eye, he observed a handsome, middle-aged man storm angrily from the restaurant and disappear into the concourse beyond. He was slender, not a Latin American, and dressed in a dark charcoal-gray suit. A cleric's collar and bib ringed his neck.

Guess he's not hungry, Cory thought caustically. But the man gone, he could now no longer resist a furtive look at the woman. Making a point of relighting his pipe, he casually glanced over his left shoulder, his interest piqued.

He turned back to the front and took a sip of his coffee.

Monika, he remembered the man saying. Rather plain in appearance and wearing no makeup. Provincial, but so very Latin. Age? Cory suspected somewhere in that enigmatic 38 to 42 bracket. That time when hopes become memories, causes important, and loneliness a frame of reference.

She was small and dark. Dark eyes, dark, shortly tousled hair, dark Latin skin.

But the clothes? He couldn't remember.

He glanced again.

They seemed to match the body. Modest clothes, all black. A simple black sweater, black pants, nurse-type shoes, only in black.

Another glance. She caught him this time, but looked away first.

Her eyes were deep-set, yet sensitive and indeed intelligent. Latin middle-class breeding in the nose. Loose skin at the cheeks and under the chin. Compressed lips, a hint of weakness. A short neck, small ears, no jewelry, and thick unattended eyebrows.

She was not a vain woman, Cory decided. Just the Central American version of a Midwestern farmer's wife. One who expected no callers.

Opinion? Probably a teacher, perhaps some kind of social worker. Someone who cared and could be found feeding homeless children after natural disasters. A follower in greater situations, a leader in lesser.

But where was she in the Nicaraguan context? Surely aware, her argument with the priest indicated this. But the church and revolution? Why that? Moreover, why was she even interested?

Cory needed to know. He had already predicted her suitability. If his appraisal bore fruit, he could cleanse himself in *her* emotional backwaters. And if he did, could she handle the abandonment? Would she?

Cory puffed on his pipe and imagined her questions: *Why did he leave? What did I do?* He felt a measure of poignancy in his loins. Would this one elect suicide? Would he again be the catalyst for that most loathsome expression of despair? In the past one had actually committed suicide, and he had thought himself nudging the cusp of insanity. But the madness was not drawn from the realization that he had been responsible for her death; it was spawned from the irony of it all. He needed the women to escape the pressure of his calling. Yet when he learned of her death he found the cleansing to be even more exquisite, more primal, than when the woman did *not* die. Raw and dominant, it was an emotion he had never before experienced. So very good, but too, so excessively corrupt.

The riddle of catharsis, he told himself. The imperative in his hedonism.

Cory stood from his table and picked up his bill.

"Quite the revolutionary, aren't we?" he mentioned, as he passed her shoulder.

She looked up, a wide I-beg-your-pardon expression on her face.

Cory repeated the question in Spanish.

She answered, obviously to show him she could, in heavily accented English.

"We were too loud?"

"Not really." Cory stood motionless for a moment, then, not quite on impulse, sat down in the chair vacated by the priest. She seemed not to mind.

"I just like to eavesdrop," he added, continuing in Spanish.

The woman smiled at the admission. Cory noticed her teeth were small, stained, and suggestive of a slight overbite. Poor hygiene, but the smile softened her features. Cory decided her the type of person who rarely indulged in something as trivial as a smile.

"Your Spanish is excellent," she said. "Where are you from?"

"Here, the United States," Cory told her. "Southern California originally. I'm Brian Kellogg."

"Monika Sotelo." She offered her hand. Cory took it briefly, squeezing tenderly as if palpating for splinters of glass. Her palm was moist, and he noticed that the fingernails were chewed to the quick.

She noticed him looking.

"It's a horrible habit. I've tried, I've just never been able to stop."

Cory released her hand and returned the smile.

"Contradiction and struggle are universal and absolute."

She nodded mindfully.

"You've read Mao."

"Selectively," Cory said, easily beginning the lies that composed Brian Kellogg's cover story. "My education was at Berkeley during the Vietnam War. The chairman was more or less a required course of study."

"You were against the war?"

Cory shrugged.

"It was all rather pointless, don't you think?" Before she could answer, Cory looked over to the counter and signaled his waiter. "Could I buy you breakfast or something?" he offered.

"Just coffee," she said.

The waiter responded, and they were both well into their fresh coffees when she leaned over and placed her elbows on the table.

"So you've studied Mao, speak fluent Spanish, and are in Washington. Do you live here?"

Cory shook his head.

"No. I have a home, the family home, in California. Unfortunately, I only seem to get back there every other year or so. Most of my time is spent in South America, the lower countries: Chile, Argentina, Uruguay, sometimes Paraguay."

"Business?" she asked.

"Heavy equipment. Farming, mining, hydroelectric generators, and the like. The things people tend to forget they need."

"And you remind them?"

"I try to," Cory said, his voice sounding reasonably far away.

But Monika Sotelo seemed genuinely interested. She asked any number of questions to which Cory responded in character. As it had been for years, the agricultural consultant anecdotes remained second nature, and for the next half hour Cory lied both gracefully and convincingly.

His father, Paul Kellogg, had been a widower, his wife dying a few years after Brian's birth. In 1952, he had resigned from the State Department to accept a position with I.T.T. as a political liaison specialist to the Chilean government of General Carlos Ibañez. A former president, Ibañez had been re-elected after a heated campaign against corrupt politicians and the food shortages, inflation, and labor unrest that were then plaguing the country.

The general and Paul Kellogg had become quite close. A fact, Cory explained, attributed to two common interests: a respect for fine horses and an appreciation of falconry.

"I've always loved horses," Monika said. "I rode as a child."

"So did I," Cory nodded. Then he went on to explain how, on the occasion of his twelfth birthday, General Ibañez had surprised him by allowing him to pick for his own, one of the fine Andalusian colts from the general's private stable.

Cory had selected an arrogant sorrel two-year-old. The general complimented Paul Kellogg on his son's choice. The colt was from excellent bloodlines.

The general, from that point on, had become like an uncle.

"Wasn't Ibañez a good friend of Juan Perón?" Monika asked, after a moment.

"A very good friend," Cory told her. "In fact, the general even arranged for my father to begin doing business with Argentina."

"You met Perón?"

"Many times."

"His wife? Eva?"

"Her too."

"I think I can understand the Mao now," Monika smiled.

Cory understood her meaning. It was not entirely correct, but it did indicate she was being led to exactly where he wanted.

"Maybe a predisposition," he said slowly, choosing his words carefully. "But not to the extent of the chairman's. With Ibañez and Perón, it was a different type of socialism, more nationalistic, not quite as Spartan and more open to new ideas."

"Better?"

"For my business," Cory admitted. "At least it has turned out that way."

"So you are really a capitalist?"

"In an economic sense," he nodded. "I'm here in Washington to obtain export permits."

Monika took a sip of her coffee.

"And you continue to look for new markets," she said.

"What makes you say that?"

She reached over and tapped an index finger on the cover of the book about Mexico.

"That," she said quietly.

"I don't know," he shrugged. "You're Nicaraguan, closer to it than me. What do you think?"

"Lenin told us development and motion are absolute."

"Lenin told a lot of people a lot of things."

"And many people believed him to be a visionary."

"The reality of illusion," Cory said.

"And what does Brian Kellogg believe?" she asked quickly.

Cory paused. Interesting turn of phrase. What *did* Brian Kellogg believe?

First of all, he believed the woman was probing. Questioning him about his insights on the offensiveness endemic to Mexican politics. Perhaps he should ask Eisler to post him there and he could really wade into the morass.

Still, her question intrigued him. The woman intrigued him. She was unquestionably intelligent and, conceptually, he wanted to pursue the conversation to its logical end: relief of the imperative. The problem was, he couldn't, at least not in a satisfactory manner.

The previous night's efforts were now calling for their due. The meal had made him sleepy and he finally felt both mentally and physically exhausted. Tired to the degree where he knew he could sleep. Yet he was not quite ready to just walk away from Monika Sotelo. He would suggest a later meeting.

"Well," he began, answering her question. "Brian Kellogg believes our conversation must end on the Mexican note." He glanced at his watch, it was nearly noon. "I have another meeting at the Commerce Department within the hour and as much as I would enjoy asking you along, I'm afraid you'd only find it boring and very lengthy."

She looked down at her hands, but not before Cory noticed a flicker of something in her dark eyes. He decided it disappointment, skepticism, or, most likely, a little of both. Intellect aside, her plainness had probably seen many men walk away. It was a foreshadowing of vulnerability.

Cory exploited the moment. He smiled while inside, from somewhere near the Lucius site, he felt the tension begin to drain.

"Would you like to meet later?" he asked. "This evening? Nothing special. Dinner, maybe a movie or something?"

She looked up. Her features relaxed and Cory could detect a slight smile tugging at the corners of her lips.

"I think I would like that," she nodded. "I will meet you somewhere. Where are you staying?"

"The Stouffer's Concourse." Cory gestured in the direction of the mall. "There is a bar off the lobby, the Ondine Lounge. Seven-thirty?"

"I will be there," she said.

They left the Florakis Grill together, her surprised at Cory's height, him amazed at how short she was when standing, no more than an inch over five feet. He also noticed she walked with a slight limp, as if she had not altogether overcome some childhood muscular disease. Cory filed this away for future reference and, as they entered the concourse, he turned and looked down at her.

Emotionally, he realized that his control had now returned. As to when, he wasn't really sure. Just the same, it was present. His earlier self-indictment of the Pawpaw lapse was all but forgotten, and Monika was doing all those subtle things, those right things, to ensure it remained repressed.

She was like an analgesic, Cory realized. A graft of coherence when he needed it most.

Just two more sanctions, he told himself.

Monika, like the others, offered the gift of perspective. She would facilitate the stability necessary for him to complete the assignment.

"I'm looking forward to tonight," Cory said, surprised at the sincerity in his tone.

She took his hand, squeezed it once, and offered what Cory took to be a self-conscious but encouraging smile.

"So am I," she said softly. "We share similar interests."

"So it seems," he nodded.

As she turned to leave, Cory watched her for a long moment, then he began walking back toward the hotel at the mall's opposite end. The concourse was crowded now, the smells of holiday heavy and the sounds of happiness irrevocable.

It all felt different now, Cory decided. So much improved. No longer were the shoppers so relentlessly middle-class. No longer did they seem so incessantly alien.

First, call Defense, he thought to himself, as he found a pay telephone. Then he would sleep until tonight and the meeting with Monika Sotelo.

Development and motion were indeed absolute.

Monika would only make it more so.

***

Across the concourse, hidden behind a display in the Hallmark Card shop, the priest pulled impatiently at the starched white collar and continued his surveillance. Now, finally, his part was nearly finished. Cory and Monika had gone their separate ways: Cory had walked to a pay telephone, and Monika was moving to the right and in front of the card shop.

Stepping out from behind the display, he made his presence known and she looked directly into his eyes before giving an almost imperceptible nod of the head while continuing her slow limp to the outside parking area.

Wondering, the priest couldn't even imagine why Cory would even bother to be remotely interested in someone so nondescript as Monika Sotelo. Her breasts were small, probably sagged anyway, and her spine seemed to taper directly into legs without benefit of buttocks in between.

One question, perhaps, but then there were so many others.

How had the ambassador known to use Monika instead of some young, pretty girl? How had he known *when* to run Monika on Cory? How had he known to order the outraged priest role?

Three how's and a why. The answer to all?

Eisler. The ambassador well knew his people, for his instructions had been explicit: *Surveillance on Cory will be established and continued until contact is initiated. Once initiated, Monika will facilitate liaison with Cory.*

"Eisler," the priest whispered. He wondered what specific instructions he had given Monika. Of course, he would probably never know, for Eisler only explained in parts. Only Eisler knew the whole, the aggregate. Only Eisler held the key to disclosure.

"Man must eat," Eisler had said. "Cory is man. Cory will eat. Make the contact in a restaurant."

As for where surveillance would be established?

Eisler had this answer also.

"His vehicle," he had said. "Watch for his vehicle in the hotel garage. If Cory is out, he will return. If he is in the hotel, then he will check his vehicle before he does anything else."

Predictably, Eisler had been correct. After arriving by taxi, the priest had joined Monika in the Stouffer's garage. Waiting in her rented Toyota, they had observed Cory's return and followed him to the mall.

While trailing Cory from shop to shop, the priest and Monika had discussed the general direction of the conversation they would stage for Cory's benefit.

Eisler had defined the topic, the Catholic Church in Central America. This, he had said, would "tap" something Eisler termed as Cory's "imperative." Whatever the hell that was.

Doubtless, the priest realized, Eisler had known precisely what it was, for the guise had worked perfectly. Contact had been initiated and, at least from his vantage point in the card shop, it appeared the liaison was in effect.

But Monika Sotelo?

The man felt a chill sniff at his spine. If he was the actor-priest, then she was the certainly the grande dame of illusion. And to her, the limp, the nondescriptiveness, even her age were her most precious assets.

Eisler called her *la lagartija*, the little lizard. But a lizard with teeth who, from her home, a small apartment just off rue Sommerard, in the Parisian Latin Quarter, had done Eisler's bidding for nearly ten years.

La lagartija. Her specialty was seduction of young men. Those from wealthy South American families who hated their family money only because they had never lived without it. Eisler considered them lesser revolutionaries. Dangerously impressionable expatriates who loved the political intrigues of the Latin Quarter and saw themselves as the next Che or Marighella.

"Like weeds," Eisler had once said. "These boys must be plucked before their politics take root, for the roots search for water and the fountain is insurgency."

An Eisler garden, the priest remembered. And once identified as weeds, Monika would be ordered to search out the young men amid the smoky bistros, restaurants, and back alleys of Paris. At Eisler's behest, she would listen to their conversations. Share their dreams. Allow them too much drink on too little sleep, then take them home for a sexless night where they slept apart.

Morning would bring fellatio. Additional mornings, the trust that came with the morning ritual. Soon, like all young men, the weeds would beg to touch her. Monika would tell them she wanted it to be special. Something to be consummated in a special place.

Never, the priest knew, had even one of the youths declined to accompany her to the old abandoned gristmill near L'Aigle, some seventy miles west of Paris.

And once there?

The priest shuddered.

The weeding was pro forma in nature.

Sitting on a checkered picnic blanket, Monika would undress the youth, tease him with her tongue, then persuade him to lie back, close his eyes, and wait until she disrobed. The priest knew of at least seven young men who, while waiting, had died as Monika perfunctorily sliced their throats with a four-inch, commercial-grade straight razor before dusting their bodies with lye and burying them inside the mill.

La lagartija in Washington?

The priest suspected where this was leading. Cory would kill the five Russians, and Monika, should Eisler deem it necessary, would now be in a position to prosecute the prosecutor, thus severing the evidentiary blood trail.

"And what then?" the priest whispered as he left the Hallmark Card shop.

Who could venture a prediction? Not himself. His cards seemed dealt at random, but he knew this was certainly not the case. It was Eisler's deck and Eisler's deal. It always had been.

For over two decades now it had been like this, an introduction here, a small guise there. Nothing too brazen; but nothing too trivial either.

Eisler had termed it the "commerce," and he worked it with a subtle hand.

No, it was not a "commerce" based upon money or greed. On the contrary, the Eisler "commerce" was drawn from the sharing of a common ideology, the straightforward, sometimes ruthlessly direct protection of democracy. Despite the world's increasing economic problems, despite its political vagaries, even despite the seemingly continual realignment of world order, many still schemed for some measure of domination. So while the majority of official Washington did little more than buy new maps and ponder nebulous economic forecasts, Eisler declined reaction in favor of more proactive confrontations.

To be sure, he regretted neither the commerce nor his sharing of Eisler's approach to political expedience. After all, in the most personal sense, it had proven central to achieving his current position.

Walking by a mall trashcan, Jonathan Weall reached up, removed the stiff cleric's bib and tossed it into the container. Another guise abandoned. Another assignment finished.

And how many had there been now? he thought.

He couldn't recall. Since first meeting Eisler, the intervening years seemed to have passed with alarming speed.

"Over a decade," Weall whispered, as he walked on through the mall.

It had begun as a chance meeting, he remembered. 1969. Salvador Allende, a Marxist, was coming to power in Chile. President Nixon wanted him stopped. To do so, the president established a five-agency back-track committee to evaluate the situation and propose alternatives.

In addition to State, Defense, and CIA representatives, Eisler occupied one of the National Security Council chairs and Jonathon Weall, having just rotated back from the attaché office in Santiago, was one of three FBI delegates.

But it was a committee of confusion, Weall recalled. More arguments than agreements. And while the committee continued to squabble, Allende was elected president of Chile.

Nixon was outraged and the back track committee shifted gears. Eisler assumed control and a coup d'etat was planned. It moved along successfully and soon, the troops of General Pinochet had the presidential palace surrounded. But inside was Allende. If Pinochet could usurp power, would he in fact be strong enough to ward off a counter-coup attempt by Allende and his Marxist supporters?

The committee consensus was generally no.

As to how to deal with Allende?

Two options emerged. One, exile; two, abdication. Abdication by assassination.

To Jonathon Weall, who had learned to disdain Communists even while dining with them at various embassy functions, the choice was uncomplicated. Option two.

But as it came to pass, Weall, along with only two other voices, one each from the CIA and State, found himself in the minority. Eisler recommended exile to President Nixon.

Within the week, Salvador Allende was dead, reportedly by suicide, and Agusto Pinochet was securely ensconced as the new president of Chile. And it was that same evening, during a private, one-on-one meeting in Eisler's apartment, that Jonathon Weall first mentioned that Allende's death had been merited.

Eisler, in response, had smiled demurely.

"If you will remember Dracula, Jonathon," he had said. "You will remember it was necessary to drive a stake though his heart to preclude a continuation of his crimes. With respect to Allende, I believed a more humane death was in order."

Jonathon Weall had understood the meaning as Eisler continued what turned out to be a thinly disguised, if tender, offer of recruitment.

"Do you remember Catherine Howard, Jonathon?" he had said. "Catherine and Anne Boleyn?"

"They were wives of Henry the Eighth," Weall answered. "Both were beheaded."

Eisler had smiled at the correct answer.

"Well, then, you will remember they were imprisoned in the Tower of London before being taken to the scaffold. In any case, there was a phrase that became quite popular during that period, Jonathon. It was the Queen Walk, and it referred to the path they followed from the Tower to the headsman."

"Similar to the last mile?" Weall had said.

"Yes, Jonathon, similar, but different. Different in the sense that their death was sanctioned by the Head of State. Only Henry had the power to order the Queen Walk. Am I making myself clear, Jonathon?"

To Jonathon Weall it was perfectly clear.

"Then Allende," he had asked. "His death was a contemporary Queen Walk?"

Eisler had said nothing, and Weall ventured an observation.

"Some would consider it a conspiracy."

"Not at all, Jonathon. How high does a conspiracy have to reach before it becomes public policy?"

There had been silence for a long moment before Eisler continued.

"Consider QUEENWALK, Jonathon. A vehicle free to operate anywhere. A vehicle free to counter our enemies wherever. Free for preemption. Free from diplomatic and legal meddlings and operating with total impunity. It is the solution, Jonathon. It is what is necessary."

Jonathon Weall, in all candor, could only agree. And when Eisler had asked, "Will you support me in this endeavor, Jonathon?" Weall had immediately acquiesced. And although he had never been asked to personally kill, he had become Eisler's confidant, and eyes, within the Federal Bureau of Investigation.

Eisler's rule. The ambassador could touch the untouchables. The ambassador could solve the intrigues.

And during the past decade? The introductions and the guises?

Jonathon Weall had no complaints, the ambassador always reciprocated.

Eisler's insights, his suggestions and his ability to make the complex comprehensible, all of these things had only served to raise Jonathon Weall through the FBI ranks to where he was now. The future? With Eisler's help, even becoming director was well within the realm of possibility.

The "commerce," Weall smiled, as he walked toward a pay telephone. A little give, a little take. The Russians, in this context, the icing on the cake.

Reaching the phone, Weall checked his watch. 11:48 a.m.

He needed to get back to his office before Franco missed him. But first he had to call Eisler and let him know the lizard had the scent.

Eisler would be pleased.

His Jonathon had once again performed.

CHAPTER 26

FBI Headquarters, 11:55 A.M.

There were but three sounds in Sal Franco's tiny office. Above his head, the heater duct breathed softly; on his desk, a computer terminal hummed restlessly; and, from his lips, a toneless rendition of "glow little glow worm, glitter, glitter" continued to repeat like a raspy broken record.

It was dark in the room. Franco required the darkness and had turned off all other lighting. It obliged him to remain focused on the cursor-worm and, hence, the task at hand. The cubicle was now illuminated by only the pulsing white on blue of the twenty-inch video monitor that was interfaced with the data bank maintained at Quantico by the Bureau's Behavioral Science Unit. Having been part of the team that originally developed the application, Franco was now assessing the behavioral matrixes in an effort to classify the shooter's mental profile. The prototype Incident Based Reporting System classification was 09A. The behavior, homicide.

"Okay, worm," he whispered. "Let's go to the core and look for seeds."

Then he pressed a key and began to read:

PSYCHOLOGICAL MOTIVATION MATRIX - HOMICIDE [IBRS-09A]			
	SUICIDAL PERSONALITY	VENGEANCE SEEKER	MENTALLY DISTURBED
WHEN DOES HE KILL?	emotional state	after meticulous planning	in an aberrant mental state
WHERE DOES HE KILL?	random locations	significant location	in any setting
WHY DOES HE KILL?	self-death wish	revenge	to attain mastery
HOW DOES HE KILL?	as an irrational act	furtively or overtly	illogical impulse
BEHAVIOR PATTERNS?	doesn't care if caught	driven by single impulse	lack of judgment - anger

Franco studied the information for a long moment, then he reached to the desk and slid a yellow legal pad in front of the screen. He had two incidents from which to work: Celt at the cemetery, Pointer in the Airstream. Deliberately, impartially, these would be considered, not separately, but as an extension of the same crime.

With this in mind, Franco grabbed a pencil, wrote the abbreviation PSY at the top left corner of the pad and started with the suicidal column, top to bottom.

When? Negative. No evidence of emotion noted: signs, blood on walls, torture. This was devil worship crap. Omit this one.

Where? This should be deleted too: the shooter hit where he wanted to, planned, not random. Omit.

Why? How? Behavior?

Franco omitted these too. The shooter definitely took precautions not to be caught. And he had a cause, so no indication of irrational acts. As for the death wish thing, well, who knew? But in this context, suicidal personalities, it just didn't fit. Omit the whole suicidal category and move to the next column.

Vengeance seeker, Franco thought. Pretty close here. A lot of things could fit. He read down the column quickly and noted those factors which, at least upon a cursory examination, a reasonable and prudent man could infer from the facts:

Meticulous planning: yes.

Revenge: a conceivable yes, but based solely on the telephonic claims of responsibility.

Furtively: a definite yes.

Single impulse: another definite, as evidenced by whatever reason these particular men were being killed.

These four written on his pad, Franco looked to the third column and scanned it briefly.

Mentally disturbed? Best guess, no. Try as he could, Franco could not imagine this shooter as insane. It just didn't feel right. Nothing kinky involved so far. Nothing to indicate any aberrant behavior or impulsiveness. On the contrary, the shooter did show some a considerable measure of judgment, and his capabilities—the range of the shot at the cemetery for example—also demonstrated that the shooter was a planner.

He killed old men and he killed them purposely. But again, why them?

Franco placed a piece of gum in his mouth and evaluated the mentally disturbed category once again.

No, he decided. Nothing here. He would omit it all and move to the next matrix.

Reaching to the keyboard, he tapped in a three-digit code. Figures danced in blue and white and the second category appeared:

POLITICAL MOTIVATION MATRIX - HOMICIDE [IBRS-09A]			
	SOCIAL PROTESTOR	IDEOLOGICAL ZEALOT	TERRORIST EXTREMIST
WHEN DOES HE KILL?	to eliminate injustice	perception of being wronged	high publicity potential
WHERE DOES HE KILL?	social protest relevance	in any setting	inherent media access
WHY DOES HE KILL?	create social chaos	redress a grievance	attain political change
HOW DOES HE KILL?	part of group effort	robot-like conduct	with emotional justification
BEHAVIOR PATTERNS?	idealistic	fanatic programmed cultist	will sacrifice life for plot

Political murders, he thought. Well, according to the claims, that was exactly what these were supposed to be. But were they? Franco leaned closer to the screen and read the entries under social protestor.

When? A possible here, but based only on the claims and nothing from Shining Path inside Peru to support it. It could be bullshit, it could not be bullshit. Whatever, until something independently substantiated the claims, this could only be assumed and the assumption remained, Franco again speculated that killing people in Washington was way too far a reach for Shining Path.

He looked to the ideological considerations and smiled.

"I'm beginning to see you, my friend," he whispered, as he wrote the abbreviation POL on the pad and enumerated three of the five zealot factors he knew were applicable: the shooter killed anywhere and he killed professionally, robot-like. He was killing by virtue of some preselection process, not randomly, and while not exactly a cultist per se, he was programmed, at least to the degree of having been instructed to select these particular victims.

But was he a terrorist? Franco glanced at the third column.

"No," he said quickly. Out of the five considerations, only one seemed to have even any applicability, the why. And really, he thought, coming back to square one again, aside from the damn telephone calls, even this could not be considered factual until independently confirmed. Back to Shining Path reaching again. Always back to Shining Path reaching.

Franco tapped another set of instructions on the keyboard. The political matrix disappeared and the final profile appeared:

CRIMINAL MOTIVATION MATRIX - HOMICIDE [IBRS-09A]			
	CORNERED PERPETRATOR	AGGRIEVED INMATE	PROFESSIONAL FELON
WHEN DOES HE KILL?	believes no alternative	spontaneously	as part of a plan
WHERE DOES HE KILL?	when trapped	custodial environment	location of choice
WHY DOES HE KILL?	to effect escape	to change situation	contractual motivation
HOW DOES HE KILL?	reflexive response	with planned force	calculated manner
BEHAVIOR PATTERNS?	caught up in events	frustration	unemotional cunning

"Yes, my friend," Franco whispered. "You are getting clearer." The shooter was obviously not cornered, nor was he an inmate, at least not just yet, so Franco ignored the first two columns and directed his attention to the third.

Of the five entries under PROFESSIONAL FELON, four seemed salient. He noted them on his pad, flipped off the computer and turned on the desk lamp.

"Well," he said softly to himself. "Interesting."

Franco picked up the pad, leaned back in his chair and quickly cross-referenced the variables.

Vengeance Seeker: four entries, three if he deleted the responsibility claims which he did at this point.

Ideological Zealot: three entries.

Professional Felon: four entries.

"Three, three and four," Franco said slowly. "And they all come back to four, don't they, my friend?"

Franco glanced over to the video screen and flipped it on. It colored, but he could see only the reflection of the desk lamp. He looked back to the legal pad.

"And you're about a cold bastard too, aren't you?"

Three, three, and four. They all corresponded except one.

But it's the one thing I now understand, Franco thought. It's the programming, my friend. It's what makes you neither a zealot nor a vengeance seeker. It's the fifth factor. It is what makes you the professional.

Franco reached over and snapped off the desk lamp. To his left, the blue of the computer screen bathed his face in half shadow. He reached over and tapped his pencil point against the video monitor.

"This is where you are, my friend."

Beneath the sharpened lead point, the words contractual motivation continued to glow as Franco allowed his mind to fill with the one question that none of the matrixes could answer: *Why are you killing these old men?*

But the answer never came, the phone call did instead. Franco turned on the desk lamp and picked up the receiver on the second ring.

"Franco."

Dunnigan Cox did not bother with pleasantries.

"It's a *silver* Camaro," he said tersely.

"Where did you get that?"

"A neighbor," Cox explained. "She was awakened by gunfire, two shots, I might add, and looked out her window just in time to observe the vehicle impact her trashcan."

"She recognized the car in the dark?"

"No, not at all. She recognized her trashcan. We took it in, analyzed the damage and were able to find enough paint scrapings for an association analysis. It was a General Motors paint, their control batch SS0652, a factory bake described as dark silver metallic and available only on this year's models."

"Nice," Franco said, making note of the information. "I'll get . . . ."

"There's more," Cox interrupted. "We also located a spent shell casing."

"Match King?"

"Yes," Cox said. "And it was definitely fired from a modified Steyr, as we initially believed."

"Semiautomatic to single shot?" Franco asked.

"Most assuredly," Cox said. "Trace extractor scorings confirm the modification."

Before Franco could respond, Cox ventured a conclusion.

"If I might add something, from the evidence we've been able to isolate here, my staff has decided the suspect to be extremely flexible, as well as calculating. Do you recall my saying that the witness indicated there were two shots?"

"Yes," Franco said.

"And when you were here, I mentioned that the explosion of the Airstream should be attributed to some internal stimuli?"

"Yes," Franco said again. "Something that ignited the propane."

"Well, we have now concluded how it was effected."

"How?"

"The actual ignition source appears to have been the television set. We recovered the picture tube and conducted a cursory analysis of the non-crystalline fracture pattern. We found the shatter point with relatively little reconstruction. It was projectively unique . . . ."

"What do you mean *projectively unique?*" Franco interrupted.

"I'm referring to the fact it was uniquely, to the exclusion of all other phenomena, generated by a projectile," Cox said quickly. "In this instance, a bullet. We discovered the ingress cone near the lower center of the glass. The cone was lateral, small end to the outside, large end toward the television's interior. More succinctly, the bullet entered the television, shorted out the electronics which, in turn, self-ignited and provided the flame source which ignited the propane."

Franco considered this for a moment.

"So how did propane get into the Airstream's interior in a flammable form?"

"Quite simple, Agent Franco. Someone turned it off from the outside long enough for the heater's pilot light to burn out. Once out, the gas was again turned on. Without the pilot light, it remained in a flammable state as it dispersed throughout the trailer's interior."

"But the two shots," Franco said. "Why so?"

"Because it was cold outside," Cox explained, rather indulgently. "The deceased had the windows closed. In order to ignite the television set, the suspect first had to have a clear trajectory. Remember, the particular bullet was a hollowpoint. It would flatten, possibly splinter, when striking the window. If so, there would be no way to ensure its continuing on through the glass to the television. Two shots would ensure ignition."

Franco understood.

"The first shot shattered the window glass, and the second passed through the shattered window into the television."

"Precisely," Cox agreed. "We isolated a partial, but arguably comparable, ingress cone at the bottom-center of the window glass."

"Great," Franco said vaguely. The suspect was a trick shot on top of everything else. Still, this all but confirmed the contractual motivation theory. Someone, somewhere, for some reason, had brought in a ringer.

"As I said, Agent Franco," Cox added, after a pause. "Flexible and calculating."

"This is all starting to sound a little atypical," Franco said.

"So it would appear," Cox agreed.

"Anything else?" Franco asked. "Latents? Toolmarks?"

"Not as yet," Cox told him. "The spent casing is being further analyzed as we speak. I'll let you know if anything is developed."

"Where will you be?"

"We're enroute to headquarters now," Cox said. "So I should be back in my office within the hour. Oh, and Franco?"

"What?"

"Both of the deceased have been transported to Walter Reed for autopsy. A Major Jim McLain will be your contact. I've spoken with him this morning. Celt's examination is probably already finished. Pointer's, he assures me, will begin immediately upon the corpse's arrival."

"Fine," Franco said. Walter Reed Army Hospital was excellent. The doctor's were good and kept their mouths shut—no leaks. "Thanks, Dunnigan. I'll talk to you later."

Franco replaced the receiver, leaned back in his chair and laced his fingers behind his head.

The doctor's were good and kept their mouths shut—no leaks.

"God damn it," he said. *That* was what was wrong with this old man thing. *No leaks.* No public claims of responsibility. Not in Washington. Not in Peru. Nowhere. Just the calls to Defense. Specific emotionless calls that, if the shooter was as "calculating" as Franco believed, he would know wouldn't be made public knowledge, particularly by a federal agency.

So why, then, even bother to claim responsibility?

There were two obvious answers: one, he was simply following orders; or, two, he had elected to make them on his own, a red herring to throw any investigators off the scent.

Franco sighed heavily and glanced over at the desktop computer.

No, he knew, the computer terminal wouldn't provide the answers, garbage in, garbage out, that meager bit of reality. Besides, in either case the two other, more pivotal questions, remained: Were the shooter and the caller one and same? And the nagging—as it was rapidly becoming a fixation now—*Why these specific victims?*

The phone rang again. Franco picked up the receiver.

"Franco."

"Let's talk," Jonathon Weall said.

"You see Bechtel?"

"Two hours worth."

"And?"

"He broods your progress." The understatement spoke volumes.

"I'm on the way," Franco said. Replacing the receiver, he turned off the computer and, worried, hurried to Weall's office.

Hershel Bechtel "brooding" was never a desirable sign.

Franco had visions of the Albuquerque field office.

CHAPTER 27

Washington National Cathedral, 12:15 P.M.

After leaving the mall, Monika Sotelo had made one telephone call, then, as instructed, hailed a cab and directed the driver to take her across the District into the old St. Albans area of the city. The ride had taken no more than fifteen minutes, but it seemed an eternity. The driver was Haitian, and from two rear speakers beating reggae music blared while she, with the heater on high and the windows closed, stewed in silence and wondered what it was that enabled the man to emit that horrible, rotten egg stench.

Rankness alone merited this one a trip to L'Aigle, she thought cynically, as the driver slushed to a halt at the curb.

"Wanna me wait, lady?" he asked, leaning an elbow back over the front seat.

"No," she said. Glancing at the meter, she reached over and handed him the fare without additional comment.

Monika climbed out of the taxi and found the National Cathedral looming before her. Like similar designs the world over, it was massive, solemn, and ecclesiastically Gothic. A grand, timeless structure whose dominance was only enhanced by the dull, swirling sky and the cold north wind whipping at her face.

Monika crossed herself and with the sound of salt crunching beneath her shoes, slowly moved up the steps, pulled open one of two huge wooden doors and entered the vestibule.

At the sound of the outer door opening, Boudreaux Pock looked up from the church newsletter he had been reading.

Right on time, he thought, as their eyes locked. He had never before met Monika Sotelo, but he knew it was her. The limp, more pronounced than he expected, was unmistakable. He said nothing.

The bodyguard, she thought, dismissing Pock as nothing more as she looked away and continued on through a smaller set of doors and into the cathedral's interior.

Inside was warm and, despite the cavernous size, surprisingly intimate. Soft lighting illuminated the walls and altar, and small red and blue votive candles seemed to be everywhere, their scents mingling pleasingly with those of frankincense and old paper.

She crossed herself a second time and looked around. There were three, no, four people in the cathedral. Widely dispersed, each occupied their own darkly oiled pew and each appeared to be lost in prayer.

Three women kneeling and one man sitting.

She walked down the center aisle, genuflected and slid in next to the man who acknowledged her arrival by only the slightest nod of his head.

There, then gone, she caught a whiff of camphor and looked over to him. He was dressed in a dark suit and wore a threadbare cashmere topcoat. A black Irish walking hat and gloves were at his side, and his hands rested on an umbrella that lay across his lap. She stared at its handle. In the lesser curve of the grip the paint had been worn away and bare wood, probably pine, was now visible.

"Do you like this place, Monika?" he asked.

"Yes," she said softly. "It is very peaceful."

Eisler turned to looked at her.

"They call this America's Westminster Abbey."

"There are tombs here?" she asked.

Eisler nodded slowly.

"America, too, venerates its heroes," he said. "Cordell Hull, Admiral Dewey, Woodrow Wilson, they are all buried here. Some say the admiral's ghost still walks these chambers, that he is unrequited."

"Unrequited? Why?"

Eisler's eyes warmed with emotion.

"That is the mystery, Monika. They never say *why*. They say the only people who knew were Cordell Hull and Woodrow Wilson."

"I don't understand."

"Nor do any of us," Eisler replied. "That is the significance. America also needs its mysteries. They can be something, or they can just as easily be nothing."

"And which is the admiral?" Monika asked.

Eisler smiled.

"Some of both," he said. "Or . . . ."

"None of either," Monika added, completing the phrase.

Eisler smiled. She had pleased him. He reached over and patted her knee.

"Tell me about your morning," he said after a moment.

"It went well. I assume you've already spoken with Jonathon Weall?"

Eisler avoided the question and asked one of his own.

"Did Jonathon perform adequately?"

"Yes," she nodded. "He appeared quite priestly in his collar."

"And Damon seemed to believe it?"

"From what I could tell," Monika nodded. "We are going to meet this evening for dinner."

"And after dinner?"

Monika stared directly into Eisler's eyes. He held hers effortlessly and repeated the question. "And after dinner, Monika?"

Monika looked away, down to the umbrella. Eisler's two index fingers were tapping out a silent rhythm on the handle.

"I cannot predict what he will want," she whispered.

"He will want you," Eisler said gently. "He will have explored your mind and will want to learn your body."

Monika sighed and looked back up into Eisler's face.

"I will not sleep with him," she said, aware of the emotion in her voice.

A thoughtful expression crossed Eisler's face.

"Of course," he said softly. "The issue of, shall we say . . . your memories?"

Listening, but refusing to respond, Monika lowered her head and there was nearly a full minute of awkward silence until Eisler decided to express a conclusion.

"Fellatio will not suffice, my little one," he said. "Damon is a man. He is not one of those silly Latin youngsters. Damon will want to learn all of you."

Eisler observed the muscles in her jaw tighten. The old scar had been opened. A grim, yet all too common wound. He allowed her a moment to relive her pain while he remembered the story.

Managua, Nicaragua, 1959. Then a devout Catholic, Monika Sotelo had just celebrated her tenth birthday and was visiting her uncle who lived in Managua. The trip from her home, a tiny farming hamlet called Champa, had been a gift from her parents, and for weeks she had looked forward to the two-hour bus ride through the countryside. It was Monika's first trip away from Champa and it was to be a very special occasion. It was the week of the Festividad de Cristo, the seven-day celebration of Jesus' virgin birth, and even though the event was celebrated more modestly throughout Nicaragua, only in Managua was it such a splendid party. There would be candy, music, laughter, and dancing in the streets while, in the sky, all manner of brightly colored fireworks marked the festival's passage.

For the trip, Monika's mother had crocheted her a beautiful white lace *mantón*. As that first night began, dressed in the shawl and a plain shapeless dress and walking barefoot, Monika giggled with excitement and followed her uncle into the streets.

As she had imagined, it was a splendid affair, the crowd screaming "carnavál," and long conga-like columns of strangers dancing in time to the driving music.

Her uncle, glassy-eyed and quite *borracho* by this time, had been caught up in the frenzy. He dropped Monika's hand and disappeared into one of the conga lines. She attempted to follow, but being a stranger to such crowds, soon found herself unable to keep up, so she returned to the spot where her uncle had last seen her and waited.

Unfortunately, Eisler remembered, it was not her uncle who found her, at least not then. As she had explained years earlier, about an hour later, a voice had whispered in her ear, "Want to see the *mono*, the monkey?"

Looking up, she was surprised to see the voice belonged to a handsome boy who was probably in his late teens. He was dressed much better than most of the others and he had a nice smile. It was obvious, even to a ten-year-old that he was a member of one of the newer families that had usurped control in Nicaragua with the consent of the *presidente*, Somoza.

"I must wait for my uncle," she had said.

"The monkey can do tricks. It is a magic monkey."

Monika had looked back to the crowd, but still her uncle was nowhere to be found.

"Is the monkey close?" she had asked.

"One street away. I will bring you back here in five minutes."

"Do you promise?"

"I promise."

But the boy had lied. He had taken Monika's hand and led her to a closed produce warehouse where six of his friends were waiting. All were in their late teens or early twenties and all were sons of Somoza's political cronies.

As she was led into the warehouse office, one of the boys picked her up and stood her atop a desk. The rest formed a circle around them. He reached over, removed the lace *mantón*, and lay it on the desktop. Then he removed her dress and tossed it into a corner.

The last thing Monika could remember was him unzipping his pants and exposing himself.

"Here is the monkey," he had told her. "But the monkey is sad. Make the monkey smile."

Her aunt found her the following morning. The lace *mantón* was torn and stained with blood, semen, and feces. Her uncle reported the crime. He disappeared. Her father came to Managua and again reported the attack. He also vanished.

Monika had returned to Champa and since that incident, had never allowed another man to penetrate her vagina, nor had she ever worn lace again. Now, Eisler knew, he would have to ask her to do both.

"Do you remember our first meeting, Monika?"

"Yes," she sighed. How could she forget. It was the only time she had ever been caught. She had believed the man to be just another rich Chilean playboy. How could she have known he was really one of Eisler's people.

"Do you remember our conversation?" he asked. "The settlement?"

Monika said nothing.

"Of course you do," Eisler said softly. "You promised me something then, Monika. You pledged that if I did not bring in *le judiciaire* you would provide me certain services. Support me in particular endeavors."

She shrugged and glanced over as Eisler reached into his topcoat pocket, pulled out a small, folded paper bag, and lay it on the pew between them. Free from the pocket, the bag began to partially unfold. Blue on white, she could read the words Neiman-Marcus.

"What is that?" she asked.

Eisler offered a kindly smile and pushed the bag closer to her thigh.

"With Damon," he said again, "fellatio will not suffice."

"But I cannot," she told him, her voice small. "You cannot force me to do what I believe is . . . ."

Eisler held up a hand.

"There is never any force, Monika," he said gently. "I am only asking you to do this for me. I must know you are in place in the event circumstances license a more defensive course of action."

"But . . . ."

"Sssh, my little one," Eisler breathed, as he reached over and again patted her knee. "You must once more trust me. Will you do this for me, Monika? Will you once more believe in me?"

She looked into his eyes. They seemed remarkably warm and kind.

"Yes," she told him. "When will I . . . ?"

"Sssh," Eisler said, interrupting her again. "There may be no reason to deviate from the current scenario. Remember, I told you this is merely a precaution. If it appears Damon's loyalties are wavering, that he could possibly become untrustworthy, then and only then will you proceed."

Monika nodded knowingly. Eisler had used her for housekeeping twice before. She took a deep breath.

"How soon will you know?" she asked.

"Forty-eight, perhaps seventy-two hours."

Monika looked back to her hands and, as she did, Eisler stood and picked up his gloves, hat, and umbrella.

"Remember his mind, Monika," Eisler told her. "Damon is different than other men. To him, the body is secondary. Capture his mind, allow him to touch yours, and you will occupy his interest for as long as we deem it necessary."

She glanced up at him.

"I hope you are right," she said.

"I am seldom wrong," he countered.

"Doesn't that ever bother you?"

At the question, Eisler's eyes veiled and he tossed his gloves into the hat and squeezed by her knees toward the center aisle.

"Seldomly," he said, as he passed in front of her. "It is a quality that allows old men to grow older."

Reaching the aisle, Eisler turned and shuffled slowly to the rear of the church. Pock straightened up as he entered the vestibule.

"We leaving?" he asked, tossing the newsletter to a table.

"Yes," Eisler told him, as he paused to put on his hat and gloves.

Pock pulled open the outer door, and Eisler led the way out into the weather.

"So, Boudreaux," he asked, as they descended the steps. "What did you think of the woman?"

Pock shrugged.

"Nothing special," he said.

"Do you believe she could seduce a man?"

"Maybe," Pock answered. "Why?"

"What about a woman, Boudreaux? Do you believe she could seduce a woman?"

Pock experienced an uncomfortable sensation. He felt Eisler was again toying with him.

"I don't know."

Eisler nodded thoughtfully.

"I understand the wife of the new Jordanian ambassador has, on a number of previous occasions, participated in such activities. Have you also heard this rumor, Boudreaux?"

"No," Pock admitted. "But I guess you're thinking about running this one on her, right?"

"Many considerations are in order," Eisler said. "I find pillow talk between women much more absorbing than any other type."

Pock smiled broadly.

"Well, if you need some surveillance help, Mr. Eisler, you know who to call."

Pig, Eisler thought. But still, at least now, Pock had seen Monika. This would save time should unforeseen contingencies dictate her elimination.

"Indeed," he said, forcing himself to smile. "How thoughtful of you to offer, Boudreaux. And I will keep you in mind."

"Anytime, Mr. Eisler. Anytime."

***

After Eisler left, it was ten minutes before Monika could bring herself to even touch the bag sitting at her side. Finally, she decided it wasn't going to go away and she slowly unfolded the open end and peered inside.

"Bastard."

The gift was a pair of white lace panties.

CHAPTER 28

FBI Headquarters, 12:25 P.M.

Jonathon Weall was all but shouting into the telephone when Sal Franco appeared in his doorway. Glancing up, he motioned Franco to the chair without interrupting his conversation. Weall was livid, and Franco felt a touch of genuine sympathy for the target of his wrath. Only once had Franco been forced to suffer through one of Jonathon's legendary "counseling" sessions. It had been a remarkably humiliating experience.

"And you paid *how* much?" Weall was asking. "You idiot. Did you even bother to look at a map before doling out the money?"

Weall rolled his eyes at the explanation.

"Well," he said sarcastically. "Had you bothered to look, just maybe you would have noticed that Anguilla is not a city in Angola, it's not even on the same goddamn continent. Anguilla is a goddamned island in the Caribbean."

A shake of the head.

"I don't give a damn if you thought it sounded like they went together and I really don't give a damn about Thomas Hardy, his fucking eloquence, *or* his fucking contributions to ninteenth-century English literature. You think about this 'crushing fate,' dickhead. You think about a fucking transfer to Borneo, because if you don't find that son of a bitch and get my goddamned money back that's exactly where you're heading. You've got twelve hours and not a minute more."

Weall slammed down the receiver.

"Trouble in paradise?" Franco asked.

"It's fucking Athens again," Weall told him. "You know, one of these days, I'm going to clean out that whole little nest of incompetent bastards. I don't think there's one in the bunch who could solve a case of hives. All they do is run around in white suits like they're in some goddamn 1952 Richard Widmark movie."

Franco smiled. It was the perfect description of the Athens legal attaché staff. All four were well-born graduates of Brown University. They were also, in Franco's considered opinion, pretentious assholes.

"What this time?"

Weall held out his hands in a gesture of helplessness.

"About the usual. They *la dolce vita*-ed their way into letting some Arab businessman tap them for 10K."

"Scam?"

"Not even a good one," Weall nodded. "Some nonsense about the Iranians financing an airbase in Angola, in *Anguilla*, Angola. The Arab offered the plans. Guess the format?"

"The muses are fickle," Franco shrugged. "A Big Chief tablet and a red crayola?"

"Close," Weall said. "A goddamned microdot, of all things. Can you believe those Athens idiots actually bought the damn thing? To the best of my knowledge, I don't think there's anyone who's actually used a fucking microdot since goddamned Khrushchev."

Franco chuckled and, after a moment, Weall joined in.

"You know what was on it?" he smiled.

"What?" Franco asked.

"The first ten pages of *Wuthering Heights*," Weall said flatly. "And the goddamn idiots don't even see anything wrong with it. He tells me some crap about Hardy 'writing studies of strong men being crushed by malignant fates.' I'm surrounded by fools."

Franco laughed politely as Weall closed a folder, then leaned back in his chair.

"Linguistics finished the second tape," he said, as the smile faded from his lips. "With the exception of the victim's name, it was the same exact message. Same diction, same speech patterns, same lack of emotion. The computer says it's the same caller."

Franco nodded thoughtfully.

"I knew it would be."

"How?"

"It fits the psychological profile. He's contract, Jonathon, and very good. Cox calls him 'calculating.' He's too smart to work a tandem. He'd make his own calls, do his own shooting. No, the guy's a loner, and the shooter and caller are one in the same."

Weall's eyes narrowed.

"Proof?"

"None," Franco admitted. "At least until we get the shooter into custody and compare the speech patterns."

"But the Shining Path connection, don't you . . . ."

"They have nothing to do with it," Franco interrupted.

"That's not what Bechtel and the Defense reps think," Weall told him. "They're proceeding under the assumption it's all organized."

"It *is* all organized," Franco said softly. "Only not by anyone connected with Shining Path and not to get any of our military types out of Peru."

Franco paused for a moment and collected his thoughts.

"I assume they have their little counterterrorism working groups in place over at the White House?"

Weall knew they did, Hershel Bechtel chaired one. He nodded.

"And all the little crisis management people running around doing crisis management things?"

Weall continued to nod.

"Well, that should give you a clue," Franco said.

"What do you mean?" Weall asked.

"They've been looking for a reason to justify their existence for the past five years. No terrorists, no justification."

"Perhaps," Weall said cautiously. "But until we have some real proof otherwise, shouldn't we . . . .?"

"Goddamn it, Jonathon, look at the facts. Look at the weapon, one of the finest sniper rifles in the world. Look at the shooter's capabilities, the distance of the shot. And the trailer, Cox tells me it was a double shot, one to shatter a window, the second to explode the television to ignite the gas inside. And what about the man himself? He's a goddamn anglo."

"But the calls to Defense, why say Shining Path is responsible?"

"To screw *us* up," Franco said tersely. "They weren't public claims. The only calls have been directly to Defense and if these were an authentic terrorist stunts, doesn't it stand to reason they would want some public exposure? Christ, Jonathon, someone as good as this man is would know *we* wouldn't release it to the press."

"But that's working to our advantage," Weall said. "We would never be able to control the media."

"And that's my point," Franco said. "We're not even having to bother with controlling the press. Whoever is killing these men is not doing it for any political reasons. If he were, we would have learned about it from television."

Weall considered this for a long moment.

"Do you follow my rationale?" Franco asked.

"I don't discount it," Weall finally said. "But assuming you're right, what makes you think Shining Path just couldn't have brought in a professional and instructed him not to make the killings public knowledge?"

"To what end?"

Weall had no good answer. It went back to the media pressure aspects.

"So where is the motive?" he asked.

"I don't know yet," Franco admitted. "But it's not with the shooter though. It's something that connects the two victims together. Some link we haven't identified yet."

Weall shifted uneasily in his chair.

"The Defense relationship?"

"That's the obvious one," Franco agreed. "Then again, it just could be coincidence and I hesitate to draw assumptions between links. The real motive could be anything. Something they did, something they didn't do. Like I said, I just don't know yet."

"So where do you take it from here?"

"Study the victims," Franco said. "Try to isolate some common thread—*any* thread, for that matter—and hope it unravels back to a legitimate motive. Did you get Pointer's personnel file from Defense?"

"Just before you came up." Weall reached to the desktop, picked up a thick manila folder, and passed it to Franco.

"You know, Sal, I'm going to have to run your theory by Bechtel. He may not be in a position to go along with it. He's only got one vote on the crisis management team, and the others may think this is all way out of line."

"It's not goddamn terrorists," Franco said sharply, already regretting his tone. But before he could apologize, the phone rang. Weall immediately picked up the receiver.

"Yes. Where? No, he's here with me now. Of course."

He replaced the receiver and looked across the desk.

"There'll be a third file, Sal," he said slowly. "The call came into Defense about a ten minutes ago. They've confirmed it. A Robert Rouse. Advanced Research Projects Agency. Dunnigan Cox is already en route."

"Where?" Franco asked.

"Arlington."

Franco closed his eyes and forced the muscles in his neck to relax as he remembered his computer and the soft pulsing of the words *contractual motivation*.

"Same caller?" he asked.

"It appears so," Weall said.

Franco ran the tip of his tongue along the underside of his moustache. The cold sore felt more painful now.

"What about the wording?"

"Only the victim's name was different."

Franco opened his eyes and stood.

"I have a car waiting downstairs," Weall told him. "You can ride with me."

Franco said nothing. Tucking the Pointer file under his arm, he followed Jonathon Weall out of the office.

And now there were three, he thought sullenly.

The thread was becoming elastic.

CHAPTER 29

Arlington, Virginia, 1:30 P.M.

As Jonathon Weall pulled to a stop some fifty yards from Robert Rouse's ground-level apartment, Franco was struck by the uniquely primitive nature of the crime scene. There had been unexpected and violent death, and the carrion eaters were already in attendance.

The first to arrive were the urban hyenas: the police who rode in the mobile lab, the coroner's van, and the other marked and unmarked cars that were now jammed into the parking area closest to the scene of the kill.

Next were the vultures perched above the carnage. Here they were in the guise of Rouse's neighbors. Those curious, scared, or thrill-seeking spectators who lined the walkway on the building's second floor and would wait until the hyenas departed before swooping down and picking through whatever remained.

Franco climbed out and joined Weall on the driver's side of the car.

"I wonder if the lion will sleep tonight?" he asked, as they walked toward the apartment.

Weall glanced over, a curious expression on his face.

"What lion?"

"The one we're cleaning up after."

"I don't understand?"

Franco shrugged.

"Just a thought."

"You want to share it?"

Franco shook his head and they covered the remaining hundred feet in silence.

A tall, pleasant man with mirrored sunglasses was posted at the apartment door. He wore an FBI badge on the left lapel of a tan trenchcoat.

"Good afternoon, Sal," he smiled. "Good to see you again."

Franco nodded a greeting. He had no idea who the man was, and decided he was one of the endless faces he had lectured at one time or the other.

"Keeping out of trouble?" Franco said good-naturedly.

"I keep trying."

"I've been there," Franco smiled, as he gestured toward the apartment's interior. "Dunnigan Cox inside?"

"I haven't seen him come out," the agent replied.

Franco nodded and, with Weall following, entered the apartment just as a technician popped a flash, then another as he took photographs of a small dining area just to the right of the door. Franco looked to the left. Two fingerprint technicians were in the process of dusting the books and other items that lined a full wall in what was obviously the apartment's living room.

"Where's Cox?" he asked one of the men.

"In the bedroom," the man answered, not bothering to look up. "Straight down the hall and off to the left."

Franco looked briefly to Weall, said nothing, and together they began walking down the hall.

Reaching the bedroom, Franco paused in the doorway and allowed his senses to develop impressions. The room was a bit larger then he expected. Nevertheless, it also appeared quite overfurnished. A contemporary, light ash and ebony king-size bed dominated and matched an eight-foot dresser with mirror, a seven-drawer chest-on-chest, and the two night tables that flanked the bed's headboard. Directly across from the bed and between the closet and bathroom doors, a large color television was set atop what looked to be an old parson's table.

Franco glanced back to the bed. He counted four king-size pillows with black silk covers. The sheets appeared to be of similar material. A charcoal-colored spread was rumpled at the foot of the bed, and this matched the dark-gray, deep-pile carpeting.

On the other side of the bed, on the floor between the mattress and chest-of-drawers, lay the stiffening body of Robert Rouse. At his head knelt Dunnigan Cox. He was placing bits of fingernail scrapings onto glass slides, then into glassine envelopes which he carefully marked for identification. Franco walked over to Cox and stared down at the corpse. It appeared white, hairless, and flabby. Dried feces was visible between the thighs, and congealing blood had pooled beneath the skull.

"Head shot?" Franco asked Cox.

Cox glanced up, then returned his attention to the slides.

"No, Agent Franco," he said absently. "Puncture wound."

"Type of weapon?"

"I don't know," Cox interrupted. "We have to wait for the autopsy."

"But no gunshot?" Franco repeated.

Dunnigan Cox stood and yelled, "Alright, move him out!" to a technician standing in the doorway next to Weall.

Momentarily, two men came in with a stretcher, picked Rouse's body off the floor and lowered it into a open black plastic bag. They zipped the bag closed, lifted it to the stretcher, and carried it out.

"I'm sorry," Cox apologized. "What did you say?"

"No gunshot," Franco said, making it a statement.

"No. Definitely a puncture wound. Larger than an ice pick, maybe a stiletto or something similar."

"Any forced entry?" Franco asked.

"No," Cox answered. "All the windows still have paint around the seals. It looks as if they haven't been opened for years."

"What about the door? Tool marks? Any signs of picking?"

"None," Cox said. "Nor was there any indications of the deceased putting up a struggle."

Franco considered this for a long moment. *No struggle, no forced entry.* Why?

Two reasons: Rouse knew his killer and let him in or, Rouse had no reason to think someone he didn't know would do him any harm. Problem. Why in the bedroom? Franco looked back to Dunnigan Cox.

"Was he killed here, or brought in here?"

"He was killed in here," Cox said quickly.

"What was he doing?"

"I have no idea," Cox admitted. "Most likely, he was standing in front of that chest-of-drawers."

"Facing the attacker?"

"It appears not. From the positioning of the body and the angle of the wound, I would say the attacker approached from behind."

"So he was definitely awake?" Franco pressed.

Cox's eyes narrowed.

"What are you getting at?"

Franco nodded back toward the hallway.

"Well," he explained. "It's only about twenty feet from here to the front door. It seems to me he would have heard the front door opening. Did you note any evidence of his wearing a hearing aid?"

"No," Cox said.

"So even if the attacker used a key, it stands to reason Rouse would have heard him. Correct?"

Cox shrugged.

"Your extrapolating, Agent Franco. I don't believe in. . . ."

"I know that," Franco interrupted. There was no reason to pursue it. In the larger sense, he knew Rouse hadn't known the attacker. In the more direct context, he knew Rouse had allowed the attacker entry. He changed the subject.

"The neighbor canvassing in progress?"

"Yes," Cox told him. "And everything even remotely portable in this room will be tagged, brought in, and analyzed."

Franco grunted his approval.

"Rouse is being taken to Walter Reed like the other two?"

"Yes," Cox said. "A Major . . . ."

"McLain," Franco nodded. "I remember. Thanks, Dunnigan, I'll be at Walter Reed if you need me."

Turning away, Franco looked back to the hallway. Weall was gone. He found him waiting outside talking with the agent in the sunglasses.

"Are you ready?" Franco asked.

"More than ready," Weall admitted. "I couldn't stand the smell in there."

"A little ripe for me, too," the agent cheerfully chimed in. "That's why I'm glad I'm standing out here."

The feces, Franco thought. Strangely enough, he hadn't even noticed the odor.

Once upon a time he *had* noticed and, once upon a time, like Weall and Sunglasses, he, too, had loitered at crime scenes and exchanged these same kind of juvenile *seeing something nasty* comments.

Once upon a time, Franco thought, as he looked down and fingered the wedding band on his right hand. But not now. Not ever since Puerto Rico.

"How'd you stand it, Sal?" Sunglasses grinned.

Franco looked to the agent, then to Weall who also had a smile on his face.

"Let's just get the fuck out of here," he said, already walking away.

Weall caught up with him a few steps later.

"What's the matter with you?" Weall snapped.

"Nothing," Franco whispered.

"You're acting like some dilettante."

"I just want to get over to Walter Reed."

Weall thought for a moment.

"I'm not sure I can go with you."

"Don't worry, Jonathon. I don't particularly need you to come along. Just drop me back at the office and I'll get my car."

Weall could think of nothing to say and there was no conversation on the drive back into Washington.

Franco thought it just as well. At Walter Reed there would be autopsies and organs, liquids and odors. Jonathon would probably find it all snickeringly nasty.

Body fluids and little boys.

Such were the eyes of a child.

CHAPTER 30

Walter Reed Army Hospital, 2:45 P.M.

"... kidneys are similar in size, shape, appearance and together weigh, uh, 190 grams. The capsules strip with ease and reveal a smooth, homogeneous, cortical surface. Upon sectioning, the gross renal architecture is not remarkable and the ureters and urinary bladder remain intact, the latter containing, uh, say about 300 milliliters of amber fluid. The prostate gland is not remarkable, and the testes are similar in size, shape and appearance. The tunica is intact and upon section, the tubules string with ease. The epididymides are not remarkable, appearing nearly . . . ."

Only vaguely aware of specifics, Franco continued to stare out the fourth-floor window while behind him Robert Rouse, in a pathological sense, revealed secret after secret. Franco experienced a strange awareness. It was as if he were standing in the margin that demarcated two, totally discordant spheres.

Inside the VIP autopsy suite, livers were smooth and glistening, spleens beefy red and diffluent, and aortas, elastic and patent. This was the sphere in which the private became public and all was duly examined, dissected, and transcribed.

The second sphere, that which he could observe through the window, was just the opposite. It seemed as lenient as inside did stern.

Authorized by Teddy Roosevelt and named for the U.S. Army officer credited with conquering yellow fever in the early 1900s, the grounds more resembled a college campus and still comprised over 200 orderly, landscaped acres less than thirty minutes up 16th Street from the White House.

To the public, Franco knew, the facility was little more than another stop on the tour bus. And indeed, the tourists came in droves. The reason was curiosity. Walter Reed offered a splendid geek show, and in one of its museums there existed the world's largest collection of actual human and animal anomalies. From tumors the size of watermelons to two-headed babies to three-legged men, all were on display to shock, educate, or fascinate.

But what the tourists did not see were the closed VIP facilities sponsored by Walter Reed's Armed Forces Institute of Research. Why? The reason was rather self-serving. The institute was dependent on federal funding, and there was little humanitarian rationale behind the congressional largesse. The fact of the matter, Franco knew, was that Walter Reed was where most presidents, statesmen, and senior military officers went to receive treatment for those maladies which could be interpreted as being *controversial* in nature. Neurosis, psychosis, even schizophrenia—for more than seventy years these potential embarrassments had been secretly and efficiently addressed. And if its museums had skeletons, Franco would bet their numbers would pale when compared to those locked within the institute's executive files.

"The invisible touch," he whispered to himself. Discretion was a financially profitable enterprise. The institute had no need for want.

". . . the heart weighs 300 grams and there are no thrombi in any of the four chambers. The foramen ovale is not patent and valves remain intact as do the, uh, trabeculae carneae muscles . . . ."

Franco turned from the window and directed his attention back to the autopsy suite. Three stainless steel tables held the bodies of Gustav Celt, William Pointer, and Robert Rouse, respectively, shot, burned, and stabbed. The bodies remained uncovered and looked waxy-dank, not unlike cue balls on a billiard table, as the skins reflected back the glow of each table's overhead surgical light.

Their turn finished, Celt and Pointer remained partially dissected and organically hollow. Rouse continued to give up organs to Maj. Jim McLain, who now had both hands inside the chest cavity and was feeling around as if searching for something hard in a vat of soft, wet mud.

He found the item shortly. In what Franco thought to be a "Little Jack Horner" maneuver, the pathologist plucked out a small dark object and examined it closely as he shifted it from palm to palm.

". . . the thymus weighs twenty grams and is somewhat fibro-fatty and mildly autolyzed . . ."

Franco watched as McLain tossed the tissue into a clean stainless-steel bowl and reached back into Rouse's chest. Since the autopsy had been in progress when Franco arrived, the two men had not been afforded the opportunity to be formally introduced, nor had they even begun to discuss any physical findings. Nevertheless, Franco suspected he would find himself liking the officer due to his casual, yet professional approach to pathology. His attitude, Franco decided, was an almost second nature in manner, that of a man who had done this many, many times before and was prepared to stand by his decisions. Franco doubted little, if anything, would be overlooked.

" . . . the left lung weighs 400 grams and the right, uh, say 500, because, uh, the former is slightly collapsed and the latter, uh, rather hyperaerated . . ."

He was getting tired, Franco realized. No doubt, three autopsies in a row.

" . . . the trachea and bronchi contain no foreign material . . ."

Watching McLain, Franco was reminded of an old sepia Matthew Brady photograph: *Union Field Hospital, Chancellorsville, 1863*. It was not really that different. The surgeon's smock remained bloodstained, and his instruments remained large and crude knives, hatchets, and saws.

As for the surgeon himself?

Franco began to speculate. In his late thirties, McLain was a tall, lean man whose physique indicated participation in aerobic exercise. He was bearded and balding in front, and any remaining hair was streaked with gray. With dark, quick eyes behind half-frame lenses, he had the body of a dancer and moved around the corpses with familiarity and ease. Franco smiled. McLain would eat no salt or butter, no fried food, and would decline a martini in favor in mineral water. Upon the occasion of his own autopsy, he would want to give his fellow pathologists something to talk about.

McLain would have done well at Chancellorsville, Franco suspected. He appeared to concede the impermanence of life.

"Any more lined up outside?"

Franco suddenly realized McLain was speaking to him.

"I'm sorry. What did you say?"

McLain gestured a bloody finger toward the door.

"Any more?"

"No," Franco said.

A flush of relief colored the pathologist's face.

"Good. I'm two hours late for lunch. You're Franco?"

"Sal Franco, Major . . . ."

"It's Jim," McLain corrected, as he snapped off his latex surgical gloves and casually draped them across Rouse's left shin. "I wear my brass tarnished."

Franco glanced down at the officer's shoes. They looked as if they had been polished with steel wool. McLain obviously cared little about military appearance. Briefly, Franco wondered why he hadn't resigned and moved on to more profitable pastures.

"I returned my brass back in '78," Franco finally said. "I remember it being pretty tarnished at the time."

McLain pulled off the bloodied smock and tossed it atop the gloves. Underneath he was wearing a plain dark-green T-shirt and blue surgical pants.

"Then we don't have to stand on ceremony, do we?" McLain said.

"Not as far as I'm concerned," Franco shrugged.

McLain smiled openly.

"Can I buy your lunch, Franco?"

"Make it close."

"Fifth-floor commissary close enough?"

"Is the food any good?"

McLain furrowed his brow and peered skeptically over the tops of his glasses.

"Wednesday's always the Mexican fiesta," he said, already turning toward the door. "This is the army. Let your conscience be your guide."

"*Olé,*" Franco said as he followed McLain out.

***

Even at the relatively late hour, the commissary remained crowded and, upon entering, Franco was hit with the sensation of mouths either chewing or gossiping, hands either dabbing or pointing, and feet either tapping or walking. From somewhere there was a great crash of silverware, and from ceiling speakers out-of-place *mariachi* rhythms could barely be heard over the general confusion.

"This is a nice, quiet place to talk," Franco quipped, as they moved to the head of the cafeteria-style serving line. "Reminds me of a Kansas City feed lot."

McLain grabbed a wet tray, then another that he handed to Franco.

"They're all just grousing about something," he said, raising his voice. "Don't worry, we'll find a corner somewhere."

Franco nodded and looked to his left. On the wall, next to the stacked trays, was a large 1940-ish poster of a uniformed army nurse with an index finger poised to her lips. Printed at the bottom were the words, *Ssssh— Hospital.*

Franco started to say something but, looking back to his right, he could see that the pathologist was already moving down the serving line. He quickly fell in behind and, realizing just how wrong he had been about the major's diet, watched in amazement as McLain stacked dish after dish on his tray.

"You sure you're not working for the Red Cross?" Franco asked, as they reached the cashier and waited to pay.

A curious expression crossed McLain face.

"No," he said. "Why?"

Franco nodded to McLain's tray which contained at least two of everything on the Mexican fiesta menu.

"You've got enough food there to feed Ethiopia for a month."

McLain winked and indicated Franco's tray which held only a taco salad and a glass of iced tea.

"I used to eat like that," he said. "Watch everything. Do the food group shuffle. But I said screw it. I've never had a weight problem anyway and than I began to wonder why. Then something dawned on me. I even submitted an article about it to the *New England Journal of Medicine.* Of course, they rejected it. I assume they thought my thesis too uncomplicated to merit publication."

"About how to stay thin and still eat everything?" Franco asked.

McLain nodded and became serious.

"That was part of it. But it was mostly about digestion. It's a phenomenon I noticed one morning. I termed it *defikitis*."

"What was your thesis?" Franco asked, as they paid the bill and began looking for a table.

McLain sighed almost forlornly.

"That everything you eat turns to shit."

Tray in hand, Franco stopped and stared at the pathologist. At first McLain' face remained impassive. Then, first at the corners of the eyes, then the lips, Franco detected the beginnings of a grin.

He nodded knowingly.

"You reeled me in on that one, didn't you?"

McLain laughed.

"People always believe doctors," he said. "It's the American way."

"Kind of gives credence to holistic healing."

McLain shrugged.

"Makes me no difference. All my patients are already dead. Seems like if the cancers don't get you the herbal teas will."

"Or the bombs or the bullets?"

"Yes," McLain said softly. "Them too. Come on, let's eat before it gets cold.

True to his word, McLain found them a table in the corner. The problem, as far as Franco was concerned, was that it was in the corner next to the restrooms and every time the doors opened, the stench of commercial disinfectants wafted in the air. He decided not to mention it.

"So why pathology?" he asked instead.

"Inquisitiveness," McLain said, as if having answered the question many times before. "I've always wondered why things break. When I was a child, I'd take broken things apart. Radios, clocks, took an old Ford six-cylinder apart once."

Franco took a bite of his salad.

"Most kids try to fix things," he said.

"I know," McLain nodded, as he reached over picked up the pepper and doused his plates. "But I never fixed anything. Never cared to. All I wanted to know was why things broke."

"Guess the writing was on the wall early."

"So it seems," McLain agreed. "The machines got more and more complex, animals in college, cadavers in medical school, the really strange things I see here. You know, they send me bodies from all over the world?"

"I know they do research here."

"Yeh," McLain said. "It's receiving-end research. All the rockets and stuff like that? Well, when someone gets themselves killed, I get to take them apart and see, specifically, how the rockets or whatever actually killed them."

"Kind of like a quality control inspector?"

McLain smiled at the implication.

"Yes, I suppose. I've never really looked at it like that but, I guess, for the weapons industry, that's exactly what I am."

"It takes a lot of feathers to make a war bonnet."

"That's what they say," McLain shrugged. "But, personally, I try not to dwell on that part of it. I think everybody loses in war."

McLain bit off half a taco, chewing pensively as he continued.

"I guess it goes back to what I said earlier."

"Receiving-end research?"

"Before that . . . inquisitiveness. I just like to find out why things break."

Franco finished his salad and watched McLain for a long moment.

"You really do enjoy it, don't you?"

McLain nodded and wiped his mouth on a napkin.

"Yes, Franco, I do." He tossed the napkin to the table. "So, what do you need to know?"

"Your general impressions."

"Are you going to give me anything to go on?"

Franco shook his head. "Not yet."

McLain understood. Franco wanted a clean opinion. He would offer no additional background data that might prejudice the autopsy findings.

"Decedent one," McLain began, speaking in careful, measured phrases. "Gunshot wound to the upper chest cavity. Quite typical. It could have been a hunting accident, could have been a war wound. As I said, nothing special."

"You're the one who recovered the projectile?"

"Yes," McLain nodded. "They analyze it yet?"

"Yes," Franco said, offering no details. "What about Pointer."

"Yes," McLain said. "Decedent two. Pointer suffocated . . . ."

"But I thought he would have burned to death."

McLain made an obliging gesture with his hand.

"He would have, had he lived that long. The fact of the matter is that I found almost a total glazing of both the bronchi and the alveoli."

A curious expression crossed Franco's face. McLain noticed it.

"It's not really that uncommon," he explained. "It usually manifests itself in napalm attacks or when gasoline tankers explode. There is an ignition and a vacuum is created. During the vacuum, similar to being hit in the solar plexus, all air is forced from the lungs. Autonomically, the phrenic nerve responds, the intercostal muscles contract, and the lungs expand. Unfortunately there is no oxygen. There is only the burning napalm or burning gasoline or burning whatever. In this case, however, I found no petroleum residue. Of course, after the tissue samples are analyzed, I'll know for sure, but from just what I've seen, I'd say Pointer sucked in some kind of flammable gas. Am I close?"

Franco nodded as his respect for the pathologist grew.

"Very close," he said. "But we'll get back to that. Tell me about Robert Rouse."

McLain took deep breath. Glancing around, he leaned closer to Franco.

"Pathologically," he whispered. "I found him to be the most interesting."

"Why was that?"

"How he died. The others could have possibly been accidents. Rouse was murdered. I know that much."

"Want to speculate?"

McLain shifted slightly in his chair.

"No need for speculation," he said. "He died from a penetration wound to the brain. A screwdriver, a Phillips screwdriver to be exact. There were a number of metal fragments, slivers really, which have also been couriered to your lab. I would think it should be a new screwdriver."

"Why the side entry instead of the base of the skull?" Franco asked.

McLain shrugged.

"Personal preference, training, whatever, the killer was definitely right-handed though. And something else, this behind-the-ear thing? You know, it is a relatively new technique?"

"No I didn't," Franco admitted.

McLain nodded cautiously.

"Everything progresses," he said. "Korea was the throat cutting, Vietnam the base-of-the-skull penetrations you asked about, and now lateral punctures are the fashion. Each technique, at least in the pathological sense, is a bit more efficient that its predecessor."

McLain shook his head.

"What?" Franco asked.

"They call it *pithing*," McLain said.

"Who does?"

"The clandestine tactics cadre at Ft. Bragg. They're the ones who perfected it. A spike is the weapon of choice, and the indention behind the ear lobe is the point of entry. The word *pithing* refers to the fact that the spike literally eradicates the nerve ganglia that bind the brain stem to the medulla—the brain's pith, so to speak."

"How long have they been teaching it?" Franco asked.

"Oh, I don't know," McLain said. "Ten, maybe eleven years."

"And this is a course of instruction in our military now?"

"No, not for everybody," McLain said. "Just the special operations types: rangers, special forces, SEALs, Delta. I suppose they don't have anything else to do but sit around and dream up ways of killing one another.

And even I have to admit some of them are quite ingenious. You wouldn't believe what they can do with a gallon of bleach and a few Tylenol gel tabs."

Franco didn't want to know. He redirected the conversation.

"So you're saying whoever *pithed* Rouse was trained at Ft. Bragg?"

McLain shook his head.

"Not at all. Ten years ago? A qualified maybe. Now? The technique's everywhere. That kind of stuff spreads fast. In a manner of speaking, I guess you could say it becomes fashionable. The winners write the history and the losers learn the lessons."

Franco understood the meaning. Pithing was now probably both a term of art, as well as an accepted exercise for half the world's standing armies. It would prove itself a waste of time to try to locate everyone who possibly knew the technique. On the other hand, this could well become a valuable piece of information when building the case background on the assassin, presuming, of course, he ever arrested the man.

"Okay, Agent Franco," McLain said. "You want to tell me what's going on?"

"I think the same person killed all three men," Franco said softly.

McLain leaned back in his chair and sucked his teeth as he thought over the autopsy findings.

"I was hoping you could give me an angle I've overlooked," Franco added, after a moment.

"I wish I could," McLain said. "Unfortunately, pathologically, the causes of death appear totally unrelated."

"I can't buy that," Franco sighed.

"Well, then, give *me* something," McLain said. "I can keep a secret."

Franco looked across the table. Peering above the top of his glasses, there was a sincere, almost intent expression on McLain's face.

"It's not the kind of thing you can draw a nice little box around," Franco said.

"Then try for a circle," McLain smiled. "That's one big angle."

"Is that anything like a glass being half empty or half full?"

"It's everything if you're thirsty," McLain nodded.

Franco chuckled, then, for the next ten minutes, he explained the situation. He held nothing back, and the pathologist grunted responses to Shining Path, the telephone calls, the bits of previously gleaned evidence and mostly, Franco's intractable *why these particular men* question.

"I can see where you get your drift," McLain said, when Franco finished. "Their selection does seem rather remarkable. But still, it's like I said, no pathological connection. Even the toxicology findings: alcohol, serology, drug screens, nothing in common. Not even the . . . *McLain you dumb shit!"*

"What?" Franco asked, surprised by the outburst.

"Come on," McLain ordered as he stood up from the table.

"Where are we going?"

"Back to the shop."

"You've got something?" Franco asked, as they hurried toward the elevators.

"No," McLain said. "They've got something . . . something in common."

Before Franco could ask the obvious question, the pathologist turned and looked him directly in the eyes.

"They each have an identical scar in an identical location."

For some reason the word "cult" jumped into Franco's mind, but before be could wonder about its significance, the elevator doors opened. Stepping inside, he was aware of the word fading as the car jerked into motion.

Its memory left him warm.

He remembered to remember the feeling.

***

Chilled flesh on cold steel, the autopsy suite remained the same. McLain had pulled on a fresh pair of surgical gloves and was standing over the body of Robert Rouse.

"Here," he said. "Look at this."

Hands behind his back, Franco leaned over and watched as the pathologist slid his fingers between Rouse's right upper arm and chest and began to slowly pull the arm away from the torso. Holding it with one hand, he then touched a gloved finger on a point central to and perhaps three inches beneath Rouse's armpit.

"They all have one of these," McLain said matter-of-factly.

Franco inspected the blemish. It was not big, surely no larger than a quarter. But it was not round. Franco decided it more, what? *Squarish* in appearance? But not an exact square either. Mostly round and squarish at the same time.

Franco reached up and adjusted the overhead lamp, then he looked back to the spot. It was an odd color, he thought. Not red, like a welt; not blue, as from surgery. He shifted the light again and watched the scar change. Now it was different. More puffy. An ugly little ashen thing.

"Gum," he said softly.

McLain arched an eyebrow.

"Gum?"

"Yeh," Franco said. "It looks like a chewed piece of gum."

"It's a burn scar," McLain explained as he examined it between thumb and forefinger.

"It doesn't look like any burn scar I've ever seen."

"Capillarity is absent," McLain said. "The color changes when the heart ceases function."

Franco found himself wondering what Alicia Carrera's breasts looked like now that she was dead. He suspected like larger wads of gum.

" . . . to the barrel of an automatic weapon."

Franco realized the pathologist was explaining something.
"I'm sorry," he apologized. "My mind was wandering."
McLain nodded.
"I was saying the scar is quite similar to some of the facial burns I've seen. Like when someone is killed while firing an automatic weapon? Well, in many cases, when wounded, they fall over their weapon and the barrel—a red-hot barrel—touches their exposed skin. If it remains in contact with the skin, you have this general type of scaring."

McLain made a *voila* gesture with his hands. Unfortunately, from Franco's point of view, it seemed a little premature. The pathologist's opinion only added to the puzzle.

"Now," McLain went on, as they moved to next table. "Look at Celt. There is the same type of scaring."

Franco leaned over the table. In the identical location, an identical gum-like wad was clearly visible on the skin. He said nothing.

"And finally," McLain added. "Mr. Pointer."

Working swiftly, the pathologist eased Pointer's arm away from the torso. For some reason the skin where the arm touched the torso was not really burned, and Franco was reminded of someone who had fallen asleep while sunbathing. There was a distinct line between the seared flesh and that which had been touching other skin and not exposed to the flame. He asked why this was, and McLain explained it was typical for someone caught in a vapor flame. He likened it to Hiroshima where only the skin directly exposed to the blast was burned.

"He was nude when the fire flashed," McLain said casually. "Still, I doubt he felt any pain."

Pain, Franco thought. It was the furthest thing from his mind. There, on his arm, perched snugly just below the armpit, was a third piece of gum-like matter.

"Seen enough?" McLain asked.

Franco nodded and began walking toward the suite door. The pathologist joined him outside.

"So what do you think?" he asked.

"I don't know," Franco admitted. "I wanted something to link them together, but . . ." He turned and looked at McLain. "You tell me, why would all three men have a weapon scar under their armpits?"

McLain shook his head emphatically.

"I didn't say it was a weapon scar. I said it was similar. As a practical matter, anything could have caused it."

"You said metal."

"Yes," McLain nodded. "Metal, hot metal to be exact. But, regardless, you saw the scars. Not exactly calligraphy, I don't think. No, they could have been caused as easily by a fireplace poker as an angle iron."

Franco agreed. Besides, at this juncture, the *what caused it* was a long second to the *what might the scars indicate* train of thought. He decided to change the subject.

"Is there any type of surgical procedure that would result in that kind of scar tissue?"

"None currently accepted. A long time ago people used to cauterize wounds to stop bleeding."

"And how old are those scars in there?" Franco asked, nodding back toward the autopsy suite.

A whimsical expression crossed the pathologist's face.

"Not that old," he chuckled. "Cauterization's like ancient history unless you're from some island in the Java Sea. And those three weren't. There was enough fat in their arteries to deep-fry Phoenix."

Franco smiled as McLain continued.

"As for the age of the scars? Best guess, thirty-five, maybe forty years, maybe more. But, whatever, it's not cauterization. I'm sure of that."

"How so?"

"I would have noticed the evidence of any wound during the autopsies. Internal tissue also scars."

"I didn't know that."

McLain seemed to miss the comment.

"I think something was removed," he said, almost to himself. "Maybe a wart. A tumor. Hell, that's not right either, those scars aren't surgical. You know, Franco, it's almost like they all underwent some kind of ritual for something. But even if you take off forty years, they would have all still been in their mid to late thirties and that's a little old to be passing around the old fireplace poker, don't you think?"

The word "cult" flashed in Franco's mind a second time.

"What about a tattoo?" he asked.

McLain nodded slowly.

"Could be," he said. "It sure would have had to been small though."

"Yeh," Franco said. "Something small, but something probably significant. Something all three found themselves sharing sometime in their lives. Is there any way of telling for sure if it was a tattoo? Tissue samples? Some kind of microscopic analysis?"

McLain shook his head.

"Not in this instance," he said slowly. "The scars are too traumatic. There wouldn't be any ink remaining because the skin that was stained no longer exists."

"Great," Franco sighed. "I'm back to scars for scars' sake. I feel like a blind man in a swimming pool. I know the steps lead out, but I can't find the corner."

"I wish I could give you more."

"You've done your part. I wanted a connection; you've given me one."

As Franco's voice trailed off, both men fell silent, each sensing the conversation had run its course.

"So," McLain said, after a moment. "How about a slice of cheesecake? There's always chocolate cheesecake on Wednesday."

"I wish I could," Franco answered. "But I need to be getting back. Besides, I've got a cold sore on my tongue. Chocolate would only make it worse."

"Let me see," McLain ordered.

Franco glanced around, then stuck out the tip of his tongue.

McLain leaned closer, cocked his head to one side and uttered a clucking sound as he studied the tiny white canker.

"Umm," he nodded with recognition. "The sly and elusive *Aphthous stomatis*. An exquisite little virus, I must say."

"Think I'll live?" Franco asked.

"You just need some steroid creme," McLain smiled. "Stop by the first-floor dispensary on your way out. I'll call down and tell them to give you a tube of Lidex on my tab."

"I appreciate it."

The pathologist dismissed the remark with the wave of a hand.

"Nonsense," he said. "I kind of like to keep touch every now and then. You're the first live patient I've had in ten years."

"That's comforting," Franco chuckled, as they began walking toward the elevators.

"It's what Hippocrates would want," McLain shrugged. "Oh, and just so you'll know, the canker? Probably caused by stress compounded with a bad diet."

"It comes with the territory," Franco said.

As they reached the elevators, Franco shook the pathologist's hand before stepping into an open car.

"I'll call and let you know how this works out," he said.

Behind the glasses, McLain's eyes sparkled as his face split into a wide grin.

"Call me for cheesecake. I'd like that best."

Franco only smiled as the doors slid closed.

He knew he'd just met an honest man.

Cheesecake it would be.

CHAPTER 31

Georgetown, Washington, D.C., 4:50 P.M.

Martin's Tavern was exactly what a Georgetown pub should be, dark, wooden, a long venerable bar, and waiters in dark-green jackets. Since its opening in 1933, it had catered to Washington's sports aficionados. Even after five decades, most of it had been left unchanged. It was masculine, clubby, and tobaccoishly rugged. It was also quite crowded.

Shoving through the Wisconsin Avenue entrance, Franco paused and looked around. Across the room, at the far end of the bar, he could see Jonathon Weall perched atop a weary barstool. Through talking heads and mingling bodies, Franco threaded to Weall's side where a second stool was tipped forward against the bar.

"I see you've been back to the office," Weall said, as Franco pulled the vacant stool upright and sat down.

Franco nodded. After returning from Walter Reed, he had found the third personnel file, Rouse's, on his desk. Paper-clipped to one corner was one of Jonathon Weall's typical typed notes: `Martin's, till seven, Weall.`

Adding the Rouse file to the previous two, Franco had immediately left for Georgetown. He was feeling tired again, and at least at a tavern he could drink while trying to outguess Jonathon's second guessing.

"So?" Weall asked, as Franco settled in. "Buy you a drink?"

"A tall scotch and water."

Weall summoned the bartender and ordered Franco's drink, then a white wine for himself. Franco noticed Weall still had a full glass of wine sitting in front of him.

"Going to one of your disease-of-the-month benefits tonight, Jonathon?"

Weall smiled politely.

"No," he said. "I have a meeting at seven. Some old associates from State."

Franco nodded knowingly.

"Let me guess," he teased. "I'm envisioning a private room at La Maison replete with chamber music and a bunch of Foggy Bottom types wearing old school ties and nibbling mushrooms stuffed with little green things."

Weall chuckled.

"Something like that," he said. "You want to come along?"

"I'd rather spend a year in a Turkish prison," Franco said, as the bartender returned with the drinks. Reaching over, Franco swirled his scotch once, then raised his glass to Weall.

"Thanks for the drink, sailor," he smiled.

Weall returned the toast and took a sip of his wine.

"You know something, Sal?"

"What's that?"

"You're making me get that feeling again."

"What feeling?" Franco asked.

"The one that makes me think you've been out doing something I really don't want to know about."

"Not this afternoon," Franco said. "I don't even think I inadvertently hurt any feelings."

"Hope springs eternal," Weall said thoughtfully, becoming serious. "So how was Walter Reed? Anything positive?"

Franco flipped a palm back and forth.

"*Más o menos*. But I don't know what it means yet."

"It would be nice if you told me about it. I am your supervisor, in case you've forgotten."

Franco took a quick sip of his scotch.

"What do you know about scars?" he began.

A blank expression crossed Weall's face. Franco recognized it for what it was and began to elaborate. For the next few minutes he briefly touched on, in order, armpits, cauterization, pithing, and, finally, the mole, tumor, and tattoo speculation.

"One would think the pathologist could have narrowed it down more than that," Weall said, after Franco finished. "Perhaps we should have someone more schooled evaluate his findings?"

"Well, unless they can read tea leaves, it's not going to do any good. Nobody can evaluate something that isn't there anymore."

"Just a thought," Weall shrugged, wishing he hadn't mentioned it in the first place.

"No, Jonathon," Franco added. "The answer's got to be in their files someplace. I've got all three out in the car and I'm not going to sleep tonight until I find it."

Before Weall could respond, Franco abruptly stood.

"What?" Weall asked.

"I'll be at the house," Franco told him.

"Don't you want another drink?"

"It doesn't taste right tonight. Thanks for the thought anyway."

Weall glanced back to Franco's glass. It remained three-quarters full. He turned back to say something, but Franco was already gone.

Somewhat miffed, Weall checked his watch. 5:20 p.m.

From Georgetown, it would take no longer than fifteen minutes to reach the meeting. But Franco had been wrong. Tonight there would be no old school ties nor chamber music. Tonight's meeting would be a two-man session in the open cold of the Jefferson Memorial.

Weall took a sip of his wine.

And what to do until time to leave?

Weall summoned the bartender.

"My usual," he told the man. "A double order."

Martin's served excellent crab cakes; he would sample them at leisure. And later, before the meeting, he would remember to eat a mint.

Eisler despised fish breath.

CHAPTER 32

The Stouffer's Concourse Hotel, 5:45 P.M.

Jerked from a very small place, Cory's eyes snapped opened. The rapping at his door continued. He felt fear, then irritation, as he recognized the now familiar surroundings.

Instinctively he raised his watch to his eyes.

"Shit." The wake-up call wasn't scheduled for another half-hour yet.

The DO NOT DISTURB sign?

Three thoughts: someone had removed it, someone couldn't read, someone who knew Brian Kellogg was registered in the hotel.

He considered the third option: Pock, Eisler, possibly the woman. Out of the three, he knew Pock would be the most likely. Of course, if the sign was missing, he would no doubt find the knocker to be another of housekeeping's domestic staffers.

Curious now, and speculating on the odds, Cory threw back the covers and walked nude to the door. The sleep had worked its magic. He felt rested, alert, and surprisingly buoyant.

"Yes?" he called through the door.

"Pock," came the muffled reply.

Should have taken the bet, Cory told himself, as he removed the security chain and unlocked the door.

As usual, Boudreaux had not dressed for the occasion. Beneath an old army field jacket, he was wearing a faded pair of jeans, a plaid woolen shirt, and old cowboy boots. On his head was a navy-blue baseball cap with the words DODGE—TOUGH TIMES, TOUGH TRUCKS stitched in gold across the front. In his left hand he carried a small, black plastic briefcase.

"I thought you were a Ford man," Cory said, indicating the hat.

"I'm going over to one of those cowboy joints in Maryland tonight," Pock grinned. "It's Dodge night. The cap always gets the ladies' attention."

"What about the redhead at your apartment?"

"Naw," Pock said. "I need variety. You know that. Why don't you go? I promise, I'll find you a big old mean one, too."

"Can't," Cory said. "Plans."

"Aw, come on, Damon. These cowboy ladies are fine specimens. Hell, you've had worse before."

"Maybe so," Cory said, doubting he could remember when. "But, really, I can't. I've someone meeting me in about an hour."

"That little Korean?"

Cory shook his head.

"Someone I don't know?" Pock asked, probing.

"I hope so," Cory smiled.

Pock nodded knowingly and looked around the room.

"Well, if you're planning on any kama sutra dancing in here tonight, you may want to get someone hot with a mop first. This place smells like dirty feet."

"You've got a lot of room to talk, Boudreaux."

"Hey," Pock said. "Big difference, Damon. I just breed them, you court them. Courting men need clean sheets."

Cory chuckled. The comment was more right than wrong.

"I'll get it taken care of," he said, turning toward the bathroom. "Come shoot the shit with me while I get cleaned up."

"I'll pass," Pock said. "I just came up to get your car keys so I could lock this in the trunk. I tried to telephone you from downstairs, but they told me you didn't want any calls."

Cory glanced back over his shoulder. Pock was holding out the briefcase.

"What's in there?" he asked.

"Your antipersonnel device," Pock said casually.

"The MON?" Cory said, as he walked over, took the briefcase, and set it on the unmade bed.

"No," Pock said. "I got to thinking about it and this is probably better. It's more directional."

Cory snapped open the suitcase and raised the lid. Inside, protected by a spongy Styrofoam collar, was a small, plastic, drum-like object. About eight inches in diameter and no larger than half that in height, the top "lid" of the mine was simply a black latex sheet secured to the casing by a thin metal clasp. From the side of the casing a small firing mechanism protruded maybe two inches. Similar in appearance, it reminded Cory of a tiny microwave timer control.

"What is this?" Cory asked. "Kind of looks like an old Soviet PNM."

"Same principle," Pock said. "Only this is an updated, Austrian version containing about a quarter-kilo of shape-cast C-4 instead of the TNT."

"Does it arm like the Soviet version?" Cory asked.

"Yeh," Pock nodded. "Just twist the arming switch. The rest is all done under the rubber. You'll need about two pounds of pressure and the striker released into the percussion cap. After that, instant detonation."

"Is anybody going to miss this?"

Pock shook his head.

"No," he said. "It's from my personal collection."

"I hate to take your only one," Cory said.

"You're not," Pock smiled slyly. "Just use it in good form. You'll have about 26,000 feet per second of velocity coming straight through that rubber lid like smoke through a chimney. It's a damn fine piece of equipment, Damon. Just remember, once it's activated, it's tough to disarm."

Just like the PMN, Cory remembered, as he snapped the briefcase closed.

"You sure you don't want me in on this thing?" Pock asked.

Cory considered his answer. He did, but he couldn't request it without Eisler's prior authorization.

"Does it show?" he asked.

Pock nodded and gestured toward the briefcase.

"You're holding that thing like you've never seen one before."

"I haven't," Cory said. "You said it was new."

"You know what the fuck I mean, Damon."

Cory felt his sense of buoyancy beginning to dwindle.

"I've got to grab a shower," he said, avoiding Pock's suggestion.

"I'll stick around if you really want to talk."

"No," Cory said. "That's okay. The keys are on the dresser over there. I'd appreciate it if you'd leave them at the front desk. Do you mind?"

"Whatever you need," Pock said, reaching over to the dresser and picking up the Camaro's keys. "Don't be afraid to get . . . ."

Pock was interrupted by the sound of water running in the bathroom and realized Cory was no longer listening. Walking to the bed, he picked up the briefcase and moved to the bathroom door. Eyes closed, Cory was leaning over the sink and appeared to be breathing the vapors of steam drifting up from the faucet.

"Keep your powder dry, Damon."

Raising his head, Cory looked over to Pock.

"I will," he said softly. "And Boudreaux?"

"What?"

"Until it's cleared, I have to travel this road alone."

Pock smiled slightly, offered an abbreviated salute, and let himself out of the room.

At the sound of the door closing, Cory looked back to the front and slowly wiped the steam from the glass. Cold blue eyes stared out at him. They mocked him. Made him angry.

"The mission, Damon," Lucius Aemilius intoned. "You have a new toy now. Yet you defer the mission in favor of the woman."

Cory said nothing and allowed the steam to remist the mirror.

"*Ira furor brevis est*," he whispered.

Anger was indeed a brief madness.

Besides, he needed the woman first.

CHAPTER 33

Falls Church, Virginia, 6:15 P.M.

Franco noticed that the Volvo was gone as he pulled the Corvette to a stop under the portico. He was not really surprised. Judging from the time that he usually arrived home, tonight was a marked exception. He was inordinately early.

Karen was probably shopping, visiting friends, or auditing some art class taught by somebody who actually knew less about whatever topic than she did.

No matter. He'd forgotten to call again and would no doubt hear about it later. Taxes notwithstanding, if anything was more certain than death, he supposed it was the inevitability of Karen's complaints about his *lack of common courtesy.*

Forgetfulness had long ceased to be a viable excuse and, once again resigning himself to this fact, Franco gathered the three personnel files, climbed out of the Corvette, plodded to the front door, unlocked it, and entered the darkened foyer.

Closing the door behind him, Franco paused to inhale the aromas of the old house: the wools, woods, even the stillness. He decided not to fumble for the light switch and soon his eyes adjusted to the gloom. Aware of deep cushioning underfoot, he walked directly to the kitchen at the far end of the hall and flipped on the overhead light.

The kitchen felt chilly, considerably colder than the foyer. Deciding to prepare a cup of tea, Franco tossed the files onto the long, scrubbed-pine dining table and moved to the sink where he filled a copper kettle and placed it on the stove. While he waited for the water to heat, he leaned against the counter and stared out the large bay window that overlooked the grounds beyond the rear of the house.

Just after dark, it was an enchanting, nearly surrealistic nightscape. The sky was clearing, and slivers of moonlight now bathed the trees and snow in the low wash of vapor drifting up from the pond and swirling into nothingness as it cooled in the northern wind.

The ducks were gone now, and the frogs and turtles were hibernating.

In another month the pond would be frozen over. Karen, of course, would be out there on the ice, chopping holes to feed the dozen large carp she had bought and nurtured and over which she continued to dote.

Franco smiled. At times, it seemed that she worried to excess. Would the ducks return from migration? Would the frogs awake from their annual nap? Would the fish need more to eat?

To be sure, Franco knew none of these answers. Yet, purposely, he acted as if he did: *yes, yes,* and *no*. If it was important to her, it would be important to him.

In the distance, Franco heard a dog barking and found himself wondering about the shooter, about the man he was hunting. Did he have a Karen somewhere? Did he indulge his mate as well? And what about children? One? Two? None? Many?

And what was the shooter doing at this precise moment? Where was he hiding? Was he lying in wait someplace? Planning? Eating? Sleeping? Considering those already dead, or stalking the next victim?

Behind him the kettle began its steamy whistle, and Franco realized that the guesses, the speculations, the feigned answers to fickle questions were getting him nowhere. The new ground was in the files, and it was time to begin reading.

Moving to the sink, he quickly fixed the tea, then returned to the dining table, sat down, and arranged the files three abreast before him. Since he had previously studied the Celt file, he decided to use it as the measure with which to compare and contrast the others.

Appropriate, he thought, as he began to read.

The files even smelled like yesterday's news.

CHAPTER 34

The Jefferson Memorial, 6:55 P.M.

Although he had driven past the columnar rotunda on hundreds of occasions, Jonathon Weall had never actually ever taken the time to visit the monument dedicated to America's third president. Tonight, early for the meeting anyway, would change all that and, turning up his collar to ward off the gusting wind off the Potomac River, he climbed the steps and entered the deserted but well-lighted inner rotunda.

On a placard next to the closed gift shop, historical information was displayed. Weall read it carefully:
Dedication, 1943
Cornerstone laid by Franklin Roosevelt.
Constructed on land reclaimed from the Potomac River Tidal Basin.
Statistics: 121 feet tall, 152 feet in diameter.

"And it's a goddamned cold 152 feet," Weall whispered, as the wind surged into a low moan as it whipped through the columns.

Shivering, Weall shoved his hands deep into his overcoat and began looking for a spot out of the wind. There was only one, the south side of the statue itself.

He moved in close and, directly beneath the monument dome, stared up at the figure towering above him.

The placard had indicated the effigy was "19 feet of bronze set atop a 6 foot pedestal of black Minnesota granite."

Odd, Weall thought, but this close the statue looked to be at least three times that height. Craning his head even farther back, he began to wonder. Was it the dome that caused the illusion, or was it the massiveness of the bronze itself?

But Jonathon Weall's questions went unanswered for, at that moment, the hairs at his nape began to twine. The voice came a moment later. It was soft and breathy.

"Good evening, Jonathon."

Weall spun to his left. Standing less than three feet away, Eisler was wearing a dark, full-length overcoat and black Irish walking hat. Eyes sparkling and with a somewhat bemused set to his lips, he was leaning forward on an umbrella and staring up toward the monument dome.

They call this place our Pantheon," he said. "You have been to Rome, Jonathon?"

"Many times."

"And the Pantheon?"

"There too."

"Can you can discern the similarities?"

"Yes," Weall remembered. "The columns. Domical roof. Perhaps the porticos."

Eisler nodded in approval.

"And the differences?"

"Well, the general appearance . . . ."

"Wait," Eisler interrupted, raising a cupped hand to his ear. "Listen, Jonathon. Can you hear it?"

Weall stopped talking, but he was aware of nothing but the low, modulated windtones.

"What?" he asked.

"The sound of homage, Jonathon," Eisler said, making a sweeping motion with his hand. "Homage and the absence of differences."

"I don't understand."

"The Pantheon, Jonathon? Was it not a place of worship? A place where each Roman god held an individual niche?"

"Yes," Weall said.

"Of course it was, Jonathon. It was an earthly Olympus. Do you not find it intriguing that we, here, should want to venerate Jefferson in the same manner as those in Roman antiquity venerated their gods?"

Weall said nothing. Eisler chuckled, raised his umbrella, and pointed it up at the statue. His voice became a whisper.

"He would have heard the homage, Jonathon. For he lived the contradiction. Against slavery, he owned slaves. Against war, he was forced to wage one."

"The Tripolitan War," Weall nodded.

Eisler did not immediately respond. Seemingly lost in thought, he paused for a long moment before looking over to Weall.

"Do you believe the contradiction was a good thing, Jonathon?"

"I suppose," Weall shrugged. "I've never thought about it."

Eisler nodded slowly.

"Perhaps I think about it to excess," he said, rather prophetically.

"And what are your thoughts?" Weall asked.

Eisler looked back up to the statue.

"That, for Jefferson, living the contradiction was the attainment of fulfillment. With contradiction comes altars like this and the Pantheon. Can you hear the homage now, Jonathon?"

Realizing he still had no idea as to the direction of this particular line of thought, Weall could manage only another feeble shrug.

Eisler accepted it with benevolent patience and, once again, indicated the statue.

"Never the mind, Jonathon. I'm sure he listens for many of us. But enough of this. Come, walk with me. Let us discuss our endeavor. Tell me about this investigator of yours. You indicated his name is Franco?"

"Sal Franco," Weall said as, together, they began to walk counterclockwise around the black marble pedestal.

Almost immediately, at least to Jonathon Weall, it became evident that the idea of a "discussion" was actually a misnomer, for what resulted during the next twenty minutes was more like an interrogation, a meticulous debriefing tempered with rigorous cross-examination.

Eisler? The wizened grand inquisitor: specific and derivative.

Himself? A witness being led: honest, yet servile.

Had Cory been identified?

Had his motive been determined?

Could Franco be recruited?

Fine lines and finer deductions, the responses to these and most of the other questions were *no* and, generally, this seemed to placate Eisler.

"Then our network remains closed," he smiled. "Is that correct, Jonathon?"

Weall thought back over the previous few minutes and attempted to remember whether he had left out some detail Eisler would view as important.

"As far as Cory goes, I don't think Franco is actually any closer than he was after the first shooting. But that is only *one* track."

Eisler paused and looked up into Weall face.

"One track?"

Weall nodded.

"There is a second track relating to the Russians' personnel files," he said. Franco is attempting to isolate any similarities."

Eisler's eyes narrowed and he began walking again. As before, Weall fell into step beside him.

"Tell me about these 'tracks,' Jonathon."

Briefly, Weall explained Franco's opinion: that the assassin was a professional who would make few, if any, mistakes. Consequently, Franco was now directing his efforts to locate some feasible reason to explain the victims' selection.

"But did not Cory manufacture a cover story?" Eisler asked, when Weall finished.

"Yes," Weall said. "And it sounded viable to me."

"But not to this investigator Franco?"

"No."

"Why is that, Jonathon?"

"I don't know."

At the answer, Eisler felt a spark of aggravation. He forced himself to not let it show.

"Nor should you be expected to," he smiled. "But this 'second track,' as you term it. Is it leading somewhere which may expose our endeavor?"

"Not as yet," Weall said. "But when I spoke with Franco earlier, he indicated he had found something which was leading him to believe that all three of the victims were somehow connected."

"And what is this connection, Jonathon?"

"It's a scar. A small scar, as Franco described it."

Eisler nodded thoughtfully.

"Beneath the right armpit, correct, Jonathon?"

Weall stopped dead in his tracks.

"Yes," he said, raising his voice a bit. "You knew about them?"

Eisler walked a few steps farther, then stopped and turned back.

"What does Franco believe is the genesis of these scars?" he asked.

"The removal of something," Weall quickly answered. "Some growth, perhaps a tattoo or . . . ."

Weall's voice trailed off as he observed Eisler reaching into his breast pocket and extracting the nub of a pencil and a small scrap of paper. Curious, he waited while the old man scribbled something on the paper then passed it over.

"That was the tattoo," Eisler said softly.

Weall glanced down at the drawing. It was a crude five-sided star with a Cyrillic letter in its center.

"Russian script," Eisler explained. "The letter B."

"What does it mean?"

"A man's initial, Jonathon. Do you recall mention of a Soviet intelligence officer named Lavrenti Pavlovich Beria?"

"Of course," Weall said. "He directed the Cheka under Stalin."

"But first under Vladimir Ilich Lenin," Eisler corrected. "Have you forgotten the history, Jonathon?"

"Of course not," Weall said tersely, offended by the question. "I *am* the Inspector in Charge of Special Intelligence."

Insolent fool, Eisler thought. Evidently Jonathon now believed he had attained his capacity by virtue of his own talents. A normal human response, but still, a bit of humiliation was unquestionably in order.

"Yes," he said softly. "A lesser position in one of the world's more mediocre intelligence agencies."

Weall bristled, but Eisler continued.

"Tell me the history, Jonathon," he said, his voice filled with disdain. "Share with me the insights of the FBI's *chief* intelligence expert."

"Don't fuck with me," Weall said coldly. "I'm not one of your military lackeys."

"You are whatever I instruct you to be," Eisler said quietly. "Tell me the history, Jonathon. I will not ask a third time."

Weall stared into Eisler's eyes. He found no emotion, no traces of compassion or understanding, only indifference, menace. Subliminally, the words collected in his mind as he lips began to move.

"Upon seizing power," he whispered. "Lenin required a mechanism with which to ferret out any counterrevolutionaries he suspected might challenge his absolute control. His model were the Jacobins, the radical French revolutionaries who employed terror as the means to their ends. Lenin's counterrevolutionary organ became the Cheka and, as it turned out, the Cheka was in itself the infrastructure upon which the KGB was later built."

Eisler said nothing as Weall, his voice becoming more confident, continued the discourse.

"Upon Lenin's death a power struggle ensued. It began to end with Trotsky's expulsion from Russia being ordered by Stalin and two other old Lenin cronies, Kamenev and Zinoviev, who then, at least in theory, ruled Russia in a kind of disproportionate triumvirate."

"And did Stalin have the greatest influence?" Eisler asked, testing his knowledge.

"No," Weall answered. "It was more fluid than that. I suppose it could best be explained by saying that Kamenev and Zinoviev began having less and less influence."

"Well put," Eisler said, offering a slight smile. "Do you recall their fates, Jonathon?"

"Lavrenti Beria sealed them," Weall said. "Beria was an early Cheka functionary who had aligned himself with Stalin in the early days. As Stalin's star rose, Beria's kept pace to the point where he eventually emerged as Stalin's linchpin when dealing with the more distasteful matters of state."

"Like Kamenev and Zinoviev," Eisler said.

"Yes," Weall nodded. "Them and a dozen or so other former Lenin comrades. At Stalin's bidding, Beria rounded up the entire group, tried them for treason, then executed them, thus ensuring Stalin's absolute control. For his efforts, Beria was appointed chief of Stalin's secret intelligence service."

Sensing, correctly, that he had plumbed the depths of Jonathon's knowledge, Eisler picked up the story.

"Beria was a man of purpose, Jonathon. Powerful, brilliant, ruthless. It was Beria who personally tracked Trotsky from Turkey to Germany to Denmark and finally to Mexico, where the assassination was effected. Elsewhere, his operations were equally ambitious: penetration of the Spanish Falangists, the Italian Facists. He even infiltrated the Nazi

Chancellery Building in Berlin. Do you remember the London *apparat*, Jonathon? Maclean, Philby, Burgess, and Blunt?"

"Yes," Weall nodded. "Very well."

"It was Beria who controlled them," Eisler said softly. "But never mind; back to the tattoos. The men who wore them were like Beria's cadre, Jonathon. The men he trusted implicitly. Proven agents who, like a monk unto his abbot, swore a blood oath to both Beria and the Soviet Union. In the cant of the times, these few, probably no more than fifty, were known as the *sosedy*, the neighbors. And to them, the tattoo was a badge of honor."

"Then why remove it?" Weall asked.

"Expediency," Eisler explained. "And also to mitigate security concerns. The *sosedy* were responsible for Beria's more surreptitious, yet grander, pursuits. There was Richard Sorge who fronted as a Nazi journalist while running a Soviet spy network in Tokyo; Manfred Weiss who attained field-grade rank on Rommel's staff; Hans Maier, the Reich's *chargé d'affaires* in Lisbon; all were *sosedy*, Jonathon. All remained in place for years. But to do so, and not be inadvertently compromised, the tattoo had to be removed, for a Russian letter in a Soviet star, well, I'm sure you can visualize the problems it could create?"

Weall nodded and Eisler continued.

"So to thwart any complications, in preparation for the deeper penetrations, there was a ritualistic cleansing wherein Beria would remove the tattoo by searing the flesh with a white-hot sickle. A few weeks later, only the scar tissue was visible."

"Does Cory know all of this?" Weall asked, as Eisler finished.

"No," Eisler said. "There was, and is, no need. The only reason I am telling you now is to explain the scars which seem to be of such interest to your Mr. Franco."

"So what would you have me do?" Weall asked, as he indicated the scrap of paper. "Tell him about this?"

Pausing, Eisler stared up at Jefferson's statue for a long moment before answering.

"No, Jonathon. I think not. I would have never known of the *sosedy* group had it not been offered by a potential KGB defector. That being the case, Mr. Franco should never be able to resolve the significance of the scars. Do you not agree?"

"I suppose," Weall said. "So what posture shall I adopt?"

"Jonathon, Jonathon," Eisler smiled, as he reached over and patted Weall's forearm. "And what is it I've have always told you?"

"To protect the network?"

"Protect the network," Eisler repeated. "I will be speaking with Cory tomorrow. He will be instructed to dispatch the remaining two Russians posthaste. You will press Mr. Franco along the lines of his second track.

Since that is the direction he is following anyway, it should be simple enough to do. Correct?"

Weall nodded.

"Yes," he said. "And while Franco moves toward a dead end, Cory will be able to complete his assignment. Tomorrow is Thursday, Jonathon. I will suggest to Cory that he be out of the country by Sunday and I assure you, my suggestion will be given his most serious consideration."

Weall had no doubt.

"As for you, Jonathon," Eisler continued. "Your nose is red. Go someplace and get warm. Will you do that for me, Jonathon?"

Weall mumbled an affirmative sound. Clearly Eisler was dismissing him. He turned to leave.

"Jonathon?" Eisler called after him.

Weall turned back.

"You are an exceptional intelligence operative, Jonathon," Eisler said. "And at the appropriate time, I shall make mention of your qualifications to the president."

"Thank you," Weall said.

Eisler's eyes sparkled.

"I want to be able to do this, Jonathon. And I thank you for allowing me the opportunity to remain your advocate."

Briefly, Weall thought to respond, but judiciously decided against it. Offering a curt nod, he walked directly to his car, started the engine, and drove into the evening.

Some minutes after Weall had left, Eisler began to once again slowly shuffle around the black marble pedestal.

Protect the network. Protect the network.

The words seemed to whisper from the cold, damp wind, and Eisler again found himself staring up to the shadow-streaked profile of Thomas Jefferson.

"It is homage we share," he said to himself, then waited.

From somewhere, the roof, the river, or maybe the rock itself, the low wind responded with desire.

Protect the network. Protect the network.

Eisler shivered, yet welcomed the cold with a satisfied smile. Three more days, and all was proceeding as planned.

The homage? he thought, as he turned to leave.

In this time, in this place, it was his alone.

QUEENWALK.

In this time, in this place, he was the network.

CHAPTER 35

The Stouffer's Concourse Hotel, 7:10 P.M.

"Ten twenty," Cory said for the third time, hoping to finally observe some flicker of understanding cross the concierge's blank face. "Maid service? Now?"

Cory was again disappointed. The man only blinked and began to thumb through some papers on his desk.

Idiot, Cory decided. Despite the black tuxedo, the ornate desk and the forehead dot, the concierge was about as impressive as a Bombay dung dealer. His teeth were bad, his breath was worse, and his eyes rotated like those of some reptile from the Kiribati Islands.

Cory looked back to the main registration desk. Jammed with late arrivals, it still looked like termites swarming beneath a rotted board. This, plus the fact that housekeeping wasn't answering the phone, is what brought Cory to the concierge in the first place. Reaching into his pocket, he pulled out a crisp $50 bill and placed it on the desk. The concierge's eyes followed the movement with a smooth independent roll while the bill was pocketed in an even smoother motion.

"Ten-twenty?" the concierge asked.

"Yes," Cory nodded. "Ten-twenty."

"You Mr. Kellogg?"

"Right again," Cory said. "I need my room cleaned within the hour."

"I will see to it immediately."

"Thanks."

Cory left the concierge to his mission and walked across the lobby to the Ondine Lounge. It, too, was relatively crowded, and, realizing he was late, he stepped just inside the door and looked for Monika Sotelo. He saw her immediately. She was sitting at the same table he and Boudreaux Pock had shared.

"Did you think I'd forgotten?" he asked, as he moved to the table and sat down across from her.

"Not at all," she smiled. "I was early."

Cory nodded to the drink on the table before her.

"Ready for another?"

She shrugged and raised her glass.

"I will be by the time you get yours. Gin."

"Gin and what?"

Her expression, not in the muscles, but in the eyes, appeared to tighten.

"Just gin," she said. "On the rocks. Do you mind?"

Admittedly, Cory thought it a bit heavy, as well as being a bit unusual. Most of the straight gin drinkers he'd met were on the way down and heading slowly toward out. This morning he hadn't noticed either direction. Curious.

"Not at all," he told her. "Mad dogs and Englishmen and noonday suns, right?"

"So it was written," she smiled, the tension gone now. "But the sun's been down for two hours. Perhaps we should start a more original story?"

There was no mistaking the innuendo in her voice. Cory returned the smile and summoned the waitress: bourbon with water, a fresh gin on ice.

"So how was your meeting?" Monika asked, when the waitress left.

"Like I thought it would be." Cory sighed. "The only thing duller than a Washington bureaucrat are his forms."

"And the only thing duller than forms is filling them out, true?"

"Too true," Cory agreed, pleased with her wit. "But what about you? How did you spend the afternoon?"

"Sightseeing," she said. "I've never been to Washington before."

At this, Cory suddenly remembered he knew absolutely nothing about Monika Sotelo other than she was Nicaraguan and interested in Central American politics. He mentioned this to her, and after the waitress returned with the drinks, sipped his quietly while she attempted to compress forty years of life into five high-pointed minutes. And although Cory wasn't aware of it at the time, her story, like his own, was substantially more fact than fiction.

Born in Nicaragua, the majority of her family had died at the hands of Somoza's soldiers. Monika, outraged, had joined the Sandinista ranks in the early seventies and had fought with them, first in the hitherlands and finally the cities.

But the revolution's success soon proved to be failure, and within weeks she faced the painful realization that with the junta firmly ensconced, the people, the poor, would fare no better and probably worse than they had under Somoza. The signs had been everywhere. The economy became a memory; medicines and doctors disappeared; and education, if one could read, was but a passing reference in a censured book of history. In the end, she who had nothing found herself with even less. Disillusioned and demoralized, she had fled Nicaragua for Paris where she now lived earning a livelihood by selecting and translating Spanish-language poetry into French for the Sorbonne's College of Contemporary Arts.

"Do you enjoy the work?" Cory asked, noting that she also spoke French.

"Sometimes," she said. "It depends on the particular text."

"I don't know anything about poetry," Cory admitted. "What if there isn't a comparable word?"

Monika smiled and took a long sip of gin.

"I make something up," she said.

A realist, Cory thought. And although she made light of it, her eyes offered opposite signals. Dark and dilating, he could almost feel the bitterness and the resignation. Looking away, he waved to the waitress and held up two fingers.

"What about the movie?" Monika asked, after a moment.

"We'll find one," Cory smiled. "Unless you're in a rush?"

"Not at all. Are you?"

Cory shook his head and lowered his voice.

"I never rush into anything."

Monika arched an eyebrow, but before she could comment, the waitress returned and placed full glasses on the table.

"So," Cory said. "What kind of sights did you see today?"

"Museums," she told him. "Art galleries. I went to the Freer first, then the Hirshhorn. I think I enjoyed the Freer most, the oriental art? I can see why . . . ."

But Cory was not as much listening as he was allowing himself to experience her persona. It was the little things to which he paid the most attention: the casual wave of her hand, a chewed fingernail, a subtle shift in posture, and the sometimes defiant tilt of the chin quickly followed by the self-conscious smile.

She seemed different than she had at breakfast, he thought. Then again, everyone seemed different at night. Most usually looked better, sounded more intelligent. Still, was it her? Or was it only what he wanted her to be?

He took a sip of his drink.

No, he decided. It was neither of these things. It was simply her and the arguably lackluster life she had allowed herself to live. If the Sorbonne was a high point, he wondered what it was that she *wasn't* telling him.

A failed revolutionary now translating poetry?

The very notion was absurd, but not altogether impossible. It was his experience that most Latinos, particularly the pseudo-revolutionaries, were predisposed to misery and the only thing they could do better than lament their destiny was to fashion even more misery.

Still, he thought. The feeling—the imperative—was present, for he could sense it coursing through his veins. In Chile, it had been the married women. In Manila, the widow. And in Guatemala, the defrocked nun, the suicide, who he had lured away from the bed of the Maryknoll priest in Antigua.

Yes, he remembered. And although a few years older, Monika Sotelo was indeed grown from the same lonely Latino seed as the others. Forgetting vows as they had been forgotten, they were old and getting older, sad and getting sadder.

Eisler, of course, had noticed his choice of women and had cared enough to mention it during one of their quarterly briefings.

"I do not understand this, Damon," he had said. "Are not their bellies loose? Their breasts distended and arid? Their hands impracticed and tentative?"

Yes, he had truthfully answered. Was that what made him covet them?

Cory remembered Eisler pausing for a long, thoughtful moment before reaching over to pat his arm and responding with a gentle: "You are too wealthy to buy, Damon, and too intelligent to insult. I will attempt to do neither. You may have these woman, but they must remain an avocation and not allowed to become an obsession. Do you understand this requirement?"

Cory had nodded and Eisler continued.

"And I must also require that they never be allowed to come between us. Discretion, Damon. If you must have them, then do so. But never permit your diversion to harm our endeavors. Take them in darkness, for in shadow commitment remains obscure. If you do this for me, if you keep your perspective, then I will always be there for you. Do you also understand this, Damon? Will you abide by my proscription?"

To both questions, Cory had answered yes, and, true to his word, Eisler had allowed the women to coexist with various assignments. From the nun, to the widow, to the two Chilean wives, Eisler had watched from afar as they were selected, seduced, and subjected to Cory's criteria.

And after they had been given some measure of companionship and pleasure? After they had been given the *Corylove*, any and all of whatever it took to give new hope to dead eyes and fresh life to melancholy hearts? Then and only then did Eisler chance to intercede and require a termination of the relationship.

And how did Eisler discern when a continuation would become counterproductive?

Cory had never known, for, depending upon the woman, times had varied. Sometimes it was a month, sometimes a year. Regardless, when Eisler determined the *Corylove* had run its useful course, he quietly intervened and Cory heeded the call, leaving the woman behind and finding his emotions again secure and indeed less confusing than those of the woman he had deserted.

And now there was Monika Sotelo, Cory thought, as he took another sip of bourbon and looked across the table. Smiling frequently, she was continuing to speak of museum exhibits.

Yes, he told himself. This one would be next. Despite being older, she was plainer than ones before. Plainer with even sadder eyes. She could be even more indebted than the others. And to make sure her indebtedness did not evolve into obsession? Perchance into suicide? He could always ask Eisler for a Paris posting.

And after the eyes began to laugh?

After he had given her the *Corylove*?

Only Eisler and Lucius would know. Only Lucius would understand.

He watched her face and imagined her nude. Desire and need, flesh and mind. They all swirled together as Cory pondered the richness of his find. God, she was so common, yet so flawlessly compelling.

" . . . to the Smithsonian, Brian?"

"I beg your pardon?" Cory said, realizing Monika had asked a question.

"I was wondering if you had ever visited the Smithsonian castle?"

"Many times," he told her.

"Tell me about it."

Cory nodded and began to stuff his pipe.

They would leave the lounge two drinks later.

CHAPTER 36

Falls Church, Virginia, 8:40 P.M.

Sal Franco dabbed an excessive amount of Lidex to the tip of his tongue. Little do little good, he thought wryly. Like most people, he hoped the more medicine he applied, the more rapidly the canker would heal. Of course he realized the senselessness of this line of thought; nevertheless, somehow the effort made the bitter, alum-flavored cream nearly palatable. Resigning himself to another hour or so of styptic mouth, he put the tube back into his shirt pocket and turned his attention back to the kitchen table and the three dossiers lined up before him.

One file read, two to go. Initially, because he had fallen asleep during the first attempt, he had reread the Celt file in its entirety. Finished now, that folder lay face down to his left. As before, nothing conspicuously unusual or, for that matter, even remotely interesting was ascertained.

"Well, let's see what you have to show," he whispered, as he leaned over the center file, Robert Rouse's dossier, and flipped open the cover. The first item was a request for annual leave dated August 1982.

Franco paused and considered the date. 1982 wasn't going to get it. On impulse, he thumbed to the last page of the document. As a change of pace, he would read Rouse's file from back to front. At least then, maybe it would be more like a story and less like an accumulation of government forms.

The last item in the dossier, the one which predated all that followed, was a carbon copy on flimsy yellow paper. It was a memorandum and it was old. Franco scanned it quickly:

DATE: 17 October 1946
TO: Commanding Officer, Fort Strong, Massachusetts
COPY: Commander, Detachment 3, OMC, SHAEF, London
FROM: American Consul General, Niagara Falls, Ontario, Canada
SUBJECT: Rouse, Robert (Autley House)
Reference the letter of understanding from the Assistant Secretary of State to the Assistant Secretary of War dated 11 September 1946. Pursuant to these guidelines, this memorandum serves as transmittal cover for the following:

1. Affidavit in lieu of passport (in duplicate).
2. Letter of invitation from U.S. Consul Berlin.
3. Four passport-sized photographs.
4. Chest x-ray and reading thereof (tuberculosis negative).
5. Blood serological report (syphilis negative).
6. Alien registration receipt.
7. Letter of entrance authorization from Chief, Immigration Inspection, Washington, to Inspector-in-Charge, U.S. Immigration Station, Niagara Falls.

Subject will be accompanied by an armed noncommissioned officer escort (plain clothes) and arrival at your station is estimated to be no later than 1400 hours 19 October 1946.

Well, Franco thought. Hadn't he just read this memorandum? Wasn't it the last item in Gustav Celt's file? Reaching to his left, he opened Celt's dossier to the last page and confirmed what his memory told him. With the exception of the name, it was an identical document. Even the date and the words *Autley House* in parenthesis was identical, as was the type font that looked like pecking from an old manual machine.

Whatever. Two for two, he thought. Let's try for the trifecta.

Reaching to his right, he grabbed Pointer's file and flipped to the last page.

"Got it," he said. There, again with a variation in the name, an identical yellow carbon copy was in place.

But as he leaned back in the chair, Franco suddenly realized what was wrong with all three files. Sure they told of what the scientists had done since joining the government—where they had been assigned, what they had accomplished—but utterly nothing to indicate from *where* they had come.

Hunching forward, he shuffled through the three dossiers with both hands. He was searching for something specific: Standard Form 171, the personal qualification statement that all government employees were required to update every five years and which served as the core of most personnel files.

So where were they? Franco wondered as he completed the search and evaluated the information. It didn't make any sense. Here were three men who, together, had worked for the United States government for over a century and had never been asked to bother with 171s? Who had decided they were qualified for anything? And *immigrants*? What about security clearances? The most essential questions? Where were they born? What kind of educational qualifications did they have? And, even more significantly, how and why did they get hooked up with the Defense Department in the first place?

He glanced back over the memorandum in Rouse's file and picked out a few key words: *Alien registration receipt; Berlin; entrance authorization;*

AUTLEY HOUSE

armed noncommissioned officer escort. No answers, just more questions. *Niagara Falls; Ft. Strong; Autley House; Detachment 3; London.* Nothing.

Then, almost viscerally, the significance of the old yellow memorandums slowly dawned on him. They were like a birth certificate. Before 19 October 1946 there was nothing; but after that date, there were three new conscripts in the Department of War.

The connection to their deaths, like the scars, was glaring in its subtlety. The correlation, he now knew, was in what the yellow documents represented and in whatever Autley House had been or still was.

Where to begin?

Commanding Officer, Ft. Strong, Massachusetts.

Franco stood from the table and gathered the files.

The Pentagon was twenty minutes away.

CHAPTER 37

Crystal City Underground Mall, 9:30 P.M.

Giving the weather and the whiskey as reasons, Cory had suggested they see a movie in one of the mall's ten theaters as opposed to someplace farther from the hotel. Monika had immediately agreed and, after leaving the Ondine Lounge, they finally decided on a French import called, as she translated it, *The Moth*.

Initially Cory had looked forward to the movie, envisioning some mad scientist belting his hapless assistant with radiation and thus creating the ultimate human-insect. Unfortunately, his thirst for science fiction was left unquenched, for as it came to pass, *The Moth* turned out to be a tiresome, subtitled, black-and-white misnomer in which three unshaven Corsicans sat around drinking coffee, smoking cigarettes, and discussing such esoterica as iodine being the treatment of choice for goiter.

Cory hated the movie and, after the first five minutes, passed the remainder of the film mentally conjugating Spanish irregular verbs.

Monika, on the other hand, seemed to actually enjoy the film and, as they left the theater in search of a restaurant, mentioned it was a morality play, something about the intellectual transitions in French consciousness.

Wishing lung cancer on all actors, Cory nodded in agreement.

"Penetrating," he told her.

In keeping with what she termed the "spirit of the evening," Monika asked if they could eat in a French restaurant. Cory bowed to her wishes and after checking the mall directory, they decided on Café Henri.

In Cory's opinion, Café Henri was a dreadfully cheerful place: bright, lacy, and bistroish with lime-green tablecloths, wicker furniture, and wall after wall of white painted latticework upon which framed French travel posters were displayed and available for sale.

Great, he thought as they entered the foyer. The restaurant was not even close to being romantic. No, this was the kind of ground where old widows met to commiserate and to celebrate wedding anniversaries after husbands were planted.

"Table for two?" a voice lisped from somewhere.

Cory looked to his left. Stepping out from behind yet another lattice panel, the man was small, thin, and tuxedoed. Lips pursed and eyebrows plucked, he was a forty-year-old piece of fluff who was obviously, and quite successfully, trying to look like a *Cabaret* Joel Grey.

"Let me guess," Cory smiled. "Henri with an *i*, right?"

"Yes," the man answered. "Do you have a reservation?"

Cory glanced toward the cafe's interior. With the exception of a bored busboy folding napkins at a side table, the room was totally deserted.

"No," he said. "Think you can work us in anyway?"

Henri smiled a dental school smile and made a gracious gesture with his hand.

"But of course," he said. "This way please."

They followed Henri to a corner table, sat down, and ordered drinks: Cory bourbon, Monika another gin.

"He seems like a nice man," Monika smiled, as Henri scurried away.

"I guess," Cory said. "I bet if you peeled off some of his makeup, you'd find Jimmy Hoffa."

Monika failed to understand the joke, but moved the conversation along.

"I'm sorry about the movie, Brian."

"Why sorry?" Cory asked.

"You didn't enjoy it, did you?"

Cory shrugged.

"I guess this just isn't my night for French consciousness."

"So what *is* it your night for?"

At the question, Cory was somewhat taken aback, but there was no mistaking the clear meaning in her tone nor the direct challenge in her eyes. Instinctively he evaluated both, deciding them an invitation.

The answer, he knew, was *you*, but before he could speak, the moment was shattered by a burst of speaker static followed by music, then the voice of Maurice Chevalier singing *Gigi* and singing it loud, at least eight on a ten scale.

Cory could only laugh. Romance à la Henri with an *i*, he thought.

No wonder the place was empty.

"Well," he told Monika. "It's definitely not my night for *Gigi* either. Are you ready to leave?"

"And to where?" Monika asked.

"The hotel, I suppose," Cory said. "My room will be quiet."

"Do you have any gin?"

"I can find some," Cory smiled.

Monika returned the smile as she stood and followed Cory out of the restaurant and back toward the hotel.

Quand même, she thought in French. *Whatever may happen*, no doubt would.

Still, it was a physically uncomfortable charade.

The white lace panties had chafed her loins.

CHAPTER 38

The Pentagon, 10:10 P.M.

At four stories tall and ten city blocks in circumference, the Pentagon is the world's largest office building. Despite this fact, Franco knew exactly where to begin looking for information. While in naval intelligence he had worked the duty rotation, and now, even years later, the location remained the same: second floor, inner ring, suite 2A138, the door identified by the black serif caveat GENERAL OFFICER OF THE DAY—RESTRICTED ACCESS.

The suite was actually two rooms: a small, rabbit warren affair toward the rear in which the duty general passed the hours, and an even smaller anteroom in which an aide greeted visitors.

Upon entering the anteroom, Franco had been somewhat surprised, for, upon first impression it seemed as if nothing had changed. Metal desks, metal chairs, phones, and green walls appeared the same. Even the young naval ensign who filled the Sancho Panza role could have been him in an earlier life. Armed, polite, earnest, and contrite, tonight's aide wore the gold dolphin insignia indicating training as a submarine officer. Franco thought this appropriate. As tiny as the anteroom was, someone not bothered by cramped quarters was probably best suited for the Panza-of-the-evening role.

Beyond the ensign was the general's lair. Since the duty officers rotated after every shift, there was nothing personal in the room. No plants, no pictures, no memorabilia. Just metal furniture in a spartan, bland, eight-by-twelve box. Three walls and one venetian-blinded window through which, if one cared to look, the Pentagon's interior courtyard was visible. But where everything seemed unchanged in the anteroom, in here, Franco had been able to detect the progress the years had wrought. The first, and most striking difference, was the age of this shift's general officer of the day.

Remembering his own youthful service, Franco had expected the duty general to be much more seasoned. This being the case, he was quite taken aback to find Maj. Gen. T. Elliot Parkins to be probably no older than forty-five, with no gray hair. Parkins was an incredibly rough-looking man with wary eyes, a ruddy complexion, and an expression that could best be described as a cross between anger and a sneer. He was not a big man, but there was strength in the neck and shoulders. Dressed in an olive drab commando sweater, the shirt collar showing at the neck displayed two small silver stars at each tip and on the left breast there was an identification tag indicating his name, rank and branch of service, ARMOR.

The branch fit, Franco had decided. If anything, T. Elliot Parkins would have looked a hell of a lot more at home leading a tank attack in North Africa than sitting behind a desk. Nonetheless he had been, if not encouraging, at least polite and now was speaking quietly into the telephone trying to locate any material on either Fort Strong or Autley House. While waiting for answers, Franco played with his keys and it was then he realized the second change. More subtle than the first, it was probably more important. It was the maps on the walls, and Franco was still thinking about them.

Every wall had a different map. These were the flashpoints. In his day, Franco remembered, there had been the Soviet Union and Warsaw Pact countries. And although these areas were still represented, new flashpoint maps had been added: North Korea, the Iran-Iraq border, and, of course, Central America. Even a map of Mexico was attached to a tripod and pushed to a corner.

The more it changes, he thought, the more it stays the same.

Across the desk, Parkins replaced the receiver and noticed Franco gazing at the map of Central America.

"Ever been there?" he asked.

"Yes," Franco admitted.

"Is it really the shithole they say it is?"

Franco looked back over the desk. The general was staring almost wistfully at the map

"Why," Franco asked. "Planning a little trip?"

"Probably not," Parkins shrugged. "At least not me. Although it could be kind of fun to drive an armored division into Managua. I bet I could really stir things up."

Franco chuckled.

"I don't think it's going to turn into that kind of war, general."

Parkins' brow furrowed thoughtfully.

"Probably not," he said, waving a hand toward the maps. "But if I wait long enough, somebody will fuck something up, and some general from one of those countries, will get his tanks, and someone like me will get our tanks and we'll proceed to chop the hell out of each other's divisions. And when the tanks and the lasers and the rest of the machines break, we'll just fix bayonets and get on with the show."

"Maybe so," Franco nodded.

"Maybe so," Parkins softly repeated. "But that's my job. Now, about yours. Fort Strong is no longer a military installation. It hasn't been active for years. The records indicate it was closed shortly after the Korean War."

"Where was it?" Franco asked.

"Boston Harbor. It was an island, a chokepoint to protect the city from sea raiders. It was operational for decades, though. For so long, it was originally called Fort Miles Standish before the name was changed. Strong was a Union general in the Civil War."

"Heroes change," Franco said. "What about Autley House?"

"Nothing specific," Parkins told him. "But I seem to remember Fort Strong being involved in some type of intelligence activity. Might be something there." Parkins paused for a moment to collect his thoughts. "It was during the Second World War. Projects coordinated by SHAEF. That was the acronym for General Eisenhower's Supreme Headquarters Allied Expeditionary Force. It was based in London."

"Any idea what kind of projects?

"Specifically?" Parkins shrugged. "Not really. Some censorship activities; some war crimes work; recruitment of intelligence assets; kind of a mixed bag."

Franco nodded. "But no Autley House?"

Parkins shook his head. "Not that I recall. And, again, I'm not even sure your Autley House was even connected to the intelligence operations. It's just a guess on my part based on the Fort Strong reference. The people downstairs tell me most of the old intelligence material hasn't even been opened since being logged in during the summer of 1951."

"Isn't that kind of unusual?"

"Not at all," Parkins said. "The years after World War Two piled up a bumper crop of paper around here: the Yalta Conference, Potsdam Conference, Marshall Plan, the occupation of Europe and Japan. By the time all the records for all those things, plus no telling how many other projects, ended up here, we were well into the Korean War and a whole new set of files. Nobody ever took the time to go back through all that old stuff.

"Anyway, and I know it's not much, but if you're still interested, all the old files are stored in the SHAEF archives downstairs."

"Do you mind if I take a look?" Franco asked.

"Not at all," Parkins answered. "Room BB100. I'll call down and authorize clearance."

Franco stood.

"You mean you're not going with me?" he smiled.

"Not tonight," Parkins said, returning the smile. "I get paid to worry about the next war, not to be in the history business."

"Well, thanks for your help," Franco said, as they shook hands.

"Good luck to you," Parkins nodded. "And come back any time. We're open twenty-four hours a day."

"I'll keep that in mind," Franco said.

Leaving the general's office, Franco curtly acknowledged the aide waiting patiently outside the door and walked quickly to the elevators.

Franco was pleased with his progress. He had found the trail to follow. Autley House.

Luck had nothing to do with it.

CHAPTER 39

The Stouffer's Concourse Hotel, 10:50 P.M.

A reflection of excess, Monika thought, as she stepped from Cory's shower and stood nude before the mirror. Since returning to the room, she had finished two gins and a third sat three-quarters empty next to the sink.

But the hot water had worked its witchery, and now the glow she had been feeling only in her ears was spreading throughout her body. It was a feeling she described as vapid and it was exactly what she required at this point in the evening.

Fellatio will not suffice.

Eisler's words had been echoing in her brain since again seeing Cory in the hotel lounge and, even as they had talked, the only thing she could visualize was the *mono*—the monkey—tearing at her and doing ugly things to her.

And for this?, she thought, studying her body in the mirror. *But why?*

The monkey is sad. Make the monkey smile.

"No," Monika groaned softly, as leaned over the sink and wretched. There will be no monkey. Not now. Not ever.

Bracing herself against the sink, she waited until the waves of nausea passed. Then stood, avoiding her eyes in the mirror while she rinsed her mouth with water and took a gulp of her drink.

Fellatio will suffice, she told herself, as she set down the glass and grabbed her purse from the back of the toilet. Fumbling inside, she found a small metal carrying case, snapped open its lid, and extracted three Tylenol caplets.

She inspected her appearance in the mirror. Satisfactory. She would be naked and wet when she went back into the room.

Monika picked up the glass, tossed the pills into her mouth, and gulped the remainder of the gin. Then she turned off the bathroom light, opened the door, and stepped into the darkened room.

Peculiar, she thought. The bed was empty. For that matter, the sheets hadn't even been turned down.

"Over here."

Monika looked to her left. Although the room lights were off, she could clearly see Cory's silhouette. He had opened the curtains and was nude, standing with his back to the glass. There, with all detail masked by shadow and back-lit by the glare of outside lights, it was a powerfully suggestive image that reminded her of a dark-blue Kirlian photograph.

Saying nothing, she walked quietly to his side.

As she approached, Cory reached out, touched her hand and, entwining his fingers in hers, led her around in front of him so, together, they could look out the tenth-floor window.

"You smell of soap," he whispered as he moved in behind her, put his arms around her shoulders and pulled her back into his chest.

"And you of cherry tobacco," she said, snuggling into him.

"Maybe I should take . . ."

No," she told him. "It is a good smell. It reminds me of a small shop just off the *quai Saint-Michel*.

"A tobacco shop?"

"A book store, Yasnev's."

"That doesn't sound very French."

"It is not French at all," Monika said softly. "Yasnev is a Bolshevik. He too smokes a pipe and always smells like you do now."

"A lesser man might be jealous." Cory teased.

"Of what"

"Your mad Russian friend."

"Yasnev?" Monika laughed and reached up and touched Cory's cheek. "You have no reason to be jealous of Yasnev, Brian. He is a ninety-year-old man with dry skin and gum disease."

Cory chuckled and Monika breathed what he thought to be a contented sigh as she pressed her buttocks into his loins. At this, he began to explore her body, allowing his fingers to trail over her breasts, across the surprising tautness of her stomach and down into the damp mound of her pubis.

Almost imperceptibly, Monika began to feel a familiar uneasiness and forced herself not to recoil from his touch. She willed herself to relax. To endure.

But Cory sensed her discomfort. He considered the apprehension a positive factor. At this early juncture it was something to be understood and, in his judgment, even appreciated. He leaned forward and allowed his lips to brush the nape of her neck.

"No pressure," he whispered.

He slowly led her to the bed and a certain quietness filled the room as they moved under the sheets and arranged their bodies close together. Cory was aware of her breathing. Of small sobs and a slight tremble in her shoulders. He wondered what she was thinking. What she was feeling.

He moved his lips to her head and gently kissed her hair.

"Let the demons go," he said softly.

"I'm not sure I can," she said. "For so long, there have been so many."

Cory listened to the inflection in her voice. There was clearly something there, but what? Something akin to sorrow? Contrition?

"How many demons?" he asked, needing to draw it out of her.

She said nothing for a long moment, then he heard her whisper, "More than few, less than many."

Cory said nothing and pulled her closer into him, wrapping himself in her warmth. For the next half hour he lay absolutely motionless, listening to Monika's breathing as she slept in his arms. Then, as he himself began to doze, he abstractly recalled the last bits of their previous conversation.

What was it she had said?

More than few, less than many.

He felt the recognition run the course of his spine. As long as he could remember, the only person he had ever heard use this phrase was Eisler. Coincidence? Conceivably. Words were just words, weren't they? Maybe he was just reading too much into them.

But the more he thought about it, the less viable a sheer coincidence seemed. If it *wasn't* a coincidence, then why Monika in the first place? And he had initiated their meeting, hadn't he? Of course, he had. She had just been sitting there with . . . .

No, he decided. There was no coincidence in Eisler's world and, with this realization, he became aware of a thready pulse beating in his ears and of a cool film of perspiration forming on his skin. Still, he did not move.

More than few, less than many.

He stared at the ceiling in silence.

CHAPTER 40

The Pentagon, 11:40 P.M.

The sign on the door read BB100—ARCHIVE ACTIVITY and earlier, when he had first arrived, Franco found the section to be much as he expected. Large and remarkably dismal, it reminded him of an underground parking garage: damp brick walls, chipped concrete flooring, a low ceiling from which bare light bulbs hung like nooses, and exposed pipes and ducts that made weary mechanical noises. Around the lights dust motes frolicked, while in the air, scents of things electrical mingled with the more chemical and papery odors.

Like a garage, but not a garage. Most definitely a document storage facility. A fact made patently obvious by the legions of tall, olive-green file cabinets that stood side by side, back to back as far as the eye could see.

But activity? Franco had decided the door sign ludicrous. All but deserted, the archives were about as active as a slow night in Grant's Tomb and, to this end, the appearance of Dewitt Lester, the section's sole staffer, had done little to change his mind.

Somewhere in his early fifties, Lester was neat, clean little man with an academic demeanor. A civilian employee, his hair was a bit long, graying, and blow-dried. Instead of a uniform, he wore a long white lab coat set off by a bright red paisley bow tie.

Of course, after being called by the general he was cordial enough, but this aside, Lester, by nature, was a lecturer. He was also, in Franco's considered opinion, possibly the most boring man on the face of the earth. This, when coupled with the long white coat, left Franco with the impression of being enlightened by one of those actors who played doctors on television laxative commercials.

"I'm looking for a file," Franco had originally asked.

"We don't have files here," Lester responded. "Our records are stored in cubic yards."

"Well, that then," Franco had replied. "I believe you spoke with General Parkins? It's those records. Fort Strong?"

"As I explained to the general," Lester commiserated, "that particular material would be under the 319 Records of the Army Staff, Assistant Chief of Staff for Intelligence, Historical Studies and Related Records of G-2 Components, 1918 to 1959."

Lester had said this proudly, as if having just having solved the riddle of perpetual motion.

"Think you could narrow it down a little more?" Franco asked. "I'm interested in something that happened in 1946."

"Historical Studies and Related Records Concerning G-2 Components, 1945 to 1959?"

"How about just 1946?" Franco pressed.

Lester had pondered this for a moment.

"No," he finally said. "The 319 Records have not been subsectioned into anything less than the 1945 to 1959 grouping. Would you care to review those files?"

Franco had nodded. That was well over an hour ago and now, as he sat at a long metal table, he was wondering if he was ever going to find anything that meant something. As it turned out, the records mentioned by General Parkins, those of the Supreme Headquarters Allied Expeditionary Forces Europe, were those of whatever 319 was. The problem, as far as Franco was concerned, was that they were in no particular order, and around him, stacked on the desk, stacked on the floor, and still being brought to him by Lester, were long cardboard boxes that gave Franco a new respect for the term *cubic yard*.

"Are you sure you don't have an index or something like that?" Franco asked, as Lester dollied up another stack of boxes and piled them next to the rest.

"No," Lester said. "Not specifically."

"Then how do you know that any material involving Fort Strong is in these boxes?"

A disdainful look crossed Lester's face.

"Because I checked the master index to the G-2 Studies group and the index says so."

Franco decided on a new tack.

"Does the master index indicate if there are any specific indexes anywhere?"

"Of course not," Lester said tiredly. "One cannot put an index in an index. If one did, then one would have to begin a new index to index the indexes. It would never end. Surely you can understand the difficulty that would ensue?"

Franco shook his head, deciding not to even justify the question with an answer. The bottom line, he painfully realized, was that the Fort Strong, and hopefully the Autley House information, was in these boxes somewhere; but there was no way to further identify which particular box.

He took a deep breath and dabbed a bit of Lidex to his tongue as Lester wheeled the cart away.

So far, all of the boxes had SECRET stamped on each end, and under the stamp various titles had been stenciled in indelible red ink:

CPII BRANCH, MIS, G-2, WDGS
MISCELLANEOUS INSTRUCTION GROUP
ECONOMIC EVALUATIONS
MESSAGE CENTER BRANCH, MIS, ADCOPS
OVERCAST RELATED MATERIALS
EUCMIRS ORDER OF BATTLE

These, and at least thirty other boxes now, and still not one with any indications of Fort Strong or Autley House materials contained therein.

Franco sighed heavily.

If the master index was accurate, an optimistic assumption at best, he should eventually be able to find the Fort Strong information in one of the boxes.

Eventually. He wished he had never heard word. And with this in mind, he dutifully leaned back over the desk and unsealed another box:
JANIS JOINT COMMAND, OPLANS

Great, he thought, as he glanced over the first document.

Here was everything he had ever wanted to know about rebuilding Hamburg's bombed-out port facilities.

It was to be a long and very monotonous night.

CHAPTER 41

THE SIXTH DAY
Thursday, November 27, 1982

The Stouffer's Concourse Hotel, 2:40 A.M.
Not realizing he had been sleeping, Cory awoke with a start and looked to his right.

Monika was still sleeping soundly on the bed next to him. She was still nude; the top covers had slid down and her breasts were visible. In repose, the nipples were somewhat indented as they rose and fell with her breathing.

More than few, less than many.

Quietly, Cory slipped from the bed and moved to the bathroom. Closing the door, he flipped on the overhead light. Monika's clothes were hanging from a hook on the back of the door. He reached up and began to carefully inspect, in order, the dress, coat, and undergarments.

He was looking for one thing, manufacturer's labels.

He found none. All had been removed from the fabric.

He next turned his attention to the shoes. In the corner, away from the tub and under the door hinges, he squatted down and examined them quickly. Again, there was no manufacturer's label, only a small, pale, rectangular spot outlined by small needle holes.

Cory stood. The purse. Stepping over to the toilet, he picked it up from the top of the tank and moved to the sink where, after spreading out a towel on the counter, he dumped out the meager contents: a wallet, a small zippered bag, and a tubular plastic case with the word Tampax stamped along its side.

He opened the zippered bag first. Nothing. Just makeup. Three lipstick tubes, eyeliner, a tiny vial of perfume, and a matching comb-brush set. He returned the items to the bag, zipped it closed, and reached for the wallet.

It was a traveler's wallet, passport to the right, credit card slots and a coin purse to the left. Folding money behind the card slots. Expensive, he thought, as he snapped it open. Some kind of reptile skin and doubtless too expensive for a translator. A gift? Stolen?

He extracted the passport. It was French. He thumbed it open and began to read:

NOM: Sotelo, Monika Gabriela Abbes-Garcia
LIEU DE NAISSANCE: Champa, Nicaragua
DATE DE NAISSANCE: 11-11-1949

1949? thought Cory. She looked older. No matter.

He quickly read the remainder of the passport information: issue date, expiration date, various addresses. Nothing. She was a naturalized French citizen.

He flipped to the back. No travel to speak of, only a visa stamp from the U.S. Embassy, Paris, and the U.S. Immigration stamp: three days ago, Dulles Airport.

Could it be counterfeit?

He ran his fingers over the paper and checked the printer's marks, the cut of the paper, the registration of the punch holes, nothing. How about the photo? He raised it to the light. No. It was her image and the embossing was legitimate, evenly raised, spaced, and crisp. A perfect stamp, a genuine passport.

He slid the passport back into its place and checked the credit card slots: a French driver's license, some voting card, a university identification card, two laundry claim checks, and a slip indicating a dental appointment in three weeks. Still nothing.

Somewhat frustrated, Cory dropped the wallet to the towel and picked up the Tampax tube.

He snapped it open and found an unexpected item. There were no tampons, only a short, slender, folding straight razor reminiscent of the type usually found in barber shops.

Gripping the white—*was it ivory?*—handle, he deftly pulled the blade from its side and carefully scraped it across the back of his hand. Hair was severed at the skin. The blade was indeed razor sharp.

But why would she be carrying this? To shave her legs? Her underarms?

A possibility, but still . . . .

Perhaps as a weapon, for protection?

No. Inside the plastic case, it would take too long to retrieve if she were attacked.

Then why?

Wondering, Cory closed the razor and was patting it on his palm when he noticed the trashcan. Bending over, he looked inside. Wadded at the bottom were a pair of panties. Curious, he reached in and picked them up.

Odd. The label remained sewn atop the elastic band, Neiman-Marcus. And they looked new. Had they been worn?

Impulsively he raised them to his nose and sniffed.

Yes. But not long, not long enough to consider them soiled. Then why throw them away? And why did the label remain in a discarded item when the labels had been removed from all of her other clothing?

Cory pondered the implications, but no clear motive came to mind. Tossing the panties back into the trashcan, he then returned the razor to the tube. He then began to replace the items in the purse while again theorizing about the missing labels. Ultimately, he could think of only two excuses for their removal and neither, in reality, spoke very highly of Monika Sotelo.

The first rationale was that all the clothing had been stolen and, without identification tags, the authorities could not claim any particular garment was from any particular store's stock.

If this were the case, then Monika was a thief or, at a minimum, a recipient of stolen property. Questionable, but not really anything he couldn't live with. After all, he really did enjoy her company.

However the second reason, should it prove to be the case, would be something else entirely. Even now, he could think of only two people currently in Washington who, like Monika, had made the effort to remove labels from their clothing. One was Boudreaux Pock and the other was himself. He knew what Pock did for a living and he knew what he did for a living. Was Monika in a similar line of work? He supposed anything was possible.

How to find out?

Ask Boudreaux to initiate a surveillance.

The decision made, Cory reached to the towel and picked up the wallet. He was just about to slide it back into the purse when he realized he hadn't checked the coin nor the folding money section.

First the coins: two quarters, a dime, and a few pennies.

Next the folding money: a wad of French bills he didn't bother to count and a surprising number of American notes: three hundreds, four fifties, and seven fives. Nothing smaller. He was just about to close the wallet when inside, not quite hidden within the French bills, he noticed the credit card. He pulled it out and upon reading the bank name and account number, became aware of the sharpness that seemed to move from the card through his fingers to the base of his stomach. It was a Barclays international bank card. The name was Monika Sotelo, but the account number was 10332-222-8910.

Cory knew the number by heart. He had used the same account for the entire time he was in Chile. It was a QUEENWALK account. An Eisler account.

Pock's surveillance was not required.

Monika worked for Eisler.

Taking a deep breath, Cory slid the card back between the bills, returned the wallet to the purse, and placed the purse back on the back of the toilet. Then he leaned over the sink and stared into his own eyes as his mind began to fill with unanswered questions.

The why's? The how's? The what for's?

For a long moment he stood silently. Then, gradually, the awareness became evident. Eisler. Strange as it may seem, he felt no anger, only more curiosity than anything else.

Obviously, on whatever arbitrary grounds, Eisler had had a reason for arranging all of this. Previously his explanation had always come under the heading of *support*. Now? Here? It could only be support once again, and for him to even consider any other Eisler motive would be tantamount to what? Distrust? Treachery? Even treason?

But Cory dismissed these considerations. They were invalid. Drawn from his own *have I done something wrong* nuances and not based on anything rational or even realistic.

No. Eisler had done nothing wrong, Monika had done nothing wrong, and he had done nothing wrong. All had only done what they believed the situation, or their instructions, had called for.

So, logic over speculation, why had Eisler thought he needed Monika?

True, Eisler well aware of his need for female companionship, for someone to mirror his emotions . . . to mitigate the imperative. And it was clear Monika was not there to provide some measure of technical expertise. But could it be for something else? Something other than simple companionship? Perhaps as a spy to report back to the old man? Someone who, as Boudreaux clearly was, was *not* an old friend?

In reality, Cory suspected this to be precisely her function. Monika Sotelo was also a player . . . another of Eisler's players. And whatever her assignment might have been, it was now rendered irrelevant as Cory decided how to manage the situation. Flipping off the overhead light, he opened the door and stepped back into the room.

In the bed, Monika continued to sleep. Cory paid her little attention. Dressing quietly in the dark, he gathered his things, packed his bags, then, reaching under the bed, he retrieved the packet and slid it into his flight bag.

Moving to the door, he paused briefly and, for a brooding moment, he turned back to watch Monika sleep.

Would he ever see her again? Probably not, such were the rules in the hourglass world. But, admittedly, he would have liked to have had the latitude to explore their relationship. Only not like this, not *arranged*. And even if she hadn't shared his feelings, the time they had spent together had been what he needed when he needed it most. The laughter, the touching, even the talking. Maybe this is what the old man had intended in the first place?

Whatever, Cory decided, as he slipped into the hall and closed the door quietly behind him. Their meeting had again worked the mystic. Again buried deep, Lucius Aemilius was now in remission as his place was taken by the expectations of what might have been had the relationship with Monika Sotelo been allowed to run its course.

And what about the Russians? he thought, as he padded down the hall. Three men down and two to go and, by noon, only one would remain alive. Eisler would be pleased.

Cory took the elevator to the deserted lobby where he stopped long enough at the desk to retrieve the Camaro's keys and check out.

"There's a lady in the room," he told the clerk, as he turned to leave. "Let's let her sleep as long as possible."

The night clerk offered a lecherous wink and Cory tipped him $50 and left the lobby walking directly to the underground parking garage.

Within the hour he was forty miles south of Washington and speeding down Interstate 95 toward Richmond. Of the five targets, Steven Jarvis worked the farthest from Washington. He headed up the Defense Advanced Research Projects office at Fort Lee and lived off post on, of all things, a houseboat that was permanently moored on the southern bank of the James River at Calvert Quay.

But as he rode through the night, Cory's mind was not particularly on either Steven Jarvis nor the modified PMN mine which, if applicable, he would attempt to deploy in lieu of the Steyr.

No, the one thing that kept coming to mind was the question of Eisler and the old man's reasons for arranging the meeting with Monika.

What the hell, he decided, as he stepped the accelerator. He'd know soon enough.

Thanksgiving dinner was at noon.

Eisler would expect him on time.

CHAPTER 42

The Pentagon, 4:10 A.M.

Feeling like a clinical experiment, Sal Franco squirmed beneath the single overhead lamp and placed his elbows on the table and his head in his hands.

It was an examination of his misery quotient, he thought sourly. And surely, somewhere, someone was pushing the envelope: *Let's make the chair a little harder, the light a little dimmer, the documents a little more tedious.*

And tedious was the charitable way to put it, he decided. Five hours into the reading and he had just about completed the fifth box. One box in one hour. If he kept up the pace, he figured he'd be finished in about a month. A month, that is, if his body held out. But he doubted it would. Even at this early stage, if asked to describe his physical state in just one word, the only choice would be *fetid*. Indeed, his eyes felt like a matching set of worn-out kidneys and his neck and shoulders like something that needed to be restored by a licensed automotive mechanic.

His hands were dry, ink-stained, and paper cut, and the headache which had come and gone had again returned. Like a maggot in a peach, it was now casually feeding its merry way through his forebrain.

But it could be worse, he told himself, as he returned his attention to the final item in the fifth box. As part of the experiment, he could have been expected to remember all of what seemed to be the most irrevocably useless material:

. . . according to present evidence, the Dissemination Branch was combined with certain other functions and designated the Evaluation and Dissemination Branch, probably in the Intelligence Group. The date is uncertain, but the G-2 telephone directories for June and July indicate this could have been . . . .

Guess nobody bothered to look at a calendar, Franco thought, as he flipped through a few more pages:

. . . recommended that AR 10-15 be revised so that the distinctions between the Military Intelligence Division and the Military Intelligence Service would be properly stated. Staff Circular, 5-2 indicated . . . .

"Who cares?" Franco whispered, moving on:

. . . the offshoot of the Geographic Section of the Plans and Training Branch was the Topographic Branch which was formed in June, 1944 by separating the Map Service and Interpretation Reports Service . . . .

If they needed maps, they should have called triple-A, Franco mused, chuckling as he turned to the final page of the fifth box's last document:

. . . necessity, therefore, for employees to be of the highest character and integrity as well as being temperamentally suited to . . . .

Give 'em all a medal, Franco thought, as he closed the document and returned it to the box. So much for the MISCELLANEOUS INSTRUCTION GROUP, *nada*.

Setting the box on the floor to his left, he then looked to his right where the unread boxes sat unopened and waiting.

He listened. None seemed to call "open me next."

He listened again, as he rolled his head around on his shoulders. The only sound was the gristly popping at the base of his skull.

No point in wasting energy, he decided. He'd try the box closest to his chair.

Reaching down, he picked it up and placed it at the corner of the desk: G-3 TRANSPORTATION AUTHORIZATIONS. As he slid open the top flaps, yet another sigh escaped his lips.

Franco dipped into the box and pulled out a four-inch sheath of documents. Laying them in front of him, he leaned over the desk and began to read.

Well, he smiled. There really was a God out there.

Before him was a general index to the entire box:

AUTLEY HOUSE (LONDON)
Table of Contents
Subsection [page]
I. Policy [1]
II. Implementation and Procurement [129]
III. Security and Control [688]
IV. Immigration [1042]
V. Fiscal [1392]
VI. PEREGRINE Personnel [1791]
VII. Publicity [1803]
VIII. Endnotes [1852]

AUTLEY HOUSE

For the next twenty minutes Franco quickly scanned the various folders. None made any reference to Fort Strong. Then he extracted item six, PEREGRINE PERSONNEL. It was an incredibly thin folder containing only one memorandum of about seven pages. Flipping over the cover sheet, he quickly scanned the next page. It was short, to the point.

HEADQUARTERS EUROPEAN COMMAND
OFFICE OF MILITARY CENSORSHIP
APO 403
17 July 1946
SUBJECT: Letter of Transmittal
TO: Director of Intelligence
      General Staff, United States Army
      Washington 25, D.C.
      (ATTN: Commanding Officer, Fort Strong)

Pursuant to provisions of S-22716, the attached reflects those personnel assigned to PROJECT PEREGRINE. (Operational sub-section: Autley House)

FOR THE DEPUTY DIRECTOR, INTELLIGENCE DIVISION
W. R. Trainor
Lt. Colonel, GSC
Chief, Control Branch

And there it was: Fort Strong and Autley House. Both mentioned in one document. But what was the connection? Something called PROJECT PEREGRINE. Like the falcon? Something else?

Franco flipped to the next sheet. In no definitive order, alphabetical or otherwise, it appeared to be the beginning of a roster and, looking for the names Celt, Pointer and Rouse, he began to scan the page:

Colonel G.W. Trichel: Attached to the Office of the Chief of Ordnance, instrumental in initiating Project PEREGRINE and through the Research and Development Division, WDGS, expanded and revised program concept.

Colonel H.N. Toftoy: Office of the Chief of Ordnance. Responsible for liaison activities with the British and French occupation forces in FAIT.

Mr. Robert Frye: Office of Technical Services, Department of

Commerce. Conducted appropriate liaison between DOC and JOIA Intelligence Division.

<u>Mr. E. Allan Kightner</u>: Central European Affairs Division, Department of State. Point of liaison between DOS and European Sub-section of the SWNCC.

<u>Mr. Byron M. Stites</u>: Scientific Branch, Intelligence Division. Functions as primary liaison between Scientific Branch, ID, and Exploitation Branch, ID. Initial member of PEREGRINE Oversight Committee as suggested by Director of Intelligence.

Franco paused for a moment. *Exploitation.* A curious word. But exploitation of what? And why this unusual congregation? People from the military, the State Department, and *Commerce*?
And all the acronyms: WDGS . . . SWNCC . . . FAIT. Some he could guess at, others be had no idea. Why even PEREGRINE could be an acronym for something longer.
No matter. Celt, Pointer, and Rouse. These were the names he wanted to find.
He turned to page 1794.
More names. More descriptions. No Celt, Pointer, or Rouse.
Another page. Again no.
Another page, then another, a third, then a fourth.

<u>Captain Emile L. Berkley</u>. <u>Dr. H.B Robertson</u>. <u>Mr. Samuel Klaus</u>.

Three no's in a row.

But the fourth name on page 1799 was different. This one he did recognize:

<u>Major Blanton R. Rossett</u>: G-2 Section Liaison, European Command Intelligence Center, Office of Military Censorship.

Rossett? Franco thought. Could it be? Old Senator Rossey?
He filed it away, but not for long. The last name on the final page was another recognizable person, and Franco knew for a fact that the Rossett from then was the Rossey of now.

<u>Mr. Allen W. Dulles</u>: Formerly Head, Office of Strategic Services, Bern, Switzerland. Currently "Of Counsel" Central Intelligence Group, OSS, The White House.

Well, Franco thought. *Of Counsel*. Didn't that cover a multitude of sins?

But what did it mean? Probably the same as now. Operating from the White House, Dulles had no doubt functioned as a troubleshooter for whatever PEREGRINE had been, or still was.

Allen Dulles had done well, Franco remembered. Eisenhower had appointed him the Director of Central Intelligence where he had served for eight years. Moreover, Allen's brother, John Foster, had been Eisenhower's Secretary of State. The connection with Rossey was now obvious. Both Dulleses were from New York State. Rossey was from New York State. All were lawyers and all had together worked in World War Two's intelligence community.

For their friend in the Senate? An ally on the Military and Intelligence Appropriation Committees? Who better than someone they knew and trusted. Rossey had ridden into office on the Eisenhower tide and held his position for nearly twenty-four years.

No wonder he had been such good friends with the President.

But still, Franco reminded himself, while interesting for a change, this connection did nothing to shed any light on his current problem. What was PEREGRINE and why was the only reference he'd seen so far contained in the Autley House file? And what was Rossey's connection with military censorship?

Forty minutes later, he still didn't know. After a quick, but careful review of the entire box, he was only absolutely sure of a few isolated facts. Autley House had been situated in London and was part of Allied censorship operations during World War Two. It was staffed by about fifty U.S. Army individuals whose ranks ranged from one full colonel to three privates first class and even a chaplain. There had been medical, recreational, and food services available. There had also been dormitories and even a nursery. And this, Franco decided, was probably the most significant detail. Babies needed nurseries. So whatever Autley House was, it involved young children.

Obviously they weren't American dependents. There were none allowed in Europe that soon after the war. So who then? Refugees? Possibly, but not likely. Franco just couldn't imagine ordnance officers, intelligence officers, and OSS types being mixed up with a bunch of refugees. And even if they were, why all the SECRET markings on the files?

Maybe they were liberated concentration camp Jews? Now this *was* probable. A relatively large number of those surviving the death camps had been held in relative isolation while their statements were taken in preparation for the Nuremberg war crimes trials.

But the trials had been anything but secret, so presumably neither were the identities of those individuals who testified for the prosecution. But, back then, had their participation, either voluntary or coerced, somehow been construed to be *exploitation*?

Franco sighed heavily.

What was the connection between PEREGRINE and Autley House?

He thought back to the transmittal letter. Autley House was an operational subsection that housed people for PEREGRINE. To what end? Unknown. The file had danced around the project's real objective in every conceivable direction, and now, as he returned the documents to their box, Franco realized he was left with only two courses of action. One, open a fresh box and continue to read, or two, cut the process short and go directly to Rossey and simply ask.

He glanced at his watch. 5:40 a.m.

The decision was easy. Pushing back from the table, he walked away from the files.

It was time to go calling at 3 Bradford Lane.

CHAPTER 43

Calvert Quay, Virginia, 6:15 A.M.

Cory parked the Camaro on the highway side of the levee, climbed out, and continued on foot to the top of the berm. There, where the road continued on to the quay itself, he found a historical plaque. Moving closer, he read it with more than a passing interest.

"Finally," he whispered. After missing the unmarked easement twice, at least now he was where he needed to be.

But as he read the text, he began to shake his head rather sullenly. Like most, the story began with the word "site" and, while appropriately polite in an academic context, site, to him, had always meant someone's defeat. Now, here, in the half-light of dawn, it was clear to see this place was certainly no exception:

CALVERT QUAY
Site of collection, packaging and shipment of
tobacco grown on surrounding James River plantations.
Facilities ordered burned by General John Pelgram, CSA,
to cover retreat in face of superior Union Forces.
18 July 1864

Burn and run, Cory thought, as he surveyed the area. Constructed to protect the old plantations from the James River and its seasonal mercies, the levee was the highest point in this part of Virginia. From its top, Cory could see for miles.

The sky was clear and cold, a pinkish yellow in the east, more purple to the west. Once, thought Cory, it would have been called a plantation sky. But no more. The plantations were gone now, and to the south, from the direction of his approach, it was all strangely deserted. No houses, no people, even no animals. Only the rocky clay easement leading to the highway, the waiting Camaro, and the acres and acres of snow-patched, winter-plowed dirt and the miles and miles of broken barbed-wire fencing.

He wondered who owned all this nothing. Who had enough money to simply let it sit idle?

Foreign investors, he suspected. Probably Japanese. Absent yen czars and their little bands of banzai bankers. They were buying the whole world anyway, why not a bit of American history in the process.

Well, let them have it, Cory decided. He wasn't in the business of forgiving trespasses. Besides, he reminded himself, he had his own small measure of encroaching to worry about.

Turning back to face the river basin, Cory squatted next to the plaque and began a rapid grid analysis of the quay below. Some 200 yards away, a small lagoon formed an inverted Q on his side of the easterly flowing river. There he counted three structures.

The ruins: gutted, weed-choked, three walls down and one to go, they were nothing more than a pile of rocks from which hunks of iron jutted at odd angles. Heaped close to a rotting loading dock, this was obviously the original tobacco collection warehouse.

The shrimp boat: bow sunk and long abandoned, the out-of-the-water stern boasted the words SALLY'S CHOO-CHOO—GALVESTON displayed wreath-like around a cartoon of a buxom blonde astride a little red caboose. The paint had long since peeled away, so Cory was unable to determine whether her expression had originally been one of agony or ecstasy.

The third structure, the reason for Cory's morning excursion, was the houseboat.

Upon first impression, Cory was quite surprised. In the abstract, Eisler had used the word "houseboat" without bothering to elaborate. Reading it as it was, Cory had expected to find one of those small, metal, pontoon rentals normally seen chugging around man-made lakes. Something, perhaps, common.

What he saw was something else entirely.

First of all, Steven Jarvis' home on the water was much larger than he'd envisioned. At least sixty feet in length and a third that wide, it was an undeniably elegant craft of the type one normally associated with slow cruises through European castle country.

Painstakingly preserved and lovingly maintained, the hull, raised stern wheelhouse, and the long, low cabin were constructed of highly polished dark mahogany, which was made even richer in appearance by the contrasting light ash that constituted the cabin trim and the finely detailed gunwales.

What wasn't wood was brass. Rigging, portholes, railings. All gleamed from hours of polish and care as did the six hurricane sea lamps. Obviously antiques, there were two at the bow, two at the stern and two amidships flanking a wide ramp that ran from the deck to the bank.

At the top of the ramp a Doberman lay on the deck. It seemed concerned with only scratching an unseen parasite and then sniffing its foot before scratching again. At the bottom of the ramp, on the bank, a blue and black four-wheel drive Nissan truck was parked hood-in against an old railroad tie. It was the only vehicle in sight.

Tolerable, Cory thought. With the possible exception of the dog, all was quiet and there was no movement on the boat.

Course of action? Two.

Initially, make sure Jarvis was actually on board and, secondly, determine the most humane way of taking his life.

But Jarvis would have to be handled differently, he remembered. In the abstract's COMMENTS, Eisler had remarked: *Subject's wife resides with him. She is confined to a wheelchair and generally suffers from poor health.*

Hence the ramp, Cory thought. But its use was out of the question anyway. He couldn't actually board the boat, the dog would start barking. Shoot the dog? No. He'd always respected dogs. No point in punishing it for protecting its home. Besides, the Steyr had no silencer. The discharge would cause as much commotion as the Doberman's growling.

Option. What about waiting for Jarvis to show himself and shoot him from the levee? Two hundred yards was child's play.

Not humane, Cory decided. Oh, it would be for Jarvis, of course. He would die instantly. But what about his wife? Could her feelings be ignored?

Thinking, Cory remembered two special incidents when the wife was present at her husband's assassination: Sadat, the widow applying pressure to a lifeless heart; and Kennedy, the widow holding skull on a lifeless brain.

No, he told himself. Not humane for her. Should Cory shoot and should she just happen to be watching at the moment her husband's head exploded, his conscience wouldn't let it rest.

He would be no better than a religious fanatic or, worse, some lackluster amateur who killed just to see if he could.

Both reasons, Cory knew, were wrong. If one must kill, it should be for political reasons and not due to religious or psychological imbalances.

The widow Jarvis would be spared, Cory decided. But in doing so, the only plan, then, was to lure the target off the boat and out of his wife's line of vision. When it happened, she would hear the noise, call to him, and, getting no response, move to the telephone to summon help because she was physically unable to help herself.

Simple in theory, but how to get him off the boat? And when he was, which to use, the Steyr or the mine?

Considering this, Cory lay on his stomach and began to study the layout of the quay much more closely.

The ruins? Little use.

The shrimp boat? Even less.

The truck? Too close, as was the ramp.

Suddenly, out of the corner of his eye, Cory saw movement on the houseboat's deck. It was the Doberman. Standing, its tail was wagging, and Cory could now tell there was a chain running from its collar to the gunwale.

Steven Jarvis appeared. Stepping from the cabin, he paused to stroke the dog's head, then moved to the ramp where he stopped, untied a navy-colored bathrobe, and began to urinate in the water.

He was a big man, Cory realized. Much larger than he had appeared in the abstract's photograph.

"Younger looking too," he whispered under his breath. The abstract had indicated seventy-four, but if asked to guess, Cory would have said ten years younger. And it would have been a rigorous mid-sixties at that for, if put in the proper uniform, Steven Jarvis could have easily passed for some Soviet admiral at a May Day parade.

A beefy but trim six-foot-four, he moved with his spine erect and his shoulders level. Obviously arrogant, his face was tanned, handsomely Bohemian, and his hair was white, thick, and cut close to the head.

As Jarvis stood there, feet planted and staring toward the horizon, Cory could visualize him on the outside bridge of some Kirov-class cruiser plowing through the icy North Sea. He would speak little, ignore the frigid spray, and decline coffee, all the while scanning the sea for something to intimidate.

This one was totally different from the others, Cory decided. They had been old men, seemingly benign. Jarvis? Careful, confident, but most of all cold and cruel.

Cory felt a moment of pity for his wife.

Could he be doing her a favor?

The question passed unanswered as Jarvis finished urinating and walked back into the cabin, not bothering to pat the dog this time.

Back to getting him off the boat, Cory thought. Back . . .

Suddenly, it dawned on him. Looking to the right of boat ramp he could see the wooden pole that supported both the telephone and electrical lines. But no circuit box, he realized.

Was it on board the boat? There was probably a smaller, secondary box, but this was not the one he was looking for. Cory needed the primary converter box required by all rural electric companies before supplying current to outlying customers. It would be on its own pole and it would be located away from the houseboat proper.

How to find it? Simple: follow the power line. And this is what Cory did. Starting at the houseboat pole, the line ran to the left across a small gully and terminated at the top of a second wooden pole just to left of the warehouse ruins.

Cory nodded thoughtfully. From this wooden pole, a second, larger line also emerged. Stretching through the air, it connected to one of the giant metal skeletons that ran from the horizon to his left, bisected the river, and disappeared into the eastern horizon.

Excellent. Although through the undergrowth he couldn't see it from this distance, Cory knew only one thing could connect the overhead transformers to the houseboat—a primary circuit box. And with this in mind, he now knew how to humanely handle the matter of Steven Jarvis.

Moving quietly, Cory scrambled back off the levee to the Camaro. Popping the trunk, he shoved the Steyr package aside, pulled out the briefcase, and, leaving the trunk lid open, returned to the berm.

Bending at the waist, Cory sprinted across the levee to a point some fifty yards to the west of the ruins, carefully watching to make sure that neither the Doberman nor Jarvis was aware of his presence and to keep the old warehouse between himself and the houseboat.

The ground was damp and tangled with dead brambles, and he was forced to raise his legs high to avoid being tripped.

Just as well, he told himself. The longer strides would get him there all the faster.

As he reached the ruins, he paused to catch his breath. Overhead, the main power line was already beginning to dip down, and he knew the utility box was only a few yards away. Scratching through the rubble, he found a two-foot length of rusted metal, tested it for strength, then took it with him as he jogged the remaining forty feet to the connection point.

Cemented upright in a clump of pitch pines, he found the pole to be nothing more than a twelve-foot shaft of roughly hewn wood coated with creosote. At shoulder height, fastened to the pole with large screw clamps, was the circuit box, a battleship gray metal chest with TIDEWATER ELECTRICAL COOPERATIVE—RICHMOND stamped into the cover.

Cory raised the lid. Inside was a panel on which there were two large fuses and one lever. He placed his right hand on the lever and stepped back an arm's length. He then planted his feet as he had seen Jarvis do on the boat ramp. Satisfied with the positioning, he made a mark in the dirt with his right foot, then squatted down and began to dig a hole with the piece of scrap metal.

Two minutes later the ground was prepared. Opening the briefcase, he lifted out the small, drum-like mine, inspected it, then rotated the arming switch in a three-quarters clockwise motion. Again inspecting the device, he ensured it was operational, leveled it in his hands, and placed it into the soft earth. There was less than an inch from the rubber drum-lid to the top of the hole.

Sufficient, he thought. The covering would be well under the two-pound margin of error.

Reaching to the small pile of dirt from the excavation, Cory grabbed two handfuls and began to rub them together over the hole. He worked quickly, but meticulously, much like a baker sprinkling powered sugar atop an oven-hot strudel.

The hole was soon filled and, when the sprinkled dirt reached ground level, Cory grabbed the piece of scrap metal, turned it lengthwise, and scraped the edge across the top of the earth to further smooth the appearance. Once this was accomplished, he reached to the closest pine tree, broke off a dead lower branch, and swept the entire area.

The branch worked perfectly. Aside from removing all traces of the digging, the dead needles fell off to make the ground immediately surrounding the buried mine appear even more undisturbed.

He stood to review his work and, as he did, he was aware of the smell of bacon in the air. Breakfast on the houseboat. He hoped Jarvis had eaten fast.

Moving to the side of the utility pole, Cory reached up and pulled down on the lever. The power to the houseboat was severed. Closing the circuit box lid, he then turned and sprinted quickly to the far side of the warehouse ruins to wait.

Squatting with his back to the standing wall, the Makarov on cock and off safe, the minutes passed with the usual perceptions: sounds of the river and woods; sights of the shrubs and sky; smells of the earth and, wafting more now, the bacon.

Then Cory heard heavy footsteps crushing through the brush behind him. Considering Jarvis' bearing, he was probably incensed at having his power curtailed. Was it a malfunction on the houseboat? Or was it the responsibility of the rural power company? There was only one way for him to know. Check the circuit box. Look at the lever.

Cory knew Jarvis would be outraged at having his breakfast interrupted, and this would be to his expressed disadvantage. Outraged people did not think clearly. They lost their sense of awareness.

As Jarvis moved closer, Cory could hear, and count, the individual footfalls. It was like a marching cadence: left, right, left, right.

Cory thought of the parade field at West Point. His own marching days. The sing-along songs of trooping the line: *give me your left, your right, your left; give me your left, your right, your* . . . .

The explosion cut off Cory's final anticipatory *left*. Like a low growl, it came in a whoosh and left with a moan as it dissipated across the river.

All ashore that's going ashore, Cory thought irreverently.

The admiral was off the bridge.

Pushing off from the wall, Cory stood and moved back toward the pole. Pock had been unequivocally correct. The force of the mine had indeed come directly upward like smoke through a chimney. The pine trees, the creosote pole, even the circuit box had been left unscathed. Only Jarvis had been touched, and the touch had been with an exceptionally heavy hand.

Dead, he lay on his back, eyelids seared away, eyeballs ruptured. His left leg had been severed at the knee and the right just below the hip where a nubby thigh pointed skyward and ended in a reddish-brown twist of muscle, meat, and splintered bone.

He was still wearing the dark-blue robe, but the explosion had forced it up into a wad around his chest and his torso, that from sternum to stumps, was now exposed.

Cory glanced at it casually.

There was but one small puncture in the rigid abdomen. From it, a slender oozing of green bowel fluid dripped onto the ground while, strangely enough, the penis, testicles and scrotum remained uninjured despite their proximity to the amputated limbs.

Peculiar things happen with land mines, Cory remembered. Sometimes a body was completely destroyed, other times, like this, only partly. Of course, with an explosive this powerful, plus the fact of his having stood directly on the mine, that Jarvis would be instantly killed had been a given. Still, from a purely professional aspect, it was interesting to note how a certain device functioned when actually put to the test.

Shape-cast C-4, Cory remembered. He would not forget its efficiency.

Stepping over Jarvis, Cory opened the circuit box, flipped the lever to its original upright position and re-secured the lid. No point in making the wife suffer. Now she could have the power back on. The hiatus had served its purpose.

His work now finished, Cory took one last look at Jarvis, then walked back to the ruins, retrieved the empty briefcase, and returned to the Camaro by backtracking his original route.

One to go, he thought as he climbed inside.

Miles Wylie lived near Baltimore. If Cory allocated his time resourcefully and pushed the schedule, which he now had an inclination to do, he could still lunch with Eisler, eliminate Wylie, and be out of the country by midnight.

Puerto Rico by morning.

The thought pleased him.

CHAPTER 44

Falls Church, Virginia, 6:40 A.M.

"Shit," Franco said, as he down-shifted the Corvette into third and slowed at the city limits. He couldn't go directly to the senator's house. He'd forgotten all about Karen and, damn it all, he'd done it *again*. Out all night, and he hadn't left a note or even thought about calling.

She was going to be livid. At best, he'd suffer one of her pejorative "if you really cared, you'd call" beratings. At worst, she'd refuse to speak to him for a day or so.

His excuse: the "but I was working" explanation?

He shook his head. Better not push it.

But there had to be something he could do to offset his failing. A small trinket, flowers, something he could just kind of stop by with on the way to the senator's. Anything to cut the edge.

Great day and time for shopping, he remembered. Thanksgiving morning. Everything was closed. Maybe he should call now? No, that would be social suicide. He'd be home in five minutes. Better to hit her cold than give her five minutes to prepare.

Looking for that perfect "something," Franco cruised the Falls Church drag: Wendy's, Midas, Domino's, Gulf. Avis, Exxon, Bail Bonds, Loans.

Crap, he thought. With the exception of the Exxon station all were locked up tight.

Maybe a gift-wrapped quart of 30-weight?

Dismissing the absurd, Franco had just about given up hope when ahead, two blocks on the right, he saw the sign: DUNKIN DONUTS—24 HOURS.

Shifting into second gear, he floored the accelerator and raced toward the parking lot where, leaving the engine running, he went inside and made his purchase.

Bag in hand, and $2 poorer, he returned to the car and headed for home.

Not a great something, he thought, as he parked the Corvette next to the Volvo and climbed out. But a hell of a lot better than a quart of oil.

He found Karen in the kitchen. She was sitting on the floor with a cookbook open in her lap. All around her, on the floor, the counter tops and even the kitchen table, pans, platters, and plates were stacked, dumped, and tossed into what Franco decided was utter chaos.

"Moving out?" he said, making sure his tone was cordial as his smile.

She gave him a cold *oh, did you finally decide to come home, I hadn't noticed you were gone* glare.

"I called your office," she said. "They didn't know where you were either."

Franco put on his "it will never happen again" face.

"I know," he nodded, his tone now that of one who had just lost his immortal soul. "I was running out something on my own. I ended up spending the whole night in the Pentagon basement."

Karen rolled her eyes and, saying nothing, returned her attention to the cookbook.

"I guess I'm a bad person again," Franco added, after a moment.

"Yes, you are," Karen agreed. "You've been acting strange ever since you got back from Honduras. I know the trip's still bothering you, but that's no reason not to let me know if and when to expect you home. I knew nothing, your office knew nothing . . . I worried about you all night."

"Last night had nothing to do with Honduras," he tried to explain. "It was just something I . . . ."

"Something you cared about more than me," she interrupted, her voice a suffering sigh of resignation. "I just don't know, Sal. I really don't."

Christ, Franco thought. Karen of Arc, the ultimate martyr. But at least the "woe is me" role indicated her anger was fading.

Hanging his head, he responded in kind.

"I'm sorry," he said softly, watching her out of the corner of his eye.

"Well, you should be," she said curtly. "I feel absolutely miserable."

He nodded in agreement and reached for the bag inside his jacket.

"Then I guess you don't want this," he shrugged.

Spying the bag, her eyes narrowed.

"What's in there?"

"Apple fritters. Glazed apple fritters. I watched them come out of the oven ten minutes ago."

"Dunkin Donuts?" she asked.

Franco nodded. For Karen, he knew the only thing tastier than a cold apple fritter was a hot one from Dunkin Donuts.

"Feeling better?" He arched an eyebrow with the question.

Karen realized she'd been had.

"You're bribing me, Sal," she said. "You think you can just stroll in here with apple fritters and everything will be forgiven."

Franco put on restitution face.

"I said I was sorry," he whispered.

Karen snapped her fingers and pointed to the bag.

"Fritters," she ordered. "Give 'em here."

"So I'm forgiven?" Franco asked.

Karen breathed a theatrical sigh. The fritters had turned the battle.

"I guess," she said. "But this is the last time, understand?"

Franco grinned and tossed her the bag.

"I love loving you," he smiled.

"Because I'm easy?" Karen asked, as she pulled out a fritter and took a bite.

"That too," Franco winked. "But you never answered my question. What's all this junk doing out of the cabinets."

"I'm cooking a turkey," Karen said between mouthfuls. "I was looking for the broiler pan."

Franco walked over and looked at the oven. The temperature knob was set on 350 degrees. The selector knob on OFF. She had forgotten to turn it to BAKE.

"How long has the turkey been cooking?" he asked.

"About an hour."

"Hope you like it rare," he said matter-of-factly.

"I didn't do it again, did I?"

"Don't worry about it," Franco grinned, as he flipped the selector knob to BAKE. "It's the little things like this that make you special. Remember when you tried to microwave the soup without taking it out of the can?"

"You promised you'd never bring that up again."

"I'm sorry," Franco teased. "Have another fritter."

Karen smiled and did just that.

"Oh," she said, after a moment. "You had a call last night. A man named Doctor Cox?"

Franco tensed.

"What time?"

"About ten-thirty or so. I had just come in from the grocery store and was fixing a salad with this new low-calorie . . . ."

"What did Cox want?" Franco interrupted.

"I don't know. To talk to you. He said he would be at home and left his number. I wrote it down on the pad next to the phone."

Franco stepped over to the kitchen wall phone. Picking up the receiver, he glanced at the message pad fastened underneath and punched in the number. On the fourth ring it was answered by a sleepy female voice.

"Hello?"

"Dunnigan Cox, please. Sal Franco calling."

"Just a minute."

Cox came on shortly. He sounded as if just awakened.

"Cox here."

Franco offered no apologies for the holiday hour.

"Sal Franco," he said tersely. "You called last night?"

"Yes. I'm not planning on going in today and didn't know whether you were or not. Anyway, I have the lab results on the bullet casing found at William Pointer's trailer. Are you interested or would you rather wait until tomorrow?"

"Anything earth shattering?"

"I don't know," Cox admitted. "No classifiable fingerprints, just smudges, and you knew we already determined it to have been fired from a Steyr, didn't you?"

"Yes," Franco said.

"I thought so. Then I'll skip that and tell you about the toxicology and mineralogy examinations. Rather curious, I would think."

"What do you mean?"

"Well, mineralogically, we found a trace element in the fingerprint smudges, a crystalline sodium-chlorine, potassium-iodide compound."

"Some kind of salt?" Franco asked.

"Table salt to be exact," Cox told him.

"So what's so unusual about that? Maybe the shooter had French fries for dinner?"

"Not French fries, Agent Franco. I know because during the toxicology tests we were able to isolate an organic compound we positively identified as belonging to the plant *Anacardium occidentale.*"

"You don't really expect me to know what that is, do you, Dunnigan?"

"It's a cashew plant," Cox said indulgently. "The salt, the plant matter, and the oil base, which was also processed from the cashew plant, clearly suggest that whoever handled the casing either was or had been eating toasted cashews while, or immediately prior to, loading the Steyr."

Franco waited, but Cox added nothing else. Great, he thought sarcastically. This was exactly the kind of hopeless minutiae for which forensics was famous. And while it was important in making cases stronger for prosecution *after* an individual was in custody, at this point he could see no real value in the information. What could he do with it? Try to track down every cashew nut in the Western Hemisphere?

"Thanks Dunnigan, he said. "I'll keep it in mind. Have a nice Thanksgiving."

"You too, Sal. And I'll be here if you need me for anything else."

Franco hung up the phone, considered cashews in general, then remembered PEREGRINE specifically.

"What's Senator Rossett's number?" he asked Karen.

"Why?" Karen asked.

"I want to talk to him."

"But he'll be here in a few hours for dinner."

"I need to talk to him now."

"He may still be asleep."

"Karen, what's the number?"

"Same as ours, but with a twenty-two, forty-three."

"Thank you," Franco said brusquely, already punching the digits.

Karen had been wrong. The senator had not been asleep. He answered the phone on the first ring.

"Yes?"

"Senator? Sal Franco."

"Trying to get out of feeding me, Sal?" Rossett chuckled.

"No," Franco said. "Not at all. It's just I've got a little something I'm working on and was kind of hoping you could help me out and answer a few questions?"

"If I can, I will," Rossett said pleasantly. "What about?"

"Back in World War Two," Franco began. "Weren't you in some kind of intelligence work?"

"Yes, I was, Sal. Active times. A lot of travel, a lot of problems."

"I'm sure," Franco agreed. "And you stayed on in Europe after the War ended?"

"That I did."

"Still in intelligence?"

"That's how I spent my whole tour."

"Fine," Franco said. "Then I know you'll be able to answer this for me. What was the purpose of something called Autley House?"

There was silence on the other end of the line.

"Senator?" Franco asked, after a moment.

"Why do you want to know that, Sal? It was all such a long time ago."

"Well, it's not necessarily Autley House I'm curious about. What I really need to know is what something called PEREGRINE was, can you help me on that?"

For several seconds, Franco could hear only breathing through the receiver.

"Senator?" he pressed. "PEREGRINE?"

"Yes," Rossett finally said. "PEREGRINE. You said this is something you are working on currently?"

"Yes."

"In an official capacity?"

"Yes," Franco repeated.

"I see," Rossett said softly. "Well, perhaps you should come over and we can discuss it privately. Would that be convenient for you?"

"That's exactly what I had in mind."

"Then I'll see you in five minutes."

As Rossett hung up, Franco replaced the receiver and turned to Karen. She had finished eating the fritters and was washing her hands at the sink.

"I'll be over at the senator's," he told her, already heading for the hall.

"Neither of you better forget about dinner," she called after him.
But Franco was only half-listening.
"I love you," he yelled back, as he stormed out the front door.
Thank God for Dunkin Donuts, he thought.
With Karen appeased and the home front at peace, the hunt could now continue.

CHAPTER 45

Richmond, Virginia, 7:00 A.M.

Cory exited the expressway, drove into the center of Richmond's commercial district, and parked alongside an extremely forgettable building.

American generic, he thought, as he climbed from the Camaro and stood on the curb and stretched. Large, low, and recently built, it was a rambling, prosaic structure with tilt-concrete walls and wide expanses of green-tinted safety glass. In Omaha it could be a supermarket. In Orlando, an auto dealership. Here it served as the Greyhound Bus Terminal, desirably innocuous by virtue of its mediocrity.

Cory walked inside. There were rows upon rows of pink plastic seats. All were molded and fixed in place, and most were occupied by a wide assortment of holiday travelers: old people with faces etched with resignation; young women with squirming children on the rein; soldiers, sailors, winos, and pimps. Coming and going, and probably not caring which, all were waiting, rooted in their spots like carrots before harvest, while overhead, human-scented air carried the voice of an unseen pit boss, "Garysville, Rushmere and Norfolk. Lane number three."

It'll probably get hit by a train, Cory thought, as he moved farther inside. To the right was the ticket counter, the rest rooms, and a brace of fifty-cent lockers. On the left was a video game room, a long line of pay telephones, an unattended shoeshine stand, and the door to something identified as "Elba's Cafe." Toward the back of the lobby, the entire width was waist-to-ceiling glass through which buses, bags, and bored passengers were visible.

"Charlottesville, Waynesboro and Staunton. Lane number one."

"Three to five on the train," Cory whispered as he eased through the crowd, opened the door to Elba's, and stepped inside.

Lost in the fifties, he thought. In striking contrast to the lobby's cold, modern decor, the cafe was a small, green place with a watermarked ceiling and synthetic wood flooring. From a corner jukebox blared the voice of Elvis Presley singing "Suspicious Minds," while on every wall, large posters of Elvis, Marilyn Monroe, James Dean, and a black singing group—were they the Ink Spots?—shared space with pictures of customized old automobiles and girls with pony tails.

Glancing around, Cory began looking for a seat. A row of booths on the right, two lines of tables down the middle, a long counter to the left. What wasn't dark-green, tape-patched vinyl was either off-white Formica or chrome. The booths and the tables were occupied, and the only seats available were the stools at the counter.

Walking over, he selected the last stool at the far end of the counter next to an old black man with missing teeth, white stubble, and a bandage on his left hand.

The waitress soon appeared. She was a plump, buttermilk biscuit type of blonde who wore a starched white blouse and a gauzy purple handkerchief folded to resemble a wilted corsage. A name tag said it all: Dee.

"Coffee?" she asked, as she dealt Cory a menu from a stack of four.

"Black," Cory told her.

Dee departed and Cory turned his attention to the counter. There was a chipped plastic vase fastened to the Formica. In it, looking as if they had been dipped in dust, a handful of miniature plastic roses waited for recycling. Cory reached over and touched them. They were glued inside the vase.

Dee returned with the coffee.

"You eating?" she asked.

"I'd planned on it."

But Dee hadn't heard him. The record had just finished and she leaned across the counter and pointed to the jukebox.

"Hit B-7, Bobby," she yelled at someone. "Hit it three times."

Cory suspected what was coming and he was right. The same Elvis song again filled the room. Dee began beaming like an overripe squash.

"He's my baby, you know," she told Cory, referring to Elvis. "I've got all his records."

Cory forced himself not to smile.

"He was a saint," he reasonably replied.

Swaying with the song, Dee nodded in agreement, then jerked out her order pad. "So, you decide yet?"

"Two eggs over easy with ham and wheat toast, butter on the side."

"Hash browns or grits?"

"Neither," Cory said.

"They come with it."

"But I don't want them."

The old black man leaned over.

"I'll eat 'em if you don't want 'em."

"Fine," Cory said. "Give them to him."

"Hash browns or grits?" Dee asked Cory.

"Whatever he wants."

Dee shook her head.

"You're paying, you have to choose. Hash browns or grits?"

Cory looked to the man and nodded permissively.

"I eats 'em both," the old man said matter of factly.

"Give him both," Cory told Dee.

"It'll be extra," she said. "You can only get one with the ham and eggs."

Cory looked back to the old man.

"You hungry?" he asked.

The man nodded.

"Make it simple," Cory told Dee. "Give him the same thing I ordered. Make his with hash browns and give him my grits . . . my tab."

Dee shrugged absently and swayed to the serving window where she rang a bell and passed the order to a skinny white, professional parolee-looking cook.

"I got nothing to trade you," the old black man mentioned.

Cory looked at him.

"For what?"

"For the food. I'm poor. I got nothing anymore."

"What's your name?" Cory asked him.

"Alpheus Wheat."

"And how old are you, Mr. Wheat?"

"Eighty-nine, come Christmas."

"Did you ever have a job?"

"Long time ago. Coal handlin' over in Charleston."

"Did you pay taxes back then?"

Alpheus nodded and Cory smiled.

"Well, then, you just think of the breakfast as a way of getting back some of that money."

At the explanation a puzzled look crossed the old man's face, but Cory added nothing as Dee returned with the food. With the exception of Elvis, they ate in silence, Cory quickly, Alpheus more slowly.

The eggs were good, the ham better, and Cory finished first. Draining the last of his coffee, he declined more and gave Dee the money for the bill. When she returned with his change, he tipped her $2, then turned back to Alpheus Wheat.

"Good meeting you," Cory said sincerely, holding out his hand.

The old man took it tentatively and, when he pulled his away, there were two $20 in his palm.

He looked into Cory's face, but knew not what to say.

"You can buy next time," Cory told him.

"You a good man, mister," Alpheus smiled, as he closed his fingers around the money.

"Enjoy your breakfast," Cory said. Then he turned and walked to the door.

Leaving Elba's and Elvis, and deciding they probably deserved one another, he then moved to the row of pay telephones in the lobby.

Dropping in a quarter, he punched in a number from memory.

"Please deposit an additional seventy-five cents," a computerized voice instructed.

Cory dropped in the quarters and, a moment later, a male voice answered:

"DOD, Office of the Assistant Secretary."

Reaching into his pocket, Cory pulled out a handwritten note and began to read:

"Steven Jarvis has been executed subsequent to conviction by the people's court of the *Partido Comunista del Perú en el Sendero Luminoso de Mariateguí*. He is now the fourth to receive sentence as a result of American military oppression directed against our brothers and sisters in Peru who are now calling out for justice.

"We have but one demand. Immediate withdrawal of all American oppressors from our country. If all American military personnel are not withdrawn from our homeland within twenty-four hours, executions will continue until this demand is met. We are prepared to sacrifice ourselves for this belief."

Cory replaced the receiver without waiting for a response. He returned the note to his pocket and again picked up the receiver, wiped it with his handkerchief and walked off leaving the handset hanging by its cord.

As he climbed into the Camaro, he started the engine and lit his pipe. He felt quite content, confident, but not smug. He was warm, his stomach was full, and he had helped an old man who needed help. Christian Cory, he was.

The phone call?

He had helped *himself* there, and the Greyhound terminal had been perfect for his plan.

This was his first long-distance contact with the Defense Department. By virtue of the coins and the billing record the call could easily be traced, and the authorities, doing such, would descend upon Richmond to press the search.

They would come to the bus station, isolate the particular phone, then begin asking questions to those still around. They would learn nothing. Few would cooperate, and those who did would add nothing to what the authorities already knew.

For anonymity, Cory knew, passenger terminals held the key. Plane, bus, or train, it mattered little. It could have just as easily been the Dalai Lama making the call, for never, except while travelling, did people ever watch others harder, see nothing, and remember even less. And this is precisely why Cory had come to the bus station. While the authorities nosed around to the south in Richmond, he would be a hundred miles to the north near Baltimore.

Cory rolled down his window and accelerated onto the expressway back toward Washington. Traffic was light, and the sky was a crisp, clear winter blue.

He took a deep breath of the cold, clean air and thought of Monika, of the Russians, of Pock, and even of himself. But mostly he kept thinking about Eisler and the words the old man had said on the flight from Guatemala. *His* prediction of Cory's future.

The assignments will be become less prejudicial. Moderation will be required.

Moderation? Cory sighed heavily. And what did *that* really mean? How could he even begin to "moderate" what he had been doing for so many years now?

By default, Cory held no illusions regarding his profession. And even though his activities were cloaked in the guise, if not the reality, of national security, they all reduced down to two fundamental, and arguably traditional, functions: hunt someone down, then kill them.

Moderation? Cory wondered where he would find the courage to even begin to face the future. Wondered if the reward would be worth the effort.

Piece of shit. Not real. Have to beg off.

Mattman had tried to moderate.

Not real.

Mattman had failed.

Have to beg off.

Cory shook his head in disgust. Duty had become a licentious word. Yet he was far too old for a change.

CHAPTER 46

3 Bradford Lane, Falls Church, Virginia, 7:05 A.M.

"Milk and sugar?" Senator Blanton Rossett asked.

"Just milk, Franco answered. "I appreciate your seeing me on such short notice, senator."

"Not a problem, Sal. I always enjoy your company."

As Rossett poured coffee from silver into china, Franco took a seat in a deeply cushioned club chair, and glanced around the small, cozy study. The impression was that of money, but old wealth, reserved and unpretentious.

Diffusing the sunlight, one wall, that facing south, was recessed into a huge shuttered window. The remaining three walls collectively held the fireplace with mantel, the colorfully packed bookcases, and the dark-fabric panels upon which hunt prints hung like gallery art.

The floor was carpeted, yet it was even more softened by perhaps a half dozen or so oriental Karastan runners scattered under and between a tasteful selection of period Chippendale furniture. The woods were dark, and the leather blood red. Both smelled of power and politics.

Franco liked the room. Above his head a ceiling fan churned, and from a bookcase the gentle notes of a Viennese waltz were barely discernible.

"Thanks," Franco said, as Rossett handed him a cup, then took a seat on the opposite side of the early English partner's desk.

"There's more," the Senator told him. "Just help yourself."

Franco smiled and took a sip. It was warm and rich, Rossett's special blend.

"I've never been in here before," he said, indicating the study. "I kind of feel like I should be applying for a bank loan."

"Interesting you should say that," Rossett nodded. "At one time it was a banker's furniture. My late wife's father. He was in charge of Morgan, Grenfell and Company's London office. He had the misfortune to be aboard the *Lusitania* when the Germans torpedoed her."

"Killed?"

"So the story goes. I never knew him of course. I just inherited his furniture when I married his daughter."

"Some very nice pieces," Franco commented, as he took another sip of coffee.

"Yes," Rossett said softly. "But that was a long time ago, 1915, the First World War. You're interested in more recent history, correct?"

"Autley House," Franco nodded. "And some project known as PEREGRINE."

Rossett's eyes narrowed.

"You'll have to tell me why, you know."

"Off the record?" Franco asked.

"Let's just consider it a deep background briefing."

"It's a rather bizarre scenario, senator."

Rossett chuckled politely and leaned over the desk.

"I spent over twenty years on the Senate Select Committee on Intelligence, Sal. I can assure you, the more fantastic a story sounds, the more realistic it tends to be. Gentlemen do read other gentlemen's mail. Furthermore, they will lie, steal, and murder for the privilege to do so. Am I making myself clear?"

"Then PEREGRINE was an intelligence operation?" Franco asked.

"Yes," Rossett nodded pensively. "More specifically, it was a counter-intelligence effort structured inside the Office of Military Censorship."

"Directed to what?"

Rossett took a sip of his coffee.

"Background first," he said, making it little less than a bribe.

Franco set his cup on the desk, then for the next five minutes explained the situation. Rossett had established the parameters: deep background. Franco, following the restrictions, spoke only in generalities and about the threats, the killings, the records, and the rest, and was careful to give Rossett only enough information to facilitate his cooperation yet still hold him harmless. If, and when, the story broke, there would be repercussions. And, in Washington, repercussions meant congressional investigations, sworn testimony, and, most importantly, that certain touch of scandal that historically walked hand in hand with public scrutiny.

Rossett, a battle-scarred Senate veteran, was more than aware of how fast sterling reputations could be tarnished. So, as far as he was concerned, the fine line between curiosity and, if necessary, his "I was unaware of the specifics of that activity" testimony was vitally sensitive for reasons which Franco would shortly understand.

"So you found my name in some archive's records?" he asked, as Franco finished.

"In the Autley House files," Franco nodded.

"Yes. Autley House." Rossett turned and looked out of the window. After a moment he began to speak, his voice barely above a whisper. "Autley House was a large, 200-acre estate outside of London. It was originally built in the mid-1700s by a French Huguenot family. We leased it from the British government and had used it during the war for various intelligence and censorship activities. Because of its size, and the fact that it already possessed a high level of security, the decision was made to employ Autley for the, shall we say, *acclimation* of selected human assets, and as a staging point prior to their transshipment to the United States."

"Acclimation?" Franco repeated. "Who were these people, senator?"

"Will you indulge me for a moment, Sal?" Rossett asked, looking back to Franco. "I think it would do well to view things from a certain perspective."

Franco made a permissive gesture with his hand and Rossett began to expound in a voice that sounded like a man reciting a keepsake.

"Consider the times, Sal. The late forties. World War Two was over. Europe divided. But since Hiroshima and Nagasaki, both the East and the West realized a new definition of warfare had been coined, nuclear war. In such, existing weapons stockpiles were obsolete and even the systems under development were in jeopardy of being antiquated as each side began to modernize.

"It was the Cold War, Sal. The beginning of the arms race. The time when no amount of money was too much to keep us ahead. But something was missing. Do you know what this was? It was brainpower. At the time, man's intellect was the most precious commodity on the face of the earth."

Franco said nothing as Rossett took a sip of his coffee then continued.

"To ensure American superiority in this human element, President Truman initiated a broad-based recruitment effort as he found himself competing with both our allies and the Soviet Union for the best minds in Europe."

"And PEREGRINE was the vehicle?" Franco asked.

"PEREGRINE was part of it. There were a whole series of what were termed the 'P Projects,'" Rossett answered. "And the P-Projects themselves were part of a much more comprehensive effort operation . . . OVERCAST."

OVERCAST? Franco thought. He had seen a box with OVERCAST written on its end in the archives. He had been close. He just hadn't selected the correct box. He filed this away as the senator continued the explanation.

"Of course," Rossett said. "Being only involved with the P-Projects, I never knew everything OVERCAST encompassed. Compartmentalization was strictly enforced. Everybody thought anyone else was spying for some other party. By 1950, it had finally reached the point where, at least with respect to the P-Projects, there were only a handful of people in Washington who actually knew everyone who had been recruited."

"You?" Franco asked hopefully.

"No," Rossett said. "Not me. Oh, I do know that in all of the P-Projects combined there were somewhere between 600 to maybe 800 that were finally allowed into the United States, but beyond that, I suppose you'd have to go back and review the material in the archives. More coffee?"

"Please," Franco said, sliding his cup across the desk, thinking as he watched it being refilled. "What kind of people were recruited? Their personnel files seem to just start up out of the clear blue."

"It would depend on the particular project, the particular P designation." Rossett said casually. "PAPERCLIP, for example, directed itself to recruiting former Nazi scientists whose expertise was in rocket technology. These were the individuals like von Braun and his team."

Franco nodded. The missile experts were old news.

"What were the other projects?" he asked pointedly.

Rossett shifted in his chair and stared at Franco over the rim of his coffee cup. After a long moment a slight smile creased his lips.

"Well," he said. "There was PASTEL. I'm not very familiar with the details, as it was based in Austria. But I do know it was involved with the recovery of art and other antiquities plundered by the Nazis. Be assured our efforts had little to do with any love for the arts. Most of the inventory, after being sold through various brokers, financed covert intelligence operations throughout the entire Cold War."

Franco bristled, but said nothing as Rossett continued.

"Then there was PALACE. It concerned itself with exploiting the economic opportunities presented during the rebuilding of Europe. Some others that come to mind were PARISH, which involved the Vatican and its wartime support of the Nazis. PATCH addressed Middle Eastern contingencies, while PLUM explored various Far Eastern opportunities."

Rossett paused for a moment and stared out of the window.

"We were charged with building a new world, Sal," he said. "And we exercised our options."

Franco thought briefly of Rossett's new world. It was the world in which he himself had been conceived and grown to adulthood. A world of war, terrorism, famine, and corruption. A world where nuns were murdered and *la boya* was an inducement to conversation. But even as he pushed his cynicism aside, he remained struck by the sheer arrogance of Rossett's words. It was as if a small group of friends had gotten together and thought to impose their collective will on all of mankind. What's more, for better or for worse, they nearly did it.

"You look pensive, Sal," Rossett said, interrupting his thoughts. "You do not approve of our actions?"

"It's not my place to say," Franco shrugged. "No, I was just thinking that you left out one project."

"PEREGRINE?" Rossett chuckled softly. "I was getting to that, Sal. Suffice it to say, it was simply another exploitation project. I believe I mentioned that we were competing with our allies as well as Russia for individuals with special talents?"

Franco nodded.

"Well, in the final analysis, I suppose we got our share. But some did align with the French, others with the British, and a surprisingly large number elected to trust their fates to the Russians."

"Why was that? The Russians, I mean?"

"Two reasons, I think. The Soviets ended up controlling much of the territory which, prior to the War, had been independent countries like Bulgaria, Romania, and Albania. In some cases, these had been the candidate's original homeland. Many, I suppose, just wanted to return home and pick up whatever remained of their lives.

"The fact of the matter, that was the rationale behind Autley House in the first place. Somewhere guarded where we could hide our recruits so they couldn't be contacted by anyone else and hired out from under us."

"What was the other reason?"

"What? For Autley House?"

"No," Franco said. "You mentioned there were two reasons why some were able to be recruited by the Soviet Union."

"Oh, yes," Rossett remembered. "It was something we had done during the war. Something which had left quite a few of these men with a distinctly bad taste in their mouths about us and the British."

Franco looked puzzled.

"The bombings, Sal? Dresden, Cologne, Berlin, the munitions and aircraft plants in the Ruhr Valley? Many of the recruits had been injured by our bombs. Many others had associates or family members killed by them. With this being their only experience with America, I assume they considered the Soviet Union, with which they had had no previous negative contact, perhaps a less violent and a more discriminate place to resume their lives once the Nazi yoke was removed."

"Faulty decisions from invalid assumptions," Franco said softly.

"So it seems," Rossett quickly agreed. "But that was of absolutely no concern to us whatsoever. Our primary aim in recruitment was as much to keep Moscow from getting these men as it was to attain their services for ourselves."

"Again the Autley House isolation," Franco surmised.

"With its attendant trappings," Rossett added. "They were allowed to be reunited with any family members that could be found. Schools were opened, medical facilities, American movies, more food than they had seen in five years, and, most important to some, religious freedom was offered and encouraged."

"Des Moines in England," Franco quipped.

A sly smile crossed Rossett's face.

"Precisely," he said. "But don't be misled into thinking ours was some humanitarian gesture to, in some way, mitigate our previous bombings of their families or homelands. No, again, these were classified as exploitation projects. And the little America we built at Autley House was just one of perhaps a dozen or so similar P-Projects.

"Consider the numbers, Sal. In less than two years, through the P-Projects, we were able to identify nearly 800 special-talent candidates, convince them not to return to their homelands, and recruit them for a government that, just a few months before, had tried its level best to kill them. Moreover, we were able to do so without coercion and despite any number of Soviet attempts to penetrate their ranks and sabotage the process."

This explained the exploitation references in the files, Franco thought briefly.

"But why all the secrecy?" he asked. "If the Soviets knew and we knew they knew, it seems rather superfluous?"

"Absolutely not," Rossett shot back. "The secrecy wasn't for the Soviet's benefit, Sal. It was for the people back here in the United States. Remember, these were the same men who refined the radar that was used to shoot down American planes; who made the rockets that bombed American soldiers; who perfected the torpedoes that sank American ships. And if these were not enough, some also were the same men who developed the gases to exterminate the Jews. How many Americans had husbands and sons killed by the Germans? Had relatives gassed in the concentration camps?"

"I understand," Franco said simply, as he took a sip of his coffee. "So what was the immigration procedure?" he asked.

"After being identified, Army Headquarters in Heidelberg verified the recruit's vitae, marked him for selection and shipped him to Autley House for psychological modification. Once it was effected, he was given a new identity, escorted to Canada and authorized entry into the United States by the U.S. consul in Niagara Falls. After he cleared the border, he was housed at old Fort Strong in Boston's harbor until slotted into one the army's various development programs. Straightforward and reasonably simple."

"And his family came with him?"

"If he had one," Rossett nodded. "They were also given new identity papers while at Autley House."

New identities at Autley House, Franco thought, filing it away. Then he remembered the 17 October 1946 date on the three memoranda.

"Did the recruits travel singly or in groups?"

"Both, I believe," Rossett said. "It was more a matter of numbers than anything else. If one had a particularly large family, he may have traveled with maybe only one other recruit who had none. If a group of recruits was traveling and none had any family, then as many as five, six, even seven would be shipped at the same time."

"And on the same orders?"

Rossett thought about this for a moment.

"I'm not really sure about that, Sal," he said. "But my guess would be no. The compartmentalization I referred to earlier would have precluded putting more than one name on any particular document."

Franco understood.

"Because if the document were to be compromised, it would be better to lose only one as opposed to five or however many."

"Exactly," Rossett nodded.

"What about the dates on the orders?" Franco asked. "Would a particular group have traveled together on separate orders, but orders written on the same date?"

"Come to think of it," Rossett smiled. "I think that's exactly the way it was handled. The recruits, wives, children, each was issued separate orders even though they were all going to the same place at the same time."

"And Fort Strong was the first stop for everyone?"

Rossett nodded, but before he could comment, the telephone on the desk rang. He picked it up, said "Hello," listened for a second, then handed it over.

"It's for you."

"Karen?" Franco asked.

"A man."

As Franco took the receiver, Rossett placed his elbows on the desk and listened to one side of the conversation:

"Franco here . . . yes . . . where?"

"Yeh . . . now, I guess . . . yeh . . . no, just make it our roof pad. The weather's good and there's no traffic. I'll meet him up there in about twenty minutes.

"I know, Jonathon. I am, Jonathon. I will, Jonathon. Goodbye, Jonathon."

Franco passed the phone back to Rossett.

"We've got four now," he said quietly. "The latest is outside of Richmond."

Rossett said nothing as he hung up the receiver.

"Will you do me a favor?" Franco asked.

"Of course."

"Tell Karen I'm going to miss dinner and make her understand it's nothing personal?"

The senator smiled and nodded in understanding.

"Consider it done, Sal."

"It may not be as easy as you expect," Franco warned, as they both stood.

Rossett waved the comment away.

"I may be currently out of a job," he said, "but I'm still very much the politician. You just take care of what you have to do. Remember, I was one of the senators who ran Abe Fortas off the Supreme Court back in '68. If I could pull that off, I ought to be able to keep you out of hot water with Karen."

Franco returned Rossett's smile.

"It's in your hands then," he said, as he began moving toward the door.

Suddenly, he remembered the question Rossett had never answered. He paused and turned around.

"What was PEREGRINE's area of interest?"

Rossett shrugged. "Chemical and biological warfare applications."

"Were these recruits marked in any way?"

"What do you mean *marked*?"

Franco quickly explained about the armpit scars and the speculation regarding tattooing. As he did, he was aware of a general tightening of the older man's features. It was obvious he had hit a responsive cord.

"I know of only two groups who wore tattoos under their armpit," Rossett said, his voice coldly suspicious. "And neither did so at the request of the United States."

"Who then?"

"The first, the oldest, was a group of Soviet intelligence agents who worked for a man named Lavrenti Beria and, as a gesture of allegiance, tattooed Beria's initial under their arm. They were known as the *sosedy*."

"They were around during the PEREGRINE years?"

Rossett nodded. "Beria was Stalin's chief of intelligence."

"But why remove it?" Franco asked. "Had they defected?"

"Possibly," Rossett said, his eyes narrowing. "Or, just as likely, to destroy any evidence of Soviet affiliations prior to their undertaking some clandestine assignment. The *sosedy* were responsible for most of Stalin's more ambitious intelligence operations—extortion, penetration of foreign governments, assassination—these type of things."

"What was the second group?" Franco asked quickly.

"Nazis," Rossett told him. "Specifically, Heinrich Himmler's *Schutzstaffel*."

"The SS?"

"One and the same."

"Coincidence?" Franco asked. "Or was there some connection."

"There was a connection," Rossett explained. "Not during the war, but much earlier. Do you know anything about Himmler, Sal?"

Franco shrugged self-consciously.

"Well, no matter," Rossett said. "Suffice it to say he was nothing more than a failed chicken farmer who lived off a mistress until the Nazi Party became financially able to pay him. But this aside, he was an early friend of Hitler's and, being such, was appointed head of the SS in the late 1920s, about the same time Stalin was consolidating his power base inside Russia.

"Within a few years, it became clear to both Hitler and Stalin that Nazism and communism were on a collision course. In the German government, the Nazis outmaneuvered the Communists for control and in 1933 actually burned the Reichstag building, blaming the Communists for setting the fire. Weeks later, the democratic Weimar Republic failed and Hitler attained control. One of his first acts was outlawing all political parties except the Nazis. This done, he then instructed the Gestapo to hunt down and shoot any opponents of Nazism. The most vocal opponents, as could be expected, were the Communists.

"Anyway, back to the tattoos. For obvious reasons, Stalin wanted to know what was going on inside the Nazi Party. To do so, he instructed Beria to penetrate its ranks, which he did. As the story goes, one of his agents, a Georgian named Jundi, joined the Nazi Party of Austria, which had become Hitler's next expansion target. Operating covertly as a Nazi agitator, he took part in any number of terrorist acts against the Austrian government, acts that eventually culminated with the assassination of the Austrian chancellor by a Nazi team that included Jundi. Jundi was arrested for the crime and incarcerated until 1938 when the Nazis invaded Austria and freed all those who had been jailed in connection with the chancellor's murder.

"But something strange then happened, Sal. Whereas the other Nazi conspirators were rewarded, Jundi was removed to Berlin and interrogated at length about his Soviet affiliations."

"Sounds like someone fingered him?" Franco commented.

"Indeed," Rossett nodded. "At any rate, on one occasion, Jundi was visited by Himmler personally who, upon noticing the tattoo under his armpit, inquired as to its significance. Under drugs, Jundi explained. However, once he'd recovered, he realized he had talked and promptly swallowed his own tongue and strangled himself to death.

"Himmler evaluated what he had seen, was impressed, and decided the tattoo idea a good one with which to build morale and esprit de corps within the SS ranks."

Franco guessed the rest.

"So Himmler ordered all of his men to get tattoos."

"A small SS just under the right armpit," Rossett nodded.

"Then you think the men assassinated here are either Soviet agents or Nazis?" Franco asked.

"I'm making myself think nothing. In either case, it would indeed reflect badly upon the section I was assigned to at the time. I was in counterintelligence, and the sole reason for our section being attached to the Autley House project was to preclude penetration of PEREGRINE."

"By the Soviets?"

"By whomever," Rossett said flatly.

"Did they try?" Franco asked.

"The Soviets?" Rossett answered. "Yes, they did. We caught one. One of Beria's men. He was the one who told us the Jundi story."

"And he had a tattoo also?"

"No, Sal, he did not. He had a scar, a burn scar."

Franco thought for a moment. Soviets? Now, a definite possibility.

"Did the Nazis also try?" he asked.

Rossett nodded almost painfully.

"Two did. SS rankers."

"Burned off tattoos?"

"Yes," Rossett sighed.

"How did you catch them?" Franco pressed.

"We didn't. They passed our initial screening. They were found out only after being recognized by a few of the other recruits at Autley House."

"You realize what you are telling me, don't you?" Franco asked. "Whether you think the ones here are either Soviet or Nazi doesn't really make any difference. Somehow, someway, Celt, Pointer, and the others beat the system you designed and, now, someone has caught up with them, correct?"

"Facts tend to support that conclusion," Rossett admitted. "And I suppose if there is any blame, I . . . ."

Franco shook his head.

"Nobody's to blame, except for whoever's killing them," he interrupted. "But I've got to get moving. I have a ride to catch."

"You heard none of this from me," Rossett said, as Franco turned to go.

Franco smiled.

"You've my word on it," he said sincerely. "Thanks for the information, and don't forget to call Karen."

Leaving the study, Franco sprinted out of the front door and hopped into the Corvette.

Fifteen minutes later, he was crossing the 14th Street Bridge, back into the District and FBI Headquarters.

He now understood the scenario. Shining Path was most definitely out and something unknown was in: four dead men, linked by their past and an English estate called Autley House.

After the trip to the site out of Richmond—*a houseboat?*—he would return to the Pentagon's basement to review the OVERCAST files. In there, he hoped, should be the memos explaining who the dead men had been.

Nazis or Russians?

To him, it made little difference.

CHAPTER 47

The Watergate Hotel, Washington, D.C., 8:20 A.M.

Sixth floor, southeast view. A guest had once described the tiny L-shaped studio as "postpartum Poe." Melancholy, yet pensive; dark, but introspectively so. The visitor, a senior official in French intelligence, had said this in earnest, and Eisler considered it a compliment.

That was nine years ago, Eisler remembered. And, today, as he looked around his home, he was content to note that little had changed. The air still smelled of old men's things, and the impression remained of eclectic isolation: confinement and choice in a comfortable, if cramped, place of quiet.

The flat was divided into two parts. The kitchen, dining nook, and living area, the L's larger portion, were separated from the bed and bathroom by a tall Japanese silkscreen with split seams and colors long since faded. It was a theme repeated throughout his selection of woods, wools, and leathers that furnished the apartment.

In the living area, a tufted chesterfield sofa, love seat, and matching chair with ottoman shared space with heavy, dark, European antiques. Lamps were standing, Stiffel, and brass, and two lighted display cabinets presented a wide selection of museum-quality curios. From pre-Colombian bowls and effigies to Chinese terra-cotta figurines to Burmese coppers and vermeil boxes, all were displayed like jewels on glass.

The walls were as crowded as the floor. Frayed tapestries, old Russian icons and individually-lit seventeenth century oils seemed everywhere, as did the brass Thai pots in which large jade and ivy plants prospered solely due to the recessed ultraviolet ceiling lights that had been installed and forgotten by a previous tenant.

For all of his adult life, Eisler had eaten little and cooked even less. If a meal was required, it was always catered by the first-floor Watergate Terrace Restaurant. The food was excellent and the a la carte menu elaborate.

Since this practice fit his meager needs, the kitchen was used only to prepare coffee or tea or perhaps a slice of sugared cinnamon toast on those nights he worked late.

In a like vein, the dining nook was also quite useless. Eisler always took his meals at the large square sofa table and had no intention of ever doing otherwise. Consequently, the dining area had given way to a cluttered desk, creaking chair, and two matching china cabinets packed with leather-bound volumes of classical literature.

But this morning Eisler was not interested in the classics. Hunched over the desk he was reading the morning's *Washington Post*. The front-page article was critical of the president's policy on Thailand, and this disturbed him. Once again, another reporter had misstated the facts surrounding Washington's ability to control events in Southeast Asia.

Incredible, he thought as he lay the paper on the desk. In Vietnam, the press had criticized the White House for *getting* involved, and now, in Bangkok, they were grousing about the White House *not* getting more involved.

"She jagi panida," he whispered in Thai. *Well begun is half done.*

He would memo the president to ignore the article.

Suddenly, the telephone at the corner of the desk rang. Reaching over, he picked up the receiver. It was Monika Sotelo and she was speaking in French. Eisler responded in kind.

"What do you mean *gone*?" he said.

"Gone," she repeated. "Checked out. When I awakened . . ."

"You spent the night with him?"

"Yes."

"And everything went well?"

"I thought so . . . ."

"But what?" Eisler snapped.

There was silence on the phone.

"You provoke me, Monika. You did not follow my instructions."

"But I did," she argued. "He . . . ."

Eisler knew by her tone she was lying, that she had not, in the carnal sense, followed his instructions. This made him angry, but not to the point of becoming illogical. He would deal with it later.

"Very well," he told her, softening his voice. "But that being the situation, I suggest you go directly to Dulles and return to Paris. Remain available to me there. We shall resolve this in person. Are these instructions clear, Monika?"

Yes," she said softly, then adding, "I'm sorry."

"Yes, Monika," Eisler agreed. "I, too, feel a certain measure of sorrow."

Eisler replaced the receiver, stared at it for a moment, then stood and walked to the large window that overlooked Washington to the south. In the distance, the Capitol dome was white and stark against the clear winter sky.

The dome was perhaps America's most tangible symbol, he thought. The genesis of justice, law, order, and most of what he now held dear. Jefferson had said the Capitol captivated the eye and judgment of all, and with this Eisler could only agree.

But like the Capitol, and George Washington's rotunda crypt, Eisler felt empty inside. Monika had exercised poor judgment and it could not be excused. Somehow, Cory had discerned her affiliations; if not, he would have never abandoned her at the hotel. Her mistake was unconscionable.

How to deal with Cory when he came? *If he came?*

Straightforward honesty was the method of choice.

And Monika? Her pathetic *I'm sorry?*

She would suffer her error later.

CHAPTER 48

Calvert Quay, Virginia, 9:12 A.M.

Rotors angling, the turbines roared louder.

"Anyway," the pilot yelled. "It turned out I really screwed up not giving her a ride that afternoon. Her daddy's so rich he probably farts quarters."

Franco chuckled politely and glanced back out the Plexiglas bubble: grass, brine, and waterfowl nests. At fifty feet and 200 knots, the Virginia marshlands shot underneath like some fast-forwarded camouflage tarp. Since crossing the Potomac at Cobb Island, they had seen little else for the past half-hour.

Tidewater country, Franco frowned. He had visions of hunting and fishing and tall rubber boots and found himself thinking of Gorthram crepe soles.

"James River coming up," the pilot said, as he dipped the cyclic to the right.

Franco looked to the horizon. He could see the levee on the river's south bank.

"How much . . . never mind," he corrected himself. There, in the distance, he could see the emergency lights of a police cruiser that had been parked on the levee's river side. "Let's take it up a little so I can get a quick once-over."

"You got it, Agent Franco."

Twenty seconds later, Franco was at 300 feet and almost parallel to the ground. Looking over his shoulder, he quickly surveyed the site while the pilot kept them aloft, rotating the helicopter in tight, stomach-sucking spirals to the right.

Franco began counting:

Vehicles: five police, three marked units with lights flashing; one Nissan truck; one ambulance; two dark-green army staff cars.

Structures: two boats, one sunk, the other a house; old ruins, unknown number.

People: maybe fifteen, half in uniform. Type? State police and military.

He'd seen enough.

"Set us down on the levee by that state police unit."

"Will do."

Moments later they flared to a landing amid a rotor-whipped storm of debris. Franco waited for the turbines to whine down, then disconnected his shoulder harness and climbed out.

"*Cubano*," a voice called to him. "If I'd know you were coming, I'd have baked a paella."

Franco laughed. Only one person called him *cubano*, Elmore Lincoln Flood.

A very large and muscular black, Flood had played football at Mississippi State, served as a Marine executive officer in Vietnam, and had joined the FBI the same month as Franco. They had met in the academy, became friends, and had stayed in and out of touch for years.

Flood's current assignment, Franco knew, was heading up the "porno" squad in the Richmond field office, where his reputation was one of thoroughness and ruthlessness.

Franco turned around and smiled. Flood was wearing a long cashmere coat with a white silk scarf around his neck. His head was shaved, and there was a small gold stud in his right ear. Franco couldn't let it pass without comment.

"Well, E.L., aren't we looking prosperous," he teased. "Where's your pink Cadillac?"

"It's a gold Mercedes," Flood countered. "And it's back in Richmond. I use it when I'm doing my dirty movie deals."

"I've heard you've been making quite a name for yourself."

"I suppose," Flood nodded, becoming serious. "But it's shitty work. I'm so sick of skin flicks I don't know what I'm gonna do. You know, I actually saw one last week where some guy was getting it on with a goddamned *howler monkey!* Who in the hell would pay good money to watch that kind of crap?"

"The assholes you're locking up," Franco said quietly.

"I guess so," Flood sighed wearily. "But, anyway, that's my cross to bear and all things being equal, I'd rather be doing that than your job. This terrorism stuff scares me to death. You know how this guy died?"

"No idea," Franco admitted.

"A land mine."

"You sure?"

"I'm sure," Flood nodded. "Fourteen months in Vietnam, remember? It's not the kind of thing you forget. Come on, let's take a walk."

Franco followed Flood down the levee to where a small knot of state police and military men were standing around. Flood made the introductions, then led Franco to where, covered by a dark-green army blanket, the stiffening body of Steven Jarvis remained unmoved.

"I've seen worse," Flood mentioned, as he reached down and pulled off the blanket. "We found the left leg back over there by the wharf."

"What about the right?" Franco asked, as he squatted down next to the body.

"Just pieces. I figure that's the one that set it off."

Franco grunted a response and began to study the remains. Head to stump, shoulder to shoulder, robe to pooled dried blood.

"Do you have a stick or a knife or something, E.L.?"

"You know I do," Flood said, as he squatted down next to Franco and pulled out a long Spanish stiletto.

Taking the knife, Franco pressed a button and an eight-inch stainless steel blade shot from the tip.

"I thought these things were illegal?" he said.

"It came with the Mercedes."

Franco smiled and, reaching down, snagged a part of the robe and gently lifted it up and away from the upper body. He looked under the right arm. Like the others, the raised burn scar was clearly visible.

"Humph," he breathed, as he again pressed the button and retracted the blade.

"You acted like you knew that was going to be there," Flood said.

"I did," Franco shrugged, as he stood.

"Are you finished looking, Sal?"

"For now."

Flood jerked the blanket back over the body, stood, and walked over to Franco.

"So what does it mean?" he asked.

Franco ignored the question, asking one of his own instead.

"Answer me something, E.L. What was that old man doing tramping around out here in a bathrobe?"

"Checking the power," Flood said. "His wife said it had gone off and he'd left to check the breakers in the circuit box on that pole over there."

Franco looked to the creosote pole. *Extremely flexible*, Cox had said. It was becoming an understatement. Not only could the shooter simply kill a target, now it seemed he had developed the capability to control people's actions and movements. But why go through the trouble of drawing Jarvis so far away from the houseboat? Why not just shoot him from afar or use the mine to explode the boat or the target's vehicle?

Franco thought back to the computer and the green contractual motivation rationale. Simple. He hadn't been paid to harm the wife, only the husband.

"I guess Mr. Jarvis was a gentleman," he said, indicating the body.

"What makes you say that?" Flood asked.

"He checked the breakers himself, instead of having the wife do it."

"She couldn't do it, Sal. She's confined to a wheelchair, stroke."

Stroke? Franco thought. Then he understood. Yes, the assassin would know this and that was why he had drawn Jarvis from the houseboat. Different and yet the same, it was *justicia* now in a contract vein. It would have been wrong to harm the woman, and Franco began wondering if anyone but himself could appreciate the significance of what was a seemingly unimportant but remarkably insightful glimpse into the shooter's psyche.

Best guess? No one else.

"I want to speak with the wife," he said.

"She's on the houseboat," Flood told him.

"Cooperative?"

"She hasn't really said anything. Probably in shock."

Franco nodded in understanding and, as they began walking toward the boat, he glanced up at Flood.

"What made you think this was terrorists, E.L.?"

"I didn't, until I saw you getting off that chopper. I mean, isn't that what you're into now?"

"Weall didn't tell you anything?"

"Only to meet one of his agents and follow instructions."

Franco popped a piece of gum into his mouth.

"Well?" Flood pressed. "Is it terrorists?"

At the question, forensics information, archive data, but mostly the word *justicia* rumbled around in Franco's mind.

"No," he said softly, finally sure of it. "It's not terrorists, E.L. It's only one man doing what he knows how to do."

"But what's the motive?"

"Why do we do what we do, E.L.?"

"It's our job," Flood said quickly.

"You've answered your own question then," Franco told him.

"But it's not the same thing, Sal."

Different and yet the same, Franco thought again.

"No," he whispered. "Maybe not. But the differences are what keep men from ever looking back."

A curious expression crossed E.L. Flood's large black face. Franco was aware of it, but added nothing as they continued on to the houseboat in silence.

E.L. wouldn't have understood anyway.

It was one of those *you had to have been there* things.

CHAPTER

Calvert Quay, Virginia, 9:40 A.M.

Brass and teak and shiny black fixtures, the galley was a model of nautical efficiency. Bisected by a central hallway, one side was the kitchen, the other a heavily oiled, offset dining booth. On the two-burner stove a percolator simmered, and in the air the smell of stale coffee mingled with scents of pepper, detergent, and cooked bacon fat.

Try once more, Franco told himself, as he placed his elbows on the table and patiently repeated the question a third time.

"He said nothing to indicate that he was in any kind of jeopardy?"

Again, Valena Jarvis refused to respond. Across the booth, a wheelchair folded at her side, she continued to sit, rocking morosely and clutching an empty coffee mug with large, misshapen fingers.

Franco did not push her. But, as he waited, he found himself wondering, hoping really, that the stroke had not affected her mind to the extent it had ravaged her body. If so, then his patience and his gentleness would all be for naught and the questioning would end, as it began, in a one-sided waste of his time.

Somewhere in her early eighties, Valena Jarvis had obviously begun life as a healthy, robust woman. One which would have been described as *good peasant stock*: a big-boned, ample-breasted, wide-hipped paragon of middle-class Slavic breeding. In her youth, she would have tilled the land, tended the stock, and on weekends danced polkas or troikas for wizened village elders.

In her youth, Franco mused. But no more. Age or the stroke, or probably both, had taken what was and made it what he saw now: a pitiful shell of slackened thin skin, lifeless legs, and pores gone sour.

She would probably have to be institutionalized, he thought sadly, as a vision of his own mother passed like a kidney stone.

Florida, he remembered. His mother in the nursing home. It was all here and all the same: the aging curve of the spine; the long hair, gray and braided; the bloodless tight lips; the stubby chin whiskers; the threadbare flannel robe with flecks of dandruff on the shoulders and in the lap.

Leave a young girl and she'll cry. Leave an old girl and she'll die.

Franco swallowed hard and lowered his voice.

"Please, Mrs. Jarvis," be whispered encouragingly. "Please help me find the man who did this terrible thing."

But the response came not from across the table, but rather from the small group of official onlookers who had wandered inside to observe his questioning of the woman. The voice, loud and thickly rural, belonged to a uniformed Virginia state trooper, a stout, tobacco-chewing sergeant with mirrored sunglasses and the paunch of a panda.

"That old bitch's nuts. She don't even know what day it is. Probably thinks . . . ."

It was the wrong thing to say. Franco, whether from fatigue, frustration, or perhaps the association of Valena Jarvis with his mother, exploded and attacked. Lunging from the booth, he grabbed a handful of crotch, a second of throat, and slammed the officer into the kitchen where he held him pinioned against the refrigerator.

"The only nuts you better care about are the two I've got in my hand. You think you can figure that out, ass wipe?"

E.L. Flood was already moving. Stepping in close, he seized Franco's wrist, pivoted, and began to apply pressure as he peeled Franco's fist from around the trooper's neck.

"Back off, Sal," he threatened, twisting the wrist backwards. "He didn't mean anything. What the hell's the matter with you anyway?"

"Nothing," Franco growled, releasing the trooper only when the pain in his forearm became unbearable. "Just get this shithead out of here. Get everyone the hell out of here."

But before Flood could respond, the trooper recovered. Outraged, a drivel of tobacco juice at the corner of his mouth, he reached over and grabbed Franco's arm.

"You're under arrest," he panted. "Assaulting a peace officer."

"Fuck you," Franco sneered as he shrugged the hand off. "And how are you planning to manage that, ass wipe? Your badge says Virginia, mine says United States."

"That's enough, Sal," Flood snapped. "And enough from you, too, sergeant. This *whose badge is bigger* nonsense is getting all of us nowhere fast."

Ignoring everybody, Franco turned and leaned over the kitchen sink.

"Just get all these people out of here, E.L."

"Me too?" Flood asked.

Franco nodded without looking back.

"But Sal," Flood warned. "If she decides to make a statement, you're going to need corroboration if you're planning on . . . ."

"What I'm *planning*," Franco hissed, as he spun around, "is for you and the rest of that bunch to wait for me outside. Now, if you ever get around to doing what I've asked, maybe, just maybe, I can get on with my job. I don't need an audience, E.L., I just need my instructions followed. Understand?"

Flood understood all too well. To him, to the trooper, to everyone in the room, despite the outburst, there was no mistaking who was in charge. It was not "old friend" Sal talking now. It was the senior headquarters case agent.

"I understand," Flood nodded slowly. Then he turned to the others. "Okay boys. Let's all go outside and get a little air."

Amid murmurs and grunts and the shuffle of feet, the men allowed themselves to be herded through the main cabin to the outside dock. Franco watched them in silence, then, once alone with the woman, he grabbed the percolator from the stove, a cup from the sink, and returned to the booth and slid back into his seat.

"I'm sorry about the language," he said, as he filled her mug then his own. "I have a problem with my temper sometimes."

A brief flicker of recognition was visible in her pale blue, watery eyes. Franco caught it.

"I don't think anything's broken though," he added between sips of coffee. "How long have you lived here, Mrs. Jarvis?"

She said nothing.

"Well," Franco nodded. "It's a beautiful boat. I was in the navy, and this kind of reminds me of a place an admiral spent his . . . ."

"Did he feel pain?"

Her voice was low and weak. Not quite betrayal. Franco considered his response. He decided he would not respond. She had spoken once, she would do so again. The ice had been broken. He would allow the thawing to draw her further out.

" . . . weekends," he said, completing his comment. "I don't think his barge was this large though. Of course, his was more set up for . . . ."

"Did he suffer?"

The voice was stronger this time. More demanding. Good, Franco thought. Keep it vague. Keep her talking. Make her angry.

" . . . entertaining. A very a large area amidships. Sofas, a well-stoked bar, even a billiard table. The admiral used to sit in a big command chair and . . . ."

"Why are you doing this?" Valena Jarvis asked, as she reached over and touched Franco's hand. "Nobody has told me *how* he died. Will you show me that kindness?"

Franco took a deep breath. Her eyes were imploring and forlorn, her fingers desperate yet resolute.

"There was no suffering," Franco told her gently. "None at all."

Valena nodded stoically, glanced toward the kitchen, then back to Franco.

"We had always thought I would be the first to die," she whispered indicating the wheelchair. "He's taken care of me for twelve years now. There was never a complaint, never a self-serving remark."

"How long were you married?" Franco asked.

"Fifty years, next month."

"In Europe?" Franco probed carefully.

"Prague," Valena said, her voice sounding wistful, far away. "I was from Plzen. He was a graduate student at the Laban Institute, in Bratislava. Czechoslovakia."

As her voice trailed off, Franco took a sip of his coffee and paused for a moment of sympathy while he watched her attempting to keep her composure.

"Why did this happen, Mrs. Jarvis?" he said softly. "Why do *you* think this happened?"

"I don't know, she sighed.

"Was he worried about something? Did he ever express any concerns as to his, or your, safety?"

She shook her head.

"Did he have any enemies? Financial problems? Anything you can remember which may explain why this happened?"

"No," she said. "None of those things. He was a good man. Good to me, good to others. You're trying to make him something he's not."

"Not that at all, Mrs. Jarvis. It's only the questions I have to ask."

"I have seen television," she said sharply. "I have seen how policemen ask their questions."

To Franco this was nearly an insult, but he let it pass. She was talking now, even being combative. Speaking of her husband in the present tense, she was denying he was gone while, simultaneously, she felt anger at his being dead and her being alone.

Work the anger angle, Franco told himself. Pop the questions now, quick questions in rapid succession. Get to the meat of the matter.

"Tell me about PEREGRINE," he said gently.

She said nothing. Her eyes remained impassive. She didn't know.

"OVERCAST? What about that OVERCAST? Does that sound familiar, Mrs. Jarvis?"

"What is that?" she said.

Franco watched her closely: the eyes, the throat, the tilt of the head, the set of the lips. No response.

"Autley House?" he asked, still watching her face.

The trembling began in her shoulders and moved quickly to her throat. It was as if she were attempting to swallow a spoonful of sand.

"Tell me about Autley House," Franco repeated, venturing an educated guess. "I know your husband was there. I know you both were."

Valena took a sip of her coffee, then squeezed her eyes closed in what Franco thought must be an effort to blot out a memory.

"I have his records, Mrs. Jarvis," he lied. "I have both of your records."

"There were to be no records," she said with surprising hostility.

"No?" Franco arched an eyebrow and stroked the corner of his moustache. "And who told you that, Mrs. Jarvis?"

"My husband," she shrugged. "Steven told me that when we entered the American Sector."

"From Czechoslovakia?"

"After the war," she nodded heavily. "We were in Prague near the end. The Soviets were advancing and the American General Patton had stopped further in the east outside of Plzen. My husband and I thought the Americans would be more civilized in their treatment of refugees, so we returned to my father's farm and placed ourselves in their charge."

"And your husband came to work for the United States."

"Yes," she said. "We were moved to Heidelberg, then to Autley House in England, then finally here, to America. He was a very brilliant man. A chemist, you know."

"Yes," Franco said. "I know."

But, he thought, was it coincidence that her scientist husband had just happened to ease across the American lines? Was it true that he had fled from communist-controlled Prague in fear of the Soviet Army?

No, he decided. It was just too pat. Senator Rossett had indicated that the Soviets attempted to infiltrate Autley House. Perhaps they had succeeded and Jarvis was one of the "success" stories? One which was not identified by American counterintelligence agents?

"How far was Plzen from Prague, Mrs. Jarvis?"

"Perhaps a hundred kilometers."

"Was there anything in between? Checkpoints? Any semblance of order?"

"None," she said matter of factly. "There were thousands of people fleeing in advance of the Russians. Men, women, orphans . . . thousands."

A black-and-white image of war-torn Europe flashed in Franco's mind. Humanity on the move. Buildings bombed, children crying, the homeless plodding rutted roads with possessions stacked on man-drawn carts.

"There were rumors," Valena added. "We heard them for months. The Russians placed refugees in camps, like captives. The Americans fed them and sheltered them from the rain. What would you have done? Which side would you have chosen?"

"The shelter," Franco answered, only half-aware of the question, as he assessed the facts in his mind.

Thousands, she had said. And Rossett had admitted the screening process for PEREGRINE had been less than precise. One hundred kilometers, about sixty miles, thousands of refugees, and shitty screening. If Stalin was smart, which he undoubtedly was, he would have been a fool *not* to instruct his intelligence cadre to infiltrate the American lines at Plzen.

"Your husband worked for a man named Beria, didn't he, Mrs. Jarvis?"

A peculiar expression crossed her face, but before Franco could interpret its meaning, Valena Jarvis leaned forward in her seat.

"His name was Lavrenti Pavlovich Beria," she whispered, as if afraid he might be listening from some hidden place in the galley. "You have the records. You should know. My husband did not work for him. My husband feared him more than any person on the face of the earth."

Franco was taken aback, but he forced himself to remain impassive.

"But the scar under his armpit?" he said, probing. "The place where the tattoo was removed?"

"Yes?" Valena asked. "What about the tattoo?"

"Was it not Beria's initial? Was not your husband one of Beria's agents?"

"Of course not," she said defiantly. "My husband had been hiding from the Russians since we fled from Prague."

Franco mind swirled. The line of questioning had just run out, and he had no idea how to interpret what she had just revealed or where to take it from here.

He looked across the table. She was staring at him openly. Waiting with an expression that was somewhere between skepticism and challenge. If he didn't do something, he would lose her right now. Course of action? Bluff her into taking the lead again.

Placing his elbows on the table, Franco closed his eyes and made a grand show of rubbing his temples while lowering his voice to a tired whisper of resignation.

"Mrs. Jarvis," he said slowly. "I realize you have had a terrible shock this morning and, on that, you have my sympathy. But, as I told you, I have the records and I was simply testing you. I know your husband did not work for the Soviets. I also know what the scar represents. Now, you mentioned that you have seen the police shows on television?"

"Yes," she said.

"Well, then I'm sure you will remember the phrase *I have to hear it from you*?"

"Yes," she nodded.

"That is where we are now, Mrs. Jarvis. And the sooner I hear it from you, the sooner we can conclude this conversation and the sooner I can get on with the business of finding the man who murdered your husband. I think you want this just as much as I do. Am I correct, Mrs. Jarvis?"

For perhaps five seconds, Valena Jarvis considered Franco's words. Then, she began to nod thoughtfully.

"I suppose, now, it makes little difference," she sighed. "So, from me, you will hear it."

"Thank you, Mrs. Jarvis."

"I will begin at the beginning," she said quickly. "I am not Mrs. Steven Jarvis. That name was given to me by the Americans at Autley House. My husband was *Oberscharfüher* Erich Kleist. He was a lance sergeant assigned to a German Army unit in Bratislava, something called Einsatzkommando IV."

Franco nodded as if having heard all of this before.

"He was, of course, SS?" he asked.

"Yes," Valena said quietly. "He was German by birth, from Munich. He was one of Heinrich Himmler's protégés."

"But he still functioned as a chemist?"

"He was a brilliant chemist, as I said. He began his studies in Bratislava in the spring of 1937 and was working at the Laban Institute when the Germans seized control."

"The Germans left him in Bratislava?"

"At the Laban Institute," Valena added. "Erich had known Reinhard Heydrich from the early days when Heydrich was Himmler's principal deputy. When Heydrich was assigned by Hitler to be the Protector of Czechoslovakia, or of Bohemia and Moravia as it was called then, Einsatzkommando IV was established. A number of others, German-born scientists, like Erich, were commissioned into the SS, then assigned to the institute. When Heydrich was assassinated by partisans, the institute continued on its own. We remained in Bratislava throughout the war and left only when the Russians advanced."

Franco took a sip of coffee and considered this. Himmler? Reinhard Heydrich?

These two were certainly no sideline actors. Himmler was the one who received Hitler's orders to eliminate the Jews and who ordered the search for more efficient killing methods. Heydrich was director of Reich security, the man entrusted with implementing the decision to eradicate the Jewish population of Europe. To Franco, the next question was obvious.

"Was your husband involved with the concentration camps?"

"He knew nothing about that," she snapped. "He was a good man. I told you, he stayed in Bratislava, at the Laban Institute, and never ever wore a uniform."

"But he worked for Heydrich, and Heydrich ran the camps."

"No," she protested. "Before his assassination, others ran the education camps for Heydrich. Heydrich was removed from the training."

Education? Training? Whatever, Franco decided. There was no percentage in getting involved in an argument that ran afoul of historical reality.

"You said your husband never wore a uniform?"

"That is correct."

"And that he stayed at this Laban Institute?"

"Yes."

"What did he do there?"

"He never told me."

"What do you *think* he did there?"

"I don't know," she shrugged. "He was a scientist, always working on some project or paper or something."

"Were there other men, like your husband, who were assigned to this Einsatzkommando IV?"

"I told you there were. It was a very large institute."

"How many others?"

"I never knew. I never entered the grounds."

"Did any of the others ever come to your home?"

"No," she said. "We had few friends during the war."

"Did your husband ever speak of any of them?"

"When?"

"At any time," Franco said tersely. "At the institute, at Autley House, here, after the war?"

"No," she said softly. "We never spoke of the past."

Franco leaned back in the booth and thought over what he had just learned. There was no evidence of her having lied, nor was there any reason for her to do so. All things being equal then, he would take it on face value.

Karen knew little of his work, so it was entirely possible Valena knew nothing of her husband's. So he was left with . . . what? Steven Jarvis was actually Erich Kleist. An SS Ober-something, whatever that was, who was also a chemist who worked in civilian clothes at some Czech institute of higher learning and was chummy with butchers like Himmler and Heydrich, who themselves were the principal architects of Hitler's Final Solution.

This being the case, he thought, it then stood to reason that all four of the dead men were SS-type Nazis who had been given new identities by the U.S. government and who had been working for the Americans since the war. This, Franco knew, was a far cry from allowing the imigration of individuals who had been *forced* to work for the Nazis. These men, like Jarvis and probably the others, had not been forced to do anything. On the contrary, at least Jarvis—and possibly the others—was German-born and, in his wife's own words, a protégé of Reinhard Heydrich.

The next question was obvious.

"When you were at Autley House and received your new identities, did the Americans there know your husband had worked for Heydrich or in this Einsatzkommando IV unit?"

"No," Valena said flatly.

"Well, who did they think you were?"

"I don't know," she admitted. "Erich had obtained some new documents, but he handled everything and I don't know what they said we were."

"Was Valena the name you were given at birth?"

"Yes," she said. "Valena Ronska."

"But what about Erich's last name. Didn't you take that when you were married?"

"Kleist? I took it, of course. But when the Germans came into Prague, many of the old marriage records were misplaced. The only documents I had were those with my birth name on them. And when we were given the Steven and Valena Jarvis papers in England, well, you can understand why we never . . . well, I've told you how it was."

Franco nodded in understanding. She had just been doing what it took to survive. She would have taken any documents, any name, to be able to forget the war and get on with her life. Faced with similar circumstances, he would have probably done the same thing.

Franco sighed heavily. He realized he had learned just about everything he could from Valena Jarvis. He slowly slid from the booth and stood at the end of the table.

"I have one more question, Mrs. Jarvis, and it is something you mentioned earlier. You said your husband was more afraid of this Russian, Beria, than of anyone else in the world. Why was that?"

"Because my husband was SS."

"You said he never wore a uniform though."

"It would have made no difference to Beria. He had sworn to Stalin that he would execute every SS man who could located. When the Russians were on the outskirts of Bratislava, we heard that Beria was leading their ranks. That, more than anything else, was why Erich sought American protection."

"But why Beria's compulsion with the SS?" Franco asked.

"Erich once told me that it was Beria who began the rumor about Himmler killing those in the camps."

Rumor, Franco thought, incredulous.

"You mean you really don't believe those millions died that way?" he asked.

"Soviet propaganda," she said quickly. "My husband, Himmler, Heydrich, they were not murderers. They were heroes of the Fatherland. The SS were the chosen ones. They were the vanguards of the Reich."

At this, set back by her ignorance, Franco could only shrug and, turning, begin to slowly walk toward the door. He had just reached it when he heard the sound coming from behind him, drifting from the galley and getting louder.

Incredible, he thought. Valena Jarvis had begun to sing. But the fact of her singing was not as bizarre as her choice of song. He paused to make sure he was hearing it right. He was. It was "Lili Marlene." That haunting wartime melody sung by Hitler's troops before going off to die for the Fuhrer's greater glory:

Bugler, tonight don't play the call to arms,
I want another evening with her charms.
Then we must say goodbye and part.
I'll always keep you in my heart.
With me, Lili Marlene,
With me, Lili Marlene.

Old Nazis, at least in spirit, never die, he decided. The last time he had heard the song was when Marlene Dietrich had sung it to Spencer Tracy in the movie, *Judgment at Nuremberg.* Tracy, he seemed to recall, hadn't been too impressed with it then, and Franco was even less impressed with it now.

He shook his head sadly and wondered what it must be like to have missed the point of one's entire life.

Valena Jarvis should know. Unfortunately, she never would. *Judgment at Nuremberg* was not a television detective show.

Franco left the houseboat incensed at the Americans at Autley House who had allowed all this to happen. At least Beria, in hunting down those responsible for the concentration camps, had been trying to do the right thing.

"Finished?" E.L. Flood asked, as Franco reached the dock.

"I am here," Franco said. "Keep the woman in isolation. Get a court order if you need to, but absolutely no lawyers and no interviews unless I clear it. Do you have any idea when the forensic team will be here?"

Flood checked his watch.

"Best guess is in about an hour. They're driving in from D.C."

"Cox coming with them?"

Flood nodded.

"He'll know what to do," Franco said. "Just keep the rest of these people clear of the body."

"Can do," Flood said. "You staying around, Sal?"

"I'm heading back right now. Why?"

"What about the state trooper?"

"What about him?" Franco asked.

"Aren't you going to apologize?"

"For what?" Franco snapped. "For him not arresting me? Give me a break, E.L. I'm not running for office. He can go fuck himself. He was talking when he should have been listening."

Leaving E.L. Flood standing on the dock, Franco turned and sprinted up the levee to the waiting helicopter. Two minutes later they were airborne and flying low toward Washington.

Next stop? The Pentagon archives, the OVERCAST file, and, hopefully, the new identities of the Nazis who were now being contractually assassinated.

Admittedly, Franco was not exactly enthused by the latest turn of events. He was finding himself being lured into a situation wherein he had no choice but to locate any remaining Nazis, not only to develop affiliations that could help identify the shooter but also to *protect* them from the assassin who was still at large and who obviously possessed much more information on what the Autley House recruits had done prior to their clandestine immigration to the United States.

Had all of the murdered men been members of Einsatzkommando IV? Or had there been other Einsatzkommando units in which they had served?

Were they being punished for past offenses? Or was there another, hidden agenda connected with their deaths?

Was there a previously set number of men the shooter had been contracted to kill? Or were the four deaths, to date, simply the beginning of much more ambitious project?

Franco now knew the answer to why these particular men. They were Nazis who were doubtless connected with the concentration camps and who had escaped justice with what was evidently the full knowledge and support of the U.S. government. Their assassinations *had* to be someone's attempt to make them pay for their crimes. Based on what he now knew, this was the only remotely plausible scenario.

But who was behind it all?

Not the shooter. He was contract, working for whomever.

Who then? Some private entity? Some consortium? Could it be state-sponsored?

Franco mulled this over and began to realized that there was only one group of people who remained totally committed to the identification and prosecution of Nazi war criminals: *the Israelis*.

Could he rule them out?

Of course not. They had demanded accountability since the war. Further, with the Mossad, Israel possessed both the technical means and demonstrated ruthlessness necessary to carry out such a plan.

But, Franco reminded himself, regardless of how plausible this theory sounded, it was still a more general approach to responsibility and far beyond his initial assignment to capture the assassin. If it turned out that the Israelis were culpable, the American response would be generated at a level well above his station in life.

Put it back into perspective, Franco admonished himself. Review the OVERCAST file and find out how many Nazis came to work for the U.S. government.

Others could argue the political questions.

He would find the shooter.

CHAPTER 50

The Watergate Hotel, Washington, D.C., 11:30 A.M.

While not exactly suspicious, Cory was experiencing decidedly mixed emotions as he knocked on the door of apartment 606. Since leaving Richmond and until pulling into the hotel garage, he had been unable to stop thinking about Monika Sotelo or, most specifically, her apparent connection with Eisler.

The benefit of the doubt, he reminded himself. But this did little to help. Try as he would, aside from pure speculation, he still could not understand why the old man had gone to such unnecessary ends. Further, his earlier rationale—Monika being Eisler's spy—seemed even more ludicrous the longer he mulled it over.

Less than many, he thought again, as the door cracked open. Moodily detached, he remembered to be polite.

"Damon!" Eisler smiled warmly. "I am so pleased you could come."

"Even though I'm early?"

"Nonsense," Eisler said, as he ushered Cory inside. "Was it not Proust who told us the only thing worse than time being wasted was time spent waiting?"

"Could be," Cory said vaguely. "About the only thing I remember about Proust was that he was allergic to noise and light and spent most of his time in a cork-lined, darkened room. Of course that being the case, I suppose he would have had an inordinate number of hours to think about time."

Eisler nodded his approval and squeezed Cory's forearm.

"And while in his room, Damon. What kind of time was that? Waiting? Or wasted?"

"Both kinds," Cory said quickly. "He was waiting to waste time waiting."

Eisler's eyes danced with pleasure.

"Excellent, Damon," he chuckled. "Excellent. But on this day we shall do neither. Please, come, I have prepared refreshments."

As Eisler led him to the leather seating area, Cory glanced around the apartment. Pock had said it was small, but Pock had failed to mention it was like a small museum. Why even the air smelled priceless, and as for the furnishings, the intimate noble feel of the room, Cory could only imagine the money and effort Eisler must have expended.

"I see you are a collector," he understated, as he took the proffered chesterfield sofa. "Some of these artifacts must be invaluable."

"Vignettes of history," Eisler said proudly, taking it all in with a gracious wave of the hand as he sat on the matching love seat to Cory's right. "Many are gifts. Others, well, let us just say, on occasion, I find the process of acquiring such glimpses quite rewarding. May I offer you a cocktail?"

Cory looked to the coffee table. Like the sofas, it was a dark, substantial nineteenth-century piece with straight carved legs and a highly polished top. At one corner there was an oval brass ashtray; at a second, a copy of *Steichen: A Man and His Art*, and in the center, as in a magazine photograph, a gleaming sterling tray held two full decanters, a silver-lidded ice bowl, and two tall glasses. All were of Waterford crystal, and all were part of a matching set.

"Please," Cory said, as they selected decanters. Eisler took scotch, the lighter liquor, and Cory the darker bourbon. Twisting off the stoppers, they poured in two fingers each and tossed in a few cubes of ice.

"To whom?" Eisler asked as he raised his glass for a toast.

"Dostoyevsky?" Cory said, with something in mind.

Eisler smiled and touched his glass to Cory's.

"To Dostoyevsky," he repeated. "May we learn from what we suffer."

Eisler took a drink. Cory refrained, and Eisler suspected what was coming.

"Something is wrong, Damon?" he asked, his voice benign.

Cory nodded and began to inspect the ice in his glass.

"It was the rest of the Dostoyevsky quote," he said. "About the deceptions one endures?"

Eisler said nothing, and Cory looked up from his glass and directly into the older man's eyes.

"Have you deceived me, ambassador?" he said coolly. "Lied to me? Or will you explain to me about . . . ."

"Monika Sotelo?" Eisler breathed, completing the question. "You wonder the how's and why's of this woman, correct?"

"Yes," Cory answered. "I feel I'm entitled to wonder. Don't you?"

Eisler considered his answer. He had known Cory would eventually get to this and was thusly prepared. But he would proceed with prudence. A bit the mentor, a bit the alchemist, he would make the dark seem light and right.

"Yes, Damon," he said. "You are more than entitled to wonder. Wonderment is the logical progression of doubt, You did doubt me, did you not, Damon?"

"For the first time," Cory answered truthfully.

"Then you have again pleased me, Damon. For through this doubt, we have achieved a more absolute relationship."

"A more absolute relationship?" Cory asked. "You're telling me that doubt between us is something good?"

Eisler smiled indulgently and leaned over and squeezed Cory's hand.

"Not only beneficial," he explained. "It is the logical progression of man. You see, doubt is an essential preliminary to discovery and learning. Some, academics, term it curiosity. But it is really doubt. Doubting old theories, old knowledge, wanting to move into something new, something more valid. How could man progress and develop comparison and judgment without this questioning and doubt? He cannot, of course, and why is this, Damon? Will you share your thoughts with me?"

Cory mumbled some half-hearted nonsense about Sartre, existentialism, and man's right to individual choice. He knew not only that it had little to do with anything, but also that Eisler expected some relatively intellectual response. Since Proust and Dostoyevsky had been tapped out, Sartre was about the only person he could remember without thinking too hard. Besides, *Sartre says* was always a reasonably good answer for any rhetorical question.

"Yes," Eisler nodded pontifically. "Sartre. And back to the doubt, we must realize that doubt is to knowledge as knowledge is to trust. In a like manner, knowledge multiplies doubt and doubt leads to new knowledge. They are inseparable, Damon. And with respect to the woman, my deceiving you and your doubting me, you see, Damon, such was necessary to ensure your progress and thereby ensure completion of your assignment."

Cory took the first sip of his drink and leaned back on the couch as he allowed the liquor to burn slowly down the back of his throat. At this point, he had literally no idea as to what Eisler had been so passionately explaining. Eisler, on the other hand, seemed quite pleased with his efforts. There was a slight, telling smile on his lips, and his eyes were sparkling their *it's all so simple* expression as he waited for a response.

"What led you to believe I wouldn't complete the assignment?" Cory asked spitefully. "Have I ever let you down before?"

"No, Damon," Eisler said gently. "You have not. But your manner on the aircraft gave me cause for concern. You seemed too introspective, Damon. Too contemptuous in your regard for yourself."

"Really?" Cory said tersely. "Well, if you were so concerned, why didn't you just get someone else to do it. Pock was here. He's crying for an assignment. He wants me to intercede on his behalf."

Eisler shook his head and made a negative motion with his hand.

"I'm well aware of Pock's needs, Damon," he sighed. "He is to receive an assignment shortly. He will be traveling to Europe in a week or so."

"I'm sure he'll be pleased to hear it," Cory shrugged. "But that still doesn't answer my question. There are others besides Pock. Like I asked, if you were so concerned about my botching this, why not get one of them?"

"Because you are the best," Eisler said matter of factly.

Cory ignored the kudo.

"Why the woman?" he asked.

"Because this is perhaps the most important assignment I have ever chartered. The number of targets, their geographical location, their positions within our government, and their importance to the Russians. Very sensitive, Damon. Too sensitive to allow for any margin of error. Even for any remote possibility of error."

Cory said nothing and a tangible silence hung in the air. Eisler broke it.

"There is no shame attached to this, Damon," he said softly. "But, before, with the other women? I knew why you chose them as opposed to others younger. It was the stress, Damon. Anxiety. Frustration. But stress cannot be seen. Only the manner in which you chose to deal with it, your introspection and cynicism, only through these am I able to discern its level of persistence."

Cory glanced back into Eisler's eyes. The expression had changed. Now, they were mellowed with understanding and something very close to empathy.

"No shame, Damon," Eisler repeated, his voice a whisper as he affectionately caressed Cory's hand. "I understand and I am honored at having been selected by you as a, most times, inadequate father surrogate. Indeed, I try hard and, indeed, I value your trust. Still, I cannot become something I am not. And this, perhaps, is my greatest regret."

Cory took a long sip of his bourbon and thought about the emotions running through his mind. Oddly enough, now that the surrogate issue had been broached, he didn't feel as bad as he had always anticipated he would. And shame? None at all. It was simply his way and what was needed and Eisler indulging both in stride.

"You know," Cory said. "Without your understanding, the difficulty...."

"Understanding?" Eisler let the word out slowly. "Of course I understand. I, too, was orphaned as a child, Damon. I understand your needs only too well. In some things, only a parent can help. For you, these needs are spawned from the stress and conflict arising from our endeavors—*my* endeavors, in which you are my sword afield. I agonize for you, Damon, for I have been there. I know of the difficulties, the loneliness, the sinister questions of purpose and prejudice which trail our kind like a pack of mongrel dogs. I know it well, Damon. At times, I know it too well...."

Eisler's voice trailed off as he took a drink of his scotch.

"Was she adequate, Damon?" he asked after a moment. "Or were my efforts misspent?"

"More than adequate," Cory admitted. "Different than before. Somehow, with Monika, it seemed more mutual. More, I don't know, reciprocal. Why do you suppose this is?"

"I've told you before," Eisler said. "You are a man of purpose, and men of purpose defy convention. It simply cannot be another way because you are continually progressing, continually making judgments stemming from your doubts. This is why Monika, even though I selected her, served her purpose despite the fact you found her out. By the way, Damon, how did you find her out?"

"Something she said," Cory told him. "One of your phrases: more than a few, less than many. I started wondering about it and finally checked her purse when she was sleeping. I found the Barclay's card with one of our foreign operations account numbers on it."

Eisler chuckled wryly.

"Foiled by my own words, it would seem, eh, Damon?"

Cory returned the smile and nodded.

"The priest, I assume, was also one of yours?" he asked.

"Yes," Eisler said without further elaboration.

"So what made you think I would want to meet Monika?"

Eisler offered an indulgent gesture with his hands.

"In all candor," he said casually, "it was but a foregone conclusion. I know you well, Damon. Before, in the Latin countries, I have seen the type of women you select to facilitate your needs. Monika possessed the attributes of all of them and more. Correct?"

"Yes," Cory had to admit. "You realize it's not just a physical attraction?"

"It seldom ever is," Eisler shrugged. "Not with you, not with anybody. No, Damon, and I've mentioned this before also. You are a handsome man, an intelligent man. As to why these particular women appeal to you, well, it would be inappropriate of me to comment. In any event, after we visited on the aircraft and I observed your behavior, I began to suspect you were going to desire another shortly. If so, I wanted it to be with someone over whom I possessed some measure of influence. If this was wrong, then I am wrong. But I will not apologize, Damon. As I indicated, this is the most important assignment of our careers. Failure, however remote the possibility, had to be addressed in advance."

Cory took a sip of his drink and considered Eisler's words.

"And what if it looked as if I was going to fail?" he asked.

Eisler stared at him levelly.

"Put yourself in my position, Damon. What would you have ordered?"

"My elimination," Cory said flatly, making it a mandate.

Eisler nodded pensively.

"The mind is a fragile blossom, Damon. Acutely delicate. In another world, the blossom torn may be mended. In our world, the blossom torn is error at large and, in such a situation, the error must be corrected. Corrected by elimination and corrected before the network suffers a disservice. Can you appreciate this, Damon? And, in this context, can you now see how through doubt we achieve a more absolute relationship?"

"You make it sound even honorable," Cory said.

"It *is* honorable, Damon," Eisler whispered. "In our purpose, our calling, to know when to employ elimination is perhaps the most honorable of duties. And why is this? It is because from this tender seed, this tender network, here, in our hands, is from whence additional blossoms prosper. Promise me, Damon. Promise me you will never forget this."

"I promise," Cory said softly.

Eisler smiled a paternal smile and squeezed Cory's hand once again.

"Fine, Damon," he said cheerfully. "Now, what do you say we freshen our drinks and then you can tell me of you actions before we take our Thanksgiving meal."

"I think I would like that," Cory smiled, as he passed his glass to Eisler.

"I think I would like it too," Eisler replied.

CHAPTER 51

The Pentagon, 11:45 A.M.

While Cory sipped bourbon and communed with Eisler, Franco drank coffee and continued to read. In his mind, they remained spectrums apart. In distance, much closer: five quick minutes over holiday streets.

But Sal Franco had forgotten about the holidays. After landing atop FBI Headquarters, he had retrieved his Corvette and driven directly to the Pentagon. Briefly, he had considered telephoning Jonathon Weall and passing on the Nazi information.

He had just as quickly decided against it. *If* he called, Franco knew he would only be forced to endure a round of Jonathon questions: the *are-you-sure-what-does-it-mean-where-are-you-going-with-it* routine.

Questions to which answers could only be guesses.

Guesses to which answers would only be questions.

A pointless conversation, Franco had determined.

He needed to first review the OVERCAST file. Only then could he speak his mind with any reasonable measure of confidence.

But this was all earlier, Franco remembered as he leaned back in his chair and dabbed a squeeze of Lidex to his tongue. Now, as he had been for the previous hour, he was back in the archives, back under the overhead light, back at the cluttered archive desk.

Back in the rodent laboratory, he thought. But, this time he was alone in the rodent lab. A fact which suited Franco just fine seeing as how the previous evening's attendant, the TV laxative doctor, had been kind enough—or was it lazy enough—not to have bothered to return any of the materials to their original storage burrow.

The cardboard boxes, those Franco had already reviewed as well as those remaining, were precisely where Franco had left them, and he had found the still-classified OVERCAST file stacked upon another box just to the left of the chair.

As yet, even he had to admit the going had been dismally slow. He had finished only about a quarter of the OVERCAST materials, and still he had identified absolutely nothing with which to either confirm or contradict the story related by Valena Jarvis.

No index, no order, Franco thought, as he turned his attention back to the OVERCAST box, reached in, and withdrew a fresh sheath of documents and continued to read:

A. SCREENING
Persons brought to the U.S. hereunder shall be screened by the Commanding General, USFET, on the basis of available records (Para 5. SWNCC 257/24). No previous position or honors awarded these . . . .

Franco flipped a page:

B. MOVEMENT OF SPECIALISTS
The War Department will be responsible for moving families of specialists already in the United States (Para 2a(2) SWNTCC 257/24). Normally families will accompany specialists upon initial evacuation . . . .

Old news, Franco thought, turning through a few more pages to a memorandum:

DATE: 18 September 1946
SUBJECT: Allocation of Non-perishable Canned Goods.

"Let 'em eat cake," Franco quipped, flipping on:

TO: G-4, EUCOM LTC Madamelly
FROM: LTC Shields, OMGUS G-4

7(a). JIOA 1243, Memorandum: Proposed Procedures with Respect to the Entry into the United States for Residence of Aliens Certified as Persons Whose Admission is Highly Desirable in the National Interest . . . .

7(g). JIOA Cable, CM IN 3544, 21 January 1947: Policy Acquisition . . . .

9(C). JIOA 3435, Memorandum for Executive/Intelligence Division, GSUSA. Subject: Immigration of PEREGRINE Specialists, 19 February 1947.

Franco paused and read this last memorandum in its entirety. It seemed to provide some kind of guidelines concerning transportation of the scientist's personal effects from London to Canada. No names though and nothing really central to his investigation. However, the one thing it did do was make a reference to PEREGRINE in the OVERCAST files. This was the first time he'd come across a direct paper link and it only served to confirm

Senator Rossett's explanation. Now, at least in a documentary sense, he was able to prove the PEREGRINE-Autley House-OVERCAST connection. Anything now found in the OVERCAST files could be traced directly back to the assassinated scientists.

Franco pulled the memorandum from the rest and set it aside. Then he reached back into the box and grabbed another handful of documents. Most, he saw, were only more memoranda:

OMGUS Security Report Guidelines, 23 November 1946.
Air Intelligence Requirements Procedure, 3 January 1947.
Collection Office, ID, WDGS, Fiscal Notes, 18 March 1947.

"Nothing, nothing and nothing." Franco turned these over and continued to move down through the pile, the next item of which was a dog-eared manila folder. Across the front a label had been attached at an angle and on it were the words PEREGRINE IMMIGRATION: 1 January 1946 - 31 December 1946.

Franco held his breath and opened the file.
He exhaled slowly.
"Finally," he whispered to himself.

The folder's first item was a memorandum, an *original* memorandum dated 17 October 1946. Aware of his heart beating, he scanned the routing information at the top:

TO: Commanding Officer, Fort Strong, Massachusetts
FROM: American Consul General, Niagara Falls, Ontario, Canada
SUBJECT: Celt, Gustav (AUTLEY HOUSE-PEREGRINF)

Franco jerked this from the file and set it aside. There was another nearly identical memorandum underneath. He read it. The date was 11 September 1946 and the name Coswith, Thomas.

Unfamiliar, he thought, flipping it up and reviewing the file's third item. Again, it was an identical memorandum with the exception of the date and name: 13 October 1946, Davidson, Aaron. Once more an unfamiliar name.

The file was arranged in alphabetical order, Franco realized. The dates were unimportant. He began flipping through the sheets quickly: G's, H's, I's, J's.

Bingo on the J's. First item: Jarvis, Steven. Date: 17 October 1946. He jerked it out.

The next item: Jarvis, Valena. Date: 17 October 1946. He jerked this one out also and flipped on: K's, L's, M's, no N's or O's, then Pointer, William, 17 October 1946. Jerk and save and continue to read:

No Q's, then: Rouse, Robert. Memorandum date: 17 October 1946.
This was it, Franco knew. The connection was the 17 October 1946

memorandum. But his elation was short-lived. So what? Where to go from here? And, more central than that, why had Valena Jarvis lied? If, as Senator Rossett had indicated, the men all traveled in groups, then she should have known the others due to the fact she had come from Canada to Fort Strong with them because all the travel memoranda bore the same date. Had she lied? Could it be they were *not* Nazis? That, in fact, they were really Russians and the Nazi story had been just that, a story?

No, Franco told himself. She hadn't been lying. If she had misrepresented the truth, then he would have picked up on it. But still, all four of the dead men were connected by this date and this memorandum and it didn't . . . .

"Damn," he whispered. He had missed the obvious. *Four men?* What if there were *six*? *Eight*? Even more? He hadn't even considered this; he'd been too interested in the names. He should have been looking for the dates. Looking for anyone else who had traveled on orders dated 17 October 1946.

Turning back to the front of the file, he began to go through the documents once again, this time looking only at the date. Two minutes later, he had three additional memoranda stacked atop those of Jarvis, et al. In the order he had found them, they were:

Grawitz, Ernst
Keith, Wilford
Urbanosky, Alan
Wylie, Miles

Nine, Franco thought. Eight men and one wife, and four of the eight were now dead. Why? Still unknown. Still unknown, for that matter, was whether they were Russians or Nazis because he was not yet able to prove either with anything on paper or with any direct corroboration from the men themselves.

And what about the new names? Keith, Urbanosky, and Wylie?

What if Celt, Pointer, Rouse, and Jarvis were not the only targets? What if they were just the first four of what could be a total of seven?

At this realization Franco began to move. The memoranda clutched in his hand, he headed through the archive door and back into the Pentagon corridor.

He had one thought in his mind: *find the remaining three and find them fast.*

The shooter would already know their names.

CHAPTER 52

The Watergate Hotel, Washington, D.C., 12:20 P.M.

"Then only one remains," Eisler said casually, briefly wondering when Jonathon Weall would get around to calling to advise him of Steven Jarvis' death.

"Miles Wylie," Cory nodded, as he took a sip of his drink. "Do you still want me to go to Puerto Rico? I've made reservations for this evening's flight from Baltimore."

Eisler thought about this for a moment.

"Have you given any consideration to your next assignment?" he asked.

"Not really," Cory admitted. "I guess I've been too busy just trying to decide whether to stay in or not."

"And what did you decide?"

"Nothing yet."

Eisler nodded in understanding.

"Have you ever seen the temples of Kei Wah?" he asked, probing.

"No."

"They are quite spectacular. I believe you would enjoy them."

Cory knew where Eisler was leading.

"India?" he asked. "I think not."

Eisler smiled knowingly and leaned forward in his seat.

"I was speaking of Delhi, Damon. Not some military encampment on the Chinese border."

Cory arched a skeptical eyebrow and Eisler chuckled politely.

"Damon," he said. "I can assure you it will be much more academic than our endeavors to date."

"What is the assignment?" Cory asked, not at all believing the word "academic."

"Technology acquisition," Eisler told him, remembering a recent *Wall Street Journal* article. "In the months to come, we will see India become one of the world's major systems engineering powers—computer chips and hardware and the like. They have both an inexpensive labor base as well as access to the natural resources necessary to move into this field. You will be under embassy cloak, perhaps as an economic attaché, and assigned to monitor the Indian government's relationship with the Chinese, who, we suspect, will be their primary market. I anticipate this area will be of extreme importance to the president."

"But I don't speak the language," Cory said. "And I don't know anything about the Indian people."

"You will, Damon," Eisler said gently. "This can easily be accomplished in Puerto Rico, at the villa. Should you choose India, I shall arrange for you to be instructed in both the language and the customs of the country."

A pained expression crossed Cory's face. Eisler saw it.

"Does the idea of learning something new trouble you, Damon?"

"Some," Cory said sullenly. "I loathe tutoring."

Eisler reached over and patted Cory's hand.

"But it is always required," he smiled. "Just as, before surgery, a doctor examines the blood, bone, and tissue of a patient, we must examine the politics, religion, and customs of a people before acting. To do otherwise, to act impetuously, I think this may deny us, deny *you*, what could be a crucial measure of insight. Do you not agree?"

Cory took a drink of his bourbon.

"It is not a difficult language," Eisler added. "Why even I possess a rudimentary knowledge of its more common phrases."

"You can work crossword puzzles in six languages," Cory teased. "I'm still having have trouble with compound sentences in English."

They laughed together, then Eisler again became serious.

"So you will go to Delhi for me, Damon?"

"Can I choose my own number two?" Cory asked first.

"Boudreaux Pock?" Eisler guessed.

"How long is he going to be in Europe?"

"Not long," Eisler answered. "Surely no longer than a fortnight."

"And after that?" Cory asked.

"Very well, Damon. You may have Boudreaux."

"And how about a promotion for Pock, too?"

Eisler smiled and nodded.

"Yes, Damon," he said. "You may tell Boudreaux his past transgressions are henceforth forgiven."

"He'll like that," Cory said. "I owe you another favor."

"You owe me nothing, Damon," Eisler said with a shake of his head. "But now that all of this administrative twaddle is over, would you like to hear of my strategy in India? The predicators of your and Boudreaux's new endeavor?"

Cory didn't but knew by Eisler's tone that he would.

"Do I have a choice?" he smiled.

Eisler's eyes twinkled as he shifted in the chair.

"Perhaps we should begin with the economic realities, Damon," he said. "Specifically, Dehli's reliance upon China as a trading partner . . . ."

While Eisler continued his off-the-cuff briefing, Cory found himself only half-listening. He knew, in Puerto Rico, he would hear all of this again and more, so now he allowed himself to relax, sip his bourbon, and nod in understanding when Eisler expected a response.

But, as it turned out, there would be considerably more nods than Cory expected. The briefing continued for half an hour, ending only when Eisler looked into Cory's face and asked, "Do you eat cranberry sauce, Damon?"

"Not really," Cory shrugged.

"Neither do I," Eisler said as he stood and walked to the telephone and called the Watergate Terrace Restaurant.

"I'm ready now," he said simply, before replacing the receiver and turning back to Cory.

"You will wait in the bathroom when the meal is catered," he told him.

Ten minutes later, Cory was counting shower tiles.

Eisler, he thought fondly.

He even made lunch an intrigue.

***

The Pentagon, 12:35 P.M.

Major General T. Elliot Parkins had been more than surprised to see Sal Franco charging back into the duty office.

"You still here?" he snapped.

"I was going to ask you the same thing," Franco shot back. "Is the army running short of generals?"

Parkins snorted a gruff laugh and indicated the chair across from his desk.

"Four-day holiday," he explained. "I drew two of the four. Forty-eight hours in the building, and if I want to nap, there's a cot down the hall. Now, my turn. Why are *you* still roaming around? You stay any longer and I'm afraid I'll be forced to put you on the payroll and give you an office."

"We're already on the same payroll," Franco smiled, as he sat down. "And I haven't been here all this time. I left and came back."

"So what's the problem?" Parkins asked, his wary eyes narrowing. "I thought I put out the word for those archive people to cooperate with you. If someone isn't, you just point to the spot and they'll find out just how bright two stars can get. I'll have that hole looking like ten daytimes in about thirty seconds."

From his tone, Franco would suspect Parkins would like nothing better.

"They cooperated fine, general," Franco assured him. "The reason I'm here is to ask you to do something else for me."

"Something else meaning what?"

Franco reached into his pocket and passed a small scrap of paper across the desk. On it, in neatly printed letters, were the names Ernst Grawitz, Wilford Keith, Alan Urbanosky, and Miles Wylie.

Parkins took the paper, glanced at it, then looked back up to Franco.

"I need to locate those men," Franco explained. "They work somewhere in Defense."

"Any idea where?" Parkins asked.

"None whatsoever," Franco said. "That's why I came back to you. I kind of figured if anybody could, you'd be the person to tell me where I would be able to find a list of everybody working . . . ."

Franco allowed his voice to trail off.

"It's going to be a hell of a list," Parkins said, looking back at the names. "Taking in all the components, there's probably two million people working in, or for, the Defense Department. Do you have any identifiers? Social Security numbers? Birth dates? Anything?"

"They're going to be old," Franco told him. "Probably in their seventies."

"Old," Parkins muttered, leaning back in his chair and making sucking sounds with his teeth while mulling it over. "Well, that's something, I guess."

Reaching to his telephone, Parkins picked up the receiver and punched in a four-digit code.

"SECDEF-FOMAN," he explained to Franco while the connection was being made. "Force Management. They've got the whole world on computer. We'll try for a random run there first."

Franco nodded encouragingly, listening as Parkins began barking orders to an unseen, and probably quite intimidated, underling.

"This is General Parkins. Patch me through to the duty officer." Parkins paused, listening for a moment, then lowered his voice. "I don't give a goddamn that he's eating, if I wanted him later I'd call later. You tell him to get his face out of that feed bag and get on the horn *now*. You understand that, soldier?"

Parkins looked over to Franco, a pained expression on his face while he waited for the duty officer.

"This is General Parkins," he said, as the man came on the line. "What did you say your name was? Right. Right. Well, okay Captain Chambers, I've got a little something I need done and I need a good man to do it. Do you have your computers fired up over there? Fine, fine. Now, listen up, Chambers. I'm going to give you four names. I'm going to give them to you last name first, first name last, and I'm only going to do it once, so you get yourself a pencil and listen up.

"No, you just take down the names now, then once we get to that, then I'll tell you what I want done. Okay? You have your pencil? Good. The first

AUTLEY HOUSE

one is Grawitz, first name Ernst. I'll spell it for you: G-R-A-W-I-T-Z comma E-R-N-S-T."

As Franco watched, Parkins spelled out all four names, then asked the officer to spell them back for him.

"That's real fine, Chambers," Parkins continued. "Now, I want you to take that list and run those four names through your computer and tell me where the good gentlemen work. No, Chambers. If I knew that, then I wouldn't be calling you, would I? And, no, you may *not* ask why the general wants this information. Yes. Yes. I'm told they should all be in their seventies. Yes. Goddamnit, Chambers, use your goddamn head! I just told you they are in their seventies, right? Well, then you take this year and subtract seventy. What do you get? That's correct. Now take those names I gave you and run them through your computer and get me everything you can find on anybody with those names who is, say, sixty-five years old or older. Now, is that too difficult, Captain Chambers? Fine. You get on that right now, Chambers. I'm waiting for the information. What do mean what's my extension? I'm the goddamn General Officer of the Day. Just pick up the phone and ask for me. Oh, and Captain? Let's not keep me waiting all day, okay? That's all, Chambers."

Parkins replaced the receiver and looked over to Franco.

"Boy, they sure hate my ass," he winked wolfishly. "And that's the best part of wearing these stars."

Franco chuckled politely.

"You sure seem to enjoy your work, general."

"Just building character, Agent Franco. If there's something more worthless than a soldier with no combat time, I sure as hell don't know what it is. You know, we've got field-grade officers running around here who have never heard a shot fired in anger?"

Franco said nothing, and Parkins shook his head sadly.

"What the hell," he sighed. "I guess we've all got our own crosses to bear. You want some coffee or something? It's probably going to be a half-hour or so before the captain gets back to me."

"With a little milk if you can get it?" Franco nodded.

"Coming right up." Parkins picked up the telephone and ordered the coffee. Then he placed his elbows on the desk and looked over to Franco.

"So, Agent Franco," he said. "Are you going to tell me what all this is about?"

"I would if I could," Franco shrugged.

"But you can't so you won't," Parkins said good-naturedly. "I've already got too many worries anyway."

Franco glanced up to the flashpoint wall maps.

"No shit," he said softly.

***

The Watergate Hotel, 12:50 P.M.

The meal, thought Cory, was excellent: roast turkey, dressing, giblet gravy, corn and yams. It was not quite home cooked, but Cory had long ago forgotten that luxury.

They dined at the coffee table, dabbing soiled fingers with starched linen napkins.

"I ate too much," Cory observed as he leaned back on the sofa.

"A seasonal excess," Eisler added, as he too finished. "Quite permissible."

They chuckled together as Eisler poured black coffees.

Cory lit his pipe.

Eisler slid over the brass ashtray, then handed Cory his coffee.

"So, Damon," he said. "If it is to be India, it will be a decision I believe you will find enjoyable. It is a lovely country, a loveliness born of extremes, of the natural blend of contrasts. Winters into summer, plains into mountains. Do you know of the diversions there, Damon?"

"Not really," Cory told him. "Just the riots, the poverty, and the fact the Indian soldiers are very poorly trained."

"But India is more than that, Damon. There is a place you should occasion to visit, the mountains of the Deccan Plateau, to the east of Bombay. There are tombs there, Damon. Those of the Maratha people who, in the 1600s served as mercenary soldiers for the Yavada Prince, Sivaji, who vanquished the Moguls and sacked the port city of Surat.

"Go there, Damon. Go and pause and listen to their history. Go and see their search for truth. Their frescoed scrolls, their scriptures and all the rest. I will not tell you of what you will feel, Damon. For respect for you precludes my unnecessarily spoiling the emotion. Suffice it to say, though, what you will feel, as I did, is the India of which I speak."

Cory puffed on his pipe and nodded in understanding.

Feelings, he thought. Such a small, so very selfish word.

He wondered which Indians would die by his hand.

***

The Pentagon, 1:02 P.M.

At the corner of the desk the phone rang. T. Elliot Parkins looked to Franco, then quickly grabbed for the receiver.

"General Parkins," he growled. "Right. Right. Okay, give me what you've got, captain."

Watching hopefully, Franco felt his apprehension rise as the general began making notes on a yellow legal pad.

Definitely something new, he thought. But was it usable information?

The time seemed to hang there while the general scribbled on.

"Right," Parkins was saying. "Affirmative. Give me a spelling on that last word. Right. Okay. Fine. Is that it, Captain? Fine. You did good work, Chambers. I knew I could count on you."

Parkins replaced the receiver and looked across the desk to Franco.

"Seems like you're batting about 250."

"Two-fifty?" Franco asked.

Parkins nodded and glanced down to his notes.

"Only two were in our records as Defense employees," he said.

"Then why only two-fifty?"

"One of the two is dead," Parkins explained. "Alan Urbanosky. He worked at the Naval Air Engineering Center in Lakehurst, New Jersey. Died in 1971. Heart attack."

Franco thought for a moment.

"Any survivors? A wife? Children?"

"None of record," Parkins answered. "Want to hear about Miles Wylie? According to the computer, he's still breathing."

"Still on the job?"

The general checked his notes.

"Not anymore," he said. "He retired about six months ago from the Defense Advanced Research Projects Agency. He worked at the army's Chemical Research and Development Center. That's about forty-five minutes northeast of Baltimore."

"Where's he living now, general?"

"According to this," Parkins answered, "Middle River, Maryland. If memory serves me correct, that's a small town on the outskirts of Baltimore on the way to the center. I've got his phone number here if you want it."

"No," Franco said. "I'm going to have to make a personal call on him. You have a specific address?"

The general grunted and jotted down something on the scrap of paper Franco had given him earlier.

"Here," he said, passing it over to Franco. "That's probably good. It's where we're mailing his retirement checks."

Franco glanced down at the address: 28 Old Potters Road, Middle River, MD.

"Thanks, general," Franco said, as he put the paper in his pocket, stood and shook Parkins' hand. "You've helped me out more than you'll ever know."

"Just keeping the customers satisfied," Parkins grinned. "And don't worry about the thanks, Agent Franco. If I ever need anything from the FBI, guess who'll be the first person on my list to call?"

Franco laughed and let himself out of the general's office.

Ten minutes later, the Corvette's top down and heater on high, he was roaring out of Washington toward Baltimore and beyond.

He slid a cassette into the Corvette's tape deck and turned the volume up loud as a driving salsa beat throbbed from the speakers.

Traveling music, Franco thought, as he thumb-tapped along.

He wondered if "Lili Marlene" could be sung in Spanish.

***

The Watergate Hotel, 1:20 P.M.

Cory knocked out his pipe in the brass ashtray and drank the last of his coffee.

"More?" Eisler asked.

"No," Cory said. "It's time for me to be leaving."

A somewhat dejected expression crossed Eisler's face.

"I will remember this time together, Damon," he said sincerely, standing with Cory. "Perhaps we can steal a few more private hours in Puerto Rico?"

"You'll be coming there?"

Eisler nodded.

"It is necessary if we are to preserve your story. Again, tell those at the villa you've been in Manila and that I'm joining you shortly for debriefing."

"When will you be arriving?" Cory asked.

"Within the week," Eisler told him. "I must remain here for a few days to observe the effects of your venture."

Cory nodded in understanding as they began walking toward the door.

"About Pock," he said. "Will you tell him about India? Or do you want me to?"

"I will advise him," Eisler said quickly. "I need to explain his European assignment, so I will be speaking with him anyway."

"Well then, tell him I'll be leaving my vehicle at the Baltimore airport. The keys will be on top of the left front tire beneath the wheel well."

"Consider it done, Damon," Eisler smiled. "And I do thank you for coming here today. I have very few visitors and it is . . . oh, I nearly forgot . . . ."

Cory waited by the door as Eisler turned and shuffled toward the kitchen. He returned a moment later and in his hands, there was white wad of tissue paper no larger than a man's fist. Around its top was a thin red ribbon tied in a shoestring bow.

"A small token," Eisler explained, handing the package to Cory. "Something for your trip."

Curious, Cory untied the bow and peeked inside. He smiled. It was perhaps a quarter-pound of toasted cashews.

"Thank you," he said, sincerely touched by the gesture.

"I knew you liked them," Eisler whispered, as he reached over and shook Cory's hand. "Happy Thanksgiving, Damon."

Cory slid the package into his pocket and looked down at Eisler. His eyes were sparkling now and his face almost shining with pride.

"Happy Thanksgiving, ambassador," Cory said softly, then he turned, opened the door and quickly left the apartment.

Miles Wylie, he was thinking. Close now, he was eager to get on the road. Anxious to get it all over and done with.

For his part, Eisler too was eager, only in a more theoretical sense. And while musing on the tending of his Damon just gone, he walked slowly to the window and stared toward the distant Capitol dome.

"A more perfect Union," he whispered, as he placed a hand against the glass.

He wondered how Cory endured such perfection.

CHAPTER 53

Middle River, Maryland, 2:25 P.M.

Topped with asphalt and patched with gravel, Old Potters Road was a winding, two-lane stretch of highway that hugged the shoreline of Chesapeake Bay. It began in the small township of Middle River to the south and followed the coast until merging into an Interstate some fifteen miles to the north.

While not nearly as exclusive, Franco found the area similar to the Hamptons: a coastal plain, a narrow highway, the bay view homes atop grassy dunes. Images of soaring gulls, sun-bleached woods, and boats and weathered piers.

Cruising at seventy, Franco looked at the houses and read the numbers of their roadside mailboxes. In Middle River, they had begun with 1 and now he was approaching 23. All the houses were to his right, and all seemed to be of a distinctly different style. A-frame contemporaries to Cape Cod traditional, some were large, some small, most in-between.

Franco decided it pretty in a vacation kind of way—in that *I'm renting a house at the beach* kind of way.

But this was not summer. This was late November, and most of the houses appeared vacant. And as Franco drove along, he realized that Old Potters Road was as deserted as the highway had been crowded. If travelers had been holiday driving, it was obvious their holiday was not to be spent along Old Potters Road. He hadn't passed a car since leaving Middle River.

"... twenty five ... twenty six ...."

Franco braked, downshifted into third, then second.

"Twenty eight."

Turning in at the next mailbox, he rolled up a sand-and-shell driveway and parked to the left of an old turquoise and white Volkswagen minibus. On the wagon's left bumper a decal read: US ARMY-CRDC-EDGEWOOD ARSENAL-CR4883.

So far, so good, Franco thought, as he climbed from the Corvette and looked over to the house.

It was a small, freshly painted New England-style cottage. A cozy white bungalow with hunter's green trim, wide slatted shutters, and a tall sloped roof.

Karen would think it charming, Franco guessed, as he walked to the door and rang the bell. In addition to looks, the house even felt like that of an artist in exile.

Franco rang the bell again. Still no answer. He moved to a window and peered between the shutter slats. No lights and tidy. Very tidy. It was a living room, and it looked like an advertisement in *Architectural Digest*—the latest Henredon collection in which every item, woods, upholstered pieces, even lamps and books, had been assembled to illustrate the advantages of catalog shopping.

Franco disliked catalogs. Miles Wylie evidently relied on them. Franco suspected he would be an impulsive man.

Stepping back from the window, Franco turned and walked around to the rear of the house. There, overlooking the water, he found a raised cedar deck and a matching pair of cushioned wrought-iron lounge chairs. In one chair, that nearest the house, a man was dozing in the sun. He was lying on his back and bundled up against the chill.

Watching him, Franco put the age at eighty-plus and the weight at no more than one-twenty. He was frail and emaciated in that uniquely regressive sort of way.

His face was pinched and literally no more than skin over skull. The complexion was the color of boiled pork fat. On his head, a red stocking cap was pulled down low over the ears, and the right eye socket was concealed behind a dark blue, nearly black, nylon patch.

Chemotherapy, Franco thought, as he moved a bit closer. Another life added to the cancer coffers.

"Miles Wylie?"

From the chair, the skull lolled in Franco's direction as the good eye watered open, blinked, then focused.

It was a strange eye, Franco realized. Neither kind nor cruel nor happy or sad. In fact, there was no emotion at all. No resentment at being awakened. No surprise at the sight of an unexpected visitor. Nothing. Just a pupil, dark and watching, adrift in a capsule of faded winter blue.

"Miles Wylie?" Franco repeated.

"Yes," Wylie answered in surprisingly deep voice.

"My name's Franco. May I sit down for a minute?"

"Why?"

Franco pulled out his badge and identification wallet.

"I'm a special agent with the FBI."

Wylie briefly glanced at the credentials, then indicated the vacant chair.

"I have some questions, Mr. Wylie," Franco said as he sat down.

"We all have questions," Wylie said softly as he turned his head and gazed toward the waters of Chesapeake Bay. "Out there, sailors wonder about the land. Here, we wonder about the sea."

"I have reason to believe your life is in danger," Franco said quietly.

"My *life*?" Wylie wheezed at the irony and looked back to Franco. "You may wish to tell me a fact of which I am unaware."

"It's not the disease," Franco explained. "It's something else, something from your past."

"And what would that be, Agent Franco?"

"Autley House," Franco said simply.

A wry look crossed Wylie's bony face.

"Indeed," he said thoughtfully. "Autley House. You force me to experience a curious sensation, Agent Franco."

"Why is that?"

"Because of what you asked," Wylie said as he gazed back to the water. "It is the sensation felt by one who worried about something for years, dreaded it, tried unsuccessfully to forget about it, and just when he does forget about it, he finds it only to return in the person of you."

Wylie paused for a moment, then continued.

"But you know something, Franco? Now, here, at this point, I find that the dread is not at all what I anticipated it to be. There is no worry anymore. No apprehension. Not even the slightest twinge of misgiving. Can you appreciate what I am trying to explain?"

Franco could. It was the outlook of a man who had accepted the certainty of his own death. The inevitability of its closeness, the inability to change its course.

"I think I understand," Franco whispered, going slowly, allowing Wylie to lead himself.

There was a second or two of introspection, then Wylie broke the silence.

"It began in Czechoslovakia, you know. At the Laban Institute outside Bratislava. My name was Helmut Blobel."

"You were a Nazi?"

"A *Sturmbannführer*, Wylie grunted. "A major in the SS."

"And you were assigned to something called Einsatzkommando IV."

At the question, Wylie turned and stared into Franco's face.

"Assigned?" he said. "Not at all. I *made* the assignments, Agent Franco. Einsatzkommando IV was my command . . . ."

***

Cory took a deep breath. Through the ART scope, the old man remained in focus.

It was almost 850 yards from the deserted A-frame at 25 Old Potter's Road to Miles Wylie's cedar deck. 850 yards and two houses in between.

A long shot, Cory thought, as he continued to squat in the A-frame's kitchen window. But not at all impossible. Just, *delicate*. He would have to keep his mind clear. Stop worrying about the mustachioed man in the short leather jacket.

Still, Cory thought. *Who in the hell was he?* Eisler's abstracts had said nothing about Wylie having any immediate family. Maybe the man was a nephew or something? Maybe another Russian agent? A contact? A cutout?

"Shit," Cory whispered. He could guess all day and never know. When he had first driven past Wylie's house, Leather Jacket had been peeking in the window. By the time he had decided on the A-frame, Jacket had been standing on Wylie's deck.

"Bastard," Cory breathed, as he repositioned the Steyr against his shoulder and continued to wait. Leather Jacket was screwing up the timing. He had no orders to shoot him, and he couldn't shoot Wylie and leave Jacket as a witness.

Course of action?

Bide his time.

Sooner or later, Jacket would leave.

***

" . . . so we burned off the tattoos to preclude identification."

Franco considered Wylie's statement. It was precisely what Senator Rossett had speculated and what he, himself, believed. Now he knew. All of the dead were definitely Nazis.

"Then there was no connection with the Russians at all?" Franco asked.

"None whatsoever," Wylie said with resignation. "It was simply self-preservation. It was either the French, the British, or the Americans. The Americans offered asylum here, off the Continent, so it seemed the logical choice. Besides, the American terms were much more lucrative."

"But how were you able to pass yourselves off as scientists?" Franco asked.

"Our relationship with the Laban Institute," Wylie explained. "Even though we were all early members of the SS and German by birth, each individual in my Einsatzkommando had been a scientist or a research technicians, either in training or in practice, before the war. If we weren't, we would have never been able to evaluate the work of the conscripted scientists.

"And Einsatzkommando IV was only one unit. I don't remember how many others there were total. I probably never knew. But I do remember there was an Einsatzkommando II somewhere in Poland and another, I believe it was VII, in northern Italy."

Franco leaned forward in the lounge chair.

"What was the purpose of these units?"

Wylie thought about the question before answering.

"For all of them?" he said. "I truthfully don't know. We only concerned ourselves with our activities so I never knew."

"What was the purpose of *your* unit?" Franco interrupted.

"It had a multidisciplinary function," Wylie answered. "I directed the assembly of Eastern European scientists and technicians who were interred at the Laban Institute. Under my supervision they developed various—how shall I say it?—certain biological *windows of opportunity*.

"For example," Wylie continued, "one section could be working on a particular biological asset problem. Another, on the means to distribute the asset. As I indicated, a multidisciplinary approach."

"Chemical warfare," Franco nodded.

"No," Wylie corrected, as if insulted. "Not chemical. *Biological* assets. Biological genetic modifiers and the means to introduce them into selected population groups."

"To what end?" Franco asked.

"Control, of course," Wylie said casually. "Subjugation of will through genetic modification. Do you know anything of homozygosity and semi-dominant genes?"

"Nothing at all," Franco admitted.

Wylie turned and looked into Franco's face for a moment.

"No," he said softly. "You would not. In that case, let me just say we were attempting to develop a biological asset with which to alter genetic predispositions with certain externally induced chemical modifiers. Our particular efforts were directed to postnatal amentia."

"Amentia?" Franco asked, unfamiliar with the word.

"Similar to staged levels of mental retardation," Wylie explained. "Not, of course, to the point of any physical debilitation, but an amentia isolated within confines of the brain's left hemisphere, which, as you probably have read, controls man's . . . ."

"Creative processes," Franco said, completing the sentence. Then, stunned by the implication of this amentia, Franco sat back in his chair and attempted to put it in perspective. No *physical* debilitation, just the creative processes.

My God, he thought. Wylie was talking about making zombies, worker drones.

Hold on, Dorothy, he told himself. Laban wasn't Kansas and Wylie wasn't any tin man. These were Nazis, the gas and ovens and gold teeth bunch: the Eichmanns, the Mengeles, the Bormanns.

But genetically induced retardation? Jesus.

"You know, we almost perfected it," Wylie continued, interrupting Franco's thoughts. "We even had the chemical, a tetrahydrocannabinol acetate compound. The THC could, in fact, alter the brain's genetic makeup. Unfortunately, we were unable to find the means to introduce it into broad population groups."

"You said it was a postnatal thing?" Franco asked curiously. "Babies?" Wylie nodded academically.

"Milk was to be the medium for distribution. Oh, the THC would work on adults all right, but not that many adults drank milk at the time. Milk was saved for the children. Consequently, if introduced in a child's diet, within twenty years the children could be bred and, since the alteration was genetic in nature, their offspring would no longer require the THC. They would be born with the creative amentia already extant."

"A subhuman species," Franco said acidly.

"There are already any number of subhuman species, Agent Franco," Wylie commented. "Gypsies, Slavs, Jews, even the blacks and Orientals. Our approach was simply to preclude them from harming themselves. Just as a parent must remove sharp objects from a child, we, the *Reichmasters,* found ourselves with the obligation to remove the subhuman's capacity for inadequacy."

Franco shook his head incredulously. He could still not get over the conversational tone of Miles Wylie's voice. It was as if he were ordering a salad or discussing the scores of a sporting event. There was absolutely no measure of apology or even of contrition. Just the manner of a man who no longer feared society's sanction.

"But you were never able to refine the medium? The milk?" Franco asked, more for himself than anything else.

"There were limited successes," Wylie nodded. "But the distribution means, the problems of moving the product through whatever channels were available in the region—Russia, the Balkans, wherever—were insurmountable. Shelf life was our primary difficulty, and we were unable to attain any certain level of predictability due to factors outside our control. Heat, humidity, the environmental variances proved to be . . . ."

***

850 yards, Cory thought again. 350 over the ART's zero line.
Compensation?
About twelve inches, maybe just a hair under.
He focused through the scope again. To hit thorax center, he would have to aim for the top of the Wylie's head.

"Yes," he whispered. The top of the head. That tiny spot just beneath the tip of the red stocking cap and centerline between the eye and the patch.

Just stop talking, he thought to himself. Let Leather Jacket leave and the round would fly and his mission would be finished. So very close now.

***

Franco asked another question.

"How many men were assigned to your unit?"

"Civilian internees?" Wylie answered. "Perhaps thirty-five during the course of the war. About a third of that in the final days. It was a very selective group."

"I was speaking of the Nazi members," Franco corrected. "How many of your subordinates were SS?"

"No more than a dozen throughout the whole project. In the end, just before the Russians advanced, not even that many."

"And all of the SS ended up in the American sector?"

"Yes," Wylie nodded.

"And what happened to the internee scientists, the civilians?"

"Why they were executed, of course. It was their identities we used to deceive American counterintelligence. You must remember, after the end they had somehow assembled a roster of all SS personnel. It would have been rather counterproductive for us to attempt a deception under our German names, don't you think?"

"So you all became Czechoslovakian?"

"Not all," Wylie explained. "Some became Austrian, others Hungarian or Romanian. The sole factor was whichever internee's identity was assumed and where that particular internee had been born. You must remember, *we* had their documents: birth certificates, travel permits, even identity cards issued by the Reich. It was a simple matter to substitute our photographs for theirs, for we were the ones charged with keeping their identity documents in order in the first place."

"And who decided who became who?" Franco asked.

"That was an obvious decision. I told you we worked in sections: biological, bacteriological, genetics. Each of the SS staffers had an internee, or in many cases, a number of internees as opposite numbers . . . ."

"So you stayed within your respective fields," Franco surmised. "So each SS officer would have the actual knowledge to be able to pass himself off as whoever he was trying to be."

"Exactly," Wylie nodded. "As I've said, even my men, the SS, we were specialists anyway. It was not a difficult illusion. Not difficult at all."

"Do you know if you're still wanted for war crimes?" Franco asked.

"Helmut Blobel is," Wylie said. "Miles Wylie is not."

"And who would know that Miles Wylie is really Helmut Blobel and want to see him dead because of it?"

"I don't know," Wylie sighed wearily. "And, at this point, I really care little about any of it."

"Well, venture a guess for me," Franco said sharply.

"A guess?" Wylie closed his good eye and rested his head on the cushion. "I don't know. Perhaps the Jews. They're always living in the past."

"Do you know Gustav Celt?" Franco asked.

"Of course," Wylie answered.

"He's been assassinated."

"My condolences," Wylie said, obviously unconcerned.

"What about William Pointer and Robert Rouse?"

"Yes, yes, I know them."

"They've also been assassinated."

Wylie dismissed the statement with an abrupt wave of his hand. "It is none of my concern."

"Do you know . . . ."

"Agent Franco," Wylie interrupted. "I am extremely fatigued. I do not want to go through the list of my entire unit. If you are interested, you may feel free to go into my house. In the living room you will find a bookcase. In the bookcase, a book. The title is *Decline of the West*. It is a 1928 volume by Oswald Spengler. If you open the book, inside the left front cover you will find an envelope and in the envelope you will find a photograph. The photograph was taken in Bratislava less than six weeks before the Russians invaded. The men in the photograph are the members of Einsatzkommando IV who came with me to the American sector. Take the photograph, Agent Franco. Keep it. Study it. Frame it and pray to it for all I care. I make it my legacy to you. Now, just go and leave me be. I have too few tomorrows to bother with yesterdays."

Asshole, Franco thought, becoming angry. Wylie's condescending manner was growing very thin.

"Don't get too comfortable, Blobel," he said. "When I do leave you can rest assured you'll be leaving with me."

A dry, wheezy chuckle escaped Wylie's lips.

Seething, Franco let it pass without comment.

***

Finally, thought Cory. Jacket was moving and, through the scope, Cory watched him stand, look down at the old man, then turn and walk toward the house.

Was he leaving? Or was he just going inside to take a leak or get a drink or something? Unknown, but take it anyway. The deck was clear. Shift to the old man. Get Wylie in the sights.

Settling the Steyr into his shoulder, he aligned the scope on the occupied chair and depressed the rear trigger with a tensed middle finger. He took a deep breath, released half of it, and brought his right index finger to where it was just touching the front trigger.

He stared through the scope and took another half-breath.

In the chair, Wylie shifted a little, snuggling deeper.

Cory compensated with the Steyr: crosshairs down, just a fraction to the left.

A breath, a hold, a bit more tension on the front trigger: *one ounce* . . . 1.25 . . . 1.5 . . . 1.75 . . . .

Shit, thought Cory. It was a bad shot. Not right . . . not clean.

Lying nearly flat now, Wylie had made the angles all wrong, made the application imprecise.

Cory released the front trigger but kept the rear depressed. With the crosshairs centered on Wylie's patch, he began breathing normally again.

The waiting? The patience? Cory relaxed his cheek on the Steyr's smooth wooden stock. Neither was a problem now.

Second nature had taken the lead.

***

Franco dropped the book and envelope to the floor and turned the photograph over in his hands. It was, he saw, similar to what he had expected: a grainy, five-by-seven black-and-white print of the type normally found in the center of history books, a small knot of men standing posed around a desk.

In the background, there was a blackboard on which numbers and symbols were visible. In the foreground, on the desk, there were a few books but mostly a rather elaborate glass-tube Bunsen-burner affair which reminded Franco of something used in college chemistry labs.

What was surprising, Franco thought, was that none of the men were in uniform. Despite what Valena Jarvis had told him about the wearing of civilian clothing, he had half expected to see a brace of Nazi SS officers scowling with malice or arrogance. What he saw was a group of even pleasant-looking gentlemen who were all wearing long white lab coats. A few had pipes in their hands, and all were professorially proper in appearance.

Of the group, Franco could recognize only two.

The first was Steven-Kleist-Jarvis from the houseboat. He was by far the largest of the group. Next he picked out Miles-Blobel-Wylie. Even back then there was a patch covering the right eye.

Who were the others? Franco had no idea. There were no markings anywhere, front or back, that provided any additional information.

"Okay, Blobel," Franco yelled, as he took the photograph and began walking back through the kitchen toward the deck. "Pack it in, you're coming with me."

"I'm going nowhere," Wylie shouted, as he angrily leaned up in the chair. "You can . . . ."

***

... 1.75 ... 2.0 ... *squeeze.*

The Steyr slammed into Cory's shoulder and the hollowpoint round exploded inside Wylie's chest just at the base of the thorax. No shot had ever been cleaner.

It had been appropriate to wait, Cory thought, as he turned from the window, gathered the rifle, and began sprinting back to his vehicle. A call, this time, would serve no purpose.

Sendero Luminoso had completed the assignment.

***

Inside Wylie's kitchen, the crack of the shot had been immediately followed by the outraged cries of unseen gulls while, for Franco, there had been that infinite moment between hopeful disbelief and stinging reality.

He thought *No!*, screamed "Shit!" then drew his Browning 9mm from beneath his jacket, fell to the floor, and began low-crawling toward the deck.

He felt like a fool. His only real witness to the why's of all this was now, Franco was reasonably confident, well on his way to rotting in hell.

Wrong, Franco thought, as he reached the door. Wylie was already there. His stocking cap gone and patch askew, he lay curled on his side to the left of the chair.

Like a fetal frog, Franco decided. Still and quiet atop a spreading lily pad of arterial blood.

But where was the shooter? Still out there? Gone?

Franco stood and glanced out the door. From Wylie's positioning, the shot had come from either the water or the right.

Franco scanned the horizon. No boats within range. Only one was visible and that was at least two miles out. He peered around the doorway to the right. Nothing. No movement. Nobody on the beach and nobody visible in any of the houses.

Deductions. One, Wylie was dead, the shooter would already be leaving the area. Two, the beach and bay were deserted. Three, the shooter could only be leaving by road. Four, there was only one road passing the line of houses.

Camaro, Franco remembered. If the shooter hadn't changed cars, its color would be silver.

Gripping the pistol, Franco bolted from the door and jumped off the deck. Running around the house, he sprinted past the Volkswagen bus and down the sandy driveway to the middle of Old Potters Road.

He looked to the right, nothing, then back to the left toward Middle River.

He smiled. There, hanging low in the air and drifting toward him, he found what became his fifth deduction. It was the gravel dust kicked up by the shooter's wheels as he bumped over the asphalt patches. The shooter was driving toward Middle River.

Turning, Franco sprinted directly to the Corvette, hopped in, and started the engine. With his wheels spinning shell, he backed from the driveway, slammed the transmission into first, and floored the accelerator.

The shooter was about three minutes ahead of him, Franco suspected. If he was still in the Camaro, Franco estimated he would catch sight of the car somewhere on the road between Middle River and the main highway which led back into Baltimore.

Of course, if the shooter *had* changed vehicles . . . .

Screw that, Franco thought, as he cranked up the stereo and shifted into fourth.

Cars could change, men couldn't.

Just look at the faces, Franco told himself.

The answer would be in the shooter's eyes.

CHAPTER 54

Baltimore, Maryland, 3:40 P.M.

BALTIMORE—WASHINGTON
INTERNATIONAL AIRPORT
NEXT RIGHT

Considering tickets and baggage and planes delayed, Cory thought vaguely of travel by air and exchanged the slow but steadily moving Interstate for the grid-locked pageantry of the airport access road.

"Welcome to the human race," he said sullenly. Ahead was a magnificent collision, and police and wrecker drivers were doing their best to sort through the confusion. To the left, two of three lanes were blocked by emergency vehicles and all traffic was being diverted into a single right lane.

Cory checked his watch. Plenty of time, he thought. His flight was scheduled for six o'clock. He could waste an hour poking along here and still be early.

But, as it turned out, it was to be nowhere near an hour, as a few minutes later Cory was waved around the accident site. Interestingly enough, a small yellow Chevrolet was protruding from the rear of a UPS delivery van. How this had been accomplished was evidently still being contested, for to the right of the vehicles a harried policeman was standing between the two outraged drivers.

Cory chuckled at the scene. Jumpsuited, the UPS driver was a tall, West Indian black with an earring. The driver of the Chevy was a tiny Oriental man sporting an oversized Atlanta Braves baseball cap. Both were screaming at the top of their lungs and neither was screaming in English.

Cory thought briefly of justice being deaf, then drove on to the long-term parking area where he gathered his baggage and left the Camaro with the keys hidden on top of the left front tire. The Steyr and the remaining bullets remained locked in the trunk.

Overhead a plane roared into the eastern sky, and Cory watched it climb as he slowly walked toward the terminal.

Inside, emotionally, he felt strangely alone. Alone, but not lonely in any despondent sense. On the contrary, it was an almost romantic isolation—that which came with a job well done and from the realization that, with the exceptions of Eisler and Pock, no other person would know to share his success.

What was it they said out there in the shadow wars? The *clandestino* precept?

He remembered in a rush of vanity and warmth:
Priorities, performance, the sense of purpose.
Things the protected never even knew.

The elite, he thought, as he entered the crowded terminal. Eisler had been all too correct when he mentioned that it was pride that precluded involvement in amateurish endeavors. It was a pride spawned from priority and from the pride extended the logic of his calling.

People like Boatner? The five Russians?

This is what really kept him from quitting. His sense of purpose, of loyalty and duty.

These were what made the hard times worthwhile.

***

Franco was not happy. Some 200 yards on the grid-locked side of the wreck, he popped another piece of gum into his mouth while ahead traffic continued to jockey and jam.

For thirty minutes now, since first spotting the silver Camaro at the Interstate-Middle River cutoff, he had run a loose, rolling surveillance on the vehicle. He had stayed well back, sometimes allowing as many as twenty vehicles between his Corvette and the shooter's Camaro. He had not worried particularly about being spotted. The Camaro's rear window was low and its seat back high. Even with the rearview mirrors, the shooter's ability to look to the rear would be limited at best. Even so, Franco had also taken the extra precaution to stay to the right rear of the silver coupe. As yet, he knew he had gone undetected. A small consolation, though, considering that the wreck had now ruined everything and left him immobile while the Camaro had disappeared around the curve on the other side of the accident.

"Fucking shitheads," Franco hissed, as he moved forward three feet then stopped.

The problems. First, Franco decided he had screwed up the surveillance. In his caution, he had actually remained *too* far back. Like a damned rookie, he hadn't documented the Camaro's license plate number. If the shooter was *not* stopping at the airport, if this diversion was just a precautionary maneuver to elude surveillance, then the shooter had just accomplished his goal. While Franco remained snarled in traffic, the Camaro was probably already back on the Interstate heading for points unknown, and Franco couldn't put out a pick-up on the vehicle without the license plate number.

Incensed with himself, Franco decided that while this first problem could conceivably be considered some lesser dereliction of duty matter, his second problem clearly fell within the boundaries of professional incompetence: he still hadn't actually seen the shooter's face. His original plan, the one that had now turned sour, was to follow the Camaro until it stopped and then position himself to be able to watch the driver leave the vehicle.

This, Franco thought sarcastically, would have accomplished two minor functions: first, he would know *where* the shooter was and, second, he would have known *who* the shooter was.

"God damn it," Franco cursed. Thanks to the wreck, he'd lost the chance to put the shooter with the Camaro. If he did leave the airport then, for Franco it would be back to square one. If the shooter was staying at the airport, then he would be one of hundreds of faces milling in the crowd. That would be thousands of eyes to examine and evaluate. What if the shooter was wearing sunglasses?

"Shit," Franco said as he rolled another foot. If they awarded Nobel Prizes for inadequate investigative techniques, he should receive two for this surveillance alone.

***

Cory walked into the toilet stall and locked the door behind him. Setting his duffel bag on the tile floor, he unzipped the top and pulled out the envelope containing Eisler's identification abstracts. Unfolding them, he glanced briefly at the photographs of the dead Russians, then methodically tore the abstracts into small pieces and dropped them into the toilet. He then extracted his penis, urinated, and flushed the bowl.

Zipping up his pants, he wondered whether he should change clothes. He decided against it. The flight to San Juan was nonstop, so he would check his duffel through. Besides, he was simply too tired to bother with unlacing the high-top boots.

What to do with the Makarov pistol?

Better keep it for now, he decided. He would be waiting in the airport coffee shop until his flight was called. Just before passing through the security checkpoint, he would return to the rest room and, for safety purposes, disassemble the weapon. He would then wrap the dysfunctional assemblies in newspaper and drop them into different trash cans. Even if the components were located, the authorities could never effect a trace.

Hefting the duffel bag, Cory checked the toilet once again. Not everything had flushed. Floating on top was a shred of photograph: the ear, an eye and the cheek of . . . of . . .

"Humph," Cory snorted. He couldn't even remember which target it was. Either number two or three, or maybe even the first?

One of the early ones though; but it was not really important anymore.

"So long, my friend," Cory said. Then he flushed the toilet a second time and left the rest room for the ticket counter to pick up his first class seating pass. To be sure, traveling first class was no small measure of self-indulgence. Nonetheless, Cory was not bothered by the cost. He felt he owed himself a little excess. Besides, it was on Eisler's tab anyway.

***

Through the wreck and past the lines of quarter meters, Franco had just wheeled onto the sixth row of the long- term parking area when he saw the Camaro. He immediately committed the license number to memory: PET 296—*Pigs Eat Truffles 296 Times*.

He repeated the phrase again in his mind, then shifted the Corvette into reverse and backed into a vacant slot. Taking a deep breath, he cut the engine, climbed out, and jogged toward the terminal.

The shooter was good, but he was better.

Again it was time for playing by ear.

***

The ticket clerk was a pretty Puerto Rican girl with long fingernails and very public eyes. She reminded Cory of a prostitute he had sampled in Manila years before.

"Any other baggage, Mr. Kellogg?"

"Just the duffel."

The girl tagged the bag, then stapled the claim check to the ticket folder and seat pass.

"Here you are, Mr. Kellogg," she smiled as she handed over the packet. "You're confirmed on Delta flight 101 to San Juan. Scheduled departure is six o'clock, gate thirty one. Check in with the gate attendant no later than fifteen minutes before flight time."

"Thank you," Cory said as he took the ticket pack.

"And thank you for flying Delta, Mr. Kellogg."

Cory nodded curtly and walked away. He stopped at a newsstand, bought a copy of the *Washington Post*, then went directly to the coffee shop where he found a vacant, two chair table in a far corner.

He sat down with his back to the wall and looked around the coffee shop. It was crowded and noisy and smelled of chili and cigarette smoke.

A bandy-legged waitress feinted in his direction, walked away, then returned as if caught on a string. She was plumpness in pink and pursed her lips like a sea bass straining plankton.

"Well?" she challenged, pronouncing it "wheel."

"Iced tea," Cory said.

"Nothing to eat? We've got a special turkey dinner buffet. Everything you can get on a plate for $5.95."

"Just the tea," Cory repeated.

The waitress shrugged blankly and wandered away.

Cory checked his watch. 4:10 p.m.

An hour and twenty minutes, he thought. Then to the plane and off to Puerto Rico.

Leaning back in his chair, he lit his pipe and, after the waitress returned with the tea, settled in, relaxed, and began to browse through the newspaper:

ROMANIAN VIOLENCE ESCALATES
Government May Fall

Cory scanned the article with passing interest.
He wondered who Eisler had on the ground there.

***

Threading his way through the masses, Franco's impression of the terminal was one of near-hopeless confusion: speakers blaring flight numbers, rudely surging crowds, children in the way, and baggage underfoot. The only thing that could have made identifying the shooter more difficult would be if someone turned off the lights.

"Jesus loves you. Do you love Jesus?"

Franco looked to his left and down. The voice belonged to a homely white teenager wearing a shapeless cotton dress and beaded leather moccasins.

"I'm working for Jesus now," she reverently added.

Franco shook his head and thought *Appalachia*.

"Is that a union contract?" he asked her as he pushed on through the mob. Airport evangelists. Why were they always so young and so tenaciously cliched?

But the question went unanswered as Franco turned his attention back to the montage of migrating faces. Looking over, around, and between the heads, he mentally ticked off the shooter's description as surmised by Dunnigan Cox's forensic team:

> Race—White
> Height—6'2"
> Weight—190 lbs.
> Hair—Chestnut brown

Was it enough? Franco still didn't know as he completed his first pass by the ticket counters. As yet, nobody seemed to fit.

Where to look next? His choices were four: the gates, the newsstand, the coffee shop, and the rest rooms.

Franco turned on his heel and pushed his way toward the men's room. It was happening now, he realized. The bravado of earlier was tempering into something more realistic. Something that was not quite whispering fear.

He was aware of caution now. That heady scent of premonition that only occurred as instincts snapped to the forefront of certainty and self-preservation.

Franco took a breath and picked up his pace, while in his mind the two live-or-die alternatives sing-songed back and forth . . . the adult version of a childhood game.

Take a prisoner, take a life.

He wondered which option he would soon have to face.

The decision would be the shooter's.

Franco was prepared for both.

***

Leaning back in his chair, Cory turned a page of the newspaper and perused it casually:

ELECTIONS IN INDIA PLACED ON HOLD

He realized that he probably should glance through this article too. No point in waiting until San Juan to learn the political situation. Furthermore, Eisler would expect him to find out at least a little about the country on his own initiative.

But as he thought of Eisler, Cory remembered the gift, the cashews. While beginning to read, he reached into his coat pocket, pulled out the tissue bag, and untied it without taking his eyes from the article:

New Dehli (AP) — Indian sources confirmed a Wednesday cabinet meeting during which Indian Prime Minister Sarafat Mahir told supporters he would suspend upcoming elections pending the results of a government investigation into charges that political opponents have been jailed.

Democracy in action, Cory thought caustically as he popped a few cashews into his mouth and chewed while continuing the story:

The Prime Minister's most vocal critic, Harvard-educated Sarafat Mahira, has demanded that the whole affair should be turned over to the United Nations for investigation and resolution.

Cory read the names again. Mahir and Mahira. With the exception of the *a* at the end of the second name, both the prime minister's and the Harvard-educated critic's name were spelled identically. He wondered whether this could be interpreted as some significant political occurrence or, just as easily, perhaps as a typographical error.

But tasty cashews in either case, Cory thought, reaching for a larger handful. Did they sell cashews in India?

He would remember to ask Eisler in San Juan.

***

Franco shoved through the double glass doors and entered the coffee shop.

He scanned the room quickly, then again more slowly . . . he stopped in his tracks.

The man at the corner table, he thought. Alone, white, over six feet, and well-proportioned. He could fit, but he really wasn't what Franco had expected. He was almost intellectual in appearance: a pipe; round, wire-rimmed glasses. What with the exception of the long leather coat, he seemed quite the academic. Handsome, clean features and probably muscled under the coat.

Move closer, Franco told himself. Reaching under his jacket, he slid his fingers around the grip of the Browning. Keeping it concealed, he began to walk quickly toward the table.

Ten steps. Franco saw boots beneath the table: chain tread soles. A fit.

Twenty steps. He was eating cashews. Another fit.

Franco felt his pulse quicken as he closed the distance.

The scent was there, the feeling right. The shooter was his.

Just get closer, he told himself. Both of the shooter's hands were visible. Let him just keep them that way. Let him just keep looking at that newspaper a second longer and . . . .

***

Not alone! The impression screamed in Cory's brain, shocking him, forcing his eyes from the paper and his mind from India and cashews.

An instinctual impulse, he was reaching for the Makarov even before snapping his attention toward whatever was causing the sensations.

He began to stand, to isolate the danger.

Jacket!

Jacket moving directly at him.

Fifteen feet . . . ten . . . .

I should have called backup, Franco thought, moving in. Should have . . . his mouth went dry . . . *Christ, shooter was reaching for a weapon.*

The Browning appeared in Franco's hand without him ever wondering how.

From somewhere a woman screamed. From somewhere else a chair fell, followed by a crash of plates. Then there was silence in the coffee shop, a pregnant, paralyzed hush broken only by an overhead speaker calling boardings for Texas and the gooey coos of a happy infant.

For Cory, half out of the chair, Makarov at his side, there was that long second of decision, of choices. He could feel the coldness, read the certainty in Jacket's eyes. He was caught. If he brought the Makarov up any higher, Jacket would kill him.

For Franco, crouched across the table, the Browning centered on the shooter's face, there was an even longer second. If shooter raised his pistol any higher, Franco knew he would be forced to fire. He had no real alternative. There were simply too many civilians in the room. Too many innocent lives at stake to risk any protracted exchange of gunfire.

No, Franco knew. There could only be one shot—his, into the shooter's face. And should it pass through? No issue. It would only shatter harmlessly in the corner behind the table.

"FBI," Franco told him softly, speaking in Spanish. "I know you're contract. A professional. You don't want to hurt these people in here and you know I won't allow you to."

Franco saw the shooter's eyes flicker in recognition. He understood Spanish. This cinched it. He would continue speaking in Spanish. Hopefully, that would keep most of the public from knowing what or why this was happening.

"There's been enough killing," Franco added. "Let's not have anymore."

But Cory was not thinking of killing. As he stood there, the Makarov now useless, his thoughts were only of Eisler and how disappointed the old man was going to be when he heard of this.

Could Eisler help? Somehow make all of it right?

Cory suspected he could; but that would be up to Eisler. Here, now, he could say nothing to implicate Eisler in even the remotest sense. Hopefully, the Brian Kellogg veil could stand up to inspection until Eisler worked behind the scenes to quash the charges.

Still, Cory reminded himself, these were administrative details. Things that did absolutely nothing to mitigate his letting down Eisler or the depression he was just beginning to experience. Inside, Cory felt dirty and despondent. A lump was rising in his throat and, from his stomach, a strange metallic hollowness seemed to spread like oil on water.

He realized, possibly for the first time in his life, that he was absolutely terrified. He also realized he was still not ready to die, still not ready to beg off.

"*Como?*" he asked. *How?*

"How did I find you?" Franco asked, keeping it in Spanish. "Later.

Now, just put your weapon on the table and step back, face the wall, and assume the position."

Cory took a deep breath, released it, then lay the Makarov down and leaned spread-eagled into the corner. There were murmurs in the coffee shop now, and he knew everybody was staring at his back, whispering, pointing, and making banal comments.

Cory became aware of another new feeling and realized he was experiencing shame for the first time. He found it to be infinitely more loathsome than the terror.

Franco picked up the Makarov and shoved it into his waistband. Then he stepped over and quickly frisked Cory. Finding no additional weapons and realizing, in violation of regulations, he had no handcuffs, he ordered Cory to turn around.

"I told you I knew you were a professional," he said. "I respect you for that, but I want the same respect in return. I'm not going to handcuff you; but, just remember, if you try anything, running, any kind of that night-of-the-Ninja nonsense, I'm not going to bother to play. *Comprende?*"

Cory nodded in understanding.

"Then I have your respect?" Franco asked.

"Yes," Cory said softly. "You have my respect, if for no other reason than for sparing me the humiliation of the handcuffs."

Franco didn't comment. Shoving Cory in front of him, he reached up and grabbed Cory's overcoat collar as he nudged the Browning's muzzle into the base of Cory's skull. "Let's move," he ordered.

"Can I get my pipe," Cory asked, as Franco began pushing him toward the coffee shop door.

Franco looked to the table. The pipe was sitting in an ashtray.

"Okay," he said.

Cory retrieved the pipe, but not the cashews.

"Where are we going?" he asked, as they continued to push through the crowd.

"Not far," Franco told him. "Not far at all."

CHAPTER 55

Baltimore-Washington International Airport, 4:40 P.M.

The letters on the door read AIRPORT POLICE—INTERROGATION B. Inside it was a stuffy, one-desk, two-chair, windowless alcove with bare green walls, a coffee-stained floor, and bright lights suspended in protective wire baskets.

Three items graced the desk: an old manual typewriter, a telephone, and American passport number B161096 issued in the name of Brian Kellogg.

" . . . so do you understand these rights as I have just explained to you?" Franco leaned forward and stared across the desk.

"Of course," Cory muttered sourly.

"And do you wish to waive these rights and answer questions?"

"No," Cory sighed. "I think . . ."

Franco interrupted. He didn't want to hear any lawyer requests.

"Your name is Brian Kellogg?" he asked, as he flipped open the passport.

"I told you . . . ."

"And you entered the United States in Houston last Sunday?"

"I don't think . . . ."

"You've been kind of busy since Sunday, haven't you?" Franco asked. "Is Brian Kellogg your real name?"

"I'm not . . . ."

Franco kept pushing. Kept interrupting.

"Who do you work for, Mr. Kellogg? What are you doing in this country? Shall I tell you the what and why, Mr. Kellogg? Do you think I don't know?"

Cory shrugged wearily. He knew this routine. Why he himself had actually used it on occasion. The staccato questions. The sing-song taunting tone. Franco was trying to rattle him. To make him respond emotionally as opposed to rationally.

It wouldn't work, Cory knew. He had spent too many hours with himself on the other side of the interrogation desk. And, if Franco kept it up, well, he was already beginning to feel irritated with this FBI character.

"I don't care what you know," Cory said without rancor.

Good, Franco thought. Kellogg was becoming combative. Manifesting a previously unseen trait. The glumness and resignation of before was now transforming into contentiousness. A good sign. Work the anger. Stir it up a little more. Find that pea in his pod.

"Let me tell you something, Mr. Kellogg. One of my associates described you as calculating. I believe his exact words were flexible and calculating. Do you think you are calculating, Mr. Kellogg? Tell me about Shining Path, Mr. Kellogg. Tell me about *par-TI-dos*. And about how, in Guatemala, they pronounce the word *par-ti-DO*."

"I don't know what you are talking about," Cory said.

"Well, then," Franco continued. "Let's talk about weapons. Tell me about an Austrian weapon. A 7.62mm rifle. I believe it is a Steyr?"

"I don't know," Cory mumbled. "Do you care if I smoke?"

"No," Franco said, backing off a bit. Then, as Cory began lighting his pipe, he turned to a different line of questioning.

"How old are you, Mr. Kellogg?"

"It's in there," Cory said, nodding to the passport between puffs.

Franco tossed the passport to the floor.

"I think we both know everything in there is bullshit, right?"

Cory made a *who knows* gesture with his pipe.

"You tell me, Franco. *Is* that what we know?"

"Who do you work for?" Franco asked quickly, repeating the earlier question.

"Myself," Cory said.

"And what do you do?"

"Sell industrial equipment to Third World countries."

"It must be dangerous work," Franco said. "Is that why you were carrying a weapon?"

Cory said nothing.

"How did you get inside Robert Rouse's apartment?" Franco asked, switching subjects again.

"Robert Rouse?"

"He was killed with a Phillips screwdriver," Franco said. "And he did let you in."

"I can't help you," Cory said flatly. "I have no idea who he is?"

"Was," Franco corrected.

"Whatever."

***

The Watergate Hotel, 5:05 P.M.

Eisler picked up his telephone and dialed the number from memory. A ring. Another. Then it was answered.

"Hello?" Jonathon Weall said.

"Your ineptitude," Eisler said coldly, "is exceeded only by your manifest inattention to detail. I had to learn from Cory about the successful completion of the Calvert Quay endeavor. Why is this, Jonathon?"

There was a long pause, then the sound of Weall clearing his throat.

"But today is a holiday and I was . . . ."

"There are no *holidays* in our business, Jonathon. None for me. None for Cory. None for you."

"But I . . . I'm sorry . . . I guess . . . ."

"Never mind," Eisler sighed. "Tell me about Miles Wylie."

"Who?"

"Miles Wylie," Eisler hissed. "Outside of Baltimore? He was the last."

"But I've heard nothing," Weall explained.

Eisler thought for a moment. *Nothing?* Odd. If Cory was to leave the country as he had scheduled, Wylie should already have been attended to. Could something have side-tracked him? Something altered his plans?

"Where is your investigator?" Eisler asked. "This Sal Franco?"

"I don't know," Weall said. "The last I spoke with him was this morning when I told him about the Calvert Quay death. I've heard nothing since then."

"Nothing about Wylie?"

"No."

"Find Franco," Eisler said, making it an order. "Find Franco and find out what he is doing. Then contact the airport in Baltimore. There should be a Brian Kellogg scheduled on a six o'clock flight to San Juan. Find out if he has checked in for the flight yet. Do you think you can manage this, Jonathon?"

"Yes," Weall answered, his voice small. "Where will you be?"

"My home," Eisler said, doing nothing to conceal the aggravation in his voice. "I will be waiting for your call, Jonathon. I do not wish to wait long."

Eisler slammed down the receiver.

"Idiots," he cursed. Pock, Monika, and now Jonathon Weall. The only person who seemed even remotely able to follow orders was Damon Cory.

"It is hanging by a thread," he whispered to himself.

For Damon was mad as a hatter.

***

The Airport Interrogation Room, 5:40 P.M.

"Five men in five days," Franco said, continuing the questioning. "Why were there five, Mr. Kellogg?"

"I still don't know what you are talking about," Cory repeated. "I've told you, I sell industrial equipment."

"And why Nazis, Mr. Kellogg? Who selected Nazis for you?"

AUTLEY HOUSE 341

Upon hearing this question, Franco noticed a slight but discernable change in Kellogg's expression: a squinting of the left eye, a tightness in the throat, a barely noticeable compression of the lips and jaw.

"You didn't know that, did you?" Franco asked. "You didn't know they were Nazis?"

Cory's face went blank.

"I want a lawyer," he said softly.

Franco ignored the request. Reaching into his coat pocket, he extracted the old photograph from Wylie's book, unfolded it, and lay it on the desk.

"Those were the men," he explained. "Some were already dead, the remainder you eliminated. The photograph was taken in 1945. They were SS scientists, Mr. Kellogg. Do you know what they were working on? They were developing the means to turn normal healthy babies into zombies. They were doing it so they could be bred like cattle."

Franco stopped talking. Across the desk, the man was staring at the photograph.

"Pick it up," Franco suggested. "Look at the faces."

As Franco watched, the shooter picked up the photograph and began to study it carefully. Soon Franco noticed the shooter's fingers begin to tremble. Odd response, he thought. Totally unexpected. Then the shooter's breathing began to change. Becoming shorter, shallower.

What was going on here? Franco wondered. Could the photograph, similar to Alicia Carrera and the pistol shots, be some sort of catalyst? So it seemed.

The nervous knee bounces, the cringing shoulders, the slumping posture. It was all here in the guise of emotional release. Even the swallowings now. The attempts to retain composure.

And this was all brought on by the photograph?

Franco was admittedly surprised. Intellectually, considering the professional approach with which the assassinations had been effected, he had not expected Kellogg—or whoever he really was—to talk at all. And this behavior, the physical response to the photograph, was certainly not in keeping with his experience with other homicide suspects. Some never talked at all, and others spoke only denials.

Franco watched the shooter carefully. What was it in the photograph that had brought about the dramatic change in the his demeanor? He didn't know yet. Not enough information. Still, it presented an opening, and to exploit it, he would keep the questions revolving around the men in the white lab coats.

"Did you know they were war criminals?" Franco asked softly.

Cory said nothing. He was too preoccupied. Events were overtaking him . . . old, new, those that would surely follow. Denial? Betrayal? His mind raced as he continued to stare at the faces in the photograph and forced himself to come to terms with the cold reality of his situation.

He took a deep breath. Eisler had lied to him. Used him. But why? Why tell him Russians? And the tattoo on Eisler's forearm? Birkenau? And the photograph depicting the Nazis? It didn't make sense as much as it made perfect sense. A perfection that all but destroyed him inside.

Cory swallowed a thread of salty phlegm and looked over to Franco.

"My name is Damon Cory," he whispered. "I am a full colonel in the United States Army."

Franco thought immediately of *pithing*.

"Special Operations?" he asked, softening his approach.

"Yes," Cory said, his composure slowly returning.

Franco found himself nodding at the answer, not so much for the admission, but for the self-effacing manner in which it was said.

"Did you kill them all yourself?"

Cory nodded.

"And made the telephone calls to Defense?"

"Yes."

"No help in any of it?"

Cory thought briefly of Boudreaux Pock.

"None," he said.

"Very well," Franco agreed. "Tell me about the Nazis then."

Cory took another deep breath and relit his pipe.

"There's a saying," he whispered. "I learned it at West Point. It goes something like: *That we shouldn't be carried about by men who lie in wait to deceive.* I think, perhaps, this is the best place to begin."

***

The Watergate Hotel, 5:43 P.M.

Eisler answered the telephone on the first ring.

"He's checked in," Weall said without explanation. "Delta flight 101. They've got an on-time, scheduled departure in about fifteen minutes."

Eisler breathed a sigh of relief.

"Fine, Jonathon," he said. "What about Franco?"

"Nothing," Weall answered. "He's not at the office and not at home. The last person to see him was one of our helicopter pilots who dropped him off at our headquarters after the trip to Calvert Quay. That was about eleven this morning though."

"Isn't that rather odd for him to be unavailable for this long?"

"For somebody else," Weall said. "Not for Franco. Sometimes, when he's working something, he's out for days at a time."

Eisler mulled this over for a moment. He didn't like it, but there was really nothing he could do about it.

"Do something for me, Jonathon," he said. "Keep attempting to locate

Franco. Also, keep in touch with whomever you have to in order to be able to advise me exactly when Miles Wylie's death is discovered."

"Why don't I just drive to Wylie's house and confirm . . . ."

Idiot, Eisler thought again.

"And what would be your reason for being there, Jonathon?"

Weall said nothing.

"Just do as I ask, Jonathon. I will see that it all works out."

"Yes, sir," Weall whispered self-consciously.

"I shall be awaiting your call."

Eisler replaced the receiver and leaned over his desk while rubbing his eyes. This Franco was a wild card, and wild cards were one thing he had never suffered well.

They always popped up in the other man's hand.

***

The Airport Interrogation Room, 6:40 P.M.

Tipping back in his chair, Cory listened carefully as Franco spoke quietly into the telephone.

"Yes, captain," Franco was saying. "That is correct. No, two officers will be sufficient. They're only to escort him. No questions . . . nothing. Yes, send them in now. Yes. No, I don't expect any trouble from him. Fine, Captain. I appreciate your assistance."

Franco hung up the telephone and looked across the desk to Cory.

"You'll be going with two airport police officers," he explained.

"So I heard," Cory said softly. "But what about the rest of it? Where does it go from here?"

Franco shrugged.

"I'll try to get it all in perspective, I guess. The Russians, the Nazis, this man named Eisler? It's a hell of a scheme, Cory. It'll take time to . . . ."

Franco's words were interrupted by a sharp rap on the interrogation room door.

"Come on in," Franco yelled.

The door opened and two burly airport police officers muscled inside.

"Capt'n says you need a couple of baby sitters," one said.

Franco nodded to Cory.

"Him," he said. "You know where he's going?"

"Capt'n told us," the officer answered. "Let's move," he told Cory.

Cory stood, looked to the two policemen, then back down to Franco.

"So what do you think?" he asked. "Guilty or innocent?"

"Wrong terms," Franco said quickly. "Legally, it's guilty or not guilty. Innocence is a moral concept. And morality, colonel, is something we all have to define for ourselves."

"No guesses?" Cory asked.

Franco shook his head.

"None that I'm willing to share."

The look that passed between the two said everything: commiseration, understanding, even principle were exchanged. *Specialist-to-specialist. realist-to-realist.* The kind of *justicia* both knew was requisite.

Cory thought to say something but decided against it. Nodding with resignation, he allowed the two officers to lead him from the room.

Alone in the tiny interrogation room, Franco sat there for a long five minutes before standing from the desk and beginning the slow walk back to his car.

Shitty deal, he thought. Eisler using Cory the way that he had. Still, from his point of view, he felt neither happy nor sad. Just reconciled more than anything else. He had done what was necessary and now he would find this Eisler and finish his part of the circle.

The circle, he thought. Appropriate.

It made the *justicia* even more intimate.

CHAPTER 56

The Watergate Hotel, Washington, D.C., 7:35 P.M.

"Yes?" Eisler said, as he opened the apartment door.

Franco offered his credentials.

"Sal Franco," he said. "FBI. Your name is Eisler?"

"Er . . . yes?"

"Do you mind if I come in?"

"Not at all," Eisler said pleasantly. "Please, do. Could I get you something to drink, Mr. Franco?"

Franco declined and walked over to the sofa and sat down. Eisler, his mind swirling with questions he couldn't ask, perched himself on the edge of the loveseat.

"Is there something . . ." he began.

"I assume you know why I'm here," Franco interrupted. "So let's just get on with it."

"I'm sorry," Eisler smiled. "But the fact of the matter is I have no idea why you are here."

"Damon Cory is why I'm here," Franco snapped. "Damon Cory and the fact you ordered him to assassinate five men."

"Damon Cory? I . . . ."

"I arrested Colonel Cory a couple of hours ago. We discussed it all at length."

"I see," Eisler said cautiously.

"He cooperated," Franco added, "because you used him. You led him to believe the scientists were Russian agents when, in fact, you knew all along they were Nazi war criminals."

Eisler took a deep breath and released it slowly. So, he thought, the plan had been detected, the network compromised or at least partially exposed. An unexpected but not necessarily fatal situation. It could be salvaged. But it had to be stopped here. Stopped with Franco.

But had Franco contacted anyone else yet?

Most likely no. If he had, it would have most logically been Jonathon Weall, and Jonathon had not called. This being the apparent case, Eisler decided a question was in order.

"Who, Mr. Franco, knows of this besides Damon, you, and me?"

"No one," Franco answered.

Excellent, Eisler thought. So it could be stopped with Franco. But how? Violence? Out of the question. There were no weapons in the apartment, and even if there were, he sincerely doubted Franco would afford him the opportunity to deploy one.

Perhaps Boudreaux Pock? No. Even if Pock could be contacted, it would be hours before a reasonable plan could be effected.

No, Eisler told himself. He would have to co-opt Franco himself and handle him as he handled all of his children. A gentle hand. The ploy of reason.

Conversation. It was the most subtle of weapons.

"Are you aware of my position, Mr. Franco?"

"Something to do with the National Command Authority, I believe."

"Yes," Eisler nodded. "I possess, as it has been termed, *a flexible charter*. One that, in the most ecumenical context, concerns itself with the more sensitive affairs of state: a dialogue between world leaders; a suggestion of mutual benefit; a hint; a promise; perhaps a small favor. Any one of a hundred things which may . . . ."

"Are you explaining something?" Franco interrupted. "I don't need a civics lesson."

Insipid ass, Eisler thought, careful not to let his feelings show. Leaning over he patted Franco's hand and offered a deceptively charming smile.

"Please, Mr. Franco," he said. "I am an old man. You must take this into consideration. Indulge me for a moment. I long ago lost the luxury of impulsiveness."

"Get back to the Nazis," Franco said sharply.

Eisler's eyes twinkled as he leaned back in the chair and crossed his legs.

"Yes," he smiled. "Of course. The Nazis. You are aware, are you not, that of late many European governments are going to great lengths to find the old Nazi war criminals so as to return them to the place of their crimes to stand trial?"

"I'm aware of that," Franco said.

Eisler nodded thoughtfully.

"Well, then, let me present a scenario to you, Mr. Franco. Will you allow me this latitude?"

Franco made a permissive gesture with his hand and Eisler stood, pacing the room as he spoke.

"Consider a certain Eastern European country, Mr. Franco. A country that, during the Second World War, suffered German occupation and, after the war, found itself behind the Iron Curtain."

"Czechoslovakia," Franco said. "I'm already aware of the Laban Institute in Bratislava and PEREGRINE. I've also reviewed the Autley House material and am familiar with the other P-Projects."

Eisler's eyes narrowed, but he continued to smile.

"Good, good," he said, joining his hands together. "I had hoped you would have. And with that in mind, are you aware of the political situation in Czechoslovakia today?"

"Not really," Franco said.

"Well," Eisler nodded. "Suffice it to say there had been a remarkable resurgence of interest in Czech activities during the Second World War. Why, just last month, we concluded, along with the British, negotiations to return some eighteen tons of Czechoslovakian gold that we had held since the war."

"You want to get to the point," Franco said impatiently.

"I am, Mr. Franco," Eisler said coldly. "This *is* the point."

"How is this the point?" Franco asked.

"Linkage," Eisler said. "Particularly immigration issues. To receive the gold, plus certain other considerations, a number of Czech nationals had to be allowed to leave the country. Do you have any idea how many wish to immigrate to the United States or Great Britain? There are thousands, Mr. Franco. I know. Approximately six months ago I attended a meeting with certain high-level Czech officials. The purpose of the meeting was to arrive at some sort of agreement concerning immigration quotas. The administration's position is straightforward—we will take as many as Slovakia will allow to leave. My instructions were to see that some agreement was reached which would facilitate the president's policy."

"But they are to receive the gold," Franco said.

"The gold did not cause the impasse," Eisler explained. "It was theirs anyway. The problem emerged from the *other considerations* I alluded to earlier. While the Czechs agreed to our quotas, at least in principle, they demanded a number of additional items in exchange. Most, like economic and cultural incentives, were not considered issues. These areas, as you might be aware, are more or less pro forma when dealing with the Eastern Bloc. What was out of the ordinary, Mr. Franco, were the circumstance of the Laban Institute. Specifically, the institute's less than illustrious history."

"The Nazi factor," Franco said flatly.

"The Nazi factor," Eisler repeated. "You see, Mr. Franco, the Czechs demanded a trade. Through efforts still under investigation—we suspect thanks to a man named Gregor Bukovsky—the Czech prime minister was aware that we had allowed some former Nazi scientists, all from the Laban Institute, to come to the United States. In the simplest terms, they were demanding the return of the former Nazis in exchange for allowing the immigrants to leave Slovakia."

Franco was more than skeptical.

"And how do you suppose this Bukovsky was aware of the scientists in the first place?" he asked.

Eisler held out his hands in a gesture of helplessness as he sat down on the loveseat.

"Who can say?" he shrugged. "Bukovsky is the director of the *Statní Tajná Bezpecnost*, the Czech KGB. He would have had access to the old Soviet files. Still, it is information we did not realize was known to the Soviets. Perhaps there is a lesson in there someplace, Mr. Franco."

"Perhaps," Franco said quietly.

"Nevertheless," Eisler continued. "It was an impossible request. Our government could not admit to PEREGRINE or Autley House for fear it would open the door to scrutinize all the P-Projects. If that occurred, the problem would be compounded exponentially, touching on any number of countries."

"Like PLUM in Asia and PATCH in the Middle East," Franco added.

"Exactly," Eisler agreed. "These are volatile areas, Mr. Franco. They suffer the pangs of nationalism and, at best, only tolerate our intervention in their respective areas of world. No. The president can little afford to have these secrets become the subject of a public discourse. It would set the stage for wholesale witch hunting and literally destroy U.S. credibility in the eyes of most world leaders."

Eisler paused for a moment and look down to his hands. When he again spoke his voice was barely above a whisper.

"The president was faced with a political and intelligence Gordian knot, Mr. Franco. I was charged with finding the solution. I selected the force option."

Franco considered Eisler's explanation. On the face of it, it sounded plausible enough. He could well imagine the international outrage that would accompany release of the P-Project material. After all, it was the smoking gun that laid the foundation for American meddling—both political and economic—in virtually every world venue for decades. How many coups? How many covert actions? How many crimes? All the dirty little secrets exposed. He shook his head in disgust.

"But why not just tell Cory what you've told me?" Franco asked. "Why manufacture the whole Russian penetration ruse?"

"To add another layer of disinformation," Eisler said. "Another measure of distance between the real and the imagined."

"You mean between yourself and Cory," Franco said.

Eisler nodded pensively.

"It has been my experience that soldiers and spies make very poor bedfellows, Mr. Franco. They need one another, of course. They even, at times, depend on one another. But to make more of the relationship, to believe or even draw the conclusion that there is something equitable in their relationship is innately flawed. The military belief in duty, honor, and country is diametrically opposed to the intelligence realities of duplicity, favor, and illusion."

"So you used Cory," Franco said.

"Used?" Eisler arched an eyebrow. "Is that what he believes?"

"That is what he indicated to me," Franco nodded. "When I told him the targets were not Russian but Nazis, he nearly broke down in tears. Not because he had assassinated them but because you had lied to him, that you had them eliminated to avenge a personal affront to you."

"A personal affront to me?" Eisler asked. "In what way?"

"The number tattooed on your forearm," Franco said. "Their deaths were your revenge for being held in a concentration camp. Correct?"

Eisler sighed sadly and rolled up his sleeve. He stared at his forearm, then held it out for Franco to examine. The numbers 27675 were faded, but distinct.

"I cannot apologize for what I've done, Mr. Franco," Eisler said. "Nor can I deny a certain measure of personal satisfaction with the results of Damon's efforts. I lived the Birkenau outrage. I heard the screams. I smelled the burning flesh."

"I suspect you did hear the screams and smell the burning flesh," Franco said coldly. "Only not as a victim. As for your pipe dream about the Czechoslovakian government . . . what is it supposed to be? Another ruse? Another layer of disinformation?"

Eisler's face hardened into a mask of indifference.

"Why you pathetic little bureaucrat," he said. "What do you know about anything? I *create* policy, Franco. *Create it.* I take an idea, a vision, and mold it into something tangible. So what if five Nazi war criminals were eliminated? Do you truly believe anyone really cares?"

Eisler leaned back in the love seat, a disdainful look on his face.

"So what have you gained, Mr. Franco?" he asked, his tone reasonable. "The destruction of a fine officer's military career? My ruin? All for what?"

Franco shook his head in disbelief as he reached into his jacket pocket, then tossed a piece of paper onto the coffee table.

"I want it all, Eisler." he said, nodding to the paper. "I want the truth. Pick it up."

Confused, Eisler reached to the table and picked up the paper. Unfolding it carefully, he saw it was a grainy black-and-white photograph of a group of men wearing long lab coats.

"The Laban Institute," Franco explained. "Bratislava, 1945. Cory took the trouble to circle your face. I believe it's the third one from the left?"

Eisler face went ashen as the rush of his pulse sounded in his ears. He looked over to Franco but decided not to respond.

"You're the worst kind of man," Franco said softly, coldly. "You are a coward. Birkenau? That phony concentration camp tattoo? You even make a mockery of yourself. What was your real name, Eisler? Were you Ernst Grawitz or Wilford Keith?"

A slight smile creased Eisler's lips.

"Yes," he whispered. "Another name from the past. Wilford Keith. Wilford Keith was the name Albert Berger assumed. Albert was a genius, doubtless the most brilliant scientist of them all . . . but mentally unstable. He never made it here, to America. He committed suicide on the voyage from England. As for myself? I suppose Grawitz will do. The others sometimes mocked me. Told me I looked Jewish. So, in the end, when the Russians were advancing, I decided to become a Jew. I don't know . . . I . . . ." The words trailed off as Eisler looked back to the photograph.

"And you ordered Cory to kill the others so that they couldn't expose your lies, didn't you?"

"Yes," Eisler nodded, looking over to Franco. "The Czechs *are* pressing for release of the Autley House records. And the president, against my recommendation, has ordered their declassification."

"So your real name would have been discovered," Franco said.

"Perhaps," Eisler shrugged. "Even though I immigrated as a concentration camp survivor and not as a scientist, it would have made no difference. I, too, passed through Autley House. During the course of any public inquiry into the Laban Institute, my involvement would have been discovered. The others knew of my present position. The ambassadorship and the rest of it."

"You weren't a scientist by training?" Franco asked.

"No," Eisler said.

"Then what was your function at the institute?"

"I was the senior representative of the *Sicherheit Dienst*—the Security Service. I reported directly to Himmler on matters of intelligence. I had a clerk, a Jew. His name was Ernst Grawitz. I simply became him."

Eisler stared back to the photograph for a long moment.

"He was funny little man." he said softly, fondly.

"Who?" Franco asked.

"Ernst, my little Jew clerk. He used to make me tea, gallons and gallons of tea. I didn't kill him, you know. He had a little plot of ground. Grew tomatoes and cucumbers. The guards found him there one afternoon. He had died, alone and in peace. A few months later, when the Russians were approaching, I made the decision to assume his identity. Since he had been my clerk, it was reasonable that he would know the inner workings of the Security Service. Predictably, the Americans also thought this knowledge to be of value. I was recruited and sent to Autley House."

"So Grawitz wasn't your real name either?" Franco asked.

"No," Eisler said simply.

"Then who are you?"

"Nobody of importance." Eisler paused a long moment, then placed the photograph back on the table. "So where do we go from here, Mr. Franco?" he asked.

In answer, Franco pulled out the Makarov he had taken from Cory. Eisler's eyes widened as Franco worked the action and chambered a round.

"Surely not that?" Eisler said, his tone composed. "You do not strike me as the type."

"I'm not," Franco said disgustedly. "Cory told me you two had a conversation earlier this afternoon. Do you recall it?"

His eyes fixed on the Makarov, Eisler mumbled a qualified yes.

"And you made him make a promise?" Franco added.

Eisler shrugged, unsure of Franco's meaning.

"You told Cory something about knowing when to employ elimination was the most honorable of duties and you told him never to forget it. Do you remember now?"

"Yes," Eisler whispered, his voice far away.

Franco reached into his waistband and pulled out his own Browning, aiming it at Eisler. He then lay the Makarov on the coffee table and slid it toward the older man.

Eisler glanced down at the Makarov, then back to Franco.

"I'm not sure I understand," he said.

"It was Cory's recommendation," Franco explained. "For once in your miserable life, do the honorable thing and end this self-serving charade."

A look of bemusement crossed Eisler's face.

"Suicide?"

Franco said nothing and slowly, seemingly one muscle at a time, the expression on Eisler's face changed to haughtiness, to resignation, and ultimately to serenity.

His own fingers tightening on the Browning, Franco stared into Eisler's eyes.

Eisler understood the path being offered.

"Not to worry, Mr. Franco. I well understand the ground rules. I wrote many of them myself."

Standing, the old man reached down, picked up the Makarov and caressed it with both hands. Then he began to slowly shuffle toward the bedroom. He paused for a moment at the large window overlooking Washington.

"I can see his monument from here, Mr. Franco," he said back over his shoulder.

"Whose monument?" Franco asked.

"Jefferson's," Eisler said quietly. "He too lived the contradiction. He, too, could discern the ambiguous. Could appreciate the frailties of the human endeavor." He placed a skeletal hand against the glass.

Franco said nothing.

"Toward the end, the Führer was immersed in contradiction," Eisler continued, whispering now. "The last time I spoke with him we met in his bunker beneath the Berlin chancellery garden. He had just been advised that Mussolini had been captured and killed by partisans. He expected his own fate to be the same at the hands of the Russians. He told me, 'Destroy the Bolshevik, and attack not once, but over and over.' Do you know why he shared this, Mr. Franco?"

"No," Franco said.

Eisler turned and looked directly into Franco's eyes.

"Because he believed that from the seeds of defeat, spring the roots of victory." Eisler looked back to the weapon in his hand. "But the Führer did not know his own garden, Mr. Franco. He never knew, never even suspected, that *I* was the Bolshevik."

"*You are Russian?*" Franco asked, clearly taken aback.

"I am a *sosedy*," Eisler said proudly.

Sosedy, Franco thought. This was the group Senator Rossett had spoken of. The men who worked for Stalin's spymaster Lavrenti Beria.

"You penetrated Himmler's intelligence organization." Franco made it a statement of fact

"Yes," Eisler said softly. "Very early on. Then, after the war, I merely stayed in character with the others from Laban. It was not a difficult charade, Mr. Franco. Americans always believe what they want to believe. It was their way at Autley House, it remains their way now."

"What is your real name, Eisler?"

"As I told you before," Eisler smiled. "I am unimportant."

Franco thought to press the issue but found himself saying nothing as Eisler moved behind a tall silkscreen panel and into the bedroom. The shot came immediately. It was not particularly loud, and Franco was not surprised.

Calmly, he stood from the sofa and walked toward the bedroom. Leaning around the silkscreen, he could see Eisler lying rather neatly on his back, the Makarov on the sheets to one side.

A spreading halo of blood was seeping into the pillow behind Eisler's head. The muzzle, Franco surmised, had been placed to the rear of the palate and the round had exited through the base of the skull, lodging in the headboard. This positioning had left Eisler's facial features all but untouched.

In fact, Franco decided, he looked quite peaceful, even to the slightly bemused set to his lips. It was almost as if he had been pleased with his world, or perhaps at the roles he had played and how he had played them so very well.

Franco thought briefly of Valena Jarvis and her singing came to mind. Perhaps she, too, would someday find peace.

"Frailties of the human endeavor," he whispered. Then he turned to the desk and picked up the telephone. Jonathon Weall answered on the second ring.

"Where in the hell have you been?" Weall asked.

"It's over," Franco said simply. "I'll meet you in your office."

Without waiting for a response, Franco replaced the receiver and left Eisler's apartment. In his mind the melody continued to repeat.

With me, Lili Marlene.
With me, Lili Marlene.

CHAPTER 57

THE FINAL DAY
Monday, December 1, 1982

Dulsuna, Honduras, 6:45 A.M.

The dawn was tropical, night to day with little in the way of transition.

"We must hurry," Umberto Rico told the Honduran Air Force captain as they left the main hacienda and walked directly to the waiting blue and silver Beechcraft King Air. "I understand *el presidente* plans on attending this morning's briefing."

"Do not worry, my *coronel*," the captain reassured him. "Every Monday, we have the briefing. Every Monday, we fly to Chuloteca. Every Monday we leave at 6:45 and every Monday we arrive at 7:10. Have we ever been late, my *coronel*?"

"No," Rico admitted with a Latin shrug. "But today is special. It seems I'm to be awarded another medal . . . the American Legion of Merit."

"It is a pretty medal?" the captain asked, as they climbed into the cockpit and strapped themselves in.

"Pretty?" Rico considered this while the pilot busied himself with the preflight checklist. "Yes, I suppose it is pretty. But, then, it is American. Much too small. And even no ribbon with which to wear it around my neck. I'm to just pin it on my chest."

The captain fired up the engines, revved them, then released the brakes and began taxiing toward the far end of the runway away from the compound.

"Perhaps we can buy a longer ribbon?" he suggested.

"Yes, Rico sighed disgustedly. "I suppose that is what we will be forced to do."

Reaching the end of the runway, the captain made a tight turn to the left, lined up, shoved the throttles forward, and released the brakes.

Its turbines roaring and tires bouncing, the King Air surged forward, pressing Umberto Rico back into his seat as the aircraft lifted into a cloudless Honduran sky.

"It will be a smooth flight," the captain said as he retracted the landing gear. "The air is cool, little turbulence. I have a thermos, would my *coronel* care for coffee?"

But the question was never answered. For as Umberto Rico considered the offer, behind the seats a tiny receiver pulsed once, then again, as a low-voltage signal activated first the fuse, then the four daisy-chained bricks of Amatol 80/20.

The explosion was spectacular. A boiling, billowing fleur-de-lis of orange and black as ignition spawned ignition, filling the sky, then streaming toward earth in long fiery tongues of metal and fuel and burning human flesh.

"Whoa!" Boudreaux Pock yelled. "Check that baby out. Talk about application. See? I told you it would work. I can't believe that son of a bitch lets everyone know his schedule. Makes it a piece of cake."

Damon Cory nodded in agreement. Boudreaux had planted the explosives around three in the morning and together they had lain in wait until dawn.

"I wish you had let me pop him though," Pock added, as the echo of the explosives dissipated. "If I don't keep in practice, I'm going to lose my touch."

Cory looked down to the small transmitter in his hand.

"I couldn't let you, Boudreaux," he said. "It wasn't part of the deal. I told Franco I'd do it myself."

"And he just let you walk? Just like that?"

"Just like that," Cory said. "He called someone and told them to hold the flight. It was already taxiing to the runway and they had to turn it around. Then, after we worked out our arrangement, he had two airport gendarmes walk me to the boarding gate."

Pock shook his head in disbelief.

"I wonder what Rico did to piss that Franco guy off? It must have really been something big."

"Franco told me he was responsible for killing children."

"Sounds about right," Pock shrugged. "What the hell, at least you had enough smarts to call me from Mexico City. I wouldn't have wanted to miss this for the world."

"Who else could I call?" Cory said matter of factly. "You're better with explosives than I am. Besides, what in the hell were you going to do in Washington with the old man dead?"

Pock cleared his throat and spit.

"Damn," he said. "I still can't believe Eisler's a Nazi. And all that right-and-wrong crap he was always running off at the mouth about. Shit, Damon, you know if all that stuff about him working on making zombie babies is true—me being a half-breed and all—hell, I could have ended up being some Nazi's slave and not even known it."

Cory chuckled at the way Pock had found a way to make it personal.

"Well, that's what Franco told me," he said. "And Eisler was a Nazi. I saw a photograph."

Pock shook his head again as he glanced back to the burning wreckage.

"Well, what are we going to do now?" he asked.

"First," Cory said. "I'm going to the embassy and get a new passport in my real name. Then I need to send a cable to Washington."

Pock looked back to Cory.

"Sounds good for you. What about me?"

"Want to go back to Asia?" Cory suggested. "I figure we can hang around Bangkok for a while."

Pock mulled this over for a moment or two.

"Don't worry about money, Boudreaux," Cory added. "I've got enough to keep us in whiskey and rice."

Pock offered a wide grin.

"Just until we can get a contract or something, right?"

"Right," Cory winked. "Now, let's get back to the jeep before someone sees us and we have to start answering questions we don't want to be asked."

"I hear that," Pock nodded, as he fell into step beside Cory. "Hey, Damon. I just thought of something. You remember a major named Burns? Got out of West Point a few years behind you? Short guy with only one ear?"

"Winnie Burns," Cory nodded. "I haven't thought about him in years. What about him?"

"Well, I heard he's screwing around in Burma now. Some kind of shit with the Shan states. Seems like the drug warlords are trying to split off and start their own country along the Chinese border."

"Is this a QUEENWALK thing?" Cory asked.

"Naw," Pock said. "Burns is working liaison with the Chinese under some advisory agreement. I guess the Chinese don't cotton to the warlords either."

"What's your point, Boudreaux?"

"Why don't we call Burns and see if we can get on with him?"

"I don't know," Cory smiled. "Let's try to get to Bangkok first."

"Then what?" Pock asked.

"We'll see, Boudreaux."

Pock grinned and spit again.

"I hear that," he said.

CHAPTER 58

FBI Headquarters, 6:50 P.M.

A young, female intern appeared at Franco's door.

"Agent Franco?" she asked.

Franco looked up from a sheaf of documents.

"Yes?"

"This came in for you," the intern said, passing Franco a yellow Western Union envelope. "We signed for it downstairs."

"Thanks," Franco said, taking the envelope and tearing it open as the intern walked away. Inside, there was a single sheet of paper. It was addressed to INSPECTOR SAL FRANCO, FEDERAL BUREAU OF INVESTIGATION, WASHINGTON, D.C., USA and it was from the Western Union office in Tegucigalpa, Honduras.

Franco scanned the message quickly:

PACT SEALED STOP PLANE CRASH THIS DATE STOP STILL OWE YOU STOP IF EVER NEED ANYTHING REPEAT ANYTHING CONTACT THROUGH HONG KONG OFFICE CALDER LEBRAY LTD STOP WILL NOT RETURN USA STOP

The telex was signed simply CORY.

Will not return USA, Franco thought, as he read the message a second time. The final part of the their arrangement. The closing of the circle.

Franco wondered if Cory cared. Then, immediately, he sensed he wouldn't. Cory was the real peregrine. A wanderer and a hunter. A man of honor in a world of duplicity. A man of principle in a world of little.

No, Franco knew. Cory would survive. Peregrines always survived.

"But thank you, my friend," Franco whispered, as he lay the telegram on his desk. Rico's crimes had now been requited. He would order no more torture. Kill no more children.

Franco sighed heavily and leaned forward in the chair. He found himself reaching for an envelope and extracting the old Laban photograph.

Amentia, he thought, as he stared into the grainy faces for what seemed the thousandth time. The word made the bile rise in his throat. Children. Infants. Could anything be more abhorrent? More aberrant?

He studied the photograph closely.

Eight men pictured, eight men dead. Two earlier, five by Cory's hand, Eisler by his own.

Two, five, and one. And, like Rico's, all eight deaths were justified.

Franco could remember the look in Eisler's eyes. It was both evil and knowing at one in the same time. Saying everything even as they said nothing. He shook his head in disgust.

Autley House, one project in a war of thousands.

Laban, one outrage in a time of millions.

Angrily, and somewhat impulsively, Franco watched as his fingers tore the photograph to shreds and threw the pieces into the burn bag next to his chair. Then he looked back to the telegram. Two words seemed to stand out: PACT SEALED.

Yes, he thought. It was indeed sealed. But still, the central question lingered. Was it *illegal* to have allowed Cory simply to walk away? To have forgiven his five murders for the price of a sixth assassination?

Sal Franco knew the answer: *yes*. In fact, it was completely against everything in which he believed, and counter to every oath he had ever taken.

But then there was the larger question.

Was it the wrong thing to do?

Try as he could, after evaluating the targets, weighing the situations, and considering the motivations of all involved, he could only come up with a simple, singular: *no*. For, in the final analysis, while the law may not have been served, justice surely had. And this, Franco realized, was what it was all about anyway.

Standing, he folded the telegram and slipped it into his pocket. Then he turned off his light and left the office.

"*Justicia*," he whispered. Making things right.

It was a word with many meanings.

EPILOGUE

In the weeks following Eisler's suicide, Jonathon Weall worried in vain that his QUEENWALK connection would be revealed. It never was and, on December 12th, realizing that he had been exploited, he felt only loathing as he, along with Sal Franco, attended the private interment in a little-used section of Arlington National Cemetery. The occasion was the mass burial of five senior scientists of the Department of Defense and a man named Eisler.

Also in attendance were two general officers of the Defense Oversight Board and a navy commander who served as a military aide to the president. There were no military honors, and the grave was left unmarked.

Valena Jarvis did not attend the burial. Diagnosed as schizophrenic, she was confined in the psychiatric ward Saint Elizabeth's Hospital, where she passed her waking hours humming old German folk songs and listening to talk radio.

With the exception of Eisler's, all the deaths were carried as unsolved homicides. There were no public pronouncements, and all records were sealed in the interest of "national security." Nobody questioned the presidential order.

***

In Bangkok, Damon Cory retired his warrior's sword. He resigned his commission and began to take a more active interest in his Calder-Lebray investments, particularly those which would profit from the expanding information technology market in India. In the spring, he was observed at the Thai beach resort of Krabi on the Andaman Sea. Strolling the beach, on his arm was a rather plain, Latin woman who walked with a limp.

***

On September 3rd, three unrelated events occurred: in Washington, Jonathon Weall finally replaced the entire Athens legal attaché staff; in Falls Church, Karen Franco's pregnancy was confirmed; and in Burma, an unusual item was found on the body of an assassinated Shan warlord. It was a condom the size of a man's thigh. On its side was stenciled the words MADE IN USA—SMALL. Chinese intelligence recognized it for what it was—a psychological warfare ploy. Boudreaux Pock had found work in Asia.

***

QUEENWALK continued as a classified line item in the defense budget. However, at the request of the president and the concurrence of the Defense Oversight Board, its funds were dedicated to peacekeeping operations in support of United Nations policy goals. When asked at a news conference "How many dollars are being allocated to the U.N. efforts?" the president looked the reporter directly in the eye and smiled.

"More than few, less than many."

The phrase seemed to come to him naturally.

The End

AUTHOR'S NOTES

The facts surrounding PAPERCLIP, Fort Strong, and the American selection and covert transshipment of Nazi scientists to the United States are true. PAPERCLIP was the operation that brought Wernher von Braun and teams of V-1 and V-2 rocket experts to the United States. More recently, Dr. Author Rudolph, a senior NASA scientist, renounced his U.S. citizenship and returned to Germany to face charges that he had controlled the Mittlewerk Dora slave labor factory in the Hartz Mountains. Charged as a war criminal, Rudolph had joined the Nazi Party in 1931 and the paramilitary SA (storm troopers) in 1933. In his thirty-five years with NASA, he designed the Pershing missile and supervised the production of the Saturn 5 rocket that had put Skylab into orbit and twelve Apollo astronauts on the moon. For his efforts, he was awarded the Distinguished Service Medal, NASA's highest honor.

As for how many other PAPERCLIP recruits are currently wanted war criminals? Perhaps we will never know. The actual personnel dossiers remain unavailable under the Freedom of Information Act. The rationale, of course, is national security.

***

The fact that Soviet agents penetrated American defense scientific circles is also widely regarded as fact. In his book *Special Tasks*, Paval Sudoplatov, Soviet spymaster and a protégé of Lavrenti Beria, charges that Robert Oppenheimer, while director of the Los Alamos laboratory that designed the atomic bomb, knowingly shared secrets with the Soviets, thus enabling Moscow to create their own atomic weapons.

Additionally, the revelations surrounding CIA Soviet counterintelligence branch chief, Aldrich Ames, as well as Felix Bloch, a suspected Soviet mole inside the U.S. State Department, only make one wonder how many others have escaped the American security net and, in fact, place their allegiances elsewhere.

***

Finally, Operation QUEENWALK, too, is based upon fact. In October 1981, Congress appropriated some $90 million in support of the U.S. Army's Special Operations Division. Of this amount, some $20 million disappeared into the "black" world of intelligence activity. On February 12, 1982, the Army Chief of Staff, Gen. John Vessey, issued an order calling for the Special Operations Division's records to be routinely destroyed. In effect, the men and their missions disappeared from the public ledger.

The division had one distinct advantage over the CIA: the army is not legally bound to report secret operations to Congress in advance. This detail was exploited to the utmost as the division, working with the CIA and National Security Agency, went global, setting up operations in El Salvador, Honduras, Costa Rica, Nicaragua, the Caribbean, Lebanon, Morocco, Nigeria, Saudi Arabia, Somalia, Syria, Sudan, and Iran.

An admittedly complex web of finance and foreign intrigue, the most comprehensive public-domain inquiry into the Pentagon's black budget is the book *Blank Check* by Tim Weiner, himself a Pulitzer Prize-winning reporter.

For those interested in the subject, it provides a fascinating glimpse into shadow government.

Brett F. Woods
Santa Fe, New Mexico

ABOUT THE AUTHOR

Brett F. Woods is the author of numerous articles and books in the areas of military history, police science, and government financial operations. A Vietnam veteran of the U.S. Army Special Forces, he has held a number of law enforcement and regulatory positions, including Special Agent, U.S. Secret Service; Inspector General, New Mexico Human Services Department; and Commissioner for Law Enforcement, New Mexico Gaming Control Board. Mr. Woods' professional affiliations have included the International Association of Chiefs of Police, the International Narcotics Officers Association, and the Association of the United States Army. He lives in Santa Fe, New Mexico.